Daddy's Hobby

The Story of Lek, A Bar Girl in Pattaya

The first book in the series called

Behind The Smile

by

Owen Jones

Copyright

Copyright © Owen Jones 2025

ISBN: 978-1-0683538-3-3

Behind The Smile: Daddy's Hobby
by
Owen Jones
Published by
Megan Publishing Services
(http://meganpublishingservices.com/)

Owen Jones

Contact Details

BlueSky: owen-author.bsky.social
Facebook: AngunJones
Instagram: owen_author
LinkedIn: owencerijones
Pinterest: owen_author
TikTok: @owen_author
X: @owen_author
Blog: Megan Publishing Services

Join our newsletter for insider information
on Owen Jones' books and writing
by entering your email address here:
http://meganpublishingservices.com/

Novels in the Same Series

Behind The Smile

The Story of Lek, A Bar Girl in Pattaya

Daddy's Hobby
An Exciting Future
Maya – Illusion
The Lady In the Tree
Stepping Stones
The Dream
The Beginning

Reviews

"From the first pages I was mesmerised by Lek and the other working girls, their hard life styles and thoughts, so different from our own western way of life and aspirations. Couldn't put it down till I'd finished."
RLJ, Barry, South Wales

"I enjoyed this book very much and would recommend it. I like stories that take place in foreign countries, so this was right up my alley. It was an easy read and flowed smoothly. Owen did a great job of creating a character readers could connect with and care about. I loved learning little titbits about the Thai culture and the author's descriptions allowed me to be able to picture the scenes and get a sense of what it might be like to actually be there. I appreciated learning the back story of Lek and the circumstances that led to her working as a bar girl in Pattaya. Often we only see one side of the sex industry in countries like Thailand and the rest is left up to our own assumptions. The story ended rather abruptly (I wasn't expecting it) so I'm looking forward to the sequel and finding out what happens next!"
Vanna B., Philadelphia, PA

"I bought your book, Behind The Smile, and enjoyed it tremendously. Your writing style is the sort that I like, it does not take my mind away from the story or the characters. You certainly give the impression that the book was written with fluency although I am sure you spent a lot of time playing with it.

The book is a good read and an accurate description of the world of a Thai bar worker. It is very hard to come to terms with how bar girls live as our cultures are so very different. We may have met at the same place but we took very different routes to get there. There is very little common ground to build upon. This book gives a real insight into their lives, hopes and aspirations.

I would recommend this to anyone with a Thai girlfriend, not as a warning but as a help in understanding her life. If it saves one argument then it's money well spent. I think it would dispel a lot of prejudices if more people read it, if only those with prejudices cared enough to buy it. If you ever do a sequel put me down for one."
WD, UK.

Look out for the sequel:
<u>"An Exciting Future"</u>

Owen Jones

Dedication

This book is dedicated to all the girls in Pattaya who told me their stories and gave me the idea, and the encouragement, to write them down.

Acknowledgements

The cover was designed by GetCovers.

Inspirational Quotes

Believe not in anything simply because you have heard it,

Believe not in anything simply because it was spoken and rumoured by many,

Believe not in anything simply because it was found written in your religious texts,

Believe not in anything merely on the authority of teachers and elders,

Believe not in traditions because they have been handed down for generations,

But after observation and analysis, if anything agrees with reason and is conducive to the good and benefit of one and all, accept it and live up to it.

Gautama Buddha

Great Spirit, whose voice is on the wind, hear me.

Let me grow in strength and knowledge.

Make me ever behold the red and purple sunset.

May my hands respect the things you have given me.

Teach me the secrets hidden under every leaf and stone, as you have taught people for ages past.

Let me use my strength, not to be greater than my brother, but to fight my greatest enemy – myself.

Let me always come before you with clean hands and an open heart, that as my Earthly span fades like the sunset, my Spirit shall return to you without shame.

(Based on a traditional **Sioux** prayer)

"I do not seek to walk in the footsteps of the Wise People of old; I seek what they sought".
Matsuo Basho

"Have I not commanded you? Be strong and courageous. Do not be afraid; do not be discouraged, for the LORD your God will be with you wherever you go".
Joshua 1:9

"Whatever misfortune befalls you [people], it is because of what your own hands have done- God forgives much-"
Quran 42:30

----

xi

Myself when young did eagerly frequent
Doctor and Saint, and heard great Argument
About it and about; but oft-times
Came out, by the same Door as in I went.
Omar Khayyam
The Rubaiyat XXIX.

Table of Contents

Daddy's Hobby

1 A CLOSE CALL

"Oh, bloody hell, girl! What have you gotten yourself into this time?" thought Lek as she was waking up yet again.

She had not slept much at all that night so far. Her 'boyfriend', Ali, was still asleep and the fumes coming from his open mouth told her that he must have been very drunk the night before. She had not noticed at the time, as she had been quite out of it herself. Her backside was still throbbing though where Ali had tried to take her and had beaten her in his frustration at not being able to manage it. She could have one of the boys do him over for that, she thought with some degree of satisfaction, or even report him to the police. She decided she would, if she were bruised. Yet he had seemed such a nice man earlier that night. It just went to show that you never can tell.

She wanted to get up and leave, but she had not been paid the 1,000 Baht they had agreed on; yet she was frightened of him waking up in case he wanted to try doing it again. It was not in Lek's nature to take the money from his pocket and sneak out, even though it was rightfully hers already. There was nothing for it, but to lie there awake, watchful, letting him sleep and hoping that the sleep would put him in a better frame of mind when he did wake up. Lek gave him one more furtive glance and prepared herself for a long wait. It was 5:35 a.m. and she could not reasonably expect him to surface much before 9:00 a.m.

The night before, Lek had been working in 'Daddy's Hobby', a bar off Beach Road when a thirty-odd year old Arab, Ali, had sat down. Things had been very quiet for her up until then, although most of the other girls were 'out'. Lek had gone over to him to take his order and make him feel at home, as she had done with other customers thousands of times before. Lek and Ali had introduced themselves and Ali had ordered a bottle of '100 Pipers' whisky, soda water and ice. Within minutes and with customary Arabic hospitality, he had offered her a drink and she had accepted gratefully. After all, she had thought, you never knew where things could lead, it was getting late and she was more than a little bored.

Looking back over events, Lek thought she had seen some danger signs even at that early stage. Why hadn't she listened to her instincts? They had always stood her in such good stead before. Ali had already been drinking before he got to her bar – she had noticed that, but then he had ordered a bottle of whisky. It was not unusual to see Arabs drinking alcohol, but he was drinking this bottle too quickly and insisting that she kept up with him. Maybe 'insist' was too strong a word, but he certainly wanted her to go drink for drink with him and he did not want to take 'no' for an answer.

They had finished the bottle and Ali had asked her whether 'she would like to go for something to eat' – one of the many code expressions in her profession, which could lead to lucratively-paid nocturnal employment.

And sometimes even a meal too.

She had accepted, but instead of going to a restaurant or his hotel, he had led her into a noisy disco, where he seemed to know a group of other Arabs. (She had never found out where he actually came from because his English was poor and her Arabic was non-existent; she had guessed at Abu Dhabi).

She had not been acquainted with the establishment, but it had been too full and too noisy for her tastes. The toilets were smelly too and Ali was acting 'weird' in front of his mates, showing off; showing her off; but also just showing off in general. He had also bought another bottle of whisky and danced in an odd way, pulling her about just a little too much, pawing at her, mauling her even, parading her in front of his friends.

She should have seen it all coming then, she thought. Ten years in Pattaya had taught her a lot, but she could still be too daft to listen to her inner voice. Sometimes, anyway. If she hadn't been such a good-natured person from birth, Pattaya could have done terrible things to her character.

Should she listen now? Get up, get dressed and sneak out, giving up the 1,000 Baht? No! Sod him!

She smiled to herself: 'Sod him' was a pun on what he had tried to do to her last night. The prick! But he hadn't been able to get it up! And serve him right – she had no sympathy. He had not said he wanted sodomy, if he had she would not have gone with him. Well …., not for 1,000 Baht anyway, she joked with herself. They had left the disco after an hour or so, at about 1 a.m., and had gone back to his hotel with his friends in tow. Luckily, they had not wanted to go inside with them, but they had laughed and joked in an odd way even though she could not understand what they were saying.

They had slapped him on the back and winked suggestively at her. Immature, she had thought at the time, but still weird for guys of their age. Maybe they had led sheltered lives. Maybe it was their first taste of freedom away from their village and the watchful eyes of their elders. She had seen the same sort of behaviour from some Thai villagers on their first trip to Sin City otherwise known as Fun City, Paradise or Pattaya, depending on your moral outlook. Anyway, they had eventually arrived at his room and all seemed to get a little more normal. Ali was certainly drunk, but then so was she. Ali offered her a shower and she had taken him up on the offer.

He had given her a clean towel and waited outside for her to finish and while she got into bed, he had taken a shower too. Everything back to normal, she had thought, she could handle this now – she was back on familiar territory. Then he had switched out the light and made his way over to the bed, tripping over a shoe or something in the process. He had muttered something in Arabic, she had giggled, and then he had jumped on the bed and got weird again. It was hard to explain. He had torn the sheets off her, but without hurting her. He had frightened her certainly, but not too much. At first, anyway. Then he had thrown her over onto her front and, putting an arm around her waist, had raised her bottom up towards him.

OK, she had thought: doggy-fashion – she liked that! However, he was trying to put it where she did not like and he was getting angry that she was not co-operating. He had begun muttering in Arabic again and had begun slapping her backside hard like a cowboy on a horse in the films. Very hard – much too hard. The shit! Maybe she would go to see the boys about him. The wanker!

Anyway, after 10 minutes or so, he had collapsed on the bed next to her without achieving his mission. He had said something unde-cipherable and had apparently gone to sleep fairly quickly. She had seen it all before: bloke has a few drinks, gets randy, drinks too much, can-not get it up and blames the woman in his embarrassment. The wanker! No need to get violent though, she thought.

A lot of men were just like little boys in bed, with their egos and tantrums and oh-so-easily hurt pride. One day, she would find a good man that wanted to take care of her and love her and … was not mar-ried, she smiled.

She lay there wondering whether he had bruised her or whether he had made her bleed even! Oh, she hoped not! But would she make him pay, if he had! However, she was not the vindictive type and she soon got bored planning hollow acts of revenge that she knew she was very unlikely to carry out.

It passed the time of day, well, night though and she was soon asleep again for the umpteenth time that night.

Ali could feel someone beside him when he woke up, but he could not remember who it was or even which sex it was. He had woken up facing the person, but had not opened his eyes yet. He decided to roll over, turning his back on his partner, while taking a sly peep. Please let it be a woman, he thought. He really did not want his colleagues from the oil rig to catch him with a boy. He had seen them on the way home last night, had he not?

Oh, please let it be a woman, he repeated to himself as he rolled over. Oh, thank God for that! She was pretty good looking too! In fact, very good looking and in the prime of her life, in her late-twenties, he judged. Oh, he could walk tall in front of his mates later and boast of his abilities. He could not quite remember what they had gotten up to and, for the moment, he did not care. His mouth felt as dry as the desert sand. He had to get some water and a couple of aspirins very soon. Getting up would surely wake her, but what was her name? Oh, shit! Still, he could bluff that one – at least it was not a man or a boy!

"Lak, Lek, Lik," he mused. Sounded familiar. He settled on the middle one, as he was the middle son of three. Inch Allah! He decided to go for it and leapt out of bed, picking up a towel as he headed for the bathroom. Safely inside, he downed a glass of water, grabbed the aspirins and sat on the toilet seat to recover. He had moved too quickly and his head was spinning. What a night that must have been!

No wonder The Prophet Mohammed discouraged alcohol, which itself was an Arabic word, if not an Arabic invention. He would be a good Muslim from now on he told himself and not drink ever again. His parents and the scriptures were right. He turned on the shower and sat there looking at it running for a few minutes, while he tried to piece together his movements of the night before.

He had fancied one of the katoy boy dancers in a pub called 'Night Fever' in Boyz Town and he went there whenever he could get away from his friends. He had been there last night, but surely, he had not spoken to him? No, he knew that he was too shy to 'come out' at this stage in his life. So, he had wandered about for a while and called in a quiet, empty bar on his way back to meet his friends.

That is where he must have met Lak, Lek, Lik, he reasoned. Oh, yes. He had had a bottle of whisky on top of what he had already had to drink. It was starting to come back to him as he got under the shower and the cool water began to take away some of the fog and some of the pain.

Then he had gone to meet his friends, albeit a couple of hours late and had bought another bottle of whisky by way of an apology. They had all had a good night and gone their separate ways. That was it – no harm done! He would go out now, smile at Lak, Lek, Lik; give her what she asked for, within reason and everyone would be happy. He roughly dried himself off and opened the door.

She was sitting up in bed with the sheets pulled tightly around herself up to her neck, looking at him straight in his eyes. She had the frightened look of a rabbit caught in a searchlight. It unnerved him, but he did not know why.

"Good Morning, Luaek," he mumbled, as boldly as he dared. "Did you sleep well?"

"My name Lek," she pouted, "and no. I not sleep good. You want shag me in bum and I not like. You hit me too much! I not happy. Maybe I go to police tell them 'bout you. Police take you Monkey House and man shag you in bum and you not like same same me."

Ali had thought it was going too well, but he said:

"Venez, venez. Go shower, Lek, and we talk about it after you finish."

Lek pulled the towel, which experience had taught her to keep by her pillow, around her and hobbled off into the bathroom without giving Ali another glance. She bolted the door as hard and noisily as she could and began to sob audibly.

At least, she hoped it was audible from outside. So, she turned the shower on and made even louder cries of pain, just to make sure. She inspected herself in the mirror and was pleased to see there were no signs of blood or bruising and as the cool water started to take the sting out of her beautiful bottom, her plan was unfolding.

After showering, she again donned the towel and limped into the bedroom, where Ali was sitting in anticipation, already dressed. A good sign, she thought to herself, she had escaped a replay of the previous night. She sat down gingerly; making sure that Ali was well aware of her discomfort and gave out a squeal of pain.

"Oi! Oi! Oi! I hurt!," she moaned, rubbing her right buttock. "Oh, Ali, why you hit me too much last night? I good lady for you but you hit me too much. I think you kill me. You crazy. I think I go see Mama San ask her what do. Maybe go police, you not good man, Ali."

She was getting dressed without showing a square inch of flesh, as only women brought up in a small house with a large family know how to, and Ali did not dare to ask to see the marks. In truth, Ali was a kind and decent man and flashes of the previous night had already started to filter through to his blurred consciousness making him feel quite ashamed – he could not remember ever having hit a woman before. He knew he had to appease her and he knew that that meant money, although not necessarily a lot. He said:

"Lek, I really very sorry. I not know what happen. I very drunk. J'étais mal. I think man put something in my drink, drugs or something like that. I want make you happy: buy you very good eating in good restaurant and pay you for say 'thank you' too. Je suis desolé. I very sorry, please forgive me. I have good heart, truly. I not hit mademoiselle before."

Lek looked up at him from the bed with her big, brown, doe eyes as she was combing her hair and wiped away a tear.

"OK," she simpered, "but I want you give me 2,500 Baht for go to doctor for cream and eat in 'Savoy Restaurant' and I not want see you again. You crazy sometimes. I not believe you any more! Not come to bar look for me. I have boyfriend take care me there."

Actually, that was the last thing that Ali was considering doing anyway, so he nodded his assent and looked as contrite as he possibly could. Inwardly he was relieved; he felt that he had gotten off lightly. It would cost him a quarter of a days pay on the rigs and he had escaped a brush with the police.

He knew that an unprovoked assault on a Thai was taken very seriously indeed and that it would mean at least a few nights stay in the notorious Pattaya gaol or 'Monkey House', as it was even less affectionately better known plus a fine of probably 20,000 Baht, half of which would probably go to Lek in compensation.

He could even be deported and blacklisted from re-entry into Thailand. Then his friends would have to know why he did not want to go to Pattaya on their next regular vacation. Oh, no, no, no, no, no. Better to pay up now and try to learn from the experience, if he could only remember exactly what that experience was.

Lek finished getting dressed and put on a little make up – she never used much anyway and did not really need it. Ali thought she looked a little happier, which cheered him up too and within ten minutes they were walking out of the hotel into the hot morning sunshine. Lek had already discarded any pretence of a limp as they turned left out of the hotel and started to walk the 300 metres north along Second Road towards the junction with Central Pattaya Road or Pattaya Klang, as it is known in Thai, where the Savoy is situated on the corner.

Lek loved this time of the day – about 11 a.m. – because Pattaya did not really 'get going' until about 10 a.m. and everybody and everything was full of the life, promise and hope that a new day brings – except, of course that in Pattaya it is all about the night time, so the day kicks off a little later. She sauntered along with a spring in her step and a smile on her face, keeping about two metres behind Ali.

She did this for several reasons: firstly, because she knew that most Arabs preferred to walk in front of 'their ladies'; secondly, because she did not really want to be seen with him (many men were casting appreciative eyes over her, as they always did, and from behind Ali she could smile back, without upsetting his pride) and thirdly, because of a joke she had heard a few weeks previously that always made her smile.

She repeated it to herself: 'A survey in Afghanistan revealed that most women walked three metres behind their men before the U.S. intervention, but that after the intervention this had increased to ten metres. When asked why, most Afghani women replied, smiling: "Landmines"'. She put her hands over her ears and mentally said: "Boom," giving a little hop and a smile at a passing farang (or foreigner).

She was one of the most beautiful women in Pattaya, which meant one of the most beautiful women in Thailand, which meant one of the most beautiful women in the world and she knew it.

No man would not call her beautiful and she could take her pick from any of them, and they would happily pay for the privilege. It gave her a feeling of power and a sense of self-worth, even though she realised that she had only about five years of the good life at the top left. She had led a remarkable life by the standards of most Thai women. She had met hundreds of men from almost every country in the world and most of them had been kind and generous and, unfortunately, married. None of them had ever taken her 'home' to their country, but she had stayed in the best hotels and eaten in the best restaurants for about a decade. Most of her relationships were not one-night-stands, as most people imagined.

She did not want those. Her strategy, honed over the years, was to try to find out something about the man first. She always wanted to know: how long he had left to stay in Thailand; where he came from; how old he was and whether he was married. The longer he had left in Thailand, the better a relationship she might form with him and the more chance she had of getting him to fall in love with her.

Country of origin was important, because she had preferences for where she wanted to live. She favoured Britain, but America, Canada, France or Germany would do too. Also, age was important, because it could affect his visa status in Thailand and knowing whether he was married or not was obviously essential.

Her average relationship, using the knowledge gleaned from these four questions, lasted two or three weeks. Very, very rarely had anyone left her before their flight home. Sometimes, she had been with the same man for a month or more. Some men had even taken her to other Thai cities as a companion and interpreter. She had flown to Chiang Mai, Phitsanulok, Ko Samui and Phuket at other people's expense many times.

Sometimes, men would come back and ask for her, because they had met on previous holidays. Others wrote sporadically or sent emails – not that her written English was even passable, but some of the older women specialised in reading these letters to the girls and drafting suitably romantic replies.

Lek did not often get into all that; it seemed a little bit too much like cajoling or begging and a little bit seedy or dishonest. There had been a few scary times too, but too few to mention. Not many men, it seemed, would fly all the way to Pattaya to cause trouble and risk spending ten years or more in the 'Bangkok Hilton', life in which could be likened to scenes from the film 'Midnight Express'. She had never been cut or raped as had happened to some other girls. Some girls had even been found murdered and there were rumours that some girls had disappeared into foreign slave brothels abroad against their will.

She hoped that they were only rumours, but she had never been caught up in the darker side of the sex industry. She did not even want to think about child prostitution or paedophilia, but she had always kept both eyes open for this kind of abuse. She would not have hesitated to report it to the police.

She had even managed to save a tidy sum for her contingency plan, when the inevitable retirement day arrived and she would go back to her village to live, unless she met a wealthy, single foreigner, who wanted to take her and her daughter back to his own country. That was the goal; that was the ultimate dream and she had been chasing it for 10 years. The contingency plan was to open a small shop in the village and marry a kind farmer. True, she would probably have to settle for quite an older man in this scenario, but she had had a good innings so far and she would take care of him, if he were kind to her daughter.

If she had stayed in her village, she would have been married to a farmer of her own age for about twelve years by now and have three or four children. Not that those were bad things, but she had had to leave and now she told herself that she was glad she was not bee shackled to the routines of a house and a farm, watching the world pass her by on the television screen.

She had friends who had chosen married life straight after school and she felt that most of them envied her playgirl life-style, her racks of beautiful clothes and her stories, backed-up by photographs, of fabulous locations with wealthy, generous foreigners, who thought nothing of spending as much on a single meal, a bottle of wine or a present, as most farmers earned in a month.

Her village friends and family had respect for what she had done, despite the way she had chosen to accomplish it. They were not hampered by Western morality and double standards. Were not most of the people who condemned her or 'felt sorry for her', as they more often phrased it, the frumpy wives of the very men who came to Thailand to meet girls like her? She had no time for them or how they thought.

Would they fund her lifestyle and provide for her mother and daughter if she did not do what she did? If what she was doing was so wrong, she would pay for it in Karma herself one day. She had no problem with that; so long as her ageing mother and nearly teenage daughter were all right. "Give Good, get Good. Give Evil, Get Evil" was her motto,

And the monks' motto. And what was good enough for the monks was good enough for her too.

In her state of reverie, she had forgotten about Ali and she now found herself alongside him, his arm wrapping itself around her waist to steer her into the restaurant.

"Oh well," she thought, "it's a free lunch" and Lek, like most Thais, was very reluctant to turn down a meal.

They sat in the air-conditioned section on the left and Lek ordered spring rolls and fish cakes to start; followed by a huge Red Snapper, which was to be cooked in a fish-shaped dish at the table itself and boiled Jasmine rice. Lek demonstrated her gastronomic expertise and table manners by ordering a perfect combination of sauces for the appetiser, helping Ali to titbits and attending to the cooking of the fish, while eating her own food at the same time.

They ate a fine meal, but hardly spoke, which was due equally to Ali's poor command of the English language, the tension between them and their hangovers. When they went their separate ways forty-five minutes later, both were pleased that the relationship had ended on a happier note.

Lek watched Ali turn right, presumably to go back to his hotel by Soi 9, gave him a small wave and dashed across the busy Second Road weaving in and out between the dozens of motorbike taxis and Baht buses that were waiting at the lights. She turned right into Pattaya Klang and walked the two hundred metres east looking in the shop windows to the next turning on the right, Soi Buakhao. She calculated that she had taken enough precautions to shake Ali off, if he had decided to follow her. She did not like men knowing where she lived.

She was as happy as a songbird and it radiated out from her. She felt that everybody could see how happy she was. She had landed herself in a tricky, potentially dangerous, situation, because she had not listened to her instincts, but she had played the bad hand she had been dealt like a Mississippi card-shark and had come out of it with as much money as many Thais earned in a month and she had eaten well.

Lek was waiting at the junction of Soi Buakhao and Pattaya Klang for a 'Baht Bus' to take her home, but she changed her mind and decided to walk around the corner to the Thai market opposite the Naam Chai Restaurant and buy a new skirt to celebrate. It was a very hot afternoon in June, but the market was alive, as it almost always was and Lek meandered through the fruit stalls at the front buying articles of fruit here and there, chatting to the market-traders and fellow customers on her way to the clothes stalls at the back.

She spent forty-five minutes at her favourite pastime of shopping for clothes before eventually settling on a beautiful white skirt with her Western star sign embroidered in sequins on one thigh in the front. At fourteen inches long, it would show off her beautiful legs; being white, it would show off her tan colouring and the star sign would give men a reason for looking down there, if they had not thought of one already.

She was a Leo, born in early August and although she did not know a lot about western astrology, she thought she was a typical female lion. She had read about Leos being aggressive and dominant, but in her opinion that only applied to the females. After all, it was the female lion that pursued and killed the prey. Male lions slept a lot and demanded to eat first.

They only came into play if a predator or rival came on the scene and then it was only for the selfish defence of their progeny and their wives – they did not necessarily defend them for their own sakes. What a joke!

She also bought a short white blouse, which tied at the mid-rift to finish the outfit, and then hopped on a Baht taxi heading south and home.

2 THE FLATMATES

Lek hopped nimbly off the bus and nipped around to pay the driver the fare of five Baht, before crossing the road and heading to the old, but recently renovated tenement block, where her apartment was located. She bounded up the three flights of stairs and listened quietly at the door. There was not a sound to be heard, so she rummaged in her small bag and pulled out her key. It was only one twenty-five, so the girls were probably still asleep – they rarely got up before two o'clock.

She let herself in slowly and quietly and shut the door behind her. Lek could see the double bed with two lumps under the sheets and could hear them snoring softly. She got down on 'all fours' and crept up to the bottom of the bed, keeping below their line of sight. She rolled the oranges she had bought out of the bag onto the floor and, lying on her back, lobbed them grenade-fashion up onto her friends. First, the snoring stopped and then a few puzzled expressions were uttered and Lek turned over and sprang onto the bed making as much noise as she possibly could. She jumped on her friends and made as if to pull the sheet off them.

They joined in the game screaming like shy school girls, then they hugged in a triangle and bounced on the bed laughing. The three women had known each other all their lives. They had grown up in the same part of the same village and had gone to the same school and the same Wat – as their parents had all done a generation before. They were all the same age too, within twelve months, although Lek was technically the eldest. She was also the wisest and fastest learner and

Goong and Ayr acknowledged this by the high esteem in which they held her.

Although unrelated, they called her 'Big Sister' and she called them 'my darling Little Sisters' and they all looked after each other as if they were the only family they each had ever had in the whole, wide world. There was only one person allowed to break that triangle forming a square and that was Mama San, the boss and owner of 'Daddy's Hobby', the bar where they each worked, but Mama San was older, more of a friend than a mate and, at the same time, more of a mother than a friend and she also came from the same village.

Suddenly and in unison, Goong and Ayr grabbed Lek, threw her onto her side and started to 'tan her behind'. Lek let out an involuntary yelp and the girls stopped immediately, sensing that something was wrong because they knew Lek to be a 'good sport', always ready to join in the fun.

"What's the matter, Big Sister?" asked Goong, "You're not going soft in your old age, are you?"

"No!" replied Lek, "I can still take you both on any time!"

"But why the punishment?" she queried, already suspecting the answer.

"What is our first principle? Never to be broken?" asked Ayr.

"Oh, yes. Ummm, sorry about that" said Lek, "I didn't have any reception on my phone. I did try to let you know where I was though."

"Bullshit, Big Sister! Why didn't you phone from the hotel lobby or make an excuse to phone from a bar nearby, like you trained us and insist we do?" argued Goong.

"Yes, well, I'm very sorry. It won't happen again," replied Lek.

"Oh, I shouldn't think it will," said Ayr, "Mama San had us combing the streets for you until four in the morning and she's tamping mad with you. Maybe a trip back home for a month would be enough, just about, for her to cool off. Anyway, that's up to you – you'll get your comeuppance when Mama San sees you. Why did you flinch when we slapped your bum?"

"Ah, that's a long story," said Lek, thinking as quickly as she could. "Last night, I left the bar with an Arab named Ali, but we didn't hit it off very well so we decided to part company before we got back to his hotel. I thought about walking back to the bar, but it was already late, so I called in to see an old friend working in a bar off Soi 8. She was chatting to two dreamy Englishmen and before I knew it, we were walking back to their hotel. Well, to cut a long story short ...,"

"Don't," interjected Ayr "we want to hear everything!"

"Mine was a schoolteacher and when we got to his room, I mean his classroom, he put me over his knee, pulled my knickers down and made me suck his thing while he spanked me for not having my English homework with me. Woaoy! Was he kinky! It was lovely!"

"Tell us more about the professor, you lucky so and so. Was he tall and handsome? Did he have a big muscle ..., I mean big muscles?" giggled Goong.

"Don't be rude," said Lek, "you know we're not supposed to talk about our men friends, but just between us, eh? He was dishy, handsome, generous and umm, big. Very energetic too, so maybe I'd better get a little sleep before work later. Why don't you two go and shower while I pop out to get us something to eat. What do you fancy? Anything special?"

"Just an omelette for me," shouted Ayr from the bathroom.

"Me too" added Goong from her supine position on the bed next to Lek.

Lek and Goong just chatted, passing the time of day, while Ayr showered and when she had finished, Goong took her place and Lek went to the small restaurant in the next block. She was soon back in their room and, while the two girls ate, Lek showered again, changed her underwear in their small, shared bedroom and wrapped a towel around herself.

'Apartment' was probably too grand a word for what they had, although they did have decent accommodation by many standards. It often looked like a small room in a Chinese sweatshop laundry with bras, panties and slips hanging out to dry everywhere, for they were far too modest, believe it or not, to allow men to ogle their underwear drying on the veranda.

The apartment consisted of one fairly large room, about six metres by five, a small en suite bathroom with shower and WC and a tiny balcony, where they could dry their outer clothes. Furniture consisted of one double bed; a fridge; a fan; a wardrobe; a chest of drawers; a table; three chairs and an electric ring. They had also bought a kettle for hot water and tea; a rice boiler (considered an essential in Thailand nowadays); a TV; cutlery and crockery. They paid 3,500 Baht a month for this plus bills, but they had been there for five years and had three years left on the lease.

It was central and they didn't have far to go to work. They shared the bed, but none of them minded that – usually, one or more of them was 'out', so it was rare to sleep three in the bed. When they did have to though, they got very little sleep, because it was like the first night in a dormitory on the first day of term with all the giggling and chatting.

They had obtained the room with the help and guarantee of Mama San, who seemed to know just about everyone and everything worth knowing in Pattaya. They shared everything: clothes, food and money; they split all the bills and they all had the same ambitions: to quit their jobs and get out of Pattaya with a decent, well-heeled man who loved them.

They shared thirty combined woman years of failure at that too.

They had an hour before they usually set off for work and so, as usual, to the tunes of some pop programme on the television, they read bits of articles from magazines to each other, put their make up on and laid out their working clothes, more than several times. Lek decided not to wear her new clothes that day, but modelled them for her friends anyway. Both Ayr and Goong thought she looked gorgeous – so did Lek.

"You can wear them any time, Little Sisters, 'though maybe you'd better not," joked Lek.

"Why ever not? Don't you think they would look good on us too?" pouted Ayr.

"It's not that," quipped Lek, "but you aren't Leos, are you?"

They each knew that they would look just as good on any of them. They were all three stunningly beautiful women.

At three forty-five, they locked their inadequately secure apartment door behind them and started off to work. It was only a short walk to Soi Diana, named after the murdered Princess of Wales, where they could cut through to Second Road, but they decided to take a Baht Taxi along Soi Buakhao to the newly developed Pattaya New Plaza just across Second Road from where they worked off Soi 7 at the Beach Road end. Lek paid the fifteen Baht for the five-minute ride and they turned left into the Plaza. The right-hand side of the road housed a dozen or so large stalls each stocking dozens and dozens of items of ladies' clothing.

Most of it was cheap and cheerful, short and revealing and aimed at the hundreds of bar girls that used this thoroughfare to the main girly districts of Soi 7, Soi 8 and Beach Road. But now it had another advantage, bars were going up on the left opposite the stalls, and the three friends loved the attention they got from there, while they in-dulged in a bit of window shopping on their way to work.

They walked side-by-side, wiggling their bottoms and flouncing their skirts just like fashion models on their runway, while swinging their handbags in perfect rhythm to a tune that only they could hear. All the men were watching them and they loved it. They pretended not to notice the attention while at the same time revelling in it; trying all the while to catch sly glimpses of the men who were looking at them - playing it super cool.

After all, their shift had not started yet

Walking this route, took them past at least fifty bars with probably three or four men in each at this early hour of the late afternoon. Most of these early-starters would be British - the target market for Lek and her friends. By walking this way, she could eye the latest fashions on the stalls while allowing British tourists the opportunity to eye her and, maybe, follow her to work, if they were keen enough. On the way home at night, if she left work before one a.m., she could triple those odds, but she would not have much opportunity to assess her suitor, which is where experience or / and desperation came in.

They arrived at Daddy's Hobby in high spirits. Lek was expecting a dressing-down and Ayr and Goong were looking forward to it. No sooner had Lek said 'Hello' to Joy, one of their colleagues, than a voice boomed out:

"Lek! Get your sorry little arse in here right now! Right now, I said."

Everyone knew who it was and Lek scurried in to see Mama San, making her friends smile with her imitation of a timid little mouse.

"Hello, Beou." said Lek "How are you today? Takings good yesterday, were they?"

"Don't give me all that crap! What happened to you last night? You went off with that drunken Arab, which I thought was stupid, but up to you nevertheless. He paid the bar fine for you, so OK. You gave him the benefit of the doubt. I wouldn't have. Why didn't you get the name of his hotel before you left with him? Why didn't you phone it back to someone when you got there? You stupid cow!

"How do you think we would have felt if anything had happened to you? What if we'd read in the papers this morning that an unidentified girl had been found dead in a hotel? You stupid, selfish cow! You know how much the other girls look up to you and admire you. What sort of example do you think you're setting them, eh? Eh?"

Lek tried: "I'm sor…," but was cut off.

"Shut up when I'm speaking to you. Do you have any idea what you have put us through? Any idea at all? Ayr, Goong and I walked the streets from one until four this morning looking for you, asking if anybody had seen you and the other girls used up all their phone credit asking around after you and pestering me till noon today wondering whether you had deigned to inform us that you were OK!"

"Sheesh, girl. Don't ever do that to us again" she added in a much quieter, more affectionate voice and gave Lek a hug. Lek squeezed her back.

"Sorry, Beou, really, I am " she whispered in Mama San's ear.

"OK, darling. OK," said Mama San. "You are my Number One Head Girl and I need you to help me keep the others in line. I need you to help me keep them safe. I rely on you to help me keep my promise to their mothers to keep them safe. I need you to set not only a good example; I need you to set a perfect example. I need you to be their rôle model. I am too old for that now. They see me as a 'has been', their boss. I can only scare them into being sensible. You can do more. Please try for me, for them, but above all for yourself, eh? Oh, and no more bullshit stories about giving teachers' blow jobs in hotel 'classrooms' either."

Mama San let go of Lek, took her arm and led her forcefully back into the bar, where the other girls were pretending to put the finishing touches to their make up, but were really straining to hear what was being said.

"Lek has something to say to you all" said Mama San, as she let go of Lek's arm. "Go on!"

"I'm really terribly sorry for worrying you like that last night. It was unforgivable" Lek blurted out, trying to put pathos into her voice, but she was being seriously distracted by what Mama San had just said. How the hell did she know that the teacher story was a fabrication?

"I don't know how or why I didn't call in, but there's no excuse. Sorry for putting you through the worry and, so I understand, the expense. As a gesture of my gratitude, I propose to share my bar takings from yesterday with you all! How's that? OK?"

Lek looked around smiling; expecting to see the same response back, but it was not there.

"Mama San has already left us all a packet with an eighth each of your share" interposed Joy. "Thanks for the thought anyway, though."

That would have been about 300 Baht, she thought. After all, she had had a very good day, she reflected. There had been a guy who had bought her a few Lady Drinks early on; then another and lastly Ali: they were worth 30 Baht each to her and her half of the bar fine, which was 400 Baht. So, all in all 250-300 Baht — just above average daily takings. Oh, well.

That's how it goes, she thought, easy come; easy go, although it was more than she had wanted to lose.

Mama San smiled, tapped Lek on the shoulder in mock commiseration and went back into her cubbyhole to finish preparing the till.

Lek was considered a high earner on her level of play. She could probably have made it big time as a 'resident' in one of the larger hotels in Bangkok or even Pattaya, where girls were expected to have a passport, a driving license, ball gowns and decent jewellery, but Lek had never pursued that line and had never been offered it either. If she had been offered the position, she would probably have stayed with Mama San anyway, who was from her village too. She owed her a large debt, or felt she did, which was the same in her eyes.

Lek earned the 'basic wage', the same as the other girls like her, of

3,000 Baht per month for attracting customers, keeping them talking and 'being available to escort'. Those who preferred not to be considered for escorting services, say married ladies, got 2,500 Baht per month. On top of this, both classes of employee were encouraged to ask the men to buy them drinks called 'Lady Drinks', which were usually mildly alcoholic cider or perry, but in fancy champagne-type bottles. The girls got 30 Baht for each for these. If the customer bought them a beer or a coffee they got nothing, although they would sit there and keep him company anyway, at least until a better prospect sat down.

Then there was the bar fine. A bar girl was being paid by her boss to work in the bar, if a man wanted to take her out for the evening, then the boss wanted compensation for the wages she had paid. This is called a 'bar fine' or a 'bar find'. It is typically between about 300 and 1,000 Baht and is paid by the man. The boss will split this with her employee later.

Escorting services are nothing to do with the bar, are negotiable between the customer and the escort, and range between 300 and 1,500 Baht or more per night. It could be a lot more or even a little less. Lek always pulled at least 1,000 Baht per customer, after first making sure that she had had as many Lady Drinks as she could get, before leaving her home bar.

No girl got paid for drinking in another person's bar. If Lek had a 'boyfriend' for an average of say, 20 days a month, she would earn at least: 3,000 basic; say, 4,500 in Lady Drinks; 4,000 in bar fines and 20,000 in escort fees totalling, about 30,000 Baht per month, which is four times what an armed rookie policeman with a family and a mortgage would earn in a month. Staying in good hotels and eating in the best restaurants were almost everyday occurrences; presents of gold and clothing were bonuses, but regular.

The bar girls trickled into work between four pm and 6 pm. Lek,

Ayr and Goong liked to get in early, because many of the early drinkers were British, other nationalities tended to come out later. British people tended to be the most generous holidaymakers too, meaning higher drinks payouts at the end of the month. The British were well liked in Pattaya, probably more so than any other nationality, but they were harvested just the same as anyone else.

When the average British male gets to Pattaya he has flown 11,500 km and has been travelling for 20 hours. He is exposed to sun, sand, good, cheap food good, cheap accommodation and thousands of beautiful women, all of whom will happily talk to him for hours for the price of a cheap, 100 Baht drink.

This bowls the average British male over. It is virtually impossible to spend 7,000 Baht a day (a typical single holiday maker's budget), so he becomes generous and everybody wins. Catching them early enough is the trick, while they can still speak and have not lost their wallets. Not that Lek ever 'caught' anyone; she prided herself on giving value for money. She wanted people to come back for her, she wanted a permanent falang boyfriend.

Once the girls had settled in and everybody had caught up on what everyone else had been doing for the last fifteen hours, Lek went back to see Mama San to apologise again. Mama San was smoking a cigarette, as usual when working, and she eyed Lek approaching her.

"Hi. You OK with me giving your money away like that? If you're short, I'll pay it to them, but I had to make an example of you. I would never be able to go back to the village and look their parents in the eyes again if anything happened to one of them while she was in my care, so to speak. I guess you're wondering how I knew you'd slept with that Arab fellah? Ali, wasn't it?"

"Mmm," replied Lek. "Yes, I'm OK about the money and yes, I am curious to know how you knew about the teacher and Ali, but if you don't want to tell me that's OK too. I know that you like to keep some things secret, that you have your ways and means. I really came in to say that I'd go cashier for the night, if you wanted to get off and catch up on your sleep after last night."

"Aw, thanks, love," said the boss, meaning it. "I really could do with putting my feet up and watching a good film after I've put the baby to bed. I can give the sitter the night off too then. She's been moaning a bit recently that she never has any time. But who does? That's what I say. OK, I'll take you up on that. Give me twenty minutes to get my things together and I'll be gone."

She had not said anything about how she knew about the teacher and Lek knew better that to pursue it. Beou never forgot anything, so, if she had not answered the question, it was because she did not intend to. Lek returned to the bar.

The night watch woman had put some rice in the steamer and Beou had bought a bag of pork curry and a bag of cooked vegetables for whoever felt hungry. It was usually the younger girls that did not have cooking facilities or were temporarily short on funds that needed this and some were eating now, taking advantage of the quiet early evening. Most of the girls had eaten in 'Mama's Kitchen' at some time or another. It cost only pennies to provide, but it meant that no one went hungry and that everyone had enough energy to work until one a.m.

Mama was no-one's fool.

Mama San came out at that moment with her shopping bags and the keys to her motorcycle.

"OK, ladies, I'm off now. Be good." she announced. "Lek has offered to stand in for me tonight, so get yourselves decent fellahs while she's out of action. See you all tomorrow. Oh, and Lek! I nearly forgot. Your teacher man came by at about two o'clock and said to give you this. Apparently, you left it on his bedside table." She nonchalantly tossed over a small bone hair grip and left.

"Woo, woo, woo, woo, woo," the girls all ululated at once.

The story had got about already and Lek rubbed her bottom and pretended to be embarrassed.

The early afternoon session started very well - mostly middle-aged Brits, mostly drunk and mostly amazed that they were in a country where the bars were full of young, friendly women willing to talk with them, and that they were open all day long, selling beer at reasonable prices. Lek played her rôle as hostess well; she had done it many times before. She might offer a cigarette to those that sat there a while or introduce a girl or offer to find a partner for a bar game. She had volunteered to be the cashier as atonement and that meant sitting at the back of the bar, controlling the money and the girls, but not often coming to the bar itself.

In Daddy's Hobby, like most bars, the girls pulled the punters in by dancing, shouting or posing, took the orders and then delivered the drinks. They also sat with the drinkers, if they wanted, and tried to get Lady Drinks out of them. The order went to the cashier, who wrote a chit for it, she also noted it in a ledger or had a duplicate.

The customer got a copy in a beaker in front of him. When he wanted to cash up, a girl added the chits up and took his payment to the cashier, who checked that all was in order, marked his bill as paid and supplied his change, which the girl took back to him, hoping for a tip. So, the cashier was tied to the till, being the only person with access to the takings and consequently had small chance of any action. For this reason, and the responsibility and trust necessary, a cashier usually earned twice a normal bar girl's basic salary.

Mama San usually worked as cashier.

Lek sat behind a medium sized desk, on which were arranged a duplicate chit book, a sales ledger, a desk diary, a tape deck, a CD player and the remote control for the TV.

She was in charge of the audio visual entertainment as well as the nocturnal entertainment.

Work was rhythmic. Seven girls were bringing orders on a regular basis; chits had to be written; entries made in the ledger; tapes or CD's changed; change given; TV channels changed; introductions made; pleasantries exchanged. It all made the time pass quickly.

The regular 'boyfriends' of two of the girls, Joy and Deou, Barry and Nick, arrived to take them out at nine o'clock. Lek considered it important to make a special fuss of regular boyfriends, as Mama San did too. 'Regular boyfriends' were the girls' equivalent of a salesman's hot lead. Every regular boyfriend was a potential ticket out of Pattaya.

A man was considered a regular boyfriend if he came back for the same girl several nights in succession. The best were men that had just arrived, in which case a girl had up to four weeks to get him to fall for her, to say nothing of the 28 days regular salary.

Often, a regular would arrange to meet his lady in the home bar at eight or nine o'clock; they would have a few drinks (and Lady Drinks) and the bar fine would be discretely made along with his first order. Later, they might go off for a meal and or a show, although the girl would have been working there since four or five o'clock, as usual, just in case he was a 'no show'. The house rule was to make these men feel special: all the girls chatted them up; all the girls offered to play bar games; all the girls treated them like part of the family.

Part of the family, but not part of the sorority!

Not only gender excluded them from that. Being foreign or falang (as Caucasians are called) excluded them too. It is important to realise the difference. None of the girls would try to steal a colleague's boy-friend. Every girl wanted the same and every girl would do all she could to help a friend achieve her ambition. If a boyfriend called by when his lady was, say, shopping or something else, all the available girls would make a fuss of him, while Mama San discretely phoned her to tell her to get back to base at break-neck speed. Many girls would try to hedge their bets by going 'short-time', if they were not sure of their mark.

Lek took a couple of minutes off to go over; take their order personally; shake them by the hand; ask them if they were going anywhere special later and offer them a cigarette; then she went back to her paperwork. The rest was up to them now and they were doing all right so far.

Lek looked the party of four over; noticed their body language and weighed them up: they had been seeing their boyfriends for about a week already and had seen them every day and night, which was a very good sign. They were staying in the Marriott and so were not short of money; they were about forty-five years of age, and so were probably not 'butterflies' like most younger men and could even be divorced. They dressed smartly. They both came from the same town in South Wales and had flown over together. It was their first time in Thailand and they were into the third week of a four-week stay.

Textbook stuff, she thought, the girls had every chance of success – the boys were as good as married.

She flicked through the TV channels to see if she could find some football, perhaps then they would stay a little longer – after all, all Brits liked football, didn't they?

Two of the other girls, Porn and Or, seemed to be doing well too, out the back, playing pool with two nice enough looking Englishmen. They had a good chance. The rest of the girls were out the front, cajoling passers-by to come to the bar. Mott was attempting to pole dance. She was not very good at it, but to be fair, the pole was not long enough either. Still, she was having a go and it was funny, if not sexy.

Ayr and Goong pulled in two drunks at about eleven thirty and seemed happy enough, although Lek thought they were beneath her friends. Still! Up to them – she didn't always get it right either. They ordered a round and straight away they called for the Mama San. They obviously had some experience in Thailand, although not in Daddy's

Hobby.

"What's the bar fine on these two wee girls?" one of them slurred.

"And do they speak English?" the other chipped in.

Lek walked over. She could see that this needed delicate handling so she called Fa to take over the till.

"Why you not sit talk with Ayr and Goong first? Have drink. Make friends," she suggested, making herself comfortable opposite them.

"They lovely Ladies and speak English OK. My name Lek, I very good friend from them. What name from you?"

"Ach, this is Dougal and yous can call me Jock" one said. "Hello Ayr, hello Goong, you beautiful young things. You want a drink? And you, Ayr? And you? Lek, did you say your name was? You ready for another, Dougal?"

Dougal nodded and shook hands with Ayr.

The men's Scots accents would be difficult for Ayr and Goong to follow, thought Lek. It was hard enough for her. Still, the girls did speak English, so they could have a sort of one-way conversation, if that's what they wanted. Lek took the gamble that the Scotsmen could not understand Thai, although they could well be residents of Thailand and spoke to her friends in their mother tongue:

"Are you sure you want to go through with this? They're a bit drunk and they're already man-handling you, in full view too. Why not have a few Lady Drinks; have a laugh; go for a tip and let them wander off later? There's not long to go now and we can get off home together."

Fa called for Lek's attention to a similar matter in the back bar.

"Don't go anywhere or promise anything until I get back. Tell them the bar fine is 500 each. Talk about anything, I won't be long" advised Lek.

"Sorry, boys, I come back in five minutes," she apologised in English as she headed for the back bar.

The two Englishmen were waiting with Porn and Or, who, knowing the routine had delayed asking for the customers' bill. Lek looked the girls in the eyes as she approached and silently asked them if they were happy with the situation. They said that they were equally silently, and so Lek motioned for them all to sit around the nearby corner of the bar behind the cashier's chair.

"Hello! My name Lek," she said to the Englishmen, "You like ladies? What name from you?"

They introduced themselves as John and Bob and shook hands with Lek.

"What you want to do with ladies?" she asked cheekily, but without any hint of insinuation.

"Umm, well, we were thinking of going for something to eat and perhaps on to a club later" said Bob.

"Oh, no problem. Up to you. Porn and Or know Pattaya very well. Show you good restaurant, good club. They working here now; you know you must pay me for let them go early? Not big money. Four hundred Baht each or they lose money. Understand? What ladies want to do after finish working up to them. You must talk to them what they want. You understand?" said Lek trying to make the circumstances crystal clear.

"Yes, I think I understand" said Bob "What do you reckon, John?"

"I'm OK with that," he replied catching on a little more quickly than his friend.

"Yes, fine" he said to Lek and he smiled at each of the girls, who were beaming back at him. "Very happy." Porn put her arm around his waist and hugged him.

"OK. Good. You all happy! You handsome men. You want one more drink here or you want check bin now? Drink cheap here, but expensive in restaurant?"

Bob opted for another beer and offered drinks all round. Lek accepted and nodded to Fa to put the bar fine tab into their beaker.

She smiled graciously, took a sip from the glass and slipped into the conversation:

"Where you stay? You here long time already?" eyeing her colleagues.

"Oh, we're staying at the 'Pig' up the road. We've been here three days. Three weeks to go" replied Bob.

Lek had the information she wanted and she excused herself to return to the Scotsmen. They had been sitting around the corner out of sight however her spirits fell as she turned the corner and saw that they were no longer where she had left them.

"Fa, where are Ayr and Goong?" she asked.

"Oh, they left with those men about ten minutes ago. They told me you said to write a bar fine chit out for 1,000, is that right? The men had two more rounds, putting two drinks in for you, paid the bill and said they couldn't wait any longer, they had to get going. Is that OK? Have I done anything wrong, Big Sister? Oh, and Ayr told me to give you this."

Fa handed Lek a piece of paper, on which was written the name of a hotel and a kiss sign.

"No, no, everything's fine, Little Sister. You did well. I'm just a bit tired, that's all. Go and keep Mott company and break open half a bottle of whisky for the three of us. It looks like everybody else has deserted us."

It was twelve thirty in the morning and the new law required that they close at one a.m.

Not that it was widely adhered to or enforced.

The only concession that most bars made to the new law was to turn the lights and the music off at the official closing time.

Having no customers, Lek moved to the front of the bar and sat with Mott and Fa, who had poured her a whisky and soda with ice. The girls that were still in the bar after midnight often shared a bottle of whisky. Lek told them her joke about the landmines and they all laughed. Not much was going to happen now, so Lek offered the other girls an early finish.

As she did so, the night watch woman, Noi, arrived. Mott and Fa were about 22 and 20 years of age respectively and thought they would go and chance their luck in Walking Street. Freelance, as it was called. It was only five minutes away by taxi. As they left the bar, Mott said:

"If we see your teacher, should we tell him you still haven't done your homework?"

Lek threw a bottle top at her and they scurried away laughing.

Lek and her old friend, Noi, the night watch woman were left alone – not for the first time.

Noi's job was to look after the bar after the regular bar staff had left. She slept there, but if any stragglers wanted a drink at any time of the night, she would serve them. The bar was hers for about fifteen hours – from about one o'clock in the morning until about four o'clock in the afternoon. Noi was also from the same area, although not the same village as Lek, and they chatted about their families back home, catching up on the latest gossip.

Lek had been busy when she normally phoned her daughter to wish her goodnight and ask about her day and she was not happy with herself for not having made the time to do it. It was not the first time Soomsomai had gone to bed without her mother's blessing, but it did not happen often.

"Soomsomai understands you have to work, I'm sure. She's a bright kid," Noi consoled her. "What does she want to do when she leaves school? Has she ever said anything about it? Nurse, teacher, something like that?"

"No, she hasn't really talked about a career" said Lek, finishing the bottle into her glass. "She's still young and has plenty of time. I don't mind what she does, so long as she is happy and doesn't work in a bar like me. She likes tending animals. She looks after Mum's chickens and keeps a few pigs in with her uncle's herd. She goes there straight from school to feed them and talk to them. Maybe, she will think about being a vet.

"Her favourite subject in school is computing. Somebody donated a couple of computers to the school and the kids are learning on those, but you know what it's like. The classes are too big and the teachers, with the best will in the world, don't really know much about computers themselves.

"Some of the teachers are speaking English as foreign languages themselves and have problems with computers too. Try as hard as they might, these people are not really fit to teach English and computing, which is based on English. The commands are all in English, aren't they? Perhaps, I ought to get her private lessons and a second-hand computer to practice on at home. It would give her a head start, wouldn't it? How much do you think they cost? Do you know anything about computers?"

"Sorry, I don't…"

"I certainly don't. I don't even know how to switch one on. And the Internet? Should she be on that too?"

"Oh, it's no good asking me, dear" said Noi. "I'm the same as you. They didn't have computers in school, when I was there. I don't even know anyone that has got one. My baby, Su, is 16 now and all she ever talks about is babies and houses. She'll finish school this year and soon be married, I reckon. She doesn't want a career. She's not ambitious. She likes coming to visit me once a year for a holiday, but she doesn't really like the city, not even Pattaya.

"She's happy back home in the village. Soomsomai will be all right, don't you worry too much. Why don't you get off home and have an early night? It looks like you've got the bed to yourself tonight. Go and take advantage of it. I'll tidy up a bit here and then settle down to read my magazine a while, unless some Prince Charming comes by to keep me company. I should be so lucky!"

Lek smiled at her friend and hopped off the bar.

"Mmm, yes, you're right. I know you are, but you know what it's like. I feel so guilty about working away and not spending any time with my baby. I've missed seeing her grow up and it tears me apart sometimes. Usually I'm OK, but sometimes, sometimes I just can't handle it. Sometimes, I just want to cry and cry… give it all up and go back home with my tail between my legs like a disgraced puppy. Why do we do it, Noi?"

"There, there, I know. We all get like that sometimes when we're a bit low. You have done your best for your family and you can't do more than that, can you? No one can. Get off home now and have a good night's sleep. I'll see you tomorrow afternoon," comforted Noi.

They gave each other a long hug, then Lek picked up her bag and dashed across the narrow road to one of the motorbike taxis, which stood on the rank there day and night.

Lek knew the boys well. They had often sought shelter under the roof of her bar during a storm or popped in for a coffee to help them get through a quiet spell. They looked after the local girls like big brothers - they were the local protection or mafia.

"Hi, Nong," she said, "Give me a lift home will you? I'm dead beat. Where's the boss tonight? Out on the razzle?"

"Hi, Lek, you all right, girl? As beautiful as ever. Nice enough to eat, if you get my drift. If only you could see me as more than just a taxi service home. I have more between my legs than a just a motorbike, you know. Only joking. Sure, hop on. I don't know where Bong is. You know him. He's the boss and can do what he likes. I'm just the poor hired help and I do what I'm told" he replied.

Lek slapped him playfully on the shoulder and jumped up behind him side-saddle:

"Oh, you!" she said. "One day I'll take you up on that and you'll drop dead with shock."

Ten minutes later, she was standing outside her block, wondering whether to go for something to eat or not. She felt sad and lonely, but she decided against going for food, considering herself too poor company to inflict on anyone.

The truth was that most men would have paid just to talk to her even in her melancholy mood, but she did not realise it.

Up in her room, she felt totally alone. Her friends were with some drunken louts, but at least they were not alone. She put the fan and the TV on and took her blouse and her shorts off. She looked in the mirror as she wrapped a bath towel around herself. Not bad, she thought, but for how much longer?

She removed her bra and panties from under the towel, even though there was no one there to look anyway. It was force of habit. She sat on the bed and flicked through the channels. They did not have cable or satellite, so she left it on a channel playing music and went for a shower.

She thought about her mother who was 61. How much longer did she have left to live? Would she get an awful phone call one day telling her that her mother had passed away, before she could get a chance to spend a last few years with her? Would Soomsomai get married and move away, before Lek got the chance to help her grow up? These were the possibilities that were too dreadful to think about, but which reared their heads far too often these days. She turned on the shower and begged the water to wash the thoughts away.

But it did not and Lek lay down on the bed and cried herself to sleep – alone.

Daddy's Hobby

3 SWINGS AND ROUNDABOUTS

During the night, Lek woke herself up several times from a recurring nightmare about her mother lying dead at the bottom of the stairs and her daughter crying out for her mother to come to help her. She had had the same dream before, but she was getting it more and more often now. One day she would get a telephone call to say it had come true. She was sure it was a prophesy.

She was lying awake in bed, perspiring profusely from worry about her dream but trying to watch the news on the television at midday, when Ayr and Goong came back. Their good humour soon infected Lek and the horror of the nightmare slipped into the back of her mind, where it lurked until the next time she was off her guard like a cold sore.

The Scotsmen had been far better mannered than first appearances had suggested and the girls had been treated very well. Jock had been blunt and straight talking, but was kind and generous for all that. Dougal was quieter, even a little shy, which Goong said she liked in a man. Ayr thought Jock was brave and bold for speaking out the way he did. He was not afraid of anybody and was 'his own man', as she said he had put it. Ayr liked him.

Lek asked the usual questions: where had they gone? What had they done? Before coming to the crunch – were they going to see them again? They had left Soi 7 and taken a taxi by private hire to the Naam Chai Restaurant in Soi Buakhao, before pub-crawling their way back to the men's hotel rooms in the Siam Bay View on Second Road. They had even had breakfast and lunch there and the boys had bought them a swimming costume each in the hotel shop so that they could use the pool. Lek was happy for her friends – they had not had much good luck lately and were running low on cash, as always.

Not that it seemed to bother them. Not that anything ever seemed to bother either of them. They were true adepts at the 'Why Worry? What Will Be, Will Be' philosophy of life and Lek loved and envied them for it. They had family but no children of their own, but they believed that Karma would resolve everything. Their parents' Karma, their own Karma and their families' Karma would resolve it all between themselves in time. So why worry? Lek knew this axiom to be true; she believed in Karma. She was a practising, believing Theravada Buddhist, but she still worried. She just could not leave it all to fate. She considered it a weakness and one of her failings.

She asked again "Do you think you will ever see them again?"

"I don't know," said Ayr, "I think so. They said that they are working in Thailand repairing and selling photocopiers for Xerox. They are travelling to Bangkok as we speak and are flying to Chiang Mai for a fortnight on business. They just dropped us off outside with their taxi. They said they'd look us up when they came back this way."

"'If' not 'when'," thought Lek, but she would not say it just to dishearten her friends, who were riding high at the moment. They may even have been going to Bangkok to get a flight back to Britain, she thought. Some people will tell lies just for the sake of it or to make themselves look important. Lek had been told some whoppers in her time for absolutely no reason whatsoever. It was one of life's mysteries to her why some people lied when there was no justification for doing it.

Lek got up, pulling her nearby towel around herself as she did so and went for a shower.

When she came out of the bathroom, someone had made her a cup of tea and her friends were asleep on the bed in their towels. Lek turned the television down and lay down beside them, putting her arm around Ayr. Within minutes, she was asleep again, but content this time. Glad not to be alone.

They woke up at two p.m., their internal clocks guiding them back to their normal routine. Lek dressed and went down to the street to get something to eat, while the others showered, dressed and got ready for work. Lek would meet them there as she had some business to attend to at the Bangkok Bank on Second Road. She ordered a small helping of green chicken curry and rice with a beaker of iced water, ate heartily for thirty Baht, and then jumped on the next Baht Taxi, hoping it would go her way. She knew it probably would and it did – to the end of Soi Buakhao, left into Pattaya Klang and then right at Tops Super-market into Second Road. She stopped the taxi at Soi 6, paid her five Baht and crossed the busy road to the bank.

It was the end of the month and so time to make some payments. She went inside and waited in the typically long queue until it was her turn to be served, which took about fifteen minutes. Once at the counter, she filled in four identical forms: one to send her mother 6,000 Baht; one to put 1,000 Baht into her daughter's account; one to put 4,000 Baht into her own savings account and one to pay 2,000 Baht off a loan. She handed over the forms and the 13,000 Baht – two months' money for many people, four months' for some.

She had always been determined to put as much away as possible, although not all for herself. She wanted her mother to live comfortably and to be able to look after her daughter, Soomsomai, without having to worry about money, although her mother did have a part-time job during the day earning 500 Baht a week while the girl was in school and enjoyed afternoon tea at the Wat or temple with most of the other 'older' women in the village every weekday. Then she had a 'secret fund' for Soomsomai's education and a 'retirement fund' for herself. The reason for the loan repayment was the motive for her having gone to Pattaya in the first place.

Her father had been a doting parent and a hard-working man, but, alas, no financial genius. He was dead now, Lord rest his soul, and had been dead for ten years. He had died at the early age of 51, racked with pain and remorse. One year, after having had a succession of bad crops in the previous twelve months, he had borrowed 100,000 Baht from the bank 'to tide them over' and to buy some more land 'while it was cheap'.

The bank had taken advantage of him and, not knowing any better, he had accepted an interest rate of 1.5% per month – an extortionate rate since the loan had been secured on his land and house. Things had deteriorated and when he developed secondary onset diabetes, he worried that his family was doomed. The worry of repaying the loan had eventually killed him.

That and not being able to afford the insulin that he needed.

A few weeks after the funeral, a letter had arrived from the bank threatening foreclosure and that had been the first the family had known about the loan - it had come like a bombshell from Hell. Those few weeks had been the worst time in her family's existence and they had all been lost for a solution. Until one day, Beou's mother had suggested that they ask Beou to set one of them up – or to give one of them a job in Pattaya. Beou had told her mother that there was plenty of money to be earned in Pattaya and that she was doing really well. She must be, her mother reasoned, she was sending at least 5,000 Baht home every month.

The family had had a conference about what to do. Should they sell some land? That probably would not cover it. Anyway, they needed more land to reach critical mass to become profitable, not less. Her brothers, Long and Ngat had been eighteen and sixteen respectively and her sister, little Chalita, had been only thirteen years old. Long had already left school to work with his father, now Ngat would have to leave school too to help Long.

What could Chalita be expected to do? She was already devastated over the death of her beloved father. Their mother was already working in the fields and could do no more. The only option had been for Lek to get as highly-paid a job as possible, so, after much heartache, they had decided to offer to pay Beou's fare back to the village, so that she could explain about 'working in Pattaya' and what it entailed.

Beou, Lek's cousin, had come back immediately and explained that Pattaya was best understood as a foreign man's paradise. Everything there was geared towards him. Therefore, employment opportunities were mostly limited to the entertainment and leisure industries. Beou had said that she was already actively looking for three or four extra girls at that moment and that, if Lek wanted, and if the family agreed, then they could travel back together, and that Lek could have a bed in her house. That had clinched it. They did not have many alternatives and the guaranteed 2,000 Baht per month plus tips, as it was then, was more than she could earn locally. She had had to go.

That night her family had organised a farewell party and most of the village had attended bringing their own food and drink. At the party, her two best friends, Ayr and Goong, had cried so much at the thought of losing her that Beou had offered them temporary jobs too. It would be like an adventure for them all. It would help Lek get over her husband too.

The next day the four had taken a taxi to Phitsanulok to catch the night bus to Pattaya and their adventure had begun.

Lek had been paying the loan off ever since. The bank had even put the interest rate up to 1.75% per month when they found out that Lek would be making the repayments, because they had felt that the loan was somehow less secure. Now, after 9 years and 11 months of not missing a single monthly 2,000 Baht payment, she had one instalment of 1,725.95 Baht left to make, if she had calculated correctly. It would certainly be less than 2,000 Baht. What a red-letter day that would be! She decided she would go home and roast a pig to celebrate with her family and maybe take Ayr and Goong back too.

She left the bank feeling elated, as she did every month: one more month down - one month more off the 120 months she had started with; she was honouring her father's word to pay off the loan; she was supporting her family; providing for her daughter's education and she had saved something for herself too. Not that it had always gone so smoothly – there had also been months when she had only been able to pay her mother and the loan. Not much could go wrong now though. She skipped down the steps and turned left into Second Road.

"Maybe rain later," she mused, "but who bloody cares?"

Lek arrived at Daddy's Hobby at three-fifteen and Noi was still dozing in her chair. Lek went inside and started to put the rice in the steamer to save her friend a job.

"I'm not asleep, you know. I was just about to do that, but thanks anyway," piped up Noi.

"Oh, don't worry. I'm early and could do with keeping busy. Go ahead, have forty winks and I'll make us a cup of coffee. Do you fancy a cake too? Don't bother to answer, I'll get you one anyway."

Lek put water in the steamer and in the kettle, put a spoonful of coffee in each of two cups and went to Tops to get some cakes. When she returned, her friend was swilling her face and they both sat down to drink their coffee.

"Anything happen last night?" enquired Lek.

"No, same as usual, nice and quiet - just how I like it," said Noi. "We did get a few blokes come by at about three a.m. They had a couple of quiet beers and then left. They were all right though – not like some. A bit pissed, but all right. They said they might come back later to check out the local talent. I told them we had some real stun- ners working here. They weren't bad looking themselves either.

"You could do a lot worse: polite, 40-ish, British, handsome. What more could you want? I didn't see any wedding rings either. Nor any marks of rings. Mind you, they're probably still asleep. They're staying at a hotel around the corner – over there somewhere," she said, waving over in the general direction of Second Road.

"Did you get home OK? No nonsense from Nong? I saw him yapping away at you. We all know he tries it on with all the girls. He thinks he's a real lady-killer, doesn't he? But I think he does really like you. He often comes over for a chat late at night when it's quiet or raining. He's always asking after you. He says his boss, Bong, fancies you too. Woaoy! Now he's handsome and no mistake. Don't you like him? He's got a fat wallet too. You could definitely do a lot worse than him. If I could lose ten kilos, I'd have a go at him myself, but nobody takes me seriously at my size. I can't think of a better incentive to try to lose weight though, can you?" she laughed.

Noi was a lovely woman. She was about thirty-five, but as with many over-weight people, she looked five years younger. She was about twenty kilos over-weight, but being big-boned and tall, she would prob-ably look pretty, if she could lose ten kilos, as she already knew. She al-ways had a smile on her face or a mock-frown. There was always a joke or self-effacing comment waiting to spring from her lips and everybody took to her instantly.

Men too, although everyone, of both sexes, seemed to regard her as a 'favourite aunt' rather than a potential lover. In fact, no one could remember ever having seen her with a lover of either sex in the last ten years, although she had a fifteen-year old daughter, so something must have happened all those years ago. She knew that Beou would know the full story, but she would never ask. If Noi wanted her to know, she would tell her herself soon enough.

In the bar world of Pattaya, being too curious about other people's affairs definitely did not pay.

Nevertheless, Lek sometimes got the impression that Noi would like to meet someone again. She was always joking about taking a lover; she obviously enjoyed talking to men; she liked whistling at them as they passed by; she enjoyed having a drink with them, but she always backed off at that last moment, usually making a joke of the situation and then scurrying away. They said that she had been very attractive before.

That made sense, unattractive girls just would not go to Pattaya – there was too much competition. Lek guessed that she had allowed herself to put on weight so that she could not get a man. But why would anyone do that? She didn't seem to lack confidence, but maybe that was an act. Perhaps, there was no thin woman trying to get out.

They both got up. Lek took the cups to the sink and washed them up. Noi went to the cash drawer and counted the takings. Everything over the 2,000 Baht float, she would sign for and take to Beou's house, before 'clocking off' and going home to see her daughter at about five o'clock.

Sixteen hours a day, seven days a week, everyday of the month. She didn't have much time for a love life anyway.

As Noi was getting her motorbike keys, she motioned to Lek to look down the road.

"Woaoy! That's them. Look! That's them. I told you they said they'd come back. I wonder if I made a good impression on them. I think I'll stay for just a little bit longer to get you started. He, he, he. To introduce you," she whispered, smiling.

"Woaoy! Woaoy! Woaoy! Woaoy! Woaoy! Handsome man! Where you going? Come have drink with me and my beautiful friend, Lek. I take care you last night. You mau, but I take care you. You say, you come back today, look lovely ladies. Have one now - my friend Lek. She very beautiful, no? More come now ten minutes," shouted Noi at the top of her voice to the three men who were approaching some twenty metres away.

With that, Ayr and Goong walked into the bar with Mott and Fa, whom they had met walking into work.

"Woaoy! Look have four more beautiful ladies for you to talk to now. Which one you like? Come have beer. Maybe palacetamon, eh? Have hangover? Come talk with me and I introduce you ladies. Have quiet talk." She winked at Lek.

The men walked over and sat down. Noi waaied each one and then shook his hand, before introducing him to Lek. Lek took the cue, waaied and shook hands too.

"Three beer?" inquired Lek, leaving her friend to start the conversation.

One nodded and Lek turned to get their order, place it in the ledger and write a chit. The other girls were curious about who the new men were, but were too busy adjusting their war paint to go over just yet. Noi knew that and held the fort while they got ready. Lek brought over the beers and a big smile.

"Where you come from?"

"England, Portsmouth. You hear name before? Portsmouth? South England, by the sea. Very famous. Lord Nelson. Ship 'Victory'. You know?" replied one, trying to be helpful.

"All right, Ed, all right. She's not a bleeding dummy, but I bet she's never heard of any of those things before," said another.

His assumption was correct, but Lek said: "Poltsmou? Yes, I hear before. Sou' England. Very beautiful there, eh? By the sea. Yes, lovely, I think."

The third one chipped in: "Yeah, it's all right. Plenty of night-life. You been there then, Lek?"

"Of course she hasn't been there, have you, doll? Most of them have never been out of the country. You're such a Wally, Dave. Most Thais haven't even got a passport, don't have any money and have never been abroad, let alone to Europe. Is that right, doll? You not go outside Thailand before?" He was right again.

"No, no" she smiled coyly, "I not go there before. Not go to England, Eulope. I want to go there sometime. You on holiday? How long you stay here?"

This got them talking and Noi took her leave, urging the other girls to get a move on with a flick of her eyes in the direction of the men. Fa went over, said hello and then took over the till. She put some music on and switched on the TV, looking for a football game. Mott pranced over next, said 'Hello' and hopped onto the rostrum to dance around her pole, followed by Ayr and Goong, pretending to giggle to each other at a joke, while each fixed one man's eyes with a smile.

Battle was about to commence.

"Hello, ladies. Well, hello!" Mike greeted them. "Sit down. Come and sit down. Noi was right. There are beautiful ladies working here. Look, Lek. I apologise for this pair of Wallies and their stupid questions and I humbly apologise for my attitude earlier. We're not like that really. We're just a bit mau – you know, drunk last night, have hangover today. I'm sorry. Can we get you lovely ladies a drink? Let's introduce ourselves properly.

Stand up, gentlemen. On the far left is Lieutenant David Murray; in the middle is Lieutenant Edward Riley and I am yours truly, Lieutenant Michael Smith. Three officers and gentlemen in Her Majesty's Royal Navy. We're pleased to meet you." With that, they bowed in unison, as they had obviously done many times before.

The six girls beamed with delight, especially Ayr and Goong, who were trying to find the hands of Ed and Dave again after the introductory handshake. Each of the girls had a picture in her mind's eye of a dashing, handsome, fit naval officer in a white uniform with a wallet full of lovely money. Lek was pleased too, but she had heard many stories from men trying to impress her before.

She took all stories with a few pinches of salt as a matter of course these days. Perhaps she was becoming too sceptical in her old age, but then maybe not. She asked if they had any photographs. When they did not have any on them, "What a surprise," she thought.

"How old you? Are you marry?" blurted out Mott

"38, 38, 40" answered Mike "and we're all married to The Duchess of York." The joke fell flat on the girls.

"Duchess of Yoke? Same Queen?" asked Mott hopefully, but rather naively.

"Not same Queen," joked Ed, "she has a steel bottom."

None of the girls had a clue what the men were talking about, but they were definitely intrigued – especially Mott, who shouted from her pole in all earnestness "Not steel bum, steel knickers, yes? Not see steel knickers before. I think not nice."

The men were loving it and so were the girls.

"No, darling. Only joking. We're not married. I joke with you that we are married to our ship – 'HMS The Duchess of York'. Only joking. Steel knickers, for Christ's sake. Are you for real? You're gorgeous, though, aren't you?"

They all laughed and Mike rang the bell. So, thought Lek, they have money too and are not frightened of spending it. Another good sign. Mott came down off the poll and took the men's order for themselves, before going around all the other girls and punters that were there to see what they wanted.

Ringing the bell in Thailand means you are offering everyone in the bar a drink of their choice. By six o'clock, the other two had each rung the bell as well, but the party came to an abrupt end, when Mike announced unexpectedly that it was eighteen fifteen hours and time to leave. Everybody looked disappointed, except Mike, who had been delegated to keep an eye on his watch.

"Oh, shit, Mike! Do we have to? This is the best time we've had in the whole week we've been here. I'd rather stay here. Sod 'em. Come on, me ol' shipmates, let's have another drink. What do you think, Dave?"

"Unfortunately, I think Mike's right," retorted Dave. "We promised and a promise is a promise is a promise. We can come back later. You'll still be here won't you, girls? You're not going to go anywhere are you?"

He always had been a bit slow on the uptake.

The girls smiled back weakly.

"Where you go?" asked Ayr. "You butterfly? Have other ladies everywhere? I like you. We go with you? Ayr, Lek, Goong, yes? One, two, thlee, fou', fi', sis people, yes? Have beer in other pub with you."

"Check bin, kraap" said Mike, asking for the bill and at the same time giving away that he had at least a smattering of Thai.

"We've got something to do that we can't get out of. That's all. We'll be back later. Wait for us, if you can. Otherwise, well, that's how it goes, I guess, eh? We've had a great couple of hours and we all wish we could stay here or take you with us but it's impossible, unfortunately. So, see you later. Adieu! Adieu! Adieu! Come on, me hearties."

They walked off in the same direction they had had been walking before in Indian file with hands on the shoulders of the one in front like the Seven Dwarfs, singing:

"Hi ho! Hi ho! It's off to work we go with a bucket and spade …."

The girls were disappointed to say the least, but these things happened.

Lek broke the silence with "Ah well… I thought it was too good to be true. Still, chins up. We all made some money out of the drinks and the tip and we all had a pleasant couple of hours. Well, those of us who got in early enough anyway. I made 150 Baht plus a share of the tip. So did Ayr and Goong. Mott and Fa got at least 90 Baht plus tip. Everybody else got something plus tip. So, let's look on the bright side and get on with it."

She had given the moral booster, now she rallied her troops and they all went to the front of the bar to coax the foreigners in.

Mott went back up the pole.

The evening was fairly quiet, but then it was that time of the year – the official holiday season started in late October in Pattaya. By December, hotel room prices would have doubled and you would not get in anywhere unless you had pre-booked and paid a large deposit. But those days were still a long way off and next month would be her last payment to the bank. Her reason for being in Pattaya would have expired along with the amortisation of the loan in five weeks time.

It troubled her immensely.

She wanted to go home to be with her family, but she knew she was no longer the peasant farmer's daughter of ten years before. She had become used to getting more out of life. She looked at Mott, still dancing around the pole and Fa at the till. Mott would go with man after man and really enjoy it. Fa was more like herself. Fa was a 21-22 year old woman, married to a local Thai man, who delivered flowers for a shop.

They did not have much money but they were happy. They were thinking about trying for a baby the next year. Fa did not go with other men. She would entice them, get drinks out of them, laugh at their jokes and do whatever was necessary to keep the bar busy except go home with anyone but her husband came to pick her up at random times after work.

Just to make sure.

Lek had started out in a similar way. She had been married when she had first come to Pattaya and was still married now for that matter. Sleeping with all sorts of men just because they had money had not appealed to her. People in her village did not do that sort of thing, not that any foreigners ever went there anyway. She had come to Pattaya to work 'straight' behind the bar – not in front of it, as the popular job description went.

She had worked for 2,000 Baht per month, which paid the loan and she lived off tips and Beou's charity of more-or-less free board and lodgings. She owed Beou a huge debt of gratitude, although all Beou would say was that they were family and no thanks were necessary or wanted.

She had gone there with her two best friends, Ayr and Goong, who could not bear to be parted from her. Everything had gone extremely well for a couple of months, until she realised that she was four months pregnant with the baby of her husband, Tom. She had worked right up until the week before it was due and then she had gone home to have it – her darling, beautiful baby girl, Soomsomai.

A month later, when they no longer needed her, she had gone back to work in Pattaya, leaving her mother to bring up her daughter. As far as she knew, Soomsomai's father had never seen his daughter nor even ever tried to see her. He had certainly never sent even one Baht in child support and nor did the law require him to. After her return to work, she had accepted the offer of the first man that had asked to go 'for a meal'.

She had a baby to look after now and her mother could not work because of it.

That was how she had started and many girls had a similar tale. It usually involved a loan or a debt or a child or some cocktail of the three. Ayr and Goong had not started like that. At Lek's farewell party, the three friends had cried so much at the prospect of being split up for the first time in their lives that Ayr and Goong had begged Beou to let them go too 'just to get Lek settled in and make some money before they got married'.

Their parents had relented and Beou had agreed. So they had all three shared a tiny box room in Beou's house and worked in Beou's bar. They had slept three to a bed then too, but when they decided to go full on, they had had to find their own apartment and Beou had used her contacts to help them there too. Beou could not have them coming and going at all hours of the day and night and risk their men friends coming around. After all, she had her own two daughters to consider.

She broke herself out of her reverie and mentally wished Fa good luck. Fa would need it. The temptation to 'only go with a really nice farang and only if she wanted to, once in a while' was huge and many respectable married ladies had succumbed before.

Especially the young and beautiful ones that were unaccustomed to flattery from their husbands and especially if they were kept short of house-keeping money too.

By nine o'clock, Joy and Deou were on the telephone anxiously looking for their boyfriends, Barry and Nick, who were thirty minutes late. Lek had a friendly chat with them and tried to distract them. She was sure that their friends were sincere, but just not punctual and sure enough they arrived fifteen minutes later with flowers and apologies. Lek was still with Joy and Deou when the boys arrived and she mercilessly sat there waiting to be offered a drink to boost her takings.

"Lek say you come soon," Joy told the boys. They nodded their appreciation to Lek.

The drink was duly proffered and after taking a sip she moved on.

Everyone was wondering what had become of Porn and Or, so Lek telephoned Mama San to ask whether she had heard anything. Mama San said that Porn and Or were still with the Englishmen and that they would probably not be in that evening, unless they came by much later.

Four down, four to go, thought Lek. Beou could probably do with more staff at this rate. If Lek and her friends got off with or had got off with the sailors then that would leave young Fa in charge. If Mott went, Fa could not run a busy bar on her own. She would have to have a word with Beou when she came in at about ten o'clock. There were always girls looking for work in popular bars such as 'Daddy's Hobby' so getting staff would not be a problem.

Keeping them might be.

Beou came in at ten o'clock, as she had promised, locked up her motorbike, said, "Yes, please" and jumped into the driving seat behind the cash drawer that Fa had quickly vacated. As she started to look over the takings, she lit a cigarette and a gin and tonic appeared in front of her.

"Any problems?" she asked Lek and Fa, but no one in particular.

Both shook their heads.

"I've got something I want to bring up later, but it's not pressing," said Lek, referring to taking on more bar staff.

"OK, give me ten minutes, if you're sure it can wait. Another one of these, please!" she said, holding up her glass and taking a deep draw on her cigarette.

"OK, good work, Fa. I can tell it was you by your neat handwriting. Please carry on while I have a chat with Lek. OK, girl, what's the problem?" she said getting up out of her chair and steering Lek by the arm to a quiet spot at the bar.

"Oh, nothing really" she replied, "Well, two things, I suppose. Firstly to do with your business. Joy and Deou are out almost permanently now and I think we'll lose one or both of them soon. Likewise, Porn and Or are out again, and, if they are lucky, may not be with us too much longer either, which means that if any other two of us are lucky, you have not got enough staff, unless you're here. I think you need at least two, maybe three or four more girls."

"OK, I agree. Do you know anyone back home or do you have anyone in mind, if you have, let me know? What's the other thing?"

"Mmmm, well, you remember the reason why I came here ten

years ago? It won't exist this time next month. One instalment left, then finito."

They simultaneously grinned from ear to ear and hugged each other.

"Good for you, Lek. I'm so happy for you. Let's you and me drink a bottle of scotch and get a taxi home. Will you finish working here?"

That was what Lek did not know. The answer to that question had been bothering her all day and, as usual, Mama San had hit the nail on the head first strike. What a woman, what a boss and what a friend!

"I don't know, Beou" she said "I've been thinking about it for a while now, but it always seemed so far off. Now it's next month and I'm so confused that my head hurts. Can I really go back after ten years of what I've been doing? I'm not the same woman any more, am I? Will they accept me back? Can I put up with the parochialism and narrow-mindedness? I just don't know. What do you think, Beou? Could I make it work back home? Then again, I don't want to let you down either. You have been so good to my family and me. Without you, we would have lost our home and fields – everything Dad worked and died for."

"Oh, this is worse than I thought" tutted Beou. "First of all, I strongly recommend you take me up on the offer of sharing a bottle of whisky. Then, I recommend a sensible girly chat, a good night's sleep and a decent hangover, followed by a late sleep in and two paracetamol, and if that doesn't make you see sense, the same again tomorrow, repeated ad infinitum until you do. Blow the cobwebs out of your mind. You sound as if you've become institutionalised."

They both smiled, tears in Lek's eyes and Beou got up to get the whisky, soda and ice bucket.

Lek thought for a moment about what she would do if the sailors came back. Stay with Beou or go with them? She decided she would have to 'play it by ear'.

She would not let her friend down, but the sailors were exactly her target market.

"We'll leave that one to fate," she thought.

She looked around the bar, which was busy now. Plenty of smiling faces on the punters and the girls, all of whom had someone to talk to and most of whom were playing some sort of bar game with a man.

All except Fa who was still dancing on the pole.

Most of the girls were wearing genuine smiles. They honestly did enjoy this part of the job. Socialising, keeping men happy, being girly, laughing and joking, being admired and complimented by the men was great. It is called 'sanuk' in Thai – happiness in what one is doing, whatever it is. Thai women were brought up to be good to the men-folk in this way and to be appreciated in return. It was the other part of the job that took some getting used to. That sorted the girls from the women.

There were few girls working 'in front of the bar', who had not cried themselves to sleep because of what they were doing, especially in the first few years. Most of the country girls were not brought up that way and carried a sense of shame because of it, but they bore the shame because they had a goal. They were on a mission to pay a debt or raise a child usually. There were those that enjoyed the whole job, but they were usually city girls who had seen the game from an early age or who may even have been born into it.

Goong and Ayr had taken to it quite easily although their families were respectable country farmers. Maybe their philosophy helped them. They were in for the duration. They enjoyed the job in its entirety. They enjoyed the attention, the good food, the travel, the new faces and the hotels. It was quite probable, she thought, that they would have turned down a proposal of marriage several years ago, because they en-joyed the life so much.

Nowadays, they would jump at the chance, if the right man came along with enough money, but then they were older now and could see that their days at the top were numbered. There were fresh-faced, beautiful eighteen year-olds arriving every day and the lifestyle was hard on the complexion. Late nights, too little sleep, too much alcohol and a smoky environment aged a girl prematurely.

As did not being able to trust anyone and always being watchful of your 'partner'.

There was no love from the opposite sex in their job in Pattaya. Only lust and lechery and debauchery and distrust and the threat of AIDS or some other horrible, deadly disease from a treacherous 'boyfriend' who wanted to pass his death sentence on to as many others as possible out of revenge for his own infection. Those who caught these deadly diseases usually just disappeared one day.

They could not face the shame of going home infected and treatment was unaffordable and ultimately ineffectual for most people, so they often went to Bangkok or somewhere similarly anonymous, rented a small room and quietly committed suicide. Usually with poison and died, unidentifiable, like a mosquito crushed for trying to care for its young.

Beou came back and broke her from her sombre thoughts:

"Knock that back, girl, and good luck to you. Well done for coping here for ten years and well done for paying off the loan to those shit-head bankers. Now cheer up! You've got the night off. Do you fancy going out on the town? Maybe have a dance somewhere?"

"Oh, I don't know, Beou" she said "Let's just sit here for now and have a chat. I'm feeling a bit down. Maybe later if I can shake off this mood. I really don't know what the matter with me is. I just feel like crying and I've no real reason. Like you said, the bank is as good as paid off and I'm a free woman again from next month. For the first time in ten years, I can work, if I want to or I can go home, if I want to, but for the first time in ten years, I don't know what I want. Funny, isn't it? For ten years, I had a goal or even several goals and now that I've reached them, I feel lost. Homeless even. A silly cow, aren't I?"

Lek clinked glasses with Beou, wished her 'Chok Dee" and they both emptied their glasses. Beou refilled them and, as if to echo Lek's mood, the skies opened up and it began raining heavily. As they drained the second large glass of whiskey and a little soda, Lek surmised that the sailors would not be back that night even if it had been their intention to return earlier, wherever they had gone would seem more attractive now than an open-sided beer bar.

The rain was blowing in over them and they were getting a little wet, but neither of them cared nor felt inclined to suggest that they move to a drier part of the bar. Customers were moving off to drier bars and soon Beou and her girls were left alone.

It seemed for all the world that Lek's dismay had infected the whole bar, its owner, her colleagues and even the weather itself.

4 A DREAM COME TRUE?

Lek woke up slowly and opened her eyes. They hurt, so she closed them again. Her head hurt too and so did various other parts of her body, but she recognised the room and she knew that she was safe and had been looked after. It was Beou's box room. A little bit more cluttered than when she had stayed there all those years ago, even though there had been three of them in there then.

On opening her eyes, she had seen boxes of spirits, mostly gin and whisky, piled high. It made her want to throw up. It must be Beou's storeroom now, she thought, although thinking was difficult. She felt her body. A few aches and pains and an unfamiliar garment. She still had her underwear on and what was probably one of Beou's dressing gowns on top. Good old Beou, she thought. She opened her eyes again and looked at her watch. By the light shining through the thin curtains, she could see on her wristwatch, that it was eleven thirty a.m. and she decided to get up and look for her cousin.

But slowly. Very slowly.

Lek got up, picked up the blanket and pillow and opened the bedroom door. She stopped just outside the door, as she tried to adjust her eyes to the more intense light and heard Beou say:

"Ah! So, you're awake then, Little One? Are you ready for a livener, a coffee, a coffee and a livener or breakfast, a coffee and a livener?"

"Oh, Beou! Oh dear! Oh, dear! Oh, dear! My head hurts something wicked. I don't know if I can see to come down stairs, but I've got to get to the loo. I'll tell you in a minute after I've had time to think."

She dragged herself down the stairs clutching the banister as a guide and a brake and tossed the blanket and pillow she'd slept on onto the couch where Beou was sitting as she passed on her way to the toilet.

"I won't be a minute" she said and returned five minutes later.

"Ah, that's better. I had to have a pee and wash my face. I feel a bit better now. At least I've got rid of some of that poison from my system."

"Are you saying my whisky is no good?" joked Beou. "You couldn't get enough of it last night. We had two bottles in the bar and then we sent the girls home early. It was raining too heavily and custom was thin. Do you remember? Then we caught a taxi back here after Noi arrived and I left my bike with her."

"Mmmm, vaguely."

"We sat here and watched a film or at least tried to and you wanted more to drink, so I got you an old dressing gown and a bottle of whisky and you got changed. Your skirt and top are hanging up over there. I sponged your skirt off. It should be dry soon. You can borrow one of my blouses, if you like. The kids have gone to school so we've got the house to ourselves until they get back at about five.

Noi'll be around then too for a coffee. Are you going in today? Or do you want the day off? It's up to you. If you want another session, I can get a baby sitter later. You can even go to work straight from here. Up to you, girl. Now, do you want coffee in your whisky, whiskey in your coffee or are you ready for something to eat or all three?"

"I feel awful, Beou. Really. Was I all right last night? I didn't cause any fights or anything? Or I wasn't sick everywhere, was I? I can't remember much after sending the girls home. We waited for Noi, did we? Well, of course. We had to! Silly me. I still can't think straight. Did we get a motorbike taxi? How did I stay on that?"

She curled up on the couch next to Beou; put her head on the pillow and pulled the blanket over herself.

"Oh, go on then. I'll have a little whisky in a large black coffee. I'll think about the food while I'm drinking that. Are you having one too?"

"I'm with you, kid. When you tell me that you are all right again, I'll go back to my normal life. Until then, I'll stick with you. You're my favourite cousin and number one head girl. Even if it is only for a few weeks longer. Number one head girl, I mean, not favourite cousin – you'll always be that. We have been through so much together over the last ten years. Ten years! Doesn't time fly when you're enjoying yourself?"

Lek managed a weak smile and Beou went off to make the drinks.

Beou returned, saying:

"Oh, I would not have trusted you on a motorbike taxi. Dear me! You could hardly stand upright. No, Noi went off and found us a cab. There were plenty on Beach Road. It wasn't worth the risk for forty Baht. Here are a few spoonfuls of rice and a cold boiled-egg. It'll help soak up the alcohol and give your stomach something to work with. You know what you're like with coffee on an empty stomach! It goes straight through you, burning its way through like molten lava."

"OK, thanks, Beou. I know you're right. It's just… OK, OK, I'll eat it. It'll do me good. I know it will. Thanks. Did those sailors come back last night? Did you hear about them?"

"Mmmm, Noi told me when she came around for coffee yesterday evening. You're feeling better then – asking about men. I thought you were dying. No. They did not come back. Your flatmates wanted to hang on until one o'clock to wait for them, but it was still pouring down and I could see it would be a waste of time. If they are that interested and if it is meant to happen, they will be back today."

Lek knew this was good advice and decided there and then to go into work later. She considered there to be at least a fifty-fifty percent chance that they were impostors, but then they were reasonably good odds in her world.

"I'd better go in Beou. I said I'd look for a couple of new girls for the bar. A few came by the other day and I told them to come back later in the week."

Beou pursed her lips in a sign of disbelief:

"Yeah, right! Nothing to do with sailors. Sure. OK! Up to you. If you don't want to go drinking with your old cousin, I can take it. I'm a big girl now and won't cry."

They smiled at each other.

"Beou," said Lek, "Do you mind if I just doze here in front of the TV, have a shower here later and then wander into work at about three thirty? I feel so, uh, safe and cosy here at the moment. I don't want to go back to the flat just yet."

"No, no problem. You carry on. If you want anything, just help yourself. I may pop out later and do a little shopping, otherwise, I'll be in my room catching up with the books. You get some beauty sleep you may need it. I'll see you later. Sweet dreams – of the UK Royal Navy or whatever it's called over there."

Lek awoke after an intermittent, though restful and pleasant slumber. She got up feeling a lot better, took the towel that had been placed near her head and made for the bathroom to take a shower. Lek shouted to Beou, but as there was no reply, she assumed that Beou must be out shopping. It was three o'clock. She felt almost as good as new after her shower and she went to see if there was anything she could do until Beou got back. She did the small amount of washing up that was left and folded her blanket neatly with the pillow and put them at the top of the stairs. She tapped Beou's door and looked in as she did so but saw that Beou had indeed gone out, so she went back downstairs to watch TV and wait.

Beou was not long and Lek heard the key in the latch at three forty-five.

"Yoo-hoo! You still here? Hiya, Lek. Did you sleep well? Do you still want to go into work today? All right then, we'll go in together. I'll just put these few things in the fridge and we'll share a taxi. I can get my motorcycle then too."

Within ten minutes, they were in a Baht taxi halfway down Pattaya Klang Road and well on their way to 'Daddy's Hobby'. They even had the good fortune that the taxi went straight over Second Road on the way to Beach Road and they got out a hundred metres from the bar. That did not happen often.

"Thanks for last night, Beou. I really needed that. And a friend. And you're the best."

They smiled at Noi then at each other and walked into the bar together.

"Noi," said Beou "I decided to come in early myself today, so there's no need for you to go round to my house later. Why don't you get off early for a change?"

"Oh, no thanks, Boss" she replied. "Su doesn't get home 'til about five-twenty and I'd go mad sitting in the house alone. I'll just sit here for an hour and chat, if that's all right with you."

"Whatever you like. Whatever you like. You try to help people… That's two people I've tried to give time off to today and nobody wants it. I must be paying you all too much."

She walked off muttering to herself, pretending to be puzzled.

Lek felt much better. Her head had cleared and she felt a lot happier in herself, even though she could remember only snippets of the conversations. Something had affected her consciousness; she did not know what, but it had. It was similar to going to bed troubled by something and waking up, not knowing the answer, but knowing that the problem was not as big as one had imagined. Lek had had this experience many times in her life when she felt depressed.

When this happened, she liked to think that she had visited or been visited by someone who was knowledgeable and that she had discussed the matter sensibly and rationally. Sometimes that person would not be alive in the generally accepted Western meaning of the word but would live in the Spirit World. She often felt that she had talked to her father in times of need.

This time she could only just remember talking to Beou, but it had done the trick.

She walked behind the bar, smiling at her friends and colleagues and sat down to have her fourth cup of coffee of the day. There were already a few punters drinking beer, but they were being ably looked after by the other girls.

Joy and Deou arrived beaming. Their regular boyfriends, Barry and Nick, had invited them back to Wales for an all-expenses-paid holiday. The only problem was that they only had a fortnight to get everything sorted out and it could take longer than that just to get the visas. All the girls knew someone who had fallen at that last hurdle. Great Britain was one of the hardest countries in the world for a Thai girl to visit, especially if she were young and beautiful and accompanying a middle-aged man.

Anyway, no one was going to mention this today; everybody was happy for them. They wanted to take the next six weeks off. Two weeks to get a visa and say goodbye to their families and four weeks to visit Britain. There was no question about Beou refusing. This was why all the girls were there in the first place. They would probably fight to the death to get on that plane for Britain if they had to.

Nick and Barry arrived in high spirits at about five o'clock and all the girls gathered around to wish them well. Beou went over too and shook their hands. She sat down, offered the two couples a drink, and started talking excitedly about the girls having six weeks off work.

"Joy and Deou have ask for six weeks holiday. You look after them, eh? They very good girls, but not know much about foreigners or their customs. They not go abroad before, you know? You must take care of them good. Ah, I know you, you good men. You take care of my girls for me.

"Do you want to give party for them for good luck and for say goodbye to their friends before they go? It is an old Thai tradition to have a party before a long journey to ask for good luck in travelling and say goodbye to friends. Maybe not come back, eh? Maybe you marry in Wales, eh?"

Nick looked around, saw that the bar was fairly empty and rang the bell. It was as good a way as any, he thought, to change the subject of marriage.

"Yes, OK, er, we'll have a party on the night before we leave. Can you organise that for us, Beou?"

"Sure, Nick" replied Beou, "No Problem. We will make it nice for you. Balloons, soup, chicken, rice, salad, music, a pig… You will have plenty of good luck and your sweethearts will not be afraid of flying."

"A pig!? Sounds lovely," said Barry "How much do you think all that will cost, Beou?"

"Oh," answered the Mama San, "for you and my girls only the minimum standard rate for a super de luxe 'good-luck party' for four – about 7,000 Baht. Very reasonable, eh?"

It didn't sound 'very reasonable' to Nick and Barry, but they had been out-manoeuvred. Their girls were smiling broadly at them pleading with their eyes and Mama San was also looking into their eyes waiting for an answer. They had never stood a chance, even their girls were on Mama San's side. They had not switched allegiance yet. The boys had to say 'Yes' and they did.

"OK, Beou, it's a deal" said Nick for the two of them and he rang the bell again.

The time passed slowly for Lek, as it always did when she was just working 'inside the bar' – passing the time until a new man came by, who might get her out of her predicament, even though next month that predicament would not be the same one she was in this month.

Next month she would have no reason to stay in Pattaya; she could either wait for a husband or go home.

She decided to go 'outside the bar' and camp it up in order to stave off another bout of depression, so she leapt over the bar with a 'whoop' and joined her friends who were calling anyone wearing trousers to come and join them. After a while, she noticed the three 'sailors' fifty metres up the road, engaged in a conversation with a few girls in a bar.

"Bloody typical," she thought, "I knew it."

So, she threw herself into promotion mode even more vehemently.

"Sod them."

With that, the sailors turned around, waved at her and, although pride told her not to, she waved back, tapped Goong and Ayr on their backsides, indicating to them to wave as well.

Ten minutes later, they saw the sailors turn away from the bar and start walking towards them. The girls were pleased, even Lek, but she went behind the bar anyway and pretended to be busy.

"Hello, ladies," greeted Mike, "You remember Ed and Wally, eh, sorry, I mean Dave, don't you? And myself, Mike? Hello, Lek! Are you too busy to talk to us today? Three beers for us, please, and whatever you and your two pals are having. Three bottles of ice-cold beer Chang for us. Have you all missed us?"

It appeared that they had for Ayr was holding Dave's hand, Ed was gazing shyly into Goong's eyes and Mott was doing her best to attract anybody's attention from her usual perch on the chromium dance pole.

"Oh, yes" she said, "miss you long time. Miss you vely, vely much. I not sleep good last night for thinking of you."

They smiled at her but it seemed that only Mike was readily available and he was watching Lek bring over the drinks. Lek had noticed but was studiously ignoring him.

All in good time. She brought over three bottles of beer, three Lady

Drinks and three glasses. After serving everyone, she sat down and said cheers. Everybody took a swig.

"So, ladies, do you fancy coming out with us tonight? We want to go drinking, dancing and eating. Do you fancy that?" asked Mike.

"We pay for everything" interposed Dave.

Mike shot him a glance.

"You're such a Wally, Dave; of course 'we pay for everything'. They know that, they wouldn't go otherwise, Jeez!"

"OK, OK, I was only making things clear for the ladies. I know their English isn't as good as ours is and I've told you before, stop calling me a Wally! I know I haven't been about as much as you have but that's no reason to keep taking the piss. I'm getting fed up with it…"

"All right, me hearties, calm down both of you" said Ed. "Mike didn't mean anything, did you, Mike? It's just an expression, isn't it?"

"Sure, sure, of course it is. I didn't mean anything, Dave. Jesus wept. We're on bloody holiday, mush. I'm not trying to upset you. What a Wally!

"Only joking, Dave, honestly, I don't want to upset anyone, especially my mates on holiday. OK, girls, do you fancy a night out or not?"

"Oh, I want, I want" enthused Ayr.

Goong was nodding too. Only Lek was holding back.

"How about you, Lek? Are you up for a night out?"

"Yes, I want, but we are working. We not have many ladies working tonight, but we have boss come in early. She sit over there. We talk with boss, OK?"

Mike knew the rules and nodded his approval.

"Beou, please come over here and speak with these guys about the rules," Lek asked in Thai.

Beou stood up and Fa took her place behind the desk in one seamless movement. She went over to the bar, sat down next to Lek and let Lek introduce the sailors.

"Well," she said, "how are you, boys? Lovely ladies, eh? They are very beautiful, aren't they? Great fun and good company."

A gin and tonic appeared before Beou.

"Oh, let me get that, Beou, and one for everyone else here," said Ed "Same again?"

Everyone nodded and Beou motioned for a round of fresh drinks. Mott obeyed the unspoken command.

"What you do tonight, boys?" she asked.

"We were hoping that you would release these three lovely young ladies early tonight so that we could take them dancing and then for a meal" said Mike.

"Yeah, but Lek says you're short-staffed today. Can you miss them for a few hours, Beou?" asked Dave.

Mike silently shook his head in disbelief.

"It is very difficult for me" explained Beou. "I pay them for working here monthly. I do not want to pay them for nothing. I only have small bar and cannot afford to pay for not working. If you give me compensation of wages, I can find new ladies to work here tonight and these three can have the night free. I mean 'off'. Is that fair? Only 600 Baht…. Each. 1,800 Baht for three."

"Yes, OK, Beou," said Mike. He knew it was about the going rate for a 'bar fine'.

"We'll have another round here and then we'll be off. Can we get you one too, Beou? Of course we can, what am I thinking?"

Mott was already on the case and Beou headed back to her desk. She waited while Fa finished writing the chits she had already started, one for the round of drinks and one for the girls' bar find fees. Mott put them both in the men's beaker without saying a word after she had delivered the drinks.

Lek looked at her friends in the bar. She could see the looks of envy in the faces of her colleagues. Not malicious envy, but envy all the same. These three sailors were considered eligible, single and wealthy with glamorous jobs that could take a lucky girl on expeditions all around the world, after they were married, of course. She looked at Ayr and Goong, who were already holding hands and kissing their partners and then she looked at Mike who had been watching her the whole time. She looked into his eyes and smiled.

The smile did not mean anything.

She smiled only because it was more alluring than frowning and she liked to be alluring, attractive and sexy to all men, whether she intended sleeping with them or not. In one short month, she would not 'be obliged' to do this any more. She did not really have to do it now. She had savings, but she had stuck it this far and one more month gave her time to think. It is a fallacy that the girls are obliged to sleep with men once the bar fine has been paid. The 'bar fine' only releases the girl from work for the day.

The final decision is always the girl's. She has to exercise her own judgement and discuss her own fees, if any. Girls charged 99.9% of the time, but not always and not always the same amount. Lek had liked one or two men so much that she had not charged and on several occasions, she had reduced the rate for a long-staying boyfriend. Not that it had ever got her anywhere. It had not really been worth doing it in the long run. But she was only human and all humans have emotions and emotions can lead one to making mistakes.

She was still looking at Mike and wondering about him. He was looking at her too, but she was satisfied that her features were under total control. It would take an expert to read the true meaning into any of Lek's facial expressions. Most Asians are adept at keeping their faces inscrutable and Lek was as proficient as any – she had been in this profession a long time and had had too many disappointments to allow just anyone to see the pain. She knew she had to snap out of it. She was a professional.

"OK, Lek, show-time, girl!" she thought.

"Mike, where you have in mind we go tonight?" she said.

"Wherever you like, doll," he replied. "The world's our oyster or at least Pattaya is tonight. Where do you ladies want to go? Dancing, eating, drinking, a show? What? Just say."

"We can take you girlies anywhere you want to go" said Ed, "we're lieutenants in the Royal Navy. Officers and Gentlemen. Modern day knights!"

"Where would you go on your nights off, if we weren't with you" asked Dave. "I want to go there, where a normal Thai girl would go to enjoy herself on her night off."

Lek looked at Dave and wondered if he had any idea about Thailand at all. Thailand is not like Pattaya. The Thais in Pattaya don't behave like typical Thais and yet are not tourists, she thought. Most of the working girls are there to achieve a goal. All their money goes on achieving that goal, whether it be paying off debts or buying decent clothes to attract a suitable man, whom they may have a chance of marrying. They do not have spare cash 'to go out'. Most of the girls, given a night off and enough money to enjoy it, would stay at home, watch TV and get an early night. She didn't show this thought process, but gave a stock answer:

"You are the front legs of the elephant, we are the back legs. We go where you lead us."

She looked back at Mike, who was smiling broadly at her, while shaking his head at Dave's naïve question.

Lek was warming to Mike, but she still was not sure whether she trusted him or would sleep with him. That subject had not been mentioned and no money had changed hands so she was under no obligation to do anything other than escort them around town. To be their companion, guide and interpreter.

"You want one more drink here?" she asked Dave, reasoning that

Mike would be more likely to say 'no'.

"Yes, OK then. Let's have another drink and think about where we'll go next."

Lek smiled to herself and motioned to Mott for another round. When she looked up, Mike was smiling too.

"OK," he said. "One more here, but it is eight o'clock and we ought to make a move in some direction. I don't want to sit here all night."

"Lovely as it is!" he added a bit louder, looking at Beou, but smiling at Lek.

She smiled back. She was definitely warming to him.

"OK. Do you want 'check bin', Mike?" He nodded.

"Check bin, kha!" she said to Mott, who came down off the pole and took the beaker of chits to Beou's desk, adding them up on the way.

"Can't you recommend anything, Lek? I'm sure you know some great places, don't you?"

"OK, Mike, but if you not like, not shout me, uh? Which one you want first? Eating, drinking or show/club? I think eating first. Eating late not good and maybe good restaurant close or full up."

She had everyone's attention now and Ed gave his opinion:

"OK, we'll eat first. All right with you guys? Where?"

"What you like to eat say where you must go. You want Thai food or farang food. Meat or fish? Which one you like? You want stay near here or you want to go long way?"

"Thai, fish and near by" said Dave.

"OK. No problem. OK for everybody? OK. There are three good restaurants same near here. One on Second Road and two on Beach Road. Beach Road is by the sea. Have cool sea breeze now. Maybe not too busy before nine o'clock. 'Savoy' on Second Road busy now, I think."

"Beach Road it is then" said Mike, looking at the bill. "Not too bad, just over a grand each. I'll get it, we can settle up later. OK. Job done, let's go."

"Only one minute. I just want to tell the Boss we going now and get my bag."

Lek went off to tell Beou that they were going to a seafood restaurant around the corner and that if they went on from there she would ring her.

Beou wagged a finger of admonition at her, but smiled.

The other two girls reached over the bar and grabbed their small bags too and they were all on their way arm-in-arm – Ayr with Dave, Goong with Ed and Lek with Mike.

Within minutes, they were standing on Beach Road enjoying the cool sea air outside two large outdoor seafood restaurants.

"Which one you want?" asked Goong.

"Which one very good?" asked Dave

"Both same same. Both very good" replied Goong. "This one have wishing for your food, this one not have wishing."

"What she say, Lek? 'Wishing'?" asked Mike.

"We don't have to wish for our food, we can afford to pay, can't we, lads?" he said aside to his friends.

There was a quick exchange of Thai and the three girls laughed out loud.

"Goong says that you can fish for your own food in that restaurant and you eat what you catch. In the other one you choose fish from a slab."

The men laughed too.

"Great! I love this country!" said Ed, "Especially the women. It's a laugh a minute. What do you reckon, guys?"

Mike took charge again: "I think we ought to eat in the other one where you don't have to rely on good luck to get a meal. It's getting late already and we're all hungry now. Let's go 'wishing' another day, when we have more time and aren't so hungry."

With that, he took Lek's hand and walked into the 'Pink Lady'. The others followed happily. A waiter showed them to a very pleasant table for six from where they could see the sea and they sat down: the men helping the ladies with their chairs.

"This is lovely. Thanks, Lek. What a great suggestion. What would everyone like to drink?"

With that, the waiter appeared with the menu and drinks list.

Ed suggested champagne and although the waiter nodded and went off to get a bottle, what they actually got was a sort of sweet Spanish cava, not that the girls knew the difference and at 1,000 Baht the boys didn't care either. They ordered three seafood platters, each to be shared by two people and another bottle of 'champagne'.

The seafood platters were the best any of the men had tasted before. Each platter consisting of: two rock lobsters, four langoustines, a dozen tiger prawns, a pound each of mussels and clams, two each of two different types of crab, a portion of crab sticks and a portion of squid, a few small pieces each of beef and pork; all accompanied by chips and various sauces. Each platter would have cost over £100 in the UK, if you could find all the ingredients under one roof.

An hour later they had finished their meal and the two bottles of cava and called the waiter over for coffee and brandy. While this was arriving they all got up to dance to the house band, which played a mixture of songs from around the world to suit the international audience. Another hour passed in complete enjoyment, but Mike called the waiter over and asked for the bill, which came to 6,575 Baht. They paid it and went out onto Beach Road to decide what to do next.

They chose to walk along the pavement on the beach side of Beach Road in order to look at the stars and listen to the sea. It was a beautiful, romantic night, as is it usually is in Pattaya. They walked along as three couples in Indian file, spaced by a few metres. Ed and Dave were holding their girls' hands; Mike was not. Mike sensed that

Lek liked him, but he also knew that she was no ordinary bar girl. Lek, for her part, was expecting him to make a move on her at any moment. She even felt that she would be disappointed if he did not. Not that there was much chance of him not making a play for her, if she wanted him to.

She knew that she could cause a stir in a comatose donkey.

For the time being, she was grateful that she had had a lovely meal and a decent drink in pleasant company and that it was being allowed to 'go down' in beautiful surroundings. She was walking on the left-hand side of Mike, so it was easy to look at him while she was supposedly looking out to sea. And she looked at him often, when he was not looking. Mike for his part had to purposely turn to look at Lek, but he wasn't doing it often.

He seemed preoccupied. Not with anything heavy. Just preoccupied. Or maybe he was content. She hoped that he was content. It was lovely to be where she was now: practically debt-free, walking next to a good-natured, handsome man, who was not overly demanding, with a stomach pleasantly full of good food and drink, in beautiful surroundings and in the company of her best friends.

It was Heaven to her and she thought that a good marriage must be like this.

Wedded bliss, they called it, didn't they?

It certainly had not been like this the first time for her. But then, she and Tom had been only children in those times. She wondered what he was doing nowadays. The last she had heard was four years ago, that he was a hopeless drunk continually complaining about his lot in society – always having enough money to drink, but never having enough time to work. He was probably sponging off a few lonely girlfriends he had hidden from each other around the countryside, enthralling them with stories of all the things he had never done.

She smiled to herself and put him out of her mind quickly, so as not to spoil the ambiance.

They continued walking for a few hundred metres and then they turned abruptly to cross the very busy Beech Road. Luckily, as part of the road was up at that point, the traffic soon jammed and they were able to dodge between the vehicles and cross the lanes of cars and taxis. Motorcycles were still a hazard, as they always were – weaving in and out of the cars, changing lanes as it suited them.

There were accidents on Beech Road involving motorcycles every day. They made it to the other side laughing at the near misses and skipped up onto the high pavement, which was there to keep the sea out of the shops on stormy days. Dave led the way to where their hotel – The Central - was situated in South Pattaya.

They went up to reception and asked for the keys to their rooms. While the boys were doing this, a security guard was discretely taking details from the girls' ID cards. This was standard practise in the better hotels. Some even held the cards until the girl left as insurance against a girl leaving with a wallet or passport while 'her boyfriend' was still sleeping. In this scenario, if a girl left alone, security would phone the man in his room to make sure that he was satisfied that all was well.

The six of them proceeded to Mike's room on the third floor; Dave and Ed had their own rooms nearby on the same floor. Once inside, Mike motioned towards the furniture and said to take a seat. Lek took the couch and her girlfriends sat on the armchairs; the boys crowded around the mini-bar.

"What can we get you to drink, girls?" enquired Mike, "We've got most things – the cleaner restocked the bar this morning. How about some champagne? The Heidsecker is quite nice. And you guys? A bier?"

No one objected, so Mike carried on preparing the drinks and handing them to Ed to pass around. He took Lek's drink and his own beer and sat down on the couch next to Lek. They all clinked glasses;

said cheers and took a swig. The girls giggled and loved it. They had all had champagne before and better than this brand too, but it was still enjoyable – it took them out of their predicament and made them feel special. Most men bought them a beer or two and then hurried them off to their hotel as quickly as they could. It was always refreshing to be treated like a human being with feelings. Drunken lustful men of any nationality were usually pigs, but they were an occupational hazard.

Ed and Dave sat down on the arms of the chairs that their girls were sitting on and wasted no time putting their arms around them. The sexual tension was starting to escalate, everyone could feel it coming on like the giddiness of vertigo. Ed and Dave were soon whispering in Ayr's and Goong's ears, making them giggle alluringly. Mike and Lek looked on, exchanging the odd glance with each other like parents watching their slightly wayward children being a bit naughty at a party.

Lek put an encouraging hand on Mike's, which was resting on his upper thigh He took the cue, squeezed her hand, leaned over and kissed her. She responded warmly and nestled up close to him. He disengaged his hand and put his arm around her – his right hand on her rib cage, just supporting the weight of her right breast without being too obvious. He then took her left hand in his left and kissed her again, making the presence of his right hand noticeable to her alone. She, in turn, started stroking his thigh.

Suddenly, Ed got up and asked if anyone wanted a top up. He opened the mini-bar and took out three more Singha beers and another half bottle of Heidsecker, which he opened and poured into the girls' empty glasses. On his way back for the beers, he surreptitiously dimmed the lights, hoping that the girls wouldn't notice. Fat chance, but they didn't mind anyway. Ed passed the beers around and they clinked another toast to each other's good fortune:

"Chok Dee!" they said in unison before they got back to kissing and cuddling.

"How about some music? Or a film?" asked Dave.

"Yessss!" answered the girls without expressing a preference.

"A film!" suggested Ed and Mike together.

"OK, a film it is" replied Dave with feigned reluctance. "But, I think we've only got those two we bought the other day when we were drunk. We haven't even had a chance to look at them yet. I don't even know what they're about."

He picked one at random, turned on the TV and put the DVD into Mike's portable player, which had already been plugged into the hotel TV. He quickly dashed back to his place on the arm of Goong's chair and put his arm around her.

When the light of the TV flickered into life, everyone could see that the couples were already into some heavy petting. The girls were happy and so were the men. Nobody really noticed the title of the film, 'Teenage Orgies At St. Agnes' Convent', but within a few minutes it was obvious what the film was about – blatant close-ups of group sex between the 'convent girls' and the middle-aged teachers, gardeners and medics et cetera.

The girls didn't mind. They had seen it all before – some of their friends had even taken part in similar films. It was the way they had engineered the situation that Lek found interesting.

It was typical of the British to turn the lights down in a sly fashion and to pretend they didn't know what the film was about. Americans might do the same, but a German, French man or Dutch man was more likely to be forthright and say 'Let's dim the lights and watch a porn movie to get us in the mood!'

Lek was open to either approach. She liked the honesty of the Germans, French and Dutch, but she also liked the way the British thought that they had to lure a woman into this situation, because they assumed that a lady would object. She smiled to herself. They didn't know much about women really – putting them on pedestals, constraining their true nature, forcing them to lead a lie.

They carried on with what they were doing regardless.

Until Ed suggested, "How about us all taking all our clothes off and having an orgy?"

Lek was not shocked – she had been asked the same question many times, but she was disappointed.

Every cloud may have a silver lining, but all that glitters is not gold either.

She felt stupid for having thought Mike and the others were any different from the usual foreign sex tourists.

"I sorry, Mike" she whispered in his ear. "I not do this, I not like. I not know for friends, but I go home now."

Mike didn't even argue. He just said:

"Look, I'm here for some fun. I'm not looking for a wife. I've got one of those at home. I like you, but I won't ask you to do anything you don't want to. No hard feelings, eh? Though, I don't mind admitting that I am disappointed."

Lek was already getting up, she was disappointed too.

"Hey, sisters! I'm off now. Are you staying for an orgy? I'm not into that sort of thing any more. One hole at a time is enough for me these days. Nothing against you two, of course," she quipped in Thai. "If you're staying, I'll phone into Beou for you. Well? Quickly, I just want to get out of here."

Ayr and Goong looked at each other; turned the edges of their mouths down in expressions of tacit approval and said:

"Oh, we'll stay for a while longer. See you later or maybe tomorrow. Phone Beou for us on your way home, if you would, please, Big Sister. That'll save us worrying about doing it" said Ayr.

Lek was waving to everyone as she walked to the door. Mike was with her. "You won't change your mind? Maybe I'll come by and see you tomorrow. OK?"

She nodded her head.

"Maybe I see you in bar tomorrow if you want drink."

Mike pushed his fingers into her bra.

"No hard feelings. Well, bar one and he'll be all right later. Joking aside, I've had a great evening with you. Pity it's not going to go on, but I want you to get a new pair of shoes on me – as a memento. All the best Lek. Goodnight, love. Take care."

He gave her a peck on the cheek and closed the door, leaving her feeling very lonely, standing in the corridor.

Lek retrieved the note from her bra – 1,000 Baht – and put it in her purse. She then took the lift down to the ground floor and crossed to the security guard, who nodded and smiled as she approached. She watched him cross her name off the list of visitors. They said 'Good-bye' and she walked out into the heat of the night. It was 2 a.m. and the streets were still very busy, although Lek was not really interested.

She turned right out of the hotel and continued until she got to Second Road. She was not feeling upset or even disappointed, just subdued. She was happy enough, but did not want company, although she felt completely alone in a crowd of thousands. She waited fifteen minutes for a large enough break in the traffic to cross safely in one go – she was in no hurry to get back to their empty room anyway.

Then she walked north along Second Road until she got to Soi Diana, which she followed to Soi Buakhao. She could not help thinking that she was still on her own particular 'yellow brick road'. She knew she was near the end of that road, but she still didn't know where it would come to an end or how much further she had to go. She turned right into Soi Buakhao and walked home in a trance.

As she opened the door to her flat she was still praying to Buddha to reveal to her her fate. It felt as if He was her only friend and confident at that moment, although she had not spoken to Him very often since she had lived in Pattaya. It was not that she felt that He had abandoned her since she had come to Sin City, more that she felt that she was now less worthy of His attention and she was also wondering whether her new-found financial freedom was all she had hoped it would be too.

She had a feeling that sleep would come slowly again that night.

5 REINFORCEMENTS

A few days later, while Lek was sitting alone in their flat, feeling a little better about her life, her mobile phone rang:

"Hello, Beou," she greeted her friend, "How are you today?"

"Oh, I'm fine. You too? Look, I'd like you to do me a little favour, if you've not got any plans. Are you seeing anyone right now? Good, good. Well, good for me, that is. Not good for you. I thought the bloke you have been with the last couple of days was promising. He seemed to like you a lot. No good?"

"Oh, John, yes, he was all right, I suppose. Gave me gold earrings worth three thousand and a few thousand for the three days we were together. We flew to Koh Samui for the day and a night. It was very nice, but no future in it. I want more than that these days, Beou."

"Of course you do, love. Of course you do, I know. Anyway, listen a minute. I've got some more troops coming in on the six o'clock bus from Phitsanulok this evening and I want you to meet them. OK? One of them is a cousin of yours, Noi and two of her friends, Nok and Nid. The three 'N's'. Will you do that for me, love? It was very short notice, but I've found them digs above Charli's pub on Third Road. Maybe we can get something better for them over the next few days."

"Beou, you can't put them in that smelly dump with that lecherous old git! They'd need to barricade the door and even that probably wouldn't stop him if he were drunk and knew there were three pretty girls inside. Young and innocent-ish. New faces in town. He'd want to be first. You can't do that to them. I'll ring you later and if you can't find anywhere decent for them, I'll ask Ayr and Goong if they can stay here with us for a few days, even though we're pretty cramped as we are."

"I knew I could rely on you," said Beou, chuckling to herself as her plan unfolded like a parachute. "Don't bother coming in at four, I'll be there then anyway. Pick up the girls, take them back to drop off their cases and have a shower. Then I'll see you all in the bar at seven, seven-thirty. 'Bye for now."

Lek sat back on the bed. She knew she'd just been had, but she didn't mind either. She set the alarm for five o'clock and fell asleep to dream of Koh Samui and the Big Buddha.

She got off the motorcycle taxi at the bus station on Third Road at five fifty and paid the driver the forty Baht fare. The bus pulled in only ten minutes late and Lek saw two anxious faces in the window relax into smiles when they spotted her. Lek knew her cousin and Nok, but was not sure about the other one. They were soon off the bus and crowding around Lek, waaing and saying 'Hello', while the conductor unloaded their small travelling bags from the compartment under the coach. Lek suddenly realised with horror that they were the same age as she had been when she had arrived – the same age as her darling daughter, Soomsomai, would be in about ten years time.

With that thought in mind, she hugged each one of them long and hard. A little too long and a little too hard for convention, but in a way they were entering the sorority and this was the start of their initiation even though they didn't realise it yet.

Lek approached a Baht taxi and after negotiating a fare of a hundred Baht, they all got in. En route, Lek called Beou at the bar, told her that the three new girls had been picked up safely, and asked to be put through to Ayr or Goong. After a minute or so Goong came on the line:

"Hello, Big Sister, what're you up to?"

"Oh," replied Lek, "didn't Beou tell you? I have just picked up three new girls from back home. Beou wants me to take them to Charli The Lech's place, but I can't do it. I've told them they can stay with us for two or three days. OK? Great, thanks. We'll go back there now, have a shower, get changed and come to the bar at about seven fifteen. See you then. Explain the situation to Ayr for me will you, please? See you soon." Turning, she said:

"OK, girls, you've got temporary digs, well a floor, but it's free."

The girls were wide-eyed with excitement and Lek gave them a running commentary of where they were.

"This is Third Road. The bus station was on Sukhumvit Road. Beou lives in a side street between Third and Second Road. Originally, you were going to be staying on Third Road, but we thought you'd be better off with us until you get used to the place. This is Soi Lenkee. At the end of it is Soi Buakhao. Turn left into that and our little flat is a few hundred metres down on the right. Just remember Soi Buakhao by the southern market for now and you won't get lost. Get your mobile phones out and put in my number, just in case."

They did as instructed and the bus turned left into Soi Buakhao and stopped as Lek rang the taxi's buzzer at her address. As she hopped out to pay the fare, she said:

"OK, all out. This is home for now!."

The excitement was palpable as they ascended the stairs. Had she been like this too all those ten long years ago? She couldn't really remember. Surely, she had been far more nervous than they were. Maybe, girls were more adventurous now. Braver or more worldly-wise. Perhaps, TV had done that, or perhaps, they didn't know what they had let themselves in for. She hoped that they would be able to sustain this attitude and enjoy themselves more than she had - be a bit more like Ayr and Goong, perhaps. Lek opened the door and they all took off their sandals as is the Thai custom before entering the room. Lek told them to put their bags on the blanket in the corner of the room, where she had created a space by rearranging the furniture earlier in the day. Nobody moved.

"Wow, cousin Lek. You live well! All this for just you three? And your own private bathroom and veranda too? Wow! Will we also get something like this later?"

Lek didn't want to spoil their enjoyment, so she just nodded, smiled and told them to go and have a shower so that they could go out. After showing them where everything was, Lek lay down on the bed to get out of their way and continued to answer their barrage of questions.

"Is Pattaya even bigger than Bangkok?"   - "I don't think so, no."

"Are there really thousands of very rich farangs here?" - "Yes."

"Is it true that they are all mad keen on finding a Thai wife?"   - "Yes and no! Sort of..."

"Are they more generous than Thai men?" - "Some are more generous, but they have more money to give away than most Thai men."

"What happens if they don't speak Thai, what do you do?" - "They won't speak Thai. You must learn bits and pieces of European languages – especially English. Learn it at every opportunity. Try to pick up some new words every day."

"Are they kind lovers?" - "Most are kind, but definitely not all. Some really bad ones will have come here especially to hurt you. You will have to learn how to discriminate between the good guys and the bad guys. It's tough, but most are nice."

"Are they really randy?" - "Most are, yes! When they are not too drunk...

"Stop now, please! Stone me! Questions, questions, questions. Finish showering, get dressed quickly and let's get out of here. Then you'll find out for yourselves. We're going to go to the bar, Daddy's Hobby, where Beou and all the girls are waiting for you and she doesn't like to be kept waiting. My flatmates, Ayr and Goong are there too. Don't forget to say thank you to them for letting you stay here. OK. It's seven o'clock, we ought to be leaving right now. It's not that far but I want you to walk part of the way so you can get a feel for the place and orientate yourselves."

Lek looked them over before leaving the flat. They were dressed conservatively, as most village girls would at home around their family: mid-calf length jeans with a bit of embroidery and full-sleeved blouses. She wondered how long it would take them to exchange those clothes for the more usual flashy garb of the Pattaya bar girl.

Some of them hardly wore anything at all these days although nudity or even the flashing of private parts was against the law. Outdoors, anyway. There were plenty of A-Go-Go's, indoor strip joints, where the girls walked around topless wearing a sheer, see-through loin cloth. Then the group of four women went out onto the street, turned left and walked to Soi Diana, which they entered.

Although they had already walked past dozens of girly bars, they were not prepared for Soi Diana. Lek tried to herd them along, but the three friends were awestruck by the lights, the bars, the restaurants and the sheer volume of people, most of whom were young women or older, foreign men. The three newcomers could almost taste the wealth in the air.

Once at the bottom end of Soi Diana, by Second Road, they came to a dead stop again. They were mesmerised by the lights, the hotels on the other side of the road, the bustle, the traffic... everything.

Second Road is easily one of the busiest roads in Pattaya.

Lek flagged down a taxi and off they went again for the short ride to Daddy's Hobby by Soi 7.

The girls were quieter, more intimidated than excited now. They buzzed the taxi to a stop at a convenient place, paid him and walked the couple of hundred metres to the bar. This was even busier and more intimidating. Rather like a popular market on a Saturday morning, but less polite.

In that short two hundred metre stretch, they passed dozens and dozens of bars, hundreds of very scantily-clad ladies (and lady boys) and thousands of tourists (mostly middle-aged, farang and male), all of whom were intoxicated to some degree or other. The noise was deafening and the lights blinding. Tourists milling about randomly, girls screaming for them to come and have a drink – each trying to be heard over the others and in competition with the very loud music that each bar was playing, and each bar playing it's own music – rock-and-roll, reggae, hip-hop, jazz, grunge, garage, every conceivable type was playing somewhere within earshot and all mixed into one horrible, indistinguishable noise.

Perhaps, the best description was 'The Pattaya Sound-Blend'.

Whether it was because they were stunned by the noise and lights or whether they couldn't read the bar sign because it was in English, they were surprised when Lek suddenly steered them off the street to a clean-looking bar, where several girls were smiling at them and inviting them over.

They had arrived.

Beou, Ayr and Goong were seated behind the bar, Mott was up the pole, as usual, Fa was on the till at the back and several other girls were either sitting with men or alone at various locations, but each was looking, and smiling, at them.

Each was also wondering how the new competition might affect her own earnings.

But mostly it was good-natured and Noi took her friends up to Beou and introduced them, while Lek arranged four seats and sat down opposite her flatmates. They waaied and some of the other girls waaied hello too, but everyone was smiling and after glancing around to check that the cost would be minimal, Beou rang the bell. Nick and Barry were the only two farangs who would gain and they would be paying her 7,000 Baht for a roast pig in a few days. Everybody had what they wanted.

Nobody would ask for a Lady Drink on the house!

They chatted about home and about the journey and about Soi Diana and Soi Seven, but their jobs were not mentioned. After about half-an hour, Beou motioned them to sit at the back of the bar in order to allow more room for paying customers. Business first, after all – or rather 'before all'. Nick and Barry sent over a couple of rounds of drinks and Beou opened a bottle of whisky for the seven of them. By nine o'clock, they were merry and having a great time, laughing and joking. They made a very attractive group and Beou decided to show them off a bit by organising a small pool match between the seven of them. Each was to put in twenty Baht, winner takes all. They were genuinely enjoying themselves and Beou was making thousands from the punters who wanted to join in the game, but who, after being refused, were content to sit, watch and drink.

She also made sure that the spectators knew that the younger girls had just arrived from 'up North' or 'up country' and would be back the next day.

Many of the guys sent over drinks and Beou didn't have to buy anything more for the rest of the evening. Two other girls came up and asked Beou if they could come to work for her too, because girls in her bar seemed to be very popular and always had 'sanuk'. Beou looked them over quickly, asked a few questions, gave them a whisky and soda and told them to join the party. They also joined in the following free rounds. Beou called Lek over and told her to tell the two latest girls it would probably be all right, but that they should come back tomorrow for a definite answer. She also gave her 2,500 Baht for each of her village girls as a sub on their first month's wages.

They had never seen so much money of their own in one handful and they rushed over to thank Beou, who asked them for a signature each.

Lek told the other two girls to enjoy the party for now and to bring in their identity cards the next day. Thais are required to carry their cards at all times, but some don't or forget and now wasn't the time to inspect them anyway. They had said that they had just finished working in a bar in Soi 6 and a few discreet enquiries needed to be made before any jobs could be offered.

Everybody in the bar was having sanuk, the atmosphere was infectious. 'Sanuk' is usually translated as 'joy' or 'happiness', although most translators would say that this does not quite cover it. 'Sanuk' is all of these things, but is possibly untranslatable, as is the Welsh word 'hwyl', which probably means the same.

By eleven o'clock the new girls were starting to flag due to the travelling, excitement and alcohol, so Beou told them and their hosts to get off early. Ayr went off to find a taxi, while Lek rounded up her charges, who were still wallowing in the unexpected attention of their new-found farang admirers. When the taxi arrived, Lek hustled them in and shouted:

"See you tomorrow, Beou, earlier at four o'clock."

The new girls duly repeated it after her and Beou waved them off. The other two girls waved and then wandered off together in the direction of Second Road.

When the private hire taxi pulled up outside their flat, Lek collected five Baht off each girl to pay the fare, not out of meanness, but as their first lesson in paying their own way, something they had probably never had to do before in the village, where one was still considered a child until 26 years of age. Lek paid the rest. It would be different in Pattaya, people, especially girls, grew up far more quickly there and Lek wanted them to realise it as soon as possible.

Goong offered to go to the take-away restaurant and took everybody's orders. She came back with three pork and rice and three chicken and rice dishes because she couldn't remember what they had ordered, by then the others were already undressed and wrapped in their towels watching TV. Goong gave the food to Ayr to sort out and got undressed too.

"Well, what did you think? First impressions, please?" she asked. "Do you think you'll stick it?"

"Oh, it was very exciting" answered Nid " and, how do you say his name again, Lichard, was very handsome and interested in me. Don't you think so? He said he would come back to see me tomorrow! He said I was so beautiful. I just can't wait."

"OK, OK, calm down!" said Lek. "First lesson in English: try to pronounce the letter 'r' as in 'Richard'. First lesson in Pattaya: don't get your hopes up. He's probably with someone else right now. Sorry, to be such a wet blanket, Nid, but you're better off learning that from the outset. You can't expect much loyalty from a holiday maker who probably lives 10,000 kilometres away and who probably won't come back again until next year. Neither are many of the girls loyal, before the man is on the bus to the airport, most girls are already with the next. Don't expect loyalty, honesty or the truth. If you believe them, most farang are or were Special Branch, spies, Navy Seals, S.A.S., C.I.A. or some such bull shit. None of them are just shop keepers or farmers."

She could tell that none of them was impressed by what she had just said – even Goong looked a bit disappointed although the atmosphere was still up-beat as they finished their food and took it in turns to use the shower.

Noi reached for her suitcase and extracted a brown paper bag, which she held up saying:

"Prezzy' time!."

Everybody had expected something, but nobody had liked to ask. The girls' mothers usually sent something with anyone going to Pattaya, just as the girls always gave something to take to their families to anyone going back to Baan Suay. Noi had recent photos for everyone and some banana and mango toffee sweets that Lek's mother had made from local fruit. There was also an old ice cream container of Green Chilli Chicken Curry, which Nid's mother had made for them.

By one twenty-five they were all bedded down, but far from asleep. It was like camping out with friends on the first night. Lek was looking at photos of Soomsomai and thinking how fast she was growing up without her around. She was brought back to reality by:

"I heard what you said to Nid, cousin Lek. Is there anything else we should know?" enquired Noi.

"Oh, loads ..." said Goong.

"And you will," said Lek, "but for now, the three cardinal rules are:

1] Always, always, always tell someone who you are going with and where he's staying.

2] Do not go with someone if you don't like him, learn to trust your instincts.

3] Get everything you can out of him, but do not steal under any circumstances.

"There are a few other things you'll learn as you go along too" chirped in Ayr, "Like try to get him to like you. Form a relationship. It makes rule three easier. Be his constant companion, guide and interpreter."

"Yes. Try to get something of value out of him – not only money. Gold is the easiest to get and to resell. A pair of earrings, a bracelet – 'a memento of your friendship, all-too-brief that it was'," Lek smiled in the darkness.

"If it is going fairly well, you could try getting some extra money 'for an operation that your mother has been waiting for for four years but can't afford'. The old one of 'my mum's buffalo is sick' doesn't work too well any more – it's a bit of a joke now, but 'my mum's motorcycle needs a new thingamabob still does sometimes,' said Goong.

They all laughed. Lek took it back up:

"Like I said before, don't expect too much… and don't fall in love. Most men are liars. They haven't come here looking for a wife or a girlfriend, they've already got one somewhere and no matter what they say, they won't be coming back for you. Don't fall for it. Just smile sweetly and ask for something to remember him by 'until he returns'."

"Try to stay in charge or control of the situation. Don't drink too much and don't touch drugs at all."

"Try to get a decent meal out of him," giggled Ayr drowsily. "Enjoy yourself as much as you can. Try to treat it like a game. Remember, 'We are Mountees and we always get our man to cum with us. Just not always quietly'."

"Do you mean like the Canadian Mounties?" asked Nid.

"Maybe, sometimes, but not really!" Ayr and Goong laughed at their old private joke. The new girls didn't understand it, but they all laughed along anyway.

"Yes," agreed Lek, "try to enjoy yourselves. Try to treat it like a game. There will be times when it will be very hard, it is a serious game that can have dire consequences. Always make him wear a condom too, same as you would back home, or at least, as you should be doing back home. You don't want to catch something horrible like AIDS.

"If you do get anything, get along to the clinic quickly. Don't pass it around. Nobody else wants it. And try to save some money for a rainy day" she added before drifting off into an uneasy asleep. They left a music channel on softly to muffle the excited whispers that were still coming from the blanket in the corner.

Lek suddenly saw herself lying at the bottom of some wooden staircase, but she didn't know how she had gotten there. Her head hurt, so did her left leg – maybe it was broken. She was very confused and called out for help, but nobody seemed to be around to hear her. She tried to get up, but she was dizzy, groggy and in too much pain. Then, through a haze, she saw a young girl at the top of the stairs crying out. What was she saying? It was indistinct and didn't seem to make sense,

"Grandma! Grandma!"

But she wasn't a grandmother and who was this girl anyway? She bore a familiar resemblance, but it wasn't Soomsomai. Where was Soomsomai to help her?

"Oh, yes, that's right" she remembered slowly, "she went to work in Pattaya last week… this is her daughter…"

"Oh, no, no, not that. Please Buddha, not in Pattaya!."

Lek woke up, still muttering: "Not in Pattaya!"

It was three thirty and, just as in the dream, no-one had heard her. She felt very alone, although there were five others within two metres of her.

She cried softly to herself until she was asleep again.

6 A NEW CAREER

The next day, they got up at noon, which was early for the older girls, but late for the younger ones, who were used to helping around their parents' homes and farms from about five-thirty a.m. every day of the week. Even as schoolgirls, they had had to be ready for the school bus, which had left at six-thirty a.m. to collect pupils from the surrounding villages in order to distribute them at various locations on time. Getting up early was a good habit that they would soon be getting out of.

Along with a few others that their parents had taught them.

Lek had hardly slept that night and was waiting for the chance to get into the shower without waking the others. She was first in, while the others were still yawning and stretching off the affects of a little too much alcohol. She showered quickly, but with great pleasure, aware of the fact that at ten minutes each, it would still take them at least an hour just to get washed. When she was done, she wrapped her towel around herself again and went out to supervise breakfast. She knew it was a little too early for Ayr and Goong to be of much help and the other three didn't know their way around the cupboards in the apartment yet.

Despite that, Nid had filled the kettle and was preparing to make tea and coffee, although Lek had been right about her original flatmates, who were still in bed. Noi was next into the shower. Remembering the container of Green Chilli Chicken Curry, that had been sent up by Nid's mother, Lek put six handfuls of Jasmine rice into the rice cooker along with the appropriate amount of water. She also put the curry in a pan on a low heat and then opened the veranda windows to let the smell escape.

About forty minutes later, still in their towels, they sat down wherever they could and enjoyed a lovely home-cooked curry as they would have done every day back in their village, followed by fresh fruit, tea and coffee and home-made sweets. It was everyday fare for the younger girls, but a rare luxury that made the older ones want to cry with homesickness. They talked nostalgically about Baan Suay, but Lek was only taking half of it in.

She was thinking about Baan Suay too, at least as much as the others, but she was thinking more specifically about her daughter and what would become of her. Had she had a premonition the night before or was it just a dreadful nightmare? Plans were formulating in her head, but she was still uncertain what they were leading to even herself.

Beou had asked those that could, to get in as soon after one as possible, because it was the day of Barry and Nick's party and she would need a hand with the preparations. It was also one of the reasons why she had told the younger ones to arrive when they did. It would be an easy breaking-in for them – first night off with no pressure, party second night, when it would be very easy to find a farang, especially after the build-up they had had the night before.

They may even get a short-time in the afternoon and a sleep-over in the evening. Two bar fines per girl in one day and all the Lady Drinks. She was almost too cunning for her own good, Beou had thought to herself. But the fact was that it was a good way for the new girls to get started and it happened to be good for business too – win, win, a perfect synergy in the imperfect environment of Pattaya.

The six girlfriends took the usual route, as they had done the night before, left into Soi Buakhao, left into Soi Diana and onto a Baht Taxi in Second Road to Soi Seven, from where they could easily walk to Daddy's Hobby. It was nearly two o'clock and there were half-a-dozen girls prancing about very efficiently putting up balloons and bunting as they had done many times before. The job was about half finished, judged Lek. She directed the younger girls to 'muck in' where they could and they followed Ayr and Goong to say hello to their new colleagues and help out. It was much more like having fun than working, especially the back-breaking work in the rice fields.

There were a few early customers there too and the new girls liked the attention they were getting – even when the men were trying to look up their skirts while they were on the bar hanging up balloons. It was kind of embarrassing, but also kind of exciting at the same time. Not altogether a new experience, but more intense and no parents or big brothers around to scold them for liking it. It was a new found freedom – the freedom to be sexy and to be naughty.

Meanwhile, Lek was 'around the back' talking with her boss.

"What did they think of it last night, Lek?" asked Beou.

"Oh, they had the time of their lives," she replied.

"Good, because tonight could, well, let's say should, be even more exciting. Do you think they've got what it takes?"

"It's hard to tell yet, isn't it? They are a little shy, but not too much, a little nervous, but again, not too much. Some men like shy and nerves will keep them on their toes. I think they'll be all right. No obvious negatives, anyway."

"Good. Good! I agree with you and trust your judgement" Beou said absent-mindedly, while looking through the entries in the previous night's cash book register. "Very good – takings well above average. Tonight should be a humdinger too. The girls'll be all right. How about the two from Soi 6? Have you seen them again yet?"

"No, haven't they been back here yet?"

"No," said Beou, "but I don't think I told them about the party. They'll probably wander along sometime between four and five o'clock. They're probably OK too, maybe a little more experienced, but still young. From Bangkok, I imagine. Maybe, started early, but thought the seaside would be a better place to live. It probably is too. I can't stand the hustle and bustle of Bangkok myself… and the fumes!

"Your clothes and hair smell like exhaust within the hour. Give me cool, refreshing Pattaya any time. They say Koh Samui's nice too. Never been there myself, though," Then after a moment, closing the register, "but you have, of course. Several times, eh? Recently, too. We shall see, eh? Soon enough. All things come to she who waits …"

Lek waited for her friend to stop rambling and then broke in at the first polite opportunity:

"Uh, Beou. I was wondering. I didn't get much sleep last night, thinking about the three young new girls and the two other new girls... They're going to need some training, some kind of tutor or mentor, don't you think?"

"Yes... you're right, but it's a question of time, isn't it? I'll do what I can, but I'm busy enough now with the bar and my daughters and all the piddly little 'problems' some of the dopier girls think they've got. You know, hardly a day goes by without one or another of them crying into my phone. It's not that I mind so much, as you know, I regard all of you as my family – especially you, cousin... well, you are my family, of course, but you know what I mean." Then, as she put the register back on its shelf and the pen in her blouse, she added:

"Come on then, out with it. What's troubling you?"

"Well, I'm not sure, nothing really, I suppose. It's just that seeing the new girls last night and talking to them since, I've realised how vulnerable they are. I want to help. I also had that dream again, but with a new twist. I was the grand-mother and Soomsomai was working down here… I don't..."

"OK, OK, you poor thing. Come here. Let's have a cuddle. It's only your fear that's giving you these nightmares. You would never let Soomsomai come here. It won't happen. So, hush now and think of something nice. Why don't you go home for a few days… in a fortnight's time? That'd be nice, wouldn't it and you deserve it. Let's get these new girls settled in and then you can ..."

"But that's the point, Beou! My mother let me come here and she's a good woman and she loves me and I bet it never crossed her mind that a daughter of hers would end up doing what I do. Just look at the example I'm setting Soomsomai! She's going on twelve and her mother sleeps with strangers for money.

"She didn't understand before but she will do soon and I'm tacitly telling her that it's all right to do it. I do it. How could I stop her? Girls don't even obey their parents like we did. I wouldn't stand a chance, if she wanted to do it. Would I? Go on, honestly! You've always been honest with me. Would I, having set the example I have?"

"You're too hard on yourself, Lek. We both know why you had to come here. But you're right. She might not see the reason you're here, just that you are here. To be really honest, that's why I stopped. Well, and, between you and me only, understand? I was getting too old for it too. But I'll deny I ever said that if I hear it repeated. You understand?"

That did the trick temporarily and Lek smiled.

Beou continued smiling: "After I had Shelly, who's fifteen now, I thought what you're thinking now and pleaded with her father to set me up in a bar so that his daughter would learn to know her mother as a business woman and I could set her a good example. I'm so pleased he helped me, even though I probably should have chosen a different game to be in. But this was all I knew at the time – it's probably all I'm good at now too, I suppose. OK, so what solution have you got in that still very pretty head of yours. Are you going to ask the next foreigner you meet to set you up in competition with me?"

"No," Lek laughed, "you'd beat me hands down. We'd be bankrupt within a year, even if I could find someone daft enough to back me. No, rumour has it that Fa wants to leave. Is that true? Well, you'll need a new cashier and I'm applying for the job. I want a proper, respectable job, working for you."

"OK," replied Beou without hesitating, "Good idea. I was wondering how to fill her place and didn't relish having to do more hours myself. What about money? The wages won't be what you're used to."

"I know, Beou, but it's not a bad basic wage and I have some savings and perhaps you could afford to pay a little more, if I take on the rôle of coach and nanny too. Let the girls call me with their problems in the middle of the night. Let yourself get a good night's sleep. You know you need more time with the girls now they're growing up and you'd be showing them that you are so successful that you don't have to go into work every day. What do you think? Good idea, huh?"

"It works, yes. It solves a few problems, but again, how much money? At the moment a girl working behind the bar gets 2,500 basic, a girl in front of the bar gets 3,000 basic and the cashier gets 6,000. I can pay you 7,500 plus a share of the tips, if you help out serving when it's slack and take all the girls' phone calls. You would effectively be 'Trainee Momma San Junior'."

"Make it 8,000 and I'm your Girl Friday too."

"Ah, you'll have me back working short time at that price, but we'll give it a try starting tonight. Between you and me, Fa asked if she could leave on the first of this month, a week ago, but I didn't have a replacement so she stayed on. Her old man wants her to leave because she's becoming too independent. Mouthy, he says. He says she's started answering back and he said that when he went in her bag for her wages, he found 2,500 more than he expected. He told me about it and asked if I'd given her a raise. Luckily, I twigged what he was saying and told him it was a bonus not a raise.

"He beat her up for holding back on him. I think she's been moonlighting short-time on the way home from work. She's a pretty little thing, isn't she? Well, I've checked the books against the stock and she didn't steal it from here. Not that I thought she would, but I had to check all the same, didn't I? Glad to have you on the management team! Welcome aboard Number Two, Trainee Momma San Junior. First managerial duty, go and see how that lot is doing out there and delegate someone to make us a coffee – one of the new girls, show her where everything is – your cousin Noi. Keep it in the family. I'll 'phone Fa and tell her I've found her replacement."

It was just gone four o'clock, the bar's normal opening time, and there were several more customers there than usual for that time of day, a few of whom Lek recognised from the night before. Coming back to get first pop at the new girls probably. Newbies were always in great demand and some of the resident ex-pats only went with the new ones now. They would be considered new for a month or so. They would get lots of custom and be pretty sore. They would probably take up smoking too - most did although very few women smoked in the villages.

Here, stress, strain, boredom, and sometimes a bad taste in the mouth drove a lot of girls to take it up.

Lek motioned to Noi, who was passing balloons to Nid standing on the bar trying simultaneously to hold her skirt down while pinning a balloon up. She was giggling, while a man from the night before, presumably Richard, was pretending that he was going to lift her skirt up to get a better look. He didn't look the type, or drunk enough, to carry out his threat. Nid was lapping it up and so was Richard.

Noi came inside the bar and Lek asked her to make a tea or coffee for all the girls who wanted one, showing her where all the necessaries were. Richard was finally rewarded with a flash of white panties as Nid scrambled awkwardly off the bar. He made some appropriate animal noise of appreciation and Nid giggled some more. She'd be all right, thought Lek, like a duck to water. While Noi was getting on with taking orders for refreshments and Nid was chatting up Richard, most of the

other girls were finishing chopping fruit and vegetables, putting saus-
ages on sticks and making sandwiches, while the rest were arranging it
all on trays.

The pig was almost done roasting on the spit too.

Just then, the new girls from Soi 6 arrived together and Lek asked
them if they wanted tea or coffee, before taking them round to see
Beou. They looked very nice, thought Lek, they would probably be all
right there too. They seemed to fit in straight away. Not too tarty.
Some bars went for the tarty look, others for the schoolgirl look, et cetera, but Daddy's Hobby encouraged a more natural style. Natural to
posh was their look, if it had to be described.

Sexy but respectable even, although Beou had only very rarely told
a girl that she could not wear something and even then it was usually
more for reasons of bad taste than clothing. Lek remembered that the
last time something had been banned it was a T-shirt that had written
on it: "If you like it doggy style, try the bitches in the bar next door."
Beou had said it was bad form to insult the competition.

It was five-thirty, and everything was ready for the start at seven-
thirty. Joy and Nick and Deou and Barry would probably arrive before
then, as they were paying for the bash and would want the best seats.
Most of the girls that had been there all day, decided to go home for a
shower and change of clothing. Lek, Ayr, Goong, Beou and the five
new girls stayed on to hold the fort. Nid called Lek over and spoke to
her in Thai:

"Richard has invited me back to his hotel for a drink and something to eat. What do I do next?"

"What does he want you to eat?" joked Lek.

Nid looked flustered. "I don't know. I'm not really hungry and I
don't know whether I like farang food or not. Do you think I'll like it?
Do you like it, Lek?"

"OK, OK," she soothed, "Calm down. Firstly, do you want to go?

I assume the answer's 'yes'."

Nid nodded enthusiastically.

"Secondly, find out where he is staying and, when you come behind the bar to get your bag, let one of us know. If it's not the same when you get there either dump him or ring me, but be careful. Now sit down with him, get the name of the hotel and then call me over."

Ten minutes later, Lek was called over. After the introductions, Lek asked:

"So, Richard, Nid say you want take her for a meal or something. That no problem, but she being paid to work here at the moment. You must to pay the bar compensation, we say 'bar fine' to cover her lost wages. Is that all right?"

"I guess so," replied Richard. "It depends how much."

"Not a lot, just enough so the bar not lose out. This her first day in Pattaya. Boss pay for bus, room, clothes, everything. And wages. Say 750 Baht and you must talk to lady for money for her. OK. That is business for Nid not bar. You OK? Good for new lady, yes?"

Behind Richard's back, Nid's mouth dropped wide open. 750 Baht just for her? Richard agreed and he bought one more drink for himself and a Lady Drink for Nid. Lek winked at Nid and walked away while Richard took Nid's hand. Twenty minutes later, Nid came to collect her bag.

"Hotel Fiori, Second Road." she whispered, "How much should I charge him?"

"You're on your own there, darling. Sorry. Go with your heart, but think 1,000 – 2,000 Baht. Bottom-end easy, top-end can be done. And I'm talking about the fee not your body" she laughed.

"Thanks," she giggled as she scurried out to join Richard, who was paying his bar bill.

The two couples arrived at seven o'clock. It was easy to tell that things had not gone according to plan by the look on their faces. They sat down and ordered four bottles of ice-cold beer Chang, which is made in Thailand by a firm that used to be associated with Carlsberg. It's very strong at 6.4% ABV, but doesn't taste like it.

"Everything OK, boys?," asked Lek, already knowing the answer was going to be in the negative.

"Ah," Nick replied, "you know we're going back tomorrow? Well, we wanted to take Joy and Deou back with us for a holiday, so we went up to the British Embassy in Bangkok yesterday, but were refused a visa. We filled the forms in last week and delivered them by hand saying that it was urgent. They processed the applications quickly enough, but they rejected them."

"You know why?" enquired Lek.

"Several reasons, really." grumbled Nick, "But basically, because we haven't known each other long enough quote 'to have established a long-standing relationship' unquote. We were even prepared to put our flights off for a couple of weeks so the girls could fly with us. Asking around, it looks like we'll have to try again in about six months time. So, we'll go home tomorrow as planned, leaving our beautiful ladies in your tender, loving care, Lek and we'll come back to get them in five months or so. It's July 11th today, so we could come back for Christmas. What's Christmas like here, Lek?"

"Oh, Christmas is very lovely in Pattaya. Very hot. Very busy. Have very many farang. Too much. Hotel very full and much more expensive. Price up maybe fifty percent. Good idea you book hotel before you go. Pay small money deposit. When you fly? Tomorrow?"

Their faces dropped. It wasn't really what they wanted to hear.

"We fly KLM from Bangkok at 23:30. Leave Pattaya at 18:30," said Barry.

"Good you have time to do tomorrow. Not forget, eh?"

Lek repeated the advice in Thai for their girlfriends, who were slow to see the implication, so she enlightened them. They soon perked up at the thought that Nick and Barry were more likely to come back, if they had paid a deposit on a firm future hotel booking. The advice given to the boys was valid, but with a hidden agenda to give her sisters a second chance at getting out of Pattaya.

Getting members of the sorority 'out' was often a team effort.

"Oh, Lek, I forgot to say. A friend of ours from our town came over today. He's in the hotel unpacking. He's going to have a shower and then come over. You may know him. His name's Will. He's been here before. In this bar, I mean. He mentioned Beou's name and Goong's. He should be here soon."

"I don't remember the name. Maybe when I see him I know him. Call me when he come, I want to say hello to him."

Lek accepted a drink and a smile from the group, excused herself and left to go to her new job behind the desk as cashier, which Beou was doing. They swapped places and Beou went over to talk to the foursome.

"Do you like the party?" asked Beou genuinely. "Is everything as you like? When do you want me put out food? Now or little later, say eight o'clock?"

"Sit down, Beou. Take it easy. Have a drink. What do you want? A gin and tonic, OK? Four more beers and a gin and tonic, please, Mott! You have done a very good job. Thanks, Beou. I can see you have worked very hard for us. Do you want the money now?" asked Nick.

Mott arrived promptly with the boss' gin and tonic and came back two minutes later with four more Changs.

"Thank you for gin tonic and compliments. Cheers, everyone! Pay now, pay later, up to you. All the same to me. You go home tomorrow? Take my lovely ladies with you?"

"Unfortunately, yes and no" retorted Nick. "Yes, we go home to-morrow. No, we are not taking your lovely ladies with us. I wish we could, but not have visas. Bloody embassy."

"Pity. Bad luck. Not easy get visa for UK, eh? I hear before. Many ladies try. Some pay big money for copy visa, I hear, but I don't know. I hear website for help get visa is http://uk-visas-for-thais.the-real-way.com – too late for you now, but you can look for next time you try. You come back soon, try again?"

"Yes, we will come back for Christmas to try again. Lek says it's very good at Christmas, but very busy and we should book now. What do you think, Beou?"

"Lek is very clever. She is right. It is best to book now."

At that moment a man crept up on Beou and tapped her on the shoulder. She span around, took his hand deftly and kissed him on the cheek. He hugged her in return.

"Hello! How are you?" they both greeted each other simultaneously.

"Nice to see you again, Beou." said Will, taking a stool next to Nick.

"Hello, ladies. Hiya Nick. Barry OK? Do you want a drink? Yes? OK, Five Beer Changs and a gin and tonic, please, Beou."

Beou got up to place the order and have the food unwrapped. She was back in a few minutes, once she had seen that her instructions were being carried out.

"Pity you're going back tomorrow, boys, but thanks for putting on a welcoming party for me" joked Will. "Where is Goong? Is she here tonight?"

Beou shouted the name and Goong appeared from somewhere. When she spotted Will she came running over to him screaming all the way:

"Oh, darling! Good to see you again. Why you not write? You come see me? Chup, chup ..."

"OK, chup, chup, kiss, kiss. Yes, I come see you. Why must I write? I not write Thai, you not read English! Sit down have drink. You want horrible Lady's Drink or you want lovely cheap Beer Chang same before? Beer Chang alloy mak mak."

Will winked at Beou.

"Bia Chang, kha. So, you not forget Thai you learn last year. Good for you. This year you learn more Thai, then you can write to me, if you not take me home with you. Nick and Barry good man. They try take ladies home, but can not. You not try."

"I tell you before, I can not take you home. I have two wife in the house now. Not want three. I want come here see you often. I stop working now. Can come very often for long time. Six weeks, eight weeks for one time. Can come two, three times for one year. Good, not good, huh?"

"Good, good. I like. Chawp. But I want go to UK with you, see two old wife you. I not believe you. You make joke every time too much. I love you, Will."

"Yeah, yeah. I know. I hear before. I love you too." And he had heard it all before too. Will had been coming to Pattaya for twelve years and every girl he'd met on his trips had said the same. This was the first time he'd come back to the same girl twice, but then Goong was a special lady too - bright, bubbly and beautiful.

Lek saw Will but didn't know him. She looked at him and studied him when she had a moment, which was not often as the party was in full swing and the drinks were flowing fast. She was sure she hadn't met him before. Maybe she'd been 'out' last year when he went with Goong. It was obvious that she liked him anyway. He did seem a decent sort of man and funny too.

Not that she could hear him over the din but she could see the others laughing after he had spoken. Goong had found a nice man even if he was twice her age. Maybe he was too old and wily to take Goong on full-time. She would watch out for her friend from a distance and hope for good luck for her, as she always did.

Lek looked around, all the girls, who worked outside the bar were with someone and all the girls, who worked inside the bar were serving either food or drinks. Beou was talking to Nick and his friends. She was glad that she was out of the 'cattle market'. No competition now. No more strange-smelling, sweaty, beer-swilling strangers to molly-coddle. Maybe no more nightmares. Only figures, numbers, sums, maths ...

Time passed quickly and then Nid was standing at her side beaming; waving 1,200 Baht in her hand. Lek was working so furiously that her first reaction was to take it in payment for a bill, but she stopped herself.

"Hi. You're back early. What happened?"

"We had a couple of drinks in his hotel and then went up to his room. We had a shower, made love a couple of times and then he told me he could not sleep with someone in his bed and asked me to go home. I asked him for 1,200 Baht and he just gave it to me! Just like that! 1,200 smackeroos. Wow! A week's wages in one afternoon. What shall I do now, Lek?"

"That's up to you. You didn't have to come back here. No-one would have known any different. You can slip off, help out or go and talk to one of the blokes. Whatever you like."

Nid skipped around to the other side of the bar and was being chatted up within minutes.

That one will be all right, Lek thought.

Night life officially finished at one a.m. in Pattaya, but many places ignored the rule. The same was true that night, although by one o'clock, all of the girls had found partners. Noi was on her second. The party had been a great success and there were only a few stragglers left – Nick and his party with Will and Goong, Beou, Lek and a drunken Swede, who was more asleep than awake.

Noi, the night watch woman, arrived but by then everything had been stowed away and the bar was shipshape. Mama San and her new Junior Trainee sat down with Nick and his group to enjoy a few post party drinks and let the stress ebb away.

"What's it to be, friends? Same again?," offered Beou. "That was a good night, I think. Nick, Barry, what you say? Good, not good?"

"Bloody excellent, Beou! A big 'Thank you' to you and all the girls. You made us feel really like part of the family." Tears welled in Barry's eyes.

Nick said: "It's been a long day for us, Beou, and we have a few things left to do tonight. I hope we have time to see you tomorrow before we leave. We will take your advice and book back into the Marriott for Christmas, but I want to ring the bell one more time tonight to say 'Thanks' - I'll do it now there's only a few of us here! I'm only joking, and check bin, kap. Is that right, 'check bin, kap'?"

"You are welcome! Yes, 'check bin, kap' – 'bill, please'. Lek, bill, please."

Lek walked the three metres to the desk and took her bottle of beer with her. She re-checked the bill, but it was only out of professionalism. She knew that the bill was 11,350 Baht – a fortune to Thais, but acceptable to farangs on going-away party nights.

Lek walked with the bill, put it down and took another swig of beer.

Nick picked it up, showed it to Barry and said:

"6,000 each with tip, OK?"

"No problem."

They paid the bill, shook hands, waaied and left, leaving Beou, Will, Goong and Lek behind.

This was more like a circle of friends now, although Lek and Will didn't know each other. They were friends by default, because their friends were friends. Will introduced himself for the first time and Lek shook his hand.

"You take care my friend Goong, eh, Will? She very good friend from me for long time. She very lovely lady. She like you too, she tell me."

"How come I did not meet you last year, Lek? I came here often with Goong. Not worry for your friend, I am not bad man. Are you cashier here?"

"Yes, I am cashier here. Maybe I go home see family in north Thailand when you come here last year - have holiday, understand?"

"Yeah, I guess so," he said, not totally convinced. "Anyway, I'm tired. I've been travelling for twenty-odd hours. Do you want to come with me, my darling Goong? Check bin, kap, Lek."

"Yes, my darling, I want to go home with you. Make love. Not make love long time."

Will paid the bill and took Goong away, leaving only Beou, Lek and Noi, the night watch woman, at the bar.

"Do you want to get pissed, Lek?" asked Beou, "I'm half gone anyway. Noi doesn't drink, it's only me and you. What do you reckon — a bottle of Pipers?"

"OK, Beou, but I might not be able to finish it. I feel a bit funny. Not ill, but as if something were changing. Not the menopause either — don't go thinking that, OK! I just feel weird. Watching all the girls get-ting partners like that, but not being part of it. It was definitely very strange. But also satisfying, in a smug sort of way. I didn't like the smugness. I was doing it yesterday, for Buddha's sake. Now I'm 'holier than thou'. Shit. Yes, break out the whiskey, please. I have no-one to go home to anyway. They're all out shagging. Sheesh! There I go again. Do I sound jealous, Beou? Fuck! Am I screwed up or what?!."

Her friends laughed in unison.

"Slow down, little cousin," said Beou. "You've made a big decision and had a hard day. Just stay easy. You've done well. Don't sweat it. Have a couple of drinks and then either go home or come home with me."

"Everything's going to be all right now, everything's going to be all right now, everything's going to be all right, so, no woman no cry ..," she quoted Bob Marley.

They all laughed.

But there was a tear in Lek's right eye, which she tried to hide from her friends.

"OK, OK, I give up! I'm not going to be miserable! Pity that Joy and Deou didn't get their visas, wasn't it? Changing the subject, I know. But maybe that's what I need. What do you think of Will, Beou? You've met him before apparently, haven't you?"

"OK, girl, have it your own way. Yes, I met Will last year. He seems a nice man, but not an easy fish to catch. I think that Goong will have a great time in a lovely five-star hotel with him, but she will never step foot in the UK with that one – he's a 'good time boy' or rather say old man – a very young-at-heart old man though."

The session didn't last long. Beou was more tired than she thought and Lek considered herself bad company, so before the bottle was half empty, Beou took her leave and left on her motorcycle and Lek was bidding Noi goodnight.

"See you tomorrow, Noi. Did Beou tell you that I have taken over from Fa – gone straight?"

"No, she didn't," lied Noi out of kindness, "but I would have found out tomorrow anyway. It's your job to get here first – at about three o'clock, so I can go home. Good night, love. Don't think too much. Don't worry and get a good night's sleep. See you in twelve hours. Welcome to management!."

Lek crossed the road and motioned to the motorcycle taxi drivers. A few of her admirers were there. Bong and Nong waved.

Nong deferred to his boss.

"Hi, gorgeous!" said Bong, "Are we going for a drink or a meal?"

"Hi, Bong." she answered feigning boredom. "When will you ever give up? I've told you before: I like a man with more between his legs than a motorcycle."

Lek heard herself say it as if it were someone else uttering the words.

"Buddha, why did I say that? Am I so horny or so lacking in self-confidence. Shit!"

"Just take me home, please, Bong. It's been a really hard day."

Bong knew what that meant, and, being a gentleman of sorts, he did as he was bid – no fee.

"Thanks, Bong" she said, as she jumped off the bike and went to the downstairs door.

"Good night and sweet dreams," she added guiltily.

Lek opened the door and trudged up the stairs to 'their' apartment. For the first time in a few days, there was no-one there. She had a shower and got into bed alone.

Sad, but not the same as before.

Sleep came easily.

7 THE DAY AFTER THE NIGHT BEFORE

Lek woke up at ten twelve, alone. For the first time in months, it felt strangely good. She got out of bed, totally naked, and walked over to the TV, switched it on and wondered why she was feeling so good. She had never been shy in front of her flatmates, so why did being naked feel so different this time? She did a little Thai pirouette, moving her hands in the traditional Thai way — fingers bent back in an unnatural curve for Westerners.

No answer sprang to mind

She put the kettle on to make some tea and then leapt onto the bed. She spread her legs wide provocatively and felt a little bit wicked. She felt herself too. Not enough to orgasm, but enough to want to. She was happy for the first time in what seemed like a long time. She rolled over onto her front, two fingers between her legs and five on her left breast and drifted off to sleep again to the sound of music and the automatic kettle.

An hour or so later, there was a discrete knock on the door. Lek instinctively grabbed her towel and jumped to the door feeling guilty, but not really knowing why.

It was Nid.

"Hello, Big Sister, I hope I didn't disturb you! Are you with anyone? I had another one last night after Richard. First time I've been with two men in one day! In twelve hours! In twelve days even! Wow, Pattaya's great. 2,200 Baht on my first day. Wow! My pussy's hot."

Lek could feel herself starting to get annoyed and tried to check it. Then, Nid flopped on the bed without thinking, while Lek was still holding the door open. Lek closed the door and looked at her guest, who was holding her hair out, legs akimbo. Lek could see her knickers up her short denim skirt. She switched the kettle back on and said:

"We need to talk, young lady."

While the kettle was still boiling, Lek began:

"Nid, I'm glad you enjoyed yourself yesterday and I'm glad you like life in Pattaya, but you must come down to Earth. Yesterday wasn't reality. It won't always be like that! And I NEVER bring men back to the flat, OK? Got it? NEVER! Did you just get someone to drop you off outside?"

She didn't know whether Nid had or not; she just wanted to be provocative. She could feel herself getting angry, but again wasn't sure why.

"No, Big Sister, honest I didn't." She sat up and straightened her skirt feeling that something was wrong. On the one hand, she didn't want to upset Lek, but on the other she felt so happy, tired, free, liberated and well-off. She was out of sight of her conservative family with a pocketful of money and in a place where there was an endless supply of men ready, willing and able to give her more money than she had ever dreamed of. Men who seemed to appreciate her and were willing to pay for her - in more money for one day than her father or her brothers could earn in a week.

She was exhilarated.

Naive, but exhilarated none-the-less.

"Where did you end up the second time round? Did you tell anyone? Where are your friends? Any idea? Did you use condoms? Go and make the tea and get off my bloody bed!."

Lek wanted to cry and she could see that she had made Nid upset too.

"Sorry, Big Sister." She was on the verge of tears.

Lek wanted her own room; just for herself, for the first time in her whole life.

They sat facing each other with a mug of tea each. Both sipped gingerly on the boiling liquid as a diversion. Lek began as it was obvious that Nid was waiting for her to start the ball rolling. Nid was nervously waiting to find out what she had done wrong.

"Relax, Nid – uh, Little Sister." she said, trying to calm the tension, although the nomenclature did not come easily for some reason. "I'm sorry that I got angry with you. I just want you to realise that yesterday wasn't real. I hope you never get hurt, but I know that you will be. I guarantee it. Thirty-six hours ago, you were dreaming about Richard, but went with the very next guy that smiled at you even though Richard had come back for you.

"That's OK, I've done that too, and Richard is probably a tosser anyway, but ..., but, just realise that it's not real, that's all. Now drink your tea, have a shower and get some sleep. I doubt if you slept much last night, did you?"

"Thanks, Big Sister, I am a bit tired. Maybe we can look for our own flat later, eh? One like this, or maybe a little bit bigger."

The hackles were beginning to rise again but Lek let it go. "That girl is a real pain in the arse," she thought. "Either she goes or I do. And quickly".

While Nid was showering, Lek drank her tea and thought about the situation. She felt invaded. Nid came out, flopped onto her blanket and fell asleep immediately. Lek went for a shower. She wanted to get out of the room that no longer felt partly hers – her refuge from the crap outside. Somehow she had let some of that crap creep in and she didn't like it. She knew how lucky she had been to have Goong and

Ayr for friends and flatmates and thanked Buddha for it for the ump-teenth time – tears welling up again in her eyes.

While she was in the shower, Ayr and Noi came back too. They had met in the street outside the apartment building. Apparently, Noi had been there half an hour wondering if it was the right place. Nok was still out and Goong was expected to come home only for clothes for the next four weeks. Lek tried to make polite conversation with her friend and her cousin but found it hard-going, so she made the excuse that she wanted to go shopping and left at midday.

She wandered up Soi Buakhao, keeping to the shadows so as not to get a suntan. It was very hot and she was looking in estate agents' windows, half-hoping to find a flat for the lodgers and half-thinking of one for herself. She had never lived alone before and the idea was both scary and exciting. Money, though. It would be expensive. With Goong out for a month and the lodgers gone, Lek would probably be alone at least every other night anyway, if Ayr was lucky. She noted a few ad-dresses along with their telephone numbers, judging potential flats by their location and price rather than their size.

Nid's phenomenal earnings were not sustainable. By one o'clock, she had walked up to Pattaya Klang, but it was still two hours before she had to be in work. She turned left anyway and walked down to the beach. She sat on a deck chair and watched the sea from the shade of a canopy. She couldn't remember the last time she'd done that and it felt good – very relaxing. She had a couple of hours all to herself and she wasn't too tired to enjoy them as she usually would have been. She set the alarm on her phone anyway, just in case she fell asleep.

She did fall asleep too, but when the alarm woke her at two forty-five she paid the 10 Baht hire charge for the chair and walked the 100 metres to the bar. Will and Goong were already there, being entertained by Noi, the night watch woman. Lek sauntered up went straight in to the bar, put her bag away and greeted them:

"Hello, gang. How is everyone?"

Lek sat in front of Goong and Noi went to check the float ready to sign it over to Lek and take everything over 2,000 Baht back to Beou on her way home. It had been a very good night and Beou had already taken 35,000 Baht home when she left at two a.m. There was another 7,345 Baht to be removed. New girls and a party had been a real money-spinner. Pity it couldn't be done every night. This sort of earnings was possible on a party night, because, although someone threw the party and paid for it, anyone was allowed to attend. And they did. After all, if two bars right next to each other charge the same for drinks, but one has free food, where would anyone go?

Will said: "We were on our way to the beach for a walk, but Goong wanted to stop off and see you first. She said you would be here at three o'clock. Spot on too. Very punctual – especially for a Thai. You're worse than the Spanish normally. The Spanish invented the word 'manyana', but the Thais developed the concept – sort of manyana with knobs on."

The girls smiled politely although nobody understood what he was talking about. Lek spoke to Goong in Thai:

"Hi, Little Sister, everything all right? You like this one, don't you? How long is he staying this time? Four weeks? Everybody was out last night – the whole bar. Nid twice! I had the room to myself and even enjoyed it for the first time in quite a while. I slept like a log. What did you want to see me about?"

"Oh, nothing really. I just wanted to see you were all right and to say that I'll be taking a lot of my clothes to Will's hotel. He's staying at the Marriott for five weeks. How are the new girls?"

"I've only seen Nid and she's as happy as a puppy with two tails. A bit full of herself today. She's asleep back at the flat. Oh, and Noi came back just as I was leaving. She was with Ayr and seemed happy enough too. I've been flat-hunting for them. Our place is too small for six – it takes at least an hour just for everyone to have a shower. I found three or four that look suitable Would you have time to look at them or shall we leave it up to the 'Three N's'? They'll be all right, won't they? No come back on us then either. They're going to have to learn to fend for themselves soon enough anyway."

"Is it right that you've stopped going with men, Lek? You said that 'everyone was out', but that didn't include you, did it?"

"No, it didn't include me – I told you I slept alone and enjoyed it but I'm not turning lesbian, if that's what you mean" she joked. "I don't know what I'm doing to be honest. I'm just a bit fed up with the life-style. I need a break. I still want a farang husband, so I'll have to go with some foreigners, won't I, but not the same as before. There's no point expecting a reasonable answer, because I'm not sure I have one. Something needed to be changed, so I changed that bit of my life. Per-haps, it wasn't the bit that needed changing, I don't know. Perhaps, I'm getting too old for Pattaya. I miss my daughter, that's for sure... and I have bad dreams sometimes. Too often."

"Yes, I've heard you crying out in your sleep, Big Sister, but I didn't like to say anything. I'm sure Ayr's heard you too. They sound really bad. Is there anything we, or I, can do?"

"No, darling, I don't think there's anything anyone can do except me. I'm sorry you know about the nightmares though. I didn't want to disturb you. It's embarrassing really. There's only the one dream, but it recurs often, sometimes in minor variations on the same theme. I'll tell you about it one day when we're alone. You'd better get back to your man or he'll be getting bored. Another beer, Will?"

"Yes, please, darling, and one for Goong, one for yourself and something for Noi. We haven't met properly yet, have we?"

Lek went off to get the three beers and sign for the float. Noi took the excess cash and bade everyone farewell. Lek sat back down with the couple. It would be very quiet until the girls started coming in at about four o'clock and wouldn't start getting busy until six or seven. This was to become the 'nice time' of the working day for her.

"Where you come from, Will?" came the standard opening line from Lek.

"I come from Wales. The same place as Barry and Nick. The town's called Barry too, actually. I know quite a few people from Barry who come out here regularly Another one's coming out next week. A friend of mine, Craig. You'll like him. He's very nice. A quiet man. Tall, a bit over-weight, like me, but very nice. Would you like to meet him when he gets here?"

"Oh, I not sure …," she replied and then added remembering her manners, "Yes, of course. He friend from you, yes? If you say he nice man bring him here and maybe we can talk early when I'm working and not too busy. Same now. He handsome man?"

"Average, I'd say. Not too ugly. Maybe fifty years old. Not too old. Tall, six feet; uh, let me see, maybe one metre eighty centimetres. Little bit too big; how you say, pompoy: chubby. Yes?"

Lek smiled warmly at Will's attempts to make her laugh and they both said together:

"Married?"

"No," said Will. "He never married and not have baby too."

"Why not marry and not have baby too?"

Will knew from previous talks with Thais that they found this very difficult to understand in anyone over the age of 25-30, because Thai parents had to rely on their children to fund them in their old age not having a social security system. Often the grandparents would earn their keep by looking after their grandchildren so that their own children could go out to work. This is what Lek's mother was doing and it wasn't unusual. The norm, in fact, but Lek didn't want her daughter to find out what she had done for a living.

"Oh, I think he too busy working before." This standard answer usually went a long way to satisfying a Thai's curiosity regarding the subject's sexual preferences.

"Will," asked Lek, changing the subject through genuine lack of interest, "will Nick and Barry be coming here, before they go home?"

"I don't know, love. I'll ring them and find out." A minute later, he was speaking into his mobile and waving enthusiastically. "There they are! Look, walking up from the beach with their birds. What're their names? Joy and Deou? Hey, nice to see you! How are your heads, lads? Ready to go, are you?"

The four of them looked pretty miserable, but it certainly wasn't only the hangovers. Will hadn't quite realized what they had all been through over the last two weeks trying to get visas. He could be a bit insensitive at times, always trying to play the court jester, but with no king to promise him immunity. Barry replied:

"Yeah, yeah, all right, Will. Not now, please. We'll have to leave our darlings behind in two hours and we tried like bloody hell to take them home with us. Now it won't happen until after Christmas. We've just been out booking up a couple of hotel rooms for when we come back in the second week of December. We booked for a month to be sure of enough time to get visas …. A round, please, for the seven of us, Lek, but can I have mine first, I'm sweating conkers here. That should be enough, shouldn't it, Will?"

"One beer at a time is plenty for me. You can always buy another one later. Stops it getting warm, see."

Barry was just about to protest, when Will smiled:

"All right, only joking! Yes, you should be able to get things sorted out in a month. Thais don't have Christmas holidays as such, although the Embassy may well do. You'll have to get on with it as soon as you land in Bangkok. Get the girls to meet you at the airport and stay there till it's done. I believe you can download the forms from the Internet. Make sure you know what you need and have it all with you: bank statements, mortgage papers, wage slips, photos, letter of invitation guaranteeing sponsorship and all the rest. Oh, and get the girls to get passports to put the visas in – you'd be surprised how many people forget to do that until the last minute."

"They got passports last week, but we still have a few things to sort out. Maybe we should book a hotel in Bangkok for the first three or four days, Nick, eh? We can do that on the Internet too, once we get back home. Cheers, Will. Ninety minutes to go before the taxi arrives at the hotel. Do you reckon we should use an agency to get the visas?"

"Naw, Barry. People say it's difficult to get a visa to the UK, but I think that if you provide the papers the Embassy is looking for, they can hardly refuse you. I've never tried, but it can't be rocket science, can it? Why pay someone thousands of pounds when you can do it yourself? I wouldn't anyway. You're not thick nor is Nick. Pretend you are barristers, prove everything you say and do it yourself. That's what I say."

After an hour or so, the party of four had to leave. Joy, Deou and Lek produced garlands to hang around their necks for a safe journey home and most of the girls that had arrived came over to give them a hug and a peck on the cheek, without disturbing their make-up, of course.

"Well, guys, sorry to see you go, but I'll have Craig to keep me company next week. One door closes, but another one opens. You know what I mean? I'll see you back in Barry in five weeks or so. Have a good flight both. Want one more before you go?"

"No, you're all right. See you then. Have a good holiday," said Nick and they both left with one arm waving and the other around their girlfriend.

"Poor sods," remarked Will as they walked off, "I'm glad I'm not going home for a while yet. I like it here with my little shrimp, my Goong, don't I love?" and he kissed her on the cheek.

Joy and Deou returned to the bar at seven o'clock bleary-eyed. Every one of the girls commiserated with them. There was no gloating nor jealousy. It was made worse when everybody realised that Nick and Barry had not left them any money to 'stop working'. There was a hot debate whether it was intentional or an oversight. Most said it had to be an oversight in the sad days following the refusal of a visa. But some of the more sceptical ones were not quite so sure any more.

That is what Pattaya could do to you – most dreams were shattered or just withered away, only a very few were realised.

They decided to get drunk, 'phone their men-friends in the morning and judge it by ear. They had booked hotel rooms for December after all, hadn't they? Surely, they had? They had seen them do it, but had they seen any money change hands for the deposit? They couldn't quite remember any longer.

By the end of the evening, Lek had her first real counselling job on her hands. What if Barry and Nick cancelled their bookings and went to Chiang Mai or Phuket instead. Nobody would ever know, would they? Men are all liars. They'll tell you anything.

By midnight there were two camps: one trying to make a living and the other commiserating or trying to cheer up Joy and Deou. Lek was caught in the middle, but thought that the fellahs had seemed genuine enough. She turned the music up and asked the girls to keep their voices down or go home. By one o'clock, everyone was of the opinion that they'd have to keep working until some hard cash showed up from Wales. Will tried to keep well out of the discussion even though the drunken girls pestered him for his opinion – his inside information on Barry and Nick's characters. Eventually, the girls slunk off to bed – alone or otherwise.

That left Goong, Will and Lek mopping their brows, glad it was all over for another day. Lek got a round in and no sooner had she done that than Ayr turned up – drunk but alone. She was given a drink too.

She wanted to talk about moving the new lodgers out. Stress levels were still high from before and Ayr was obviously pissed off about something too. The three flatmates tried to come to an agreement. The best they could manage, without boring Will, was to help the 'Three N's' to find a flat over the next three or four days.

It was left at that – the three had earned nearly 4,000B the day before and Beou had advanced them 7,500 collectively and maybe they had some savings. None of this was worked out with any jealousy or malice. It was just a fact that three thirty-somethings did not really want to live with three twenty-somethings, who had enough money to take care of themselves.

And if they but knew it, the feeling was mutual.

Goong called a taxi to take her and Will back to their hotel and Lek said hello to Noi, who had arrived at the tail-end of the discussion, but who had hitherto stayed discretely far in the background. They had another drink while Lek finished the books for the day shift, switched the lights and CD player off and handed the bar over to Noi.

Lek decided to walk home with Ayr later and asked Noi if they could sit as customers for an hour or until punters came and disturbed them. Noi and Ayr were happy enough to go along with it. They had nothing to rush off to. Glad of the company of her old friends, Lek wanted to be tired enough to go straight to sleep when her head hit the pillow.

"I got quite cheesed off with Nid this morning" confided Lek to Ayr and Noi, "I feel really guilty about it. It's not as if the girl did anything wrong really."

"Why? What did she do then?" enquired Ayr.

"Like I said, nothing really. She just breezed in at about ten fifteen this morning and plonked herself down on the bed. As if she owned it, I suppose. I had been so happy there fifteen minutes before and she sort of took over, I guess. I shouldn't have said anything really. She's so young and on a buzz at the moment and it was my idea to invite them to stay after all. They've only been there two days for Heaven's sake. Only slept there one night. What a selfish cow I am, aren't I?

"All right, don't all rush to defend me at once."

"You're too hard on yourself," soothed Ayr. "It's only a small flat and you were only trying to help them when you invited them in. You saved them from Charli The Lech, if nothing else. And one of them snores too!"

They all laughed and Lek calmed down again.

"Why don't you take them out flat hunting over the next few mornings?" put in Noi, "They'll need their own digs soon enough anyway. Six women using one bathroom can't be easy, I'm sure."

"Yes, we were just talking about that. I already started looking on my way in today. I have a few addresses to show them. The deposit and advance rent will take most of their money, but then, I suppose we all had to do it at one time or another. Maybe Beou will be able to come up with something. As long as it's not Charli's old dump." She didn't mention the fact that she was considering moving out herself and thus breaking up the trio – a process she had subconsciously already started by stopping 'working' and even by thinking of moving out. This was not deception, she just had not thought things through yet.

"Come on Ayr, let's get you home. We'll leave Noi to read her book or ravage the fellahs or whatever it is she gets up to when we're not around. I don't fancy walking now, do you? I feel shattered all of a sudden and just want to be home, have a shower and go to sleep. Let's hope the snorer is not in."

They all chuckled and hugged and Lek and Ayr went off to get a single, shared motorcycle home like they had used to do more often in previous years.

8 BACK TO BASICS

A few days later, without prompting, the 'Three N's' asked Lek to view a flat they had found. Things had been going all right too. People were respecting each other's space and privacy and even the snorer seemed to be snoring more quietly; whoever she was. Still, it had to be done and now was as good a time as any, even though there were rarely more than three or four of them in the flat at any given moment — night or day.

Anyway, she went and the girls had actually found something quite nice. It was not far from work, but far enough away to be quiet. It was slightly larger and more expensive than Lek's and it made her wonder whether the girls were out just to make money or to have a great time doing it too. It was a two-roomed flat. One room had three mattresses on the floor: one in each corner of a small room that the door did not open into.

There was no room for anything else but posters in there. The living room was about the same as Lek's and so was the bathroom. The veranda was slightly larger. It came 'complete' with a wardrobe, which was not large enough for three women, a table and four chairs, a sofa and a small armchair, a fridge and an electric ring plus enough plates, cups and cutlery for four.

It cost 2,000 Baht a month more than the 3,500 that Lek and the others were paying. Maybe the youngsters had the right idea. You don't have to live in a rotten flat just because you've got a rotten job. On the other hand, she had saved that extra 700B a month for ten years: 84,000 without taking interest into account. She pointed this out and read the lease. Everything seemed to be in order. Ah well, she thought, it was their money and up to them. It was also good that they were happy, even optimistic and full of the joys of life.

"See you in the bar by four thirty and don't be drunk," she warned as she left them to celebrate alone. It was only eleven in the morning, so she strolled back to the flat, knowing that Ayr was probably still asleep.

She let herself in quietly and was quite shocked to see Ayr sitting up on the bed in her towel reading a magazine. "Do you know what time it is?" she joked, "It's eleven thirty in the morning. You should still be asleep! Are you not well?"

"All right, all right, I know, Big Sister. Nothing is wrong. Well, not any more. They made such a racket leaving this morning that it woke me up. I tried getting back to sleep, but needed a pee. On my way to the loo, I opened the window, drew the curtains, and was wide-awake. It's lovely, actually, to have some time to myself; to not always be in a rush." She went back to reading her magazine.

Lek just stared at her dumb-founded. She and Goong had been tiptoeing around her for ten years so as not to wake her up in the mornings and now she comes out with this! She must be sick. "You're on the change!" she quipped and put the kettle on. It was already warm. "Crikey, and you've already made tea. Definitely something wrong."

Ayr just grinned and carried on reading.

Ayr soon got up and Lek went for some breakfast for them both. They ate rice soup and some pineapple and decided to Spring clean the place before having a shower and going into Daddy's Hobby. It wasn't dirty and it wasn't large, so it did not take long, but they both felt truly satisfied with a job well done. Lek got ready for work first then Ayr and they sat watching some rubbish on TV and chatting until two forty-five. It had certainly been an untypical day so far, but also a very pleas-ant one.

Ayr wanted to go in later, so Lek left alone and walked the usual route to the bar.

Noi was there, as expected. "You really don't have to be here by three every day, you know. I've got nowhere I need to go before four thirty. Come in at four same as before, if you like."

"Maybe I will one day, Noi, thanks, but for the moment I'm happy to come in at three. The 'Three N's' moved out today, you know? They've got a nice flat a little out past me. Not bad at all. I enjoy a chat with you early like this, before you have to rush off and while it's still quiet. Fancy a cup of coffee?"

"Sure, I like our chats too. We've always got on, haven't we? How's your new lifestyle suiting you?"

"Fine. Most of the time. I enjoy being in the flat more. Ayr and I even Spring-cleaned it today! That doesn't happen often, I can tell you. Not that it gets very dirty of course. I like running this bar too. Being its night-time manager and cashier or whatever my new job title is. Beou did have a name for it, but she was probably only joking, know-ing her.

"It's not as exciting as working with the girls but I don't miss all that. I don't even miss the travel and posh hotels. And I certainly don't miss the men, although most of them were all right really – just sad, lonely, balding, podgy, middle-aged men looking for a fling with younger women.

"Nothing wrong with that in principle. I don't know what I'm try-ing to say really. My lifestyle is vastly different now and it'll take me a while to see how I like it, I suppose. It's been good so far. Maybe I could do with a trip up country. Go see Soomsomai and Mum. Laze around up there for a few days. It's my birthday in August – maybe I could go then. That would be nice wouldn't it? I haven't been back for about a year now. When did you last go back, Noi? Longer ago than that, I reckon."

"More than two years for sure, but there's not a lot left for me there any more. My brother, you know. We were never very close. My sister's moved away to Burriram. A few disinterested aunties and uncles. My daughter's the only one that matters, and she's down here with me …. Oh, sorry, love, that was stupid of me. I know how much you miss little Soom. What a plank, I am."

"It's OK, I know you didn't say it to hurt me, but you're right, I miss her a lot, although I have sort of got used to it… but I don't want to be used to it, if you know what I mean. If I can't be with her I want to miss her. Will having more responsibility here mean that I can go home even less, do you think?

"Am I having a nervous breakdown, Noi? Am I going potty? It bloody well feels like it."

"No, darling, there's nothing wrong with you. You're concerned about your daughter like every good mother should be and you need a break. You said just now that you haven't been home for a year. It's all very well staying in some swanky hotel or flying off to Phuket with a client, but the word says it all: 'client'… you're still working, not relaxing. True or not? Call him a 'boyfriend' if you like, if it makes you feel better, but we all know he's not. He wants your body and you want his money. Plain and simple.

"You're on your toes day and night with them. Is he happy? Is he going to dump me? Is he going to pay me? Even, is he going to hurt me? It's very stressful. You need a break sometimes, everyone does. Beou will probably be in later, have a word with her. It might be difficult for a couple of weeks, but early August should be all right. You could pay off the last of your loan and go tell your Mum. That would be a really great surprise for her. She's probably forgotten when it finishes. Do you want me to mention it to Beou? Soften her up, so to speak."

"No, thanks, Noi, that won't be necessary. Beou and I have always been close. If she can spare me, she will let me go, otherwise I'll have to wait. I'll call Soom at four thirty, when she gets home from school, that'll cheer me up. Punters off the starboard bow! I'd better get started. The girls will be drifting in soon too. Time to get the rice on. See you tomorrow, if you have to disappear while I'm busy. Thanks for being a mate."

"See you tomorrow, darling. Don't thank me, we all need friends down here. Nobody could survive without them. We're each other's replacement family, aren't we? Go get 'em love."

Lek walked up to her first customer of the day: "Hello handsome, what you want to drink?"

He had a beer and she offered to play a game of dominoes with him. She had seen him playing before with one of the girls. By the end of the game three girls had come in and one relieved Lek, who excused herself by saying she had to check the books, which was a lie, but she was not a front-line trooper any longer, she was in support now.

The next few hours were routine. The only unusual thing being that Will and Goong had not popped in as they had done so every day so far. Beou turned up for a spot check at seven as she was in the area taking Sally, her younger daughter to Tops to get a new dress. Everybody loved Beou's children and someone sat Sally on the bar while her mother talked to Lek.

"Everything all right, cousin?"

"Sure, Beou. Everything's great. I see you've got Sally with you now. She is growing up quickly, isn't she? She looks more like you every day. Such a happy kid too. Beou could I have a word soon about something personal? Have you got a few minutes to spare or shall I wait?"

"Say, it now. Sally's doing fine with the girls. They spoil her rotten here and she loves it. What's up?"

"I hate to ask, what with my new job and all, but I'd like to go home and see Soom for a few days. It's been a year now and it's just too long, Beou. It's not your fault, but it's starting to get to me now. I don't mean I have to leave in the next few days, but I'd like to go within a month or so for a few days. What do you think? Is it too soon?"

"No, it's not too soon. Maybe it is a good idea to give you a break before the Christmas rush. July and August are usually quite quiet anyway because of the small monsoon, it gets too humid for a lot of people. It's hot in their own countries too. Now is actually a very good time to give you a short holiday. Good idea! Mmmm, it's the eighth or ninth of July today, eh? So, let's say the first weekend in August. Is that OK with you? Go up on the Friday and come back on Monday to start work on Tuesday. Is that OK? Good settled."

"Thanks, Beou. I really need that. I'll 'phone Soom right away and tell her the good news."

"OK, no problem. Send her my love. See you tomorrow."

Lek only had a few minutes with her daughter but they were very happy ones and Lek promised to bring her a gift from Pattaya. A few minutes later, she was back at work with a flourish. She kept the books, changed CD's and TV channels, nodded to regulars and chatted to the girls with gusto when they came to her desk. The evening passed quickly and the next thing she knew Will appeared along side her with Goong.

"Hello, Lek! A couple of beers, please. We're late on parade today. We went to the pictures for a change. Everything all right, love?"

"Yes, Will, everything lovely!" She said to Goong in Thai: "Beou's given me the first weekend in August off and I'm going home to see Soom. Great, eh? I'm so happy about it. I've already told Soom and she's as happy as ever I've heard her. If I were not so mean, I'd ring the bell!"

They both laughed and Will asked what the high spirits were all about. Lek spoke quickly in Thai: "Please don't tell anyone yet. I couldn't bear it if anything went wrong and I couldn't go." So Goong said to him: "Oh, we just happy. Our friends in our room find nice new flat today and we have more room again. Lek love her job and I love you. You not happy too, darling?"

"Yes, I very happy too, darling" and the girls smiled at each other. "And not forget my friend, Craig. He come over on number eleven, Sunday evening. He not come here before. I tell him I help him. Show him little bit Thailand... well, little bit Pattaya anyway."

"Yes, very good," Lek replied as she went back behind her desk "Good idea."

They had a short stop-on for thirty minutes but everyone that was left was happy to move on by then and Lek and Ayr went home together again.

Daddy's Hobby

9 WILL'S FRIEND

Lek slept well that night with Ayr in the flat and the day passed easily. Routinely, in fact. A heavy downpour at about four o'clock in the morning made the morning a little cooler than it would be for the rest of the day. Then shopping, a bite to eat, get changed, she chose culottes and a blouse, and off to work. Subconsciously, she was already starting to dress down – more conservatively, although she didn't even know it herself.

Lek's typical work routine started with a chat with Noi when she got in, followed by catching up on the previous night's gossip with the girls and then waiting for the punters to come in, which seemed to be getting later and later as the month went on. It was not boring, but it was not what she had expected it to be either.

Sunday began the same way and Lek found herself sitting behind the desk in the bar after Noi had left, hoping that someone would come in soon. The girls started trickling in at four o'clock as usual.

Joy and Deou were first in. They hadn't worked since Barry and Nick went home. They had phoned Wales and spoken to them and the boys had promised to send them some money, but nothing had come through yet and so they reluctantly had to go back to work.

Mott was in too, putting on her make up in the mirror near Lek's desk. She was trying to cover over a black eye. "How did you get that, Mott? It looks nasty" Lek asked.

"It's not as bad as it looks. That piece of shit I was with last night did it. He said it was an accident. He said he was drunk, but that's not true, he wasn't that drunk… He just likes knocking little women about.

Luckily he'd paid me up front and everything was fine until about two in the morning when he started getting rough. Anyway, I waited for him to go to sleep, then peed in his shoes and sneaked out. I don't think he'll be 'round here complaining though. I'm going to tell Bong about him. If he's ever seen around here again he'll be put in hospital and no mistaking."

Ayr had come in too and Or and Porn had been 'bar fined' for that day already so they didn't have to show up. Not by the two Englishmen though, they had already gone home, Porn and Or liked to work together, like a double act.

The two from Soi 6 were out for a week too, so that only left the 'Three N's', who often came in around six o'clock, but who were also often the first chosen. That was usually the way with new, young girls. Sometimes they worked too cheaply, trying to get two punters in in one day, but as often as not the foreign residents could spot the new ones and they liked to get in early.

Either way, it led the new girls to believe it would always be like that, until reality set in six or eight weeks down the line, when they would be competing with the new girls coming in after them. You had to have something special to stay at the top for ten years like Lek, Goong and Ayr had. Character, style, presence, charm, charisma. A 'je ne sais quoi'. Internal as well as external beauty. Call it what you will.

It does not come in a bottle, no matter what advertisers say.

Lek had seen it all before, but she was concerned about Mott. She spoke to her again:

"Mott, do you want to call the police about that bloke last night? 'Alan' wasn't it, staying in a hotel on the top end of Beach Road? It's against the law to hit you. You know that, don't you. Let's get the scum bag off the streets for a few days. He'll get some of his own medicine when the boys in the 'Monkey House' know what he's in there for. He deserves it. He does deserve it, doesn't he?"

"Of course he does, but I prefer to take care of this sort of thing in my own way. I didn't only pee in his shoes, I left a few reminders about the room that he'll have a job explaining to the cleaners. I know the security guard there from before and he spoke to Alan to check whether I'd stolen anything when I wanted my ID back from reception. I hadn't and he could see my eye even then so he let me pass. I'm pretty sure the hotel manager took me seriously too when I said I was going to report room 521 to the Pattaya People's News. I then had the luck to take the same taxi home as we'd used to go to his hotel.

He was very sympathetic when he saw my eye and my make-up running down my face. I don't think Alan will want to meet him tomorrow either. And then there's Bong. Bong was working not three metres from us outside here for a few hours. He won't have forgotten his face. So, all-in-all, I think Mr. bully-boy Alan had better stay in for the rest of his holiday and clean up his room."

"Sheesh, Mott! You're only small, but what a punch! Good luck to you. Still can't poll dance though" she said returning to her work.

"You have to learn how to take care of yourself here and I'll learn that bloody pole dancing too, even if it kills me trying."

Punters came and went and the girls made them feel welcome if they required it. Some didn't want to chat or play games or even take a lady out; some only wanted to sit and think or wait for a friend. It took all sorts. Many were regulars who only came in for a quick cigarette and a beer to see who was about… most often to say 'Hello' to Beou while they were in the area.

Many had not heard yet that she was taking more of a back seat now to spend more time with her daughters. Soon Lek would have a network of her own friends who would call in to see if she was about. Noi probably had a circle of night-owl friends in the same way.

It was soon six thirty and she remembered that Will had said his friend was arriving at that time. Maybe that's why he and Goong hadn't shown again up again that afternoon. She began to feel strangely nervous about meeting him. Will had gone on about him so much that he'd spooked her. That was it. Six thirty came and went and nothing happened. What an anti-climax, she thought. But what had she expected? A sign, a portent? However, she knew he would come sometime and it made her nervous.

She had butterflies in her stomach and she thought that it was ridiculous.

Time dragged on and on as if in slow motion. There were not many in, but it was still early… lately, it hadn't started getting busy until ten or even eleven o'clock. Slow motion. She even asked one of the girls to play 'Connect Four' with her, but, despite being a good player, she lost seven or eight games in a row and gave it up. She just could not concentrate.

She was starting to shake the feeling of apprehension when her mobile rang. "Hello, Lek? Goong. We're in the Pig. Will says we'll be there in five minutes. I thought I'd better warn you. Are you all right?"

"Of course I am . Why shouldn't I be? It's only a friend of Will's. I've already met at least two of them. I'll see you in five minutes." Despite what she said, she grabbed her handbag and headed for a mirror at the back of the bar. She checked the usual: hair, make-up, teeth; she lifted her breasts and bra so they rode higher and checked the contours of her bum. She was ready, but for what?

She was working as a cashier and she wasn't looking for a date. She put her bag away in a safe place, resumed her seat behind the desk and tried to look busy. She had been cashier for eight days, she told herself, it was not as if she had forgotten how to talk to a man, but she didn't sound as confident as she thought she ought to.

However, what her subconscious realised, but her head had not yet, was that she was going back longer than eight days, she was going back fifteen years to the days when she was meeting an ordinary bloke as an ordinary girl, not as a confident working girl, and she was, in fact, as nervous of meeting an older man socially now as she would have been then.

The uniform had given her confidence, but she was in civvies now.

She kept looking over the top of her pen, as if she were doing mental arithmetic, but she was looking out for Goong. Her insides were going haywire now. Why was she winding herself up? Sheesh! Then she saw Goong and Will ten metres away in the crowd, walking her way, but who was the third person? It could be any of a dozen men milling about. Here it comes, she thought and Goong turned into the bar closely followed by Will and another man, who skipped out of the crowd to catch up with Will. She licked her teeth for the tenth time feeling for food although she had not eaten for hours and popped in another mint.

Will's description had been pretty accurate except he had less hair. He was tall; a bit overweight, but not too much and had thinning brown hair with slight flashes of grey. He wore a dark blue collared shirt with the sleeves rolled up to the elbow, faded denim jeans and black leather shoes. Will lead them to seats at the bar not two metres from where she was sitting.

She looked at him but he did not look back. Will had obviously not spoken of her. She looked at him again. He was smiling even laughing as he talked with Will and he had a decent set of teeth. Mmmm, no Adonis, she thought but not bad for his age, which in many Thai women's eyes, was a good age for a man to be, because by then he'd usually had his flings and also had some money in the bank.

She grew bolder and kept glancing over furtively, but still he only had time for Will and Goong. 'How odd,' she thought. 'He is clearly very fond of Will and visa-versa… he must be treating Goong kindly because she is a friend of Will's – a Thai man would ignore another man's woman. How charming…' Will ordered a round from Ayr who had been hovering nearby hoping for such an opportunity to get a closer look.

Just as the drinks arrived, so did Beou on her motorcycle. She pulled up behind Will and joined them. Lek was watching the scene unfold, 'This is starting to look planned,' she thought, 'but what the hell? Will knew Beou and wanted her to meet his friend. Goong probably did the arranging.' In fact, it made it easier for her too.

She noted the round in the ledger and Will called out "…and one for Beou and Lek." She looked up at the sound of her name. Beou was shaking hands with them and being introduced to Craig. She looked down again, then Beou was tugging her arm saying "Come and meet Craig."

This was it. She took a big swig of the whisky soda that had arrived and at the right moment said: "Pleased to meet you!" and immediately went bright red. She didn't hear what Craig said, she couldn't concentrate. Beou held her arm which she thought was to stop her walking away, but Craig took is as an offer to shake hands and took her hand in his large fist. He smiled warmly. She couldn't remember a word of English at that precise moment, so she just smiled and sat down on a bar stool behind the bar while he released her hand.

The men talked incessantly about something in English and the ladies tried to understand, speaking every now and then in hushed Thai. As the bar filled and orders came in, Beou took over the desk, Lek just sat there mesmerised. Not necessarily by Craig but by the situation. Will held Goong's hand, Craig talked to Will and smiled at Lek every now and again, their faces were only 600 mm apart. The music was so loud the had to do that in order to communicate. Lek was gaining courage again and was waiting to smile back whenever Craig looked at her.

∞

The following morning to herself, and many, many times during her life, to her friends, Lek recalled that evening as follows:

'Will said something to Craig, he shrugged his shoulders and then nodded. He leaned over to me and said: "We're going for something to eat. Would you like to come too?" I didn't understand so he repeated it, but still I couldn't catch what he was saying. Craig leaned in and said something in my ear, but I was so overwhelmed that I had to get Beou over to translate. I was thrilled, but I said out of duty: "I cannot. I am working tonight, I work as cashier every night," or at least that was what I wanted to say.

'Beou told me that I could go if I wanted to, so I did. I didn't think about consequences or possibilities or anything, I just said 'Yes, thank you. I am happy to go'. Craig tapped my hand with his open palm which I assumed meant 'Thank you'. I waaied in response, but he didn't waai back. I wondered he knew what a waai meant. Maybe he really hadn't been to Thailand before. Most farangs would have waaied back.

'It was one of the methods of weighing them up. A farang who waais back is proving either that he has learned what it means from a Thai (lady, usually) or that he presumes he knows what it means. So, you ask whether he has been to Thailand before, if he says that he has, he has given something away about himself. Thai ladies in Pattaya always prefer a farang that has not been to Thailand before. Craig seemed to be one of those.

'I thought that I might apply more tests later, if necessary.

'Anyway, Will paid the bill and the ladies went for their bags and a little natter.

'Will and Craig had a little natter too.

'Both conversations went in a similar fashion: "What do you

think? Nice. Eh?" Both Craig and Lek answered in the affirmative, although we didn't know that at the time.

'Will asked if everyone liked seafood, we did, so we walked down Soi 7 to Beach Road and rode a Baht Taxi. Will stopped the taxi outside Walking Street and we walked in. Craig clearly didn't know the local customs, but his instincts were to shield and protect me from the jostling crowd, although it was obvious to me that I knew more about what was going on than he did. Definitely a virgin traveller in Asia, I thought. Therefore, not a liar, pretender or know-it-all.

'I watched him. He looked at women but didn't flirt. "Respect for me?" I wondered. I began to believe that he didn't know that he could have anyone on the street for the right price. I was warming to him more by the minute. Will said something to him and he took my hand. I didn't know what he was doing, but I held his hand tight anyway. Seconds later, he was steering me off to the right, following Will into a restaurant. I felt a bit of a twit, but he did not let go, so I held on.

'We were in one of the best and most romantic seafood restaurants in Pattaya - on a jetty out in the sea.

'It was fantastic. We both couples ordered the biggest platter for two they had and Will chose the wine. I was in Nirvana and I think everyone else was too. My command of the English language, such as it was, was returning and the four of us talked for hours. Wine flowed, leading to coffees and liqueurs. I had had all that before, but it had always made me wary, suspicious. This time it did not and it was lovely to have Goong there too.

'We talked until they asked us to leave and at about one thirty. Craig and Will split the bill and we walked outside. What now? No-one wanted to break up the party, but it would have to happen very soon. We got a taxi back to Daddy's Hobby. Maybe it would still be open, we all hoped so, but it was central for everyone anyway. I phoned Noi to say we were on our way, so that I knew we would have the chance to say goodnight properly.

'We got back there at about one fifty. Craig bought a round of gin and tonics and we sat down. Within ten minutes, Will announced, "Come on Goong! Tomorrow's another day. Let's leave them to it." They were gone within minutes, leaving me feeling rather awkward, although I still had Noi for support though. I felt that I could trust Craig, but I couldn't tell what he was thinking. With most men, at this time of night, in Pattaya, it was very easy. We talked a little and he had two more beers.

"Where are you staying?," I asked him. He said he was staying in the 'Pig', so I offered to walk him home as it was only fifty metres away and I wanted him to be safe. He was definitely starting to look a little ragged. Alcohol and twenty hours travelling. He paid up and we walked to his room. Once there he offered me something from the mini bar and we sat on his bed to talk again. There wasn't much furniture. We both had a beer. He didn't lay a finger on me and we talked till five in the morning.

'Craig showed me books on Thailand that he had brought from the UK, most of which had pictures. I couldn't read English well then, but what he said seemed to tally with the photos and the captions. At about six o'clock, he offered to take me home. I have never taken a man back to my room and I was not about to start now. "No," I said, "Can I sleep in your chair and go home after a few hours? Is that OK with you?" That did not happen, but we fell asleep in all our clothes and very close to each other on the bed where we had been reading.

'He sooner than I, but I was very happy to be there.

'I was also very happy that I had chosen to wear culottes rather than a skirt'.

10 A NEW DAWN OR JUST ANOTHER DAY?

She didn't know who woke up first, she was just lying there thinking, but at a given moment they looked into each other's eyes from a few centimetres, smiled and kissed lightly on the lips.

"Good morning, Lek," he said and equally predictably,

"Good morning, Craig," she replied.

"What time do you have to go to work?"

"I not know…"

Craig thought that she had meant she didn't understand him.

"What time you working today?" He had obviously learned some Thai pigeon English the previous night.

"I must phone boss, Beou, and ask," she corrected herself.

"OK, no problem It is eleven o'clock now, will you have time for breakfast or lunch?"

She replied that she was sure she would have. She didn't have to start until three after all and could always take Noi up on her off of going in at four. However, she recommended that they ought to have a shower before going down to the restaurant. Lek volunteered to go first so that he could not watch her dressing. She came out in a towel, but he took his change of clothes in the shower with him and emerged fully dressed. She remarked that she had never experienced that in a man's room before, usually they wanted to flash a bit.

Craig tidied up a little, opened the door, put his hand lightly on her shoulder and guided her through into the corridor. He followed right behind. As they went down in the lift, he said: "I had a great time last night, Lek. I'm really pleased to have met you."

"Thank you," she replied, "I happy too."

In the bar-cum-restaurant, they were shown to a table for two and he waited for her to sit down. Once seated, he asked what she wanted to drink.

"Hot tea with milk," Lek said in Thai to the waitress. 'Tea', she repeated in English for Craig. He placed the order: "One tea and one bottle of spa water, please." When it arrived the girl put the tea, with the milk in it, in front of Craig and the water in front of Lek. 'I'm so sorry', he apologised to Lek, 'the waitress must have thought the tea was for me and, because I'm British, put milk in it. I'll get you another one'.

He put his hand up slightly to attract attention and Lek took the opportunity to touch his hand and save him, and herself, the embarrassment. 'No,' she explained, 'I ordered tea with milk. Many Thais drink tea with milk, same as the British'.

She wasn't sure whether he believed her or whether he thought she was just avoiding making a fuss, but she liked him for defending her again. She took her hand off his reluctantly and they chatted for about an hour over lunch. Then she began to feel it was about time she changed her clothes, even though the 'Pig' was air-conditioned.

"Craig, I sorry, but I must go now. Put new clothes," she declared.

It didn't seem to come as much of a surprise to him and he replied: "Yes, of course. I'm sorry for taking so much of your time and you must start work again soon too'. He paid the bill and walked Lek outside. She didn't want to leave him and definitely didn't want it to end there, but she had to get changed, she had to speak to Beou and she had to work.

Life goes on, as they say, she thought

Outside the 'Pig and Whistle', she wondered how she could get to see him again? If the worst came to the worst, she thought, she could get Goong to get Will to bring him to the bar.

Satisfied that she had a decent plan, she held out her hand to say goodbye. He took her hand, shook it and mumbled something which she didn't understand. He then put something in her hand, which made her cringe. 'Horror of horrors! A thousand Baht!' she thought. She could have died there and then!

She wanted the ground to open up and take her. It was not that others could have seen. He had been very discreet about it, but she was not with him for money! She had thought that he had liked her as she liked him. 'Did he pay all his dates in Britain too? Was it some crazy Welsh custom?' she asked herself.

She was mortified.

"Why you give me this?" she blurted out. Then he got embarrassed and said: "I want you to buy something nice for yourself." That was not good enough, That did not cut it. She'd heard that phrase hundreds of times from men. She knew what it meant. "I not want. Thank you." She tried to give it back.

"Please take it," he said, not getting the point. She turned and ran with no further ado, tears were starting to well in her eyes. She had to get away. In that brief moment, Craig had managed to make her feel more embarrassed, more ashamed, more dirty, than hundreds of men collectively had over the whole ten years and they had not even had sex!

She was outside the flat before one o'clock, still on the verge of tears. Once inside, she couldn't hold the flood gates any longer and she cried like a baby. She didn't know whether she was glad the place was empty or not. She doubted whether anyone could have helped her out of the depths of despair she was falling deeper into.

Hopeless misery. Dismal gloom. Abject dejection.

She stripped off her clothes and went into the shower room. Running water often lightened her spirits. She wiped her make-up off first in the mirror and looked for where he had read the words 'WORK-ING GIRL' - it must have been stamped on her forehead somewhere! This was only the first time such a thing had happened to her, but she wondered whether it would it always be like that from now on? Could men tell women that had worked? Was she forever to be an outcast among 'decent folk'?

She got under the shower and stayed there for a long time. Until she reasoned that she had to snap out of it and hurry into work. 'WORK' would that word be the bane of her life from now on? Would she forever think of it as what she had done rather than what she had yet to do?

She dried herself, dressed and went into work.

Noi wanted to know how she had got on, as any normal female friend would. So she told her, leaving nothing out except the ending and as she relived the night in her narration, she found that she was excited all over again. The shame and disappointment at the end of her meeting with Craig did not hurt so much any longer. It was as if it had all taken place a long time ago, not as if it had finished only two and a half hours ago.

It was sinking into long-term memory rather than staying in the present, where one likes to keep happy events. She felt it was a pity really, but beyond her control. Some self defence mechanism had probably kicked in. One that she had constructed over the years, or should that be 'over the men', without realising it. Useful, but a pity nevertheless.

She tried to snap out of it, but there was nothing for her to do. The bar was clean and tidy, the rice was on, the books were straight and ready for her to sign for and there were no customers. Noi soon left and she was left with her thoughts.

She reasoned that:

A] if Craig had read 'working girl' stamped on her soul or on the Akashic Record, then how could she blame him for being perceptive, skilled, adept? She should praise him, congratulate him and like him even him more.

B] she should decide whether she wanted to see him again. The answer was 'yes'

C] the conclusion had to be: to put up with her embarrassment and be with him until she could think of a better plan

'But why should she be embarrassed?' she thought. 'We needed money to save the farm, which would provide a living for my two brothers, my mother and my sister too. I had had to work. It would have been nice to have had enough schooling and qualifications to get a decent job near the village, but the fact was that I didn't have the qualifications. There had been no choice. Therefore, there should be no embarrassment, no shame and no reproach.'

She decided to see Craig as soon as possible before he realised he was in single man's paradise, so she took the next logical step and phoned Goong. Goong and Will were at his hotel and Craig was with them; they were at the poolside with a few beers. Craig was a good swimmer apparently.

"Yes, great! That's all very well, but what are you all doing later? … Look, I can't go traipsing off to different bars and restaurants, I'm stuck here for… well, until I can make other arrangements at least. Can't you get them to come over here for a beer? Ours does taste the same, you know? ... Yes, … Yes, all right! You guessed it. I want to see him again as soon as possible, before he gets led astray by some pert little minx. I… I think we, we all, had a great night last night and I want it to happen again. … Yes, I do really like him… Thank you. Now get him over here ASAP. Bye, darling Little Sister and thank you."

Light was showing at the end of the tunnel, only a pin prick at the moment, but light nevertheless.

The girls were coming in now, and again everyone wanted to know about Will's latest friend in Pattaya. She played him up a little, but that was part of the routine – it was expected.

And allowed for accordingly.

She emphasised his good manners as befitting a 'real gentleman from the UK' not English though, she said in a worldly-wise tone, but Welsh. Nobody had heard of Wales, but that didn't seem to matter. The retelling of the previous night's episodes elicited the 'Oohs' and 'Ahhs' in all the right places and everyone was happy. The girls congratulated Lek on her good fortune and said they were jealous. They behaved impeccably – they were a good bunch. Pals, mates. Sisters-in-Arms – The Sorority. They were each other's support group, as Noi called them.

Just then Craig, Will and Goong walked up; Goong first, winking and casting her eyes back indicating Craig. Lek blushed with pride as the girls all let out a loud 'Ooh' together. Craig smiled at her too. They sat at the bar and the girls all gathered around to make a fuss of him, as they would have for any one of each other's 'boyfriends'. It was obvious that Craig was impressed and to cover it he asked Lek for a round for the four of them. One of the girls jumped up to oblige, giving Lek a moment to say 'Hello'.

"Hello, Craig, How are you? Goong say you go swimming in hotel from Will. She say you swim very good. I cannot swim but I want to learn. You can teach me?"

"I have had a lovely day. They have a great pool at Will's hotel. I'll try to teach you to swim if you like. I don't know whether I'm any good at teaching to swim though. Yeah, sure, I'd love to try. When?"

"I not know. I must ask my boss, Beou. I work here every day from three or four 'clock until one o'clock morning. Maybe, we could try tomorrow at one o'clock afternoon, but I think very hot, maybe too hot for you and I not like get black skin."

"Pardon? You not want get 'black skin'? I not understand, you have brown skin already. Oh, you mean you not want sunburn? I see. Nobody want sunburn, but when I get sunburn, I get red skin."

Everyone laughed or giggled and Lek was proud. She went back to enter the round in the ledger and the girls edged in closer giving excellent examples of what the country is famous for – smiles.

Lek had a quiet word with Ayr asking her to fill in as cashier for her while she looked after Craig.

She got out a 'Connect Four' and set it up if front of them.

"You can play?" she asked.

"OK," he replied although he was not really into such games he would have done almost anything to be at the centre of Lek's attention. In fact, if the truth be known, it had worried Craig when Lek ran off on the verge of tears and he had been racking his brains all afternoon to find out what it was he had done to upset her – something he would not have done on purpose for all the tea in China.

He was genuinely relieved that she seemed to have forgiven him for whatever it was that he had done. He imagined that he had committed a cultural faux-pas, of which he was unaware. They played for an hour or so and laughed a lot whenever one of them won and the girls egged them on, especially Craig, because they could see that he was no match for Lek. Will and Goong sat close by watching. Goong was obviously interested in her friend's future.

It was equally obvious that Will was getting bored.

Men are not so interested in their friends' love lives as women are in their friends' love lives – it's just a fact. Will said: "I want some air-conditioning, some Western food and a decent toilet, so I'm off to the Pig. Lek knew that Goong would go with him. The question was would Craig?

He said: "Well, I'm not hungry yet. I'll see you there in thirty minutes."

Lek felt a flush of a minor success and the girls reflected it. "Oh, he want stay with you, Lek. Oyeah. You want stay with Lek, Craig? Oyeah."

Lek beamed and Craig smiled broadly – the potential catastrophe of only six hour ago staved off.

"Can you get an hour off to come with me?," he asked.

Her mind raced. "Ayr can you help me for another ninety minutes or so? I'll square it with Beou."

She smiled at Craig and said: "I phone Beou now ask. Maybe."

Beou was all right about it, She sensed how much it meant to Lek and she had known Ayr and Goong as long as she had known her cousin and all three had been there ten years. It never was going to be a problem, but Lek was the sort of person who knew where her loyalties lie and tried to do the right thing.

It was one of the reasons why everybody liked her so much.

They left Daddy's Hobby and walked to the Pig and Whistle up the road.

After dinner, Will and Goong went back to their hotel to watch football on TV. It was 10pm before Craig and Lek went back to Daddy's Hobby and Craig decided to sit there until Lek finished work. It got a little busy, so they couldn't talk as much as they both would have liked, and time dragged by slowly for Craig. Lek realised this and asked some of her friends to go and keep him company when they could. Craig didn't realise that Lek had asked the girls to talk with him and the attention polished his ego a little.

When one o'clock came, they closed the bar to the public and had a few drinks with Noi. Craig invited her back to his room. Lek was very tired but he wanted to go. However, she also wanted to make it look right, so she said: "I'd love to come back for a while, put my feet up, have a coffee and maybe watch a film before going home. I'm tired but not really sleepy, if you know what I mean."

He nodded. They said goodbye to Noi and left.

Once in the room, Craig put the TV on, gave Lek the remote control and made some coffee. By the time he had finished, Lek was already asleep, so he put a sheet over her, turned the TV off and lay down on the bed to go to sleep. Minutes later, he too was snoring loudly.

So loudly, in fact that it woke her up. At first she was genuinely startled by the din and thought that Craig must be having breathing problems, but she waited a while and her fears abated. She was still working on a plan, though, and she decide to wake him up and feign being cold – that she did not know how to operate the air-conditioning. So she shook him and said:

"Craig, darling, it is very cold in room for Thai lady. I always sleep hot." It was an outrageous lie, but she guessed that he wouldn't know any better.

"OK, Lek," he mumbled, I'll walk you home now. One minute, please."

"No, no," she said hurriedly, that not being part of the plan. "I stay here with you same last night, Give me blanket, please."

Without any more ado, she rolled onto the bed next to him and pulled a blanket over herself, making sure to stay very close to Craig, who was very happy with the turn of events and with the fact that he didn't have to traipse off anywhere so late at night. He put his arm around her and said: "Good night, kid, see you in the morning."

Lek was glowing inside and out and hardly slept a wink; she felt so 'at home' with this one.

They woke up at ten a.m. – Lek had already been awake for hours, but pretended to wake up when Craig stirred and Lek kissed him on the cheek and rushed off to the bathroom for the first shower, as she had done the day before. She came out dressed and with a good idea.

"Craig, darling, can I choose clothes for you wear today, please?"

"OK, sure, that'd be nice," he replied and she ushered him into the bathroom. Now he had to come out in a towel.

Fifteen minutes later, Craig emerged wrapped in a towel, bearing his old clothes, which Lek took from him. She started to dry his back with her towel and to put her talcum powder over him.

"Please, lie on the bed, I give you massage and put powder. Very nice."

When she had finished the straight massage she told him to get dressed so that they could have breakfast on her. Lek turned her back and let him get dressed in private. While he was dressing, Lek said: "You know I work in my cousin's bar as cashier, eh? I not go with men for money. I have good job. Not pay good money, but have good job. You give me money yesterday, I not like. I not go with man for money. Sometimes, I have boyfriend, I like farang boyfriend, he not same Thai man. Thai man butterfly – he like wife for babies, but have girlfriends too. I have husband same before. I not want again now."

It was a cunning mixture of truths and half-truths without lying and it came remarkably easy to her to say it. In the short – well, very short – term it was totally accurate. Over a time span of longer than a few days the veracity of the statement wore increasingly thinner, although she did feel justified in saying it.

"Yes, OK, Lek," came the reply. "Are you OK? Did I upset you yesterday, by giving you money? It's just that when I asked Will what to do, he said he always gives Goong 1,000 Baht a night and pays a 'bar fine', whatever that is. Nobody asked me to pay one yesterday."

"No, it is OK. I not like you give me money, but you nice man. I not get angry with you." Now she knew where it had come from – Will - and she was dying to check the bar fine book, to see whether Beou had 'charged' for her and if so, how much.

She didn't offer to give Craig his 1,000 Baht back though.

At breakfast, Craig remembered offering to teach Lek how to

swim, so after he had picked up the bill, they went shopping for a new outfit and swimming costume for Lek. Craig took his wrapped in a towel from the 'Pig and Whistle'.

Job done, they made their way over to the Marriott to meet their friends. Lek adored being with Craig and would have liked to find a way not to go and share him with their friends, but it had to be done. She was also very curious about the 'bar fine' episode and could hardly wait until three or four o'clock to investigate further.

Now that she knew she was not a 'marked' lady, but had been 'unjustly fingered', she felt a lot better. She was relieved.

They met their friends at the pool side and joined in with a round of beers, even though it was barely noon. Craig and Lek slipped off to get changed. Goong went with Lek. "Have you slept with him yet? What's he like? Big and horny? Come on, tell me – I tell you everything, don't I? You've stayed with him twice now, haven't you?"

"Mmm, yes, but …, and you'll never believe this, but we kept our clothes on both times."

"Oh, I see … Kinky is he? Likes to slip it in under your knickers. I know the type. I don't mind that though. Quite nice, sometimes. He doesn't look the type, though, does he. Still, you can't always tell by appearances, can you? That's what I always say. You just cannot tell by looking at them. Men, I mean. Mind you, I'm waiting to get an eyeful when he goes swimming. Does he wear speedos or trunks? I don't suppo …"

"Goong! For Heaven's Sake, darling, slow down, will you, please. Yes, I have slept with him for the last two nights. No, he hasn't slipped it in anywhere up, over or through … yet. No, he doesn't seem kinky. He seems a bit shy if you ask me. And that's OK by me too. As for his swimwear, I don't know, look as much as you must, but please don't touch! I like this one. And I mean it. I really do – I like him a lot."

"OK, Big Sister, no offence! You know I mean that don't you?

Come on, race you back to our fellahs."

They took one last look in the mirror; adjusted their breasts in their bikini tops and checked their bikini bottoms for anything un-sightly, went outside and took off along the pool side to the far end, where Will and Craig were talking. They looked like film stars running side by side, laughing at some imaginary joke, bouncing their breasts and wiggling their behinds like Baywatch starlets as they went. Every-body stopped and looked – they couldn't help themselves. Will and Craig were the envy of the poolside loungers. And the girls knew it. After five minutes of posing and stretching, just to gain everyone's full attention, Lek asked Craig to fulfil his promise to teach her to swim.

She held his hand and walked nervously into the water up to her waist.

"You not let me die, eh, Craig?" she mewed, hoping it was loud enough for all the men to hear and be jealous of Craig.

"You hold me, please? I want try swim."

She lay in the water and blew bubbles and Craig quickly put his hands around her slim waist to support her fifty odd kilos. She made grateful noises and brushed up his ego and against the bulge in his trunks – several times, neither of which went unnoticed by most present, least of all by Craig, who was beginning to overcome his doubts about becoming a swimming instructor.

Proficient or not.

If the truth be known, she had 'learned' how to swim with many of her previous clients. She had learned to judge just how helpless or proficient she had to appear to be to enthral a man. With most she was a helpless novice with others an accomplished freestyle swimmer. It was easy to fool Western men. Most Thais do not swim readily – it is hardly a national sport, yet she had learned from excellent European, American and Australian sportsmen over the years.

She had played this game on many men before, but this time, it was not just to get his money – it wasn't even about money – she wanted him and she was prepared to do almost anything to get him. She wanted out of her old life too and she wondered whether Craig was a symbol of her 'going straight'. Maybe. The judges were still out on that one, but she did really like him too, although she couldn't say why exactly and that bothered her.

Will and Goong soon joined them and they frolicked and swam about for an hour or so, before Lek said she had to get changed for work. She had been a remarkably quick learner, although most onlookers doubted whether she had ever needed teaching at all.

They all got out of the water and, while Lek went off to get changed, the others laid on the sun beds under parasols to read. When Lek returned, she made them all promise to go to Daddy's Hobby for a beer after they'd finished, gave Craig a peck on the lips and said thanks for teaching her to swim and was gone.

Lek wanted to go home, get changed and get into work to solve her mystery but she was content that she had awoken some spark in Craig. She had contrived to get him to hold her naked mid-rift and she had brushed against him 'accidentally' a couple of times too.

The rest is up to fate – in the laps of the gods, she thought, at least until she saw him next time.

11 WHO DID IT, AND WHY?

As she walked the short distance from the Marriott to her flat, she wondered about who had said what to Craig; why they had said it and whether they had said it with malice. It had certainly caused her a great deal of pain and embarrassment whether it was intentional or not.

However, she was pretty sure of the people involved and equally sure that whatever was done was not meant to hurt her. She was over that now anyway and it was only idle curiosity that goaded her to know more. She felt that no barriers had been created between herself and Craig by the incident and she was pretty confident that if she set her mind on having him, she could.

She arrived home feeling refreshed, confident and happy. She ran up the stairs to their room and stripped off. It was empty, luckily, she thought, and went for a shower. When she came out, dressed in a towel, she hung her damp bikini on a clothes hanger behind the new damp towel outside, closed the veranda doors, which someone had left open and folded the new clothes that Craig had bought her. She looked at them and thought fondly of him – probably still at the pool drinking a beer. She was glad she was on her own, but she also wanted to talk to someone about him. She would go into work early and talk to Noi.

She chose a flouncy, A-line skirt and a short-sleeved blouse, both of which were sexy but not showy and took a motorbike taxi, sitting side-saddle, straight to Daddy's Hobby, so that she might have a good hour with Noi, before it was likely to start getting busy.

As she slipped off the bike, she heard Noi wolf whistle at her. She paid the taxi driver, who said: "You look gorgeous, darling" , did a twirl for him and Noi and went over to see her friend beaming.

"Wow," commented Noi, "and I thought you were down in the dumps about something. Not manic depressive are you? Only kidding! It's lovely to see you looking so radiant after the things we've talked about over the last couple of weeks. But, wait a minute! If you're so happy, what are you doing in work at two-thirty? Surely, it's not your new job that's put that smile on your face and that twinkle in your eyes, eh? Don't tell me! It has to be love! But if it's that why are you with me and not with him? I told you that you could come in at four or even a bit later, if you wanted to."

"Oh, Noi! I'm so happy!" she blurted out, as she flounced her way behind the bar, for the first time in ten years avoiding the admiring gazes of the motorbike taxi drivers on the rank and the passers by on the way to the beach. She hadn't dressed like this for them. She was saving it all for Craig.

"Noi! I want to sing. Do you want a cup of coffee?" She sang softly to herself while she filled the kettle, not waiting for her friend's reply. Noi looked on in feigned bewilderment and total joy for her friend's new-found happiness. She had known Lek nearly all her life and in truth wasn't that much older than her. Only three or four years, but she looked, or rather acted far older. She had a very pretty, if chubby face, but was vastly overweight and wore huge T-shirts and baggy trousers to conceal it.

But the subterfuge didn't seem to work. Her clothing emphasized her size rather than concealed it to the point where Lek had often wondered whether that was the reason for dressing like that. This way, she could laugh, joke and flirt with the men, but back off at the last moment, pretending that it had all been in jest. Maybe she feared rejection more that most. She looked at Lek singing to herself, making the coffee and hoped that nobody would disturb them until Lek had said what she had obviously come in early to talk about.

She turned around with a flourish, presented Noi with her coffee and sat down facing her, their knees touching. "Well, telak, what have you got to tell me?" inquired Noi.

"Oh, Noi! He didn't offer me money today, but bought me new clothes to go swimming in – a blouse and a skirt. He chose them himself too… he has wonderful taste and it was great. He doesn't seem to care about…, you know. What do you think?"

"I think you've been out in the sun too long It has been very hot the last couple of days and you haven't been quite yourself. Not on hashish, are you? Or drunk, perhaps? I haven't a clue what you're talking about. Why would you be happy that someone didn't pay you and what sort of a lunatic would buy a girl new clothes to go swimming in?"

"No, you're not following me are you? Listen! Last time he paid me, but this time he didn't, but he bought me some new clothes and a bikini so we could go swimming together. Except I told him I couldn't swim, so I let him teach me. You won't tell him I could swim already, will you? He …."

"Woa, Lek! Let's start here. Who is 'he'. I thought your sailor boy went home a couple of weeks ago." Noi knew it couldn't have been him, she just wanted to rib her friend.

"Oh, he was a tosser. No, not him. Craig! Will's friend, Craig. You've met him at least twice."

"Oh, I know, the fat, old, balding one with the funny English accent."

"Nooo, he's not fat, not old, is only starting to go a bit thin and that is a very slight Welsh accent. Not the same as English, you know. I think it's quite distinguished." She caught herself talking like a teenager about her first boyfriend and laughed. "OK, he is a bit chubby and a bit bald, but he's not old and I like the accent! All right?"

"All right," agreed Noi with a big grin, "proceed… enlighten me further about your hero."

Lek peered through half-closed eyes in mock warning to her friend, but continued. "Well, I met him the other night when he arrived and we four, Goong and Will too, went for a night out. It was great, but the next day he paid me as if I were still working in front of the bar. I thought I'd put all that behind me. Not that I'm ashamed of what I did, but now it's nobody's business but mine. Now I'm a cashier and that is everybody's business, not my past life.

"Anyway, I thought he'd sensed what I used to do and it really upset me for a while. Heck, it was only yesterday, but it seems so long ago. Anyway, I saw him later and he didn't seem to care and we had another great evening and I stayed there again. You know something? He didn't touch me either time, although I suppose we've all had that before too. Anyway, we got up went for breakfast, same as yesterday, and he says let's go swimming at Will's hotel and we'll get you some clothes, bikini and a towel on the way. But he didn't offer me any money.

"It felt really good, like a proper, normal boy-girl thing, you know. Not floozy and punter. Then, I let him think that he taught me how to swim and I came here. I just had to tell someone and you're it! Lucky you. He could be along soon. Please hang around for a while and meet him. I so want you to like him!"

Lek didn't have the heart to broach the subject of the bar fine yet so she bided her time and determined to look in the books at the earliest opportunity.

"Sure, I'll wait, telak. Anyway, I want to meet this man who has got you in a tizz. Do you think he's got a brother for me? Or an uncle? Even a grand-father, I'm not fussy?" Lek only smiled wanly at Noi's self-effacing joke. She wished she wouldn't always put herself down like that. Lots of men liked her, if she could but see it and accept it.

So, that off her chest, Lek began helping Noi to prepare the bar for the coming session, not that there was ever that much to do really, as Noi was very proficient at her job, but it gave them something to do together. They put boiling water on for tea and coffee, checked the rice, bought some sauces and salad stuff for the staff from a passing vendor, straightened the rows of bottles in the cabinet and polished a few glasses.

A couple of guys came in for a beer and they leered appreciatively at Lek. She hoped they'd go away before Craig got there, not that she was doing anything wrong.

Eventually, or at four o'clock anyway, Noi signed the books over to Lek and put the surplus takings in her bag, which she then hid under some towels, as was her custom. Lek sat at the desk and turned the pages nonchalantly looking for the incriminating entry. There it was! Beou had charged 400 Baht for her, but the ticket had not been put in Craig's beaker. Will had paid for both her and Goong. She was a present from Will to Craig? Or would they pay in rounds every other night, she wondered. She felt strange inside but not hurt or angry.

She had left her post the night before and Beou had the right to charge someone. Business was business. But why did Will pay for her? Maybe, Will didn't want Craig cast into the seamier side of bar business on his first day or maybe, he paid Will back later. He had certainly never brought the subject up.

She couldn't quite understand that part of the mystery. There had been a bar fine on the first night – fair enough – but not on the second, because she had worked her shift or at least most of it. So Craig probably knew nothing of bar fines nor that his friend had paid one for him. She also understood her cousin's logic in charging the bar fine and was happy with it. What she wanted to know now was how was Craig told about paying her.

In what way was that done? She didn't know Craig well enough to ask him and didn't want to rake all that up again anyway. She did not really want to ask Will, even though she thought he was approachable enough. That left Goong to find out what she could. She would ask her later to do some discreet research for her.

The girls were starting to arrive and the level of banter was rising by the minute. This attracted early drinkers, as it always had and the bar experienced the irregular bursts of business that characterised the early drinking session. Noi got out of the way and sat in the back of the bar crocheting beer mats as she had done for years to while away her time.

When Lek looked up from the ledger, she saw Will and Goong taking seats at the bar and she looked around for Craig. He wasn't there, and she felt a flutter ripple through her, but, always the trooper, she asked Noi to manage the books and she went over to her friends.

"Hi Will! You OK? I like your hotel. Very nice. Very nice pool too. I like learn to swim with Craig." She held out her hand for Will to shake, smiled at Goong and made a comically exaggerated search for Craig up and down the street with her eyes, hoping that one of them would say something.

"Yes, darling, it's a lovely hotel and a great pool. You'll have to come over again some time soon, especially now that you can swim, and appreciate it properly."

Will did not mention Craig and her friend was not helping either so she was forced to say something, "Craig stay there? He still swimming? I know he like to swim too much. He can very good swim, eh?"

"Yes, he's a good swimmer but he's not there now. He came together with us, but he's gone back to the Pig to hang up his bathers. He'll be down soon. Two beers, please and one for yourself whatever you're having."

She silently cursed herself for not thinking and showing her eagerness, but she knew it didn't matter really anyway.

"I go get your order now, Will. Goong I want speak with you, please come inside two minutes."

Lek gave Will's order to Nid, who had only just finished putting on her evening's make up and led Goong to the back of the bar, whispering to Noi as they passed the desk, that Craig would be with Will any minute.

"Goong, I have a favour to ask of you, but you have to be subtle about it, OK? Don't be too enthusiastic or pushy. The night before last, Will paid Craig's bar fine for me. I want to know why and what he said to Craig about what I do or did here. Have you told him anything?"

"I don't think I told him anything, but I should think he knows anyway. He's been here before, he's met you. We've never tried to disguise anything. I really don't know, but I wouldn't be surprised if he knows that you worked in front of the bar before you became cashier. I'll see if I can find out, but why do you want to know, Big Sister? Is there a problem?"

"No, no problem. You know me, I'm just a nosy cow and I want to know who knows what and where I stand."

"Ah, I see...," said Goong, the penny dropping. "You want to know what Craig knows about you. OK, I'll do what I can."

"Yes, OK, you guessed it. I want to know what Craig knows about it and what he thinks about it. I told you, I like him very much and I want him to like me.

"Quick! There he is now, get back over there and I'll join you in a minute." She waved demurely down the bar as she saw Craig notice her. If she took Noi to meet him, who could she get to run the till? Where the hell was Ayr? The rest of the girls in were newbies. She took out her phone, called Ayr's number by speed dial and walked towards Craig. Stopping at the desk, she asked Noi for a few more minutes and Ayr came on the line.

"Where are you? I need you here right now. Please."

"I'm here, Big Sister, where's the fire?" and she saw Ayr get off a motorcycle behind Will and wave. In a moment, Ayr was behind the till starting to adjust her make-up and Lek was taking Noi to meet Craig.

"Hello, Craig. How are you? I want you to meet my good friend, Noi."

They sat on the bar's inner ledge and were careful to keep out of Mott's way as she climbed up and swung herself around the pole, flashing her panties at Craig and Will accidentally, but not caring either, each time she did so.

"Woyyy, handsome man," Noi said to Craig, holding out her hand to be shaken. "Not too old," she remarked to Lek, but seemingly to no one in particular. "Will, you handsome man too. Sexy men!"

Will was used to this standard banter and shrugged it off. Craig was not, he just sat there smiling:

"Hello, Noi, nice to meet you. You good friend of Lek, yes? Do you want a drink? A drink everybody? Lek, can I have a round, please?"

Lek placed the order with Mott as much for safety reasons as anything else and turned to face the group.

"We're going to watch the football tonight, Lek. Manchester United and Liverpool. Do you want to come or are you working?"

"I'm working, but you can watch football here no problem. I love football. Man U number one for me."

"Not for me," interjected Will. "It's too noisy here. After about eight o'clock all the bars around are in competition with each other for who can play the worst music the loudest. Nah, not for me. I like my football, especially Man U, same as you, Lek, but I like a bit of comfort and I want to hear the commentary, not ten flavours of bloody pop music all at the same time.

"Goong and I'll go to the Pig where there is air conditioning, soft seats, sandwiches and a proper toilet if you need it. You do what you like though, Craig. You stay here with your girl, if you like and we'll meet up after the game or tomorrow, whatever you want."

Lek's heart was sinking fast until Will had said 'your girl' and none of the other girls missed it either. They exchanged glances and Noi said 'Woyyy' in a loud voice again, which pleased Lek immensely and embarrassed her at the same time.

"No, Will, you're right. Anyway, we said we would watch it together tonight and watch it together we will. Shame you can't come too, Lek, but I'll come down and see you later. What time's the game over, Will? One thirty a.m?" Will nodded.

"Oh, you'll be shut. Well, why don't you come up and watch the last bit of the game and the highlights with us?"

Lek jumped at the chance and felt the warm glow of contentment return after the bashing Will had just unintentionally given her.

Noi was the first to leave. Then the other three went their separate ways agreeing to meet up in the Pig at nine for a meal and to get good seats. Lek would join them when she could shortly after one a.m.

After Noi and the others had gone, there were only the girls left and there was almost the full crew in. Ayr was the only one of their team, but there were Joy and Deou, who seemed to be recovering quite well after their disappointing attempt to get to Britain, Mott, Porn and Or, the three 'N's', Noi, Nok and Nid, and the two recent girls from Soi 6, Dam and Din.

Everybody had had a good past few days and the atmosphere was buoyant to say the least – high-spirited with plenty of sanuk. Anyone going there that night was in for a whale of a time – even if they went home alone, because the girls were up for a good evening. They were cat-calling, wolf-whistling and shouting to the men to come over. They were dancing and strutting about and drinking and Lek was being carried along with the atmosphere almost against her will as her head was in the Pig with a guy watching football.

She was amazed to think that only a couple of weeks ago, she would have been in the middle of all that, egging them on and joining in. She missed the fun, but not the job and being management almost precluded her from being 'one of the girls'. Everyone was a member of the 'Sorority', Beou and Noi included, but not really.

Once you hung up your condoms you were no longer front-line troops and only an honorary member. She was glad she was out of it really, but she sat behind the desk and smiled with them at their antics. She really did love them all like sisters, like the brave sisters they really were.

Joy and Beou were putting a brave face on it too after having their dreams dashed by the British Embassy and their Welsh boyfriends leaving them penniless; Ayr was part of a trio, which no longer existed and Lek knew that she must be feeling lonely without her comrades-in-arms; Mott's eye was healing nicely and skilful make-up did the rest; Porn and Or were doing OK, but had also been disappointed by promises of help from a couple of English guys.

The three 'N's' were too inexperienced to know any better, but seemed to be enjoying themselves and the two new girls from Soi 6 didn't say much. They mixed in but didn't share much personal information with the others. Maybe because they were from Bangkok and all the others were from the North. They would fit in later she supposed.

Time passed quickly despite Lek's personal feelings because of the infectious good mood of the girls, which did indeed attract a lot of interest from the passing men and several of the girls were taken. Din and Dam went with two seemingly pleasant elderly Australians; Noi with an elderly Brit, who could not keep his hands off her even at the bar; Mott went with a middle-aged Indian and Joy and Deou with a lively Canadian in his fifties.

She had collected the bar fines and the hotel addresses of the clients and everything was as it should be, but she was itching to go.

When Noi came in at one o' five, the girls were still working and drinking a bottle of Pipers between themselves and there were still a few punters drinking beer, chatting up some of the ladies, but Lek's books were straight and she was ready to go.

"Do you mind if I get off now, Noi? I have a date."

"Of course not, have a good time, see you later on today."

And she was gone, hurrying to the Pig. At the door, her way was blocked by one of the waitresses: "Sorry, we are closed now. Please come back tomorrow."

"No, you don't understand," pleaded Lek, "my boyfriend is sitting over there, Craig. Go tell him I'm here, please."

The girl bolted the door and went over to Craig, who was with Will, Goong and a few other residents. She reflected that she'd used the word 'boyfriend'. It had come very easily to her, but then she had used it about hundreds of men before too. But this circumstance was different and she wanted the word to have a different connotation. The girl came back, opened the door with a smile and beckoned her in. "Please come in, Mr. Craig is waiting for you over there. I'm sorry for keeping you waiting."

She went over to the group and Craig rose, greeted her and shook her hand warmly; Will was still shaking her hand as she was sitting down and the three other men 'waaied' her. Goong smiled, but the other men's girls only eyed her over and looked away. Craig shifted up on the bench seat and Lek moved closer to him… very close, bare arms and knees touching. The bar was closed, but Craig and Will had doubled up on their drinks and Craig had got one in for Lek on the probability that she would get there sometime or other and that he would drink it if she didn't. They smiled at each other a lot, but didn't say much because everyone was concentrating on the last few minutes of extra time.

It was 2:1 to Manchester United and if Liverpool scored, it would have to go to extra time. But they didn't score and there was no extra time and after a few minutes of highlights people drifted off, some happy with their team, some not so, but everyone really happy to be in Thailand, which seemed to be more important than the mundane loyalties of team football. Will and Goong left too, promising to arrange something for the next day, which they would phone about later.

"Lek, I fancy another beer and a bit of time talking with just you. Do you know somewhere nice that is close? I want you to take me somewhere – I'll pay, of course, but I've only just got here and I don't know my way around. What do you think? Where shall we go?"

It was just the sort of question that Thai girls hate to be asked and the stock answer came out: "I done know. Up to you!." If the truth be known, she would rather have gone up to his room, had a beer from the mini bar, watched TV for a while and gone to bed with him, but she didn't feel that she could say that. She had to go with his flow. As for knowing bars or having a favourite! Well, she knew hundreds. She knew where Arabs liked to go; she knew where divers hung out; she knew American, British, Australian, German and even Finnish bars.

There were bars for every country and every interest. There were niche bars of every type, but at the end of the day, they were all only interested in one thing: selling. They 'gave away' free games of pool or live music or something else in order to attract men in; then they sold as much alcohol as was necessary to get the guy horny and then they rented out a girl with or without a nearby room.

However, she could not tell Craig that. That was something he would have to find out for himself. Favourite bars? They were luxuries she had never had. Some bars were more comfortable and some were air conditioned and some had a wide variety of foreign wines, spirits and liqueurs. Others had western food, but that was the point: these bars were small plots of foreign countries in Pattaya, where well-off foreigners could go to forget they were in Thailand while enjoying the benefits of actually being there.

The only 'ordinary' Thais who went there were girls accompanied by clients or husbands and a few social climbing Thais who had a few shekels. Ordinary Thais did not drink in bars designed for Westerners on their days off and the bars where they did go, off the beaten tourist routes, were full of Thai working class men drunk on cheap whisky and not really wanting foreigners to come in. In every country in the world, local people drink in local bars designed for them and their pockets – not in the local tourist traps.

But she could not tell him all this, not yet, so she said:

"I know, we can go for little walk and we chose bar for us together, bar you like, bar I like. OK?"

That sounded fine – a bit of a local pub crawl and get to know the area too. So they finished up, paid and headed out the back door of the Pig, turning right towards Soi 8. Immediately, there was a complex of eight to ten bars and not wanting to go too far and also wanting to be helpful, Lek suggested the last but one bar on the front, 'Tom's Bar'. The choice was a good one. Craig ordered two beers and he was happy to see Lek chatting away merrily with one of the bar girls, whose name was Nic.

This gave him time to look around and watch people, one of his favourite pastimes, he not being a big talker anyway. Lek took his hand gingerly and he squeezed it back while still watching someone in the next bar. Then he felt another hand on his shoulder and she was whispering in his ear. Well, it came across as whispering, she was actually shouting, but the music was so loud, he could just make out: "Are you OK? You happy here? Is very loud, you want to go?"

He still held her hand and went in close: "I'm fine. I like it here. You carry on talking to your friend. I like to look around, see everything. You talk to friend, Nic, and we talk later." She gave him a beautiful smile and a kiss on the cheek. Little did he know that she had never met Nic before and he didn't know what they were talking about. In fact, Nic was asking where Craig was from; how long she had known him; whether he was a kind man and whether he had taken her anywhere nice or bought her anything special. Asking whether he had any unattached friends in Thailand would be the next question.

It was routine working-girl to working-girl stuff, and although she had had these conversations thousands of times, she did not really want it now. However, she did not have anything else to talk to Nic about and Craig was obviously quite happy just looking around and that was the main objective – keeping him happy in her company. A bit like Pavloff and his dogs – conditioning the man to being happy and feeling comfortable in your presence was the way to keep him. So, she carried on talking with Nic about him and squeezed his hand, patted his knee and smiled at him regularly.

Twenty minutes passed in this fashion and Nic turned her attention on Craig. "You want to play a game, yes?" Craig looked at Lek, not for permission, and said "Yes, OK. What?" Nic smiled and rummaged behind the bar directly in front of Craig. The girls here were all more scantily dressed than in Daddy's Hobby – tiny skirts and halter tops. Nic was wearing a short, sky blue skirt made of some diaphanous material, probably Thai silk and a six-inch wide knitted band over fairly large boobs for a Thai, which she had to adjust after every few movements to stop them slipping out.

Whether she really had to do it or whether it was a ploy to attract attention, he never found out as she never did let them get out, struggle though they did. She had an infectious smile too, brown eyes and long black hair, which were standard equipment in Thailand. She seemed very nice, thought Craig, still imagining her to be a friend of Lek's. They played 'best of three' at 'Jackpot' and Craig won 2:1. Both were very happy there, but after another beer and a three-way chat with Nic, Craig suggested moving on.

They went to a far quieter bar fifteen metres on in Soi 8 where there were comfortable armchairs and a couple of tired-looking girls sitting forlornly at the bar waiting to be told they could go home. They ordered another beer, but both felt it a come-down from 'Tom's' and regretted the move. Craig was the first to speak: "Nice bar that, 'Tom's'. I liked it there, although it was a bit loud. It was nice for you to have a chat with your friend Nic too, eh? She seems lovely. Have you known her long?"

"Yes, nice bar. Nic nice too. I not know her too long. Everybody working you know? Not have big time for holiday for go everywhere talk to friends. Not same UK, eh? Work long week here." She felt she had sounded irritable and had better smile and stop talking.

"Lek," he said, "will you come back to the room with me tonight? I want to talk to you."

"Yes, OK. Pay go now? I sorry, but I tired sit in bar. Sit in bar all day."

"Sure, pay go now. Check bin, Lek."

She called for the bill in Thai, and when she told Craig the amount, he handed her his wallet for her to help herself. She thought it was a nice gesture and handed it back after paying forty Baht a beer and twenty Baht tip, which she had OK'ed with Craig first. It went against her nature to tip, but she counted on tips in her job too and she knew that most foreigners thought that it was 'the done thing'.

He would have to learn about that in his own time too, she thought.

Back in the hotel room, they sat down and began to relax. "Lek, I've been thinking. I've only known you a few days, but I think we get on well, eh? Good, I'm really pleased you agree. So, I was thinking, er, um-mm. I was wondering whether you would keep seeing me while I'm here. I've got about a month left – go home on the 12th. August." He could see by the smile on her face that his proposal, as such, so far, was being well-received, and it encouraged him to go on.

"Now, I know you've got a good job, and I'm not asking you to give it up, but do you have any free time coming? Holidays? No, I don't really mean it like that – your holidays are your own. What I would like, is for you to spend a month on holiday with me. How does that sound? I'll pay for everything… Would your boss give you the time off, do you think? We could stay in Pattaya so you could help out if they need you to fill in sometimes and maybe take a trip somewhere. Does that sound all right to you?"

She nodded and smiled, it sounded fine to her, but it was more or less what she was doing before. It seemed like a step backwards and would Beou allow it? She'd been in her new job for less than a week! It was a cheek asking for time off already, especially a month and who would fill in for her? If Ayr wouldn't do it – and she would lose money on the deal by doing so, Beou would have to hire a new girl, which could mean she would lose the job of cashier for the foreseeable future and be back where she was. Not an easy gamble to take. She could lose her new start for a month's holiday as someone's, albeit Craig's, floozy. On the other hand, something grand may come of it and she might be able to leave the bar life forever.

It could be all or nothing.

She decided to hedge her bets until she had time to think, to ask Beou, if were possible and discuss it with her friends. A few more details would be useful now though, so she offered him another beer and took one herself. "How you mean exactly, Craig? I want, but first I must talk to Mama San Beou and ask for time. She must find new girl. I must have money too, not working, not have money for room, food, clothes everything. You know? Not easy. What you thinking for idea?"

He hadn't really thought it through either, but he really did want it to happen. "Well, to be honest, I'm not 100% sure. I don't know how everything works in Thailand. Will told me something like 'You pay the

Mama San for a girl to take a night off, then you pay her any reasonable amount you both agreed on after that'. Shit! This isn't coming out right, is it? Look, all I'm saying is that I like you very much and I want to pay for you to have a month's holiday with me. If I said I could give you 500 Baht a day for twenty-eight days, is that any good?"

'He really does not have a clue, does he?' she thought, while holding his eyes with hers. She could see that none of this came easy to him and she wanted to help. She turned the proposal over in her mind: if Ayr helped her out, she would get Lek's wages, maybe not Lek's rate, but the standard 6,000 a month – 200 a day – Lek could give her, say another 200 a day; so she would get 400 a day, but lose the chance to earn 1,000 a day.

Beou would split the 400 bar fine, costing her 200 a day; so, she would earn: zero as a bar girl, and 100 from Craig: 100 whole Baht a day. If Ayr would not help out, and who would blame her, Beou would have to hire a new girl and Lek would revert to bar girl not working, at zero a day, pay half the bar fine at 200 and get to keep 300. 300 a day – also losing her job as cashier.

Craig looked on hopefully. "It not easy, Craig, sorry. I want, but I cannot say 'Yes' now. I must talk with Mama San. You understand?"

He looked crest-fallen: "Lek, if it's the money, I can pay a little more, if Mama San want more money. OK? You talk to her tomorrow."

She looked at him again and not for the first time thought: lovely bloke, but so naive in many ways. She wanted to shout: 'Of course it's the money! What else is there? Don't you know anything?', but she didn't. Instead, she took the final swig of her beer and sat on his lap. She kissed him on the lips and said: "Come on, late now. We take shower together then go to bed."

And that was what they did. It was the best shower Craig had ever had in his life. Lek washed him all over tenderly and then washed herself while he looked on and helped out a bit. Then they used his toothbrush and she put a towel on, rubbed him down with the other one and lead him out into the bedroom. She put him naked on the bed and rolled him over; took a small container of talcum powder from the room's mini shop and dusted him down while massaging his legs, back and shoulders.

Then she turned him over and did the same, but also brushing lightly against his stiff penis. "Wow, Lek, that was great! Where did you learn to do that? Let me try to do the same for you now." She lay down next to him and moved to allow him to remove the towel.

He forgot to start on her back and enthusiastically started putting powder on her breasts and massaging it in. As he got lower down, she half sat up, took his head in her hands and kissed him. He let the talcum powder fall to the floor and she put out the bedside light as he got on top of her.

After they had made love and Craig was dozing in her arms, she whispered: "What else Will tell you about Daddy's Hobby bar and me? He tell you about bar fine and pay for lady, yes?"

"Mmm," came the soft reply. "He said about bar fines and lady drinks, but nothing else. He said he meet you last week with your friend Goong. She's nice too, isn't she? You are lucky to have such good friends."

"He not say he see me working in the bar?"

"No, he only said you served him and Goong some drinks and sat down with them a few times for a chat. Why?"

"Oh, nothing. Go to sleep, darling. Tomorrow new day." She kissed him lightly as he fell asleep. 'Now I know', she thought. "What a relief!'

She wondered whether that would be the first and last time she would make love to this strange Welshman.

12 THE GAMBLE

They awoke in the morning at ten, seven hours after they had gotten to sleep. Lek was quite sure that she would take the risk, so long as it did not unduly inconvenience her cousin.

Family first, self second, old style Thai, even though she was fairly sure that this was the one. She tried to remember how she had felt for her husband, twelve or so years ago. Surely, it had seemed right at the time, but not as right as this felt now. She decided that she would 'go for it', as long as she didn't lose her family's respect. Craig was waking up too and she was looking into his eyes as he opened them.

"Good morning, darling", they said almost simultaneously.

Lek said: "Craig, I must do many things today. I must go change clothes, go see cousin, Mama San and talk to friends." It was the sort of vague, ambiguous explanation he would get used to in Thailand. She kissed him, pulled her towel around her and was into the bathroom before he really knew what was going on. Ten minutes later, she came out in towel and got dressed without showing an inch of flesh below her armpit or above her knee. It didn't bother him, but he was fascinated by how she could do it.

"OK, darling, I must go now," she said, "Please give me your telephone number and I call you later. I not sure when. OK? I want go talk to everybody now."

They swapped numbers; she kissed him and was gone. Craig lay there as if a whirlwind had just run over him, but he was happy to have her number and her promise .

Lek's first stop was Daddy's Hobby, where she knew that Noi

would be, either asleep, if there were no customers or chatting drowsily, if there were. She walked up to the empty bar and looked for Noi on the ledge where she passed the night. "Noi!," she screamed, "Where are you? Business is about! Shake a leg! There are ten men here looking for you by name! Wake up!."

Noi put her head over the bar to look straight into Lek's eyes. Noi did not drink and had had a decent night's sleep. "To what do I owe this pleasure, my friend?" she said. "And where are the ten men looking for me? You haven't told them to come back after I've put my make-up on, have you? You know that I never wear any."

Lek put the coffee on and waited for her friend to come to her. "I have a problem, Noi. A wonderful, or maybe a terrible, problem and I wanted to talk to you first. Are you wide awake yet? I'm so excited and apprehensive at the same time. I don't know whether to laugh or cry. Craig has asked me to take a month's holiday with him! All paid! What do you think?"

"Well, Little One, it was only the day before yesterday that you were upset that he did pay you. Pass me that coffee, please. What has changed?"

"I'm not really sure myself, to be honest, but I know now that he does not think bad of me in any way. He just treats me, um, er, normally. No, no, not even that. Better than that and yet… I don't know, Noi."

"I don't know what you mean, sweetheart. Do you mean that he does not know what you did before or do you mean that it's unimportant to him?"

"I'm so confused, Noi. He knows that I have worked here for a long time, but it seems never to have crossed his mind what I actually did here. He just seems to accept that I am, and always have been, the cashier here. I want to tell him the truth, but I really like him and I don't want to screw it up, but that is not being honest, is it? I've always tried not to tell lies, even when I could not be honest. 'Tam dee, dai dee. Tam choua, dai choua' and all that'.

"Last night he asked me to take a month off work. I've only had my new job for a week! Less than that! Oh, what can I do? I don't want to lose him or my new position and I don't want to let Beou down. 'Be careful for what you wish, because it may come true'. That's what they say, don't they? Well, I've wished for this for years and now I don't know what the fuck to do – excuse my French.

"What do you think Beou will say?"

Noi poured them each another coffee and said: "Lek, you are a lovely person. You are a sensible woman. Don't ask others to decide your future for you. You could be facing a huge turning point in your life and it can only be up to you whether you go for it or not. I'll be honest with you, talk it through with your friends and family, but do not ask their advice. It's just not fair. You are at a point in your life, where you do not have to be here any more. One of your problems is that you do not know what else to do.

"Another is that your mind has expanded past the expectations of the people in your village, as mine has too. We are not simple village farm girls any longer. We know too much, we have seen more than they have and we will never be the same as them again.

"Some of them resent of for that, some are jealous and some even despise us, but the real point is that we know more about what goes on in the world now than they do and it will always be difficult for women like us to go home again and be shoehorned into dreary village life.

"Going back there with nothing is no longer an option for us. If people like us go home to live we have to take a big prize with us to show, no, to prove that it was worth going away in the first place. I will never get that big prize, so I will probably be doing what I do now for the rest of my life. I'm a caretaker and that is not a problem.

"You have a different job. You were unhappy, eventually, going with clients and you got Fa's job as cashier. I think that that was a good move, especially because of your worries about Soomsomai, but now, only you can know whether the gamble on Craig is worth taking. Or any man, for that matter.

"Your cousin can say 'Yes, I'll hold the job for you', but you know that she probably can't. You and I know that she will do anything she can to help you out of this shit-hole, but she can't do everything. YOU have to grab the bull by the horns and decide for yourself whether you trust, like or whatever, this guy Craig. Only you know him, and you probably know him only a little. You are a sensible woman. The only advice I think you can expect from any of us - all of us - who love you dearly, is to do what your heart tells you to do!"

They looked at each other in silence for a while, only Noi taking a sip of coffee.

"So what you're saying basically is that it's up to me? How many times have I used that expression before to falang? It's funny! It really is. Men have told me thousands of times how annoying it is to hear 'It's up to you' from me and now I'm getting it back. Good joke, eh? One of life's little jokes. I'm not getting at you, Noi, I know in my heart that what you're saying is true, it's just that it doesn't help. I want to be told what to do. Shit! I'm in such a quandary. I suppose my next step should be to talk with Beou. What time do you think she'll be available? Ah, don't worry, I'll ring her at twelve or so. You're a good friend, Noi. I'll always listen to you."

Lek's phone rang. It was Mott: "Lek, I need to warn the bar. You know that Indian I went home with last night? Well, OK, you don't 'know' him, but you saw him, eh? We went back to his hotel and, when I got to his room, there were five others there too – all wanting to shag me for the price of one. I'm so glad I took the wanker's money up front. Six for 750 Baht? The bloody cheap Charlies!

"Three, three–and-half thousand, OK.

"Anyway, I'm all right; as I entered their room, I saw them all leering and grinning at me. Fuck that, I thought and kneed the one you met in the bollocks and high-tailed it. He followed me to the lift shouting he would report me. I'm not worried about that shit, but I just thought I ought to give you the heads-up. OK? See you later, 'bye."

And she was gone. The toughest girl in the bar, thought Lek, not for the first time.

Lek bade her friend farewell and took a motorcycle home. She was looking forward to another shower and a change of clothes. Something to eat would go down well too and this time she was hoping that Ayr would be there as well.

She was, but getting ready to go out for lunch with a girlfriend, before going to work. "Ayr," she called to her room mate in the shower, "can you hear me?"

"Yes! Are you all right? I'm going out for lunch with Jill in fifteen minutes, do you want to come along? Only for an hour or so before work, but it should be fun."

"No, I can't today, I'm sort of busy. Thanks anyway. Look, I need to talk to you a minute."

The water went off. "I'll be right out. I'm finished in here anyway. Fire away, I'm listening."

"Basically, I need a month off work starting today. Right now... but I don't want to lose the cashier's job, which I could easily do, if Beou has to hire a replacement for me. Do you follow?"

"Yes, I think so, but what can I do and why do you need a month off? You were not seeing anyone last time we spoke and I thought you had given all that up anyway."

"Mmmm, I thought I had too. Well, I have. It's complicated..."

Ayr was drying off and applying talc and deodorant.

"I still want to marry a farang, preferably British, like we've always said and that means dating, doesn't it? No-one's going to want to marry me after just seeing me sitting at the bloody cashier's desk, is he? Come on, be realistic! Anyway, Will's friend Craig and I have taken a liking to each other and he wants me to stay with him for the rest of his holiday – one month. I want to do it too. However… that means getting a month off from Beou. It drops her in it and I've only had the job a week.

"She'll be forced to get a replacement – maybe a permanent one, unless I can find someone for her. You are the only one with the experience and Beou's complete trust, Goong being with Will for the next four weeks too. You don't have to answer now. Think about it over lunch. I'll try to make up your lost earnings, but you'll definitely get at least 400 a day. I really need this chance. I promise I'll make it up to you."

Ayr was ready to go out. "Come on, I'll walk part of the way with you, then I've got to find out what Beou thinks of it all. She doesn't know anything about it yet. Pray for me." They set off together, but once outside, Lek was too het up to just walk. She wanted to be getting on with something, so she apologised to her friend and hopped on a Baht bus going north down Soi Buakhao. At the end of the road, the bus turned west to the beach, so she had to get off and catch another one heading east up Pattaya Klang.

She got off at the entrance to her cousin's soi and walked the few hundred metres to her house. Beou answered the door almost immediately with Sally in one hand. "Hello, Little Cousin, what a nice surprise. Come on in! Look, Sally, it's Aunty Lek, come to see us. 'Wadee'." Sally waaied her aunt and Lek waaied back smiling.

They went through to the lounge.

"I came without ringing first, because I know you're always here until Noi gets back. I should have rung, though, sorry."

"You don't have to book an appointment to see me, Little Cousin. Don't worry about it. Is it a social call or is something up? You look kind of agitated. Let me make us a nice cup of tea and you can tell me all about it in your own time. She left the room and Lek played absent-mindedly with Sally. Ten minutes later. Beou returned with two cups of tea, a bottle of milk and some biscuits on a tray. She gave the small bottle of milk to Sally, said 'Help yourself' to Lek and sat back into the armchair in anticipation.

"Well, Beou, you know I've been seeing Will's friend, Craig? Well, we get on really well. I like him a lot and I'm pretty sure he likes me too and… well, he has asked me to take a month off work to be with him for the rest of his holidays and I so want to do it, but I've only just star-ted as 'Trainee Mama San Junior', as you put it, and I don't want to let you down and I don't want to lose my job and I don't want to lose him and…. I want everything with no risk… I'm a selfish cow, aren't I?"

She looked down at her feet and a tear rolled down her cheek. She quickly wiped it away – it hadn't been done for sympathy – and looked at her cousin and boss.

After a few minutes with a dead-pan expression, Beou replied: "You are not making things as easy for me as I had hoped. That is true and you will need to be replaced either from outside or inside the bar. The former method poses a bigger threat to your new job than the lat-ter does. There is only one girl I can promote and still feel comfortable spending a lot of time away from the bar and I have already committed myself to spending the time you freed up for me away from that bar. So, I guess, it depends on the generosity of your friend, Ayr, doesn't it, because I'm damn sure I won't be able to get a temp at such short no-tice especially for only a month? Have you spoken to Ayr about it already?"

Lek did not want to lie to her cousin, but she also did not want to admit that she had spoken to someone before speaking to her. "Yes," she admitted for a few minutes about half an hour ago. She said she would think about it over lunch. It means a big drop in wages for her and I didn't tell her I was on more than the 6,000 you usually pay. Oh, and by the way, I'll still be your 'Agony Aunt', if you want, free of charge. That's only phone calls anyway and we'll pop into the bar every day, I promise. I feel really good about this one, I really do."

"OK, leave it with me. I need to think about it a little more and I will need to talk to Ayr before I can say 'Yea or Nay', although actually, the decision is yours at the end of the day. God, how I hate that expression, I wish I could stop myself using it. Anyway, ultimately, it is up to you. I don't run a slave camp and you are a free agent. I will do my best to secure your job. Now you had better get off and see this lucky man that has caught your eye so. Take him to our bar for a drink and wait for my phone call.

"You may have to take over from Noi as usual, if I can't sort anything out for today, but tomorrow you're free, if that's your decision. If it is, the very best of luck to you. You know you're my favourite and always have been. If you see a real chance to get out of this hole, go for it! Some make it, some fail and some just give up until they are too old. Be a trier, Lek. I envy you. Now bugger off and let me get on, I've got a time bomb to defuse. I'll see you later."

They hugged muttered a few heart-felt endearments and Lek left quickly with tears in her eyes. She honestly did not know whether that had gone well or not; whether to be sad or ecstatic. She was free, she could go if she had the courage, the decision was no one else's but hers…

And it scared her half to death.

She walked as if in a dream to Pattaya Klang and flagged down a Baht bus, which took her down Pattaya Klang, over the Second Road junction and stopped outside Tops Department Store. It was a short walk from there across the road to Daddy's Hobby. She had decided to see Noi first rather than Craig, but she rang him anyway to see what he was up to. Seated at the outside of the bar, she took out her mobile:

"Hello, Craig, how are you? You OK? You are with Will in Will hotel swimming pool? With Goong? OK. Too late for me come now, I wait here in bar for you… talk to Noi. OK? OK! See you later, telak."

'Telak' is Thai for 'darling'. It sounded more genuine to her than the English word. She had called thousands of strangers 'darling', but very few people, and only Thais, 'telak'.

This all went completely unnoticed by Craig. Things were happening that he was totally unaware of, the consequences of his actions.

"Noi, I've asked Ayr to fill in for me for a month starting today or tomorrow. She said she'd let me know later on… after lunch. It is a big favour that will cost her money. Beou said she would try to help and that the job was Ayr's if she was prepared to do it, but that 'ultimately it was my decision' because I am a free agent. Now I don't know what to do. I know what I want to happen, but it is not all up to me, is it?"

"What does Craig have to say about it all?"

"Well, no one has really asked his opinion. He made the suggestion, blissfully unaware of the consequences. He seems so naive at times. Still, I suppose he's on holiday and he just wants to spend it with me. He doesn't seem to see any further than that. I'm sure that if a Yank asked a British barmaid to go with him on a month's holiday, she would jump at it. He doesn't realise that it is probably not quite the same here.

I have an hour or two before Ayr comes in and gives me her answer. If she helps out, it will make everything so much easier for everyone. Well, except for her. If she accepts the job, I'll go for it. If she doesn't, then, … I'll work today and will have the day and night to think about it and talk to Craig, but I think I'll risk it anyway. It just feels so right with Craig, even though we have only known each other a few days.

"Am I rambling? I think I'm rambling. Oh, shit what a mess to be in!

"At least I have some savings to get me through the month, although Craig always picks up the bills anyway.

"To think that I have been trying to get into this situation for ten years and now that I'm there, I don't know what to do. I should be ready with a plan. I should have had all this worked out years ago. Plan A. Plan B. Plan C.

But what have I got? Nothing! What a stupid cow!"

"All right, Lek," Noi said soothingly, "Calm down. Stop beating yourself up. Take it easy. Things will work out as they should and there is nothing that you can do about that. 'Que Sera, Sera', as they say somewhere in Europe. Maybe in Wales, eh?"

They both laughed and Lek felt the warmth of her friend's concern lift her spirits as it had many times before.

For the second time in three days, Lek found herself sitting at the outside edge of Daddy's Hobby trying to sort out a problem concerning Craig and her future, while Craig was totally unaware that anything was going on. He was somewhere swimming about with Will and Goong or drinking a beer with Will and Goong and maybe even chatting up another girl, while she was stuck at the bar worrying.

Noi gave her some space and only spoke when Lek spoke to her first, but stopped by from time to time to refill her cup. A few men came and went and one or two tried to get her to talk or play a game, but she politely told them all that she had to start work soon.

'Maybe later', she said, which is the polite way that Thais have for saying 'no'. Time did not pass slowly, it seemed to be suspended. There was nothing around her, nobody and no bar, no sound, no music, just nothing, until Noi touched her and asked her to come inside the bar because she should start work soon.

It was a welcome release from her state of suspended animation and she flew at her job with gusto, knowing that Ayr would be in soon and that her decision would help Lek to choose a path to take and also affect the odds on her own ultimate decision.

In true trooper style, she got on with her job to the best of her ability, welcoming punters, talking to recognized faces and chatting with her colleagues.

Until she saw Ayr walking up and then her heart leaped into her mouth.

Well, Little Sister, what do you think? Can you help?"

"Of course, I can, what do you take me for? You are my Big Sister, of course I will help. You didn't seriously think I wouldn't, did you? You didn't doubt me did you? I suppose I should have phoned you an hour or more ago to tell you, but I just thought that you knew I would never let you down. Sorry, Big Sister. I have spoken to Beou and we are all so, so happy for you. You lucky so-and-so."

Lek grabbed her friend and hugged her – an unusual show of affection between Thais in public, but she could not help herself, she was so happy and so relieved.

"What do you mean 'all'?," asked Lek holding Ayr off.

"Ah, well, Beou, of course and, er …., Goong, of course. And, well, Goong just happened to be at the Beauty Salon with Mott and Porn and they said that they were very happy for you too. Er, mm I'm sorry, but have I done anything wrong? Was, it a secret?"

"No, Little Sister, you can never do anything wrong in my eyes. You have given me the chance of a lifetime. How could you do anything wrong. Come here, let me give you a hug."

And she gave her a sniff kiss too, hoping that no one would see.

"When will you start, Ayr? Is tomorrow, all right?"

"Well, Big Sister, I came prepared to start tonight, I didn't think you would want that Welshman of yours chatting up any ladies at other bars. Why do you want to wait?"

Lek gave her another sniff kiss, but this time she didn't care who saw.

Lek lead Ayr over to Noi and told her the good news. The three of them were ecstatic and Noi got up from the cashier's chair and made a grand gesture of handing it over to Ayr.

Ayr didn't need any instruction as she has stood in for people many times before, so Noi and Lek went down to the front of the bar to tell the other girls. They were all very happy for Lek and although some already knew the good news, nobody tried to steal Lek's thunder by admitting it. Lek grew in divine stature even more and in the eyes of the younger girls in particular. Everyone was very proud of her and no one was jealous in any way. They knew that their turn would come, if it was their fate and until it did, they would have as much fun as possible.

Lek decided not to go rushing off to Craig, she wanted to spend a few hours more inside the bar, she already had a feeling that it might be her last. So she rang Craig and asked her to meet him at Daddy's Hobby at eight or nine o'clock. He was perfectly happy with this arrangement, so Lek sent out for a bottle of Scotch and prepared to give the girls a small party.

At least until Craig came, if he wanted to go somewhere else.

Craig arrived with Will and Goong at nine o'clock, but Lek was not even worried that he might not come. Things seemed to be falling into place and she had already decided to go with the flow: 'Inch Allah', and that good old Welsh expression, 'Que Sera, Sera', if it was Welsh. Not that Lek cared any more.

The three new arrivals sat with the girls towards the back of the bar and Lek told Craig that she had been given a month off work, but that there were still a few details that they had to iron out. She was not sure what they were yet, but she knew that there would be some by the time the morning light came. She also explained that this was a small party, in case she decided not to come into work for a month after to-night.

Craig was delighted and Will was happy for him. Goong was

happy for Lek, because she was nearer her dream than ever before.

The party went on until four in the morning with Lek buying food from practically every street vendor that passed the bar. Will was gone with Goong by midnight, but that was his custom anyway, because he liked to get up early and swim all morning, before lunch.

Craig rang the bell a few times, after all the punters had gone, and bought the girls another bottle of Scotch, before they closed the bar and all went their separate ways. Only Craig and Lek did not walk home alone, but that was just as well, because they had to hold each other up as they walked the short distance to Craig's room in the 'Pig'.

Daddy's Hobby

13 THE DEAL

They both woke up in the morning with hangovers, but neither wanted to be the first to admit it. They looked around the room and their clothes were everywhere. Craig got up naked and saw that Lek had nothing on either. She quickly reached for a towel as he walked over to the fridge for a bottle of cold mineral water.

As he took it back to the bed, Lek said:

"You not embarrass? Falang not embarrass?"

Craig assumed she was referring to having a hangover.

"No," he said, "we are on holiday. You and me together, we on holiday together, start today. Last night, we have party because you come stay with me for one month. Do you want some cold water?"

She had not meant that.

Lek was not yet prepared to admit that she had drunken too much. She had meant walking around naked in front of her and before a window, where he could be overlooked, but she did not correct him.

Instead, she smiled and said: "Thank you. I want some water, please."

Craig handed it over and got back into bed.

She felt so good next to him.

So warm and so soft and so sexy.

He wanted to grab her and make love, but he was shy. He thought that he did not know how to treat an oriental woman. He had had mostly white friends, but from many countries and a few black friends, but the only oriental people he had ever spoken to before four days ago had worked in restaurants. He didn't have a clue, but hoped that his natural politeness would get him by.

So, instead, he said: "What you want to do today? Celebrate we have holiday together."

This was Lek's best opportunity to get things sorted out, so she said:

"Boss tell me I can go holiday with you for one month, but then I maybe lose my job, because she pay me for one month already and I give money my mother, because she no have money. My father die ten years ago and my mother cannot work. She too old now. So I have problem.

"Not work, no have money for eat now or send my Mama next month. Big problem. Not same Europe here. No holiday money."

She was testing to see if his mumbled promise of at least 500 Baht a day the night before when he was drunk was genuine.

"Yes, Lek, I understand. I tell you before, I can give you 500 Baht every day and you stay with me free in hotel and I pay for all your food and drink. Everything too. Is that OK?"

"Yes, Craig, it is OK for me and my mother, small money, because I like you, but I must pay Mama San for not working. She keep my job for me. She want 400 every day too."

Lek could see immediately that she may have over stepped the mark and she quickly said: "But maybe for one month you keep me, only 200 for one day. Good discount, eh? Eh, what you think? You want me try?"

No answer, only "Come on let's shower and go down for breakfast."

Lek was starting to worry again, so she went into the shower with him and they showered together. At the breakfast table, Lek asked:

"You very quiet, Craig. You not happy? I do, I say something wrong?"

"No, kid, it is not you. I am just thinking, that is all. Have hangover. How you say in Thai 'hangover'."

"Mau," she replied and smiled, "I mau little bit too."

After breakfast, which was quieter than usual, Craig said: "Lek, you want go home and get some clothes, put in my room? Get bikini too and see me in hotel Will. I give you 500 every day and I give Mama San 400 every day, but I want you talk to her for 200 every day, OK?"

Lek agreed and left, Craig went back up stairs, although he did not know why. The whole business of paying for company did not seem right to him, but then how else was Lek and her mother supposed to survive? The harsh realities of living outside Europe were beginning to make themselves apparent to him for the first time in fifty years.

It made him feel very uncomfortable, very uncomfortable indeed.

He entered his room, switched on the TV, took a cold beer from the fridge, even though it was only eleven in the morning, thinking what the Hell, I'm on holiday, and lay down on the bed. He propped himself up on the pillows, drank his beer and watched TV, but saw nothing. He was aware of moving lights before his eyes, but he was not using his brain to unscramble the pixels.

He was trying to unscramble life without a social security network.

It had just never crossed his mind before to think about how people outside Europe and a few other countries survived if they did not have a job. Craig himself was currently out of work, but he had worked for a construction firm as office manager for thirteen years until a few months previously, when the company had gone into liquidation. The last few months had been hard mentally but not financially. He had money in the bank, a house, a car and he was getting a little in social security. He planned to spend between £3,000 and £5,000 on this holiday and that would not hurt and here was a stunning woman asking for less than twenty pounds a day, because after ten years working, she was still not entitled to any holiday money.

It was a lot to take in. More than just culture shock. Culture shock had been the experience of going from the UK to work in the Netherlands thirty years before but there was just no comparison to this.

This was a different culture, an alien culture, something incomprehensible, something that he would never have understood from all the appeals on TV, until he had had it rammed down his throat by experience.

Although he had travelled a lot in Europe, north Africa and South America and seen 'poverty', he had not known anyone from there. Thailand is not poor by many standards, but it has many people that have to work every day to make ends meet and that does not only not include holidays abroad, it does not include any holidays at all.

At least for people who get their hands dirty when they work.

And for Lek too. He could see that she was not complaining about her situation; she was not playing for sympathy or grabbing his money. It was just a reality: she and her Mum had to eat and if Lek was not earning any money then no one from the government was going to give them any either.

It came as a hammer blow to the casing of his consciousness of the world, so he went and got another beer from the fridge and his cell phone from the table and flopped back down on the bed.

After a few seconds ringing, Will picked up: "Hiya Craig, how are you doing, mate? Up yet? I mean dressed yet? You know what I mean. Did you have a good party after we left?"

"Yes, yes, to all those things. Listen, what are you doing today? Nothing much? Good. I told Lek to meet me at your hotel for a swim later … in about two hours, but I'd like to come over earlier, if that's OK. You are at the poolside now, I can hear, or not?"

"Yes, Goong's gone off somewhere shopping. She said she'd ring later. What's the problem?"

"Oh, no problem. I'll see you by the pool in about thirty minutes. Bye."

Craig lay back and looked at the TV. A documentary on garden insects or something – aphids being tended and defended by ants.

And being eaten by them sometimes.

Anyway, he drank his beer, gathered up his bathing costume and a hotel towel and headed off to get a motorbike taxi to Will's hotel, five minutes away. When he got to the poolside, Will was ordering an early beer as well.

"Do you want one of these, Craig? Take a seat."

It was very hot and the pool was deserted except for a few Mediterranean sun-worshippers the colour of mahogany and Will who was gleaming like a greasy chip in his sun block. Craig hid under a parasol and took the beer gratefully.

"I want to talk to you, Will, about the money we give the girls. If you don't mind me asking, how much do you give Goong?"

"No, I don't mind talking about it. I've been coming here for donkey's years and this is your first trip. I give most of the girls what they ask for: five, six, seven, eight hundred and I pay the bar find: three, four, five hundred, but I try to keep the total down to about a thousand a day all-in in cash, plus I pay all the daily bills: food and drink and the odd present, you know."

"You know, Will, it hit me like a sledgehammer today, that if the girls, or any Thais for that matter, don't work, they don't get any money. I suppose, I always knew that that was how it worked in Third World countries, but it didn't sink in until this morning, when Lek sort of explained what she would need to stay with me for a month and why. I suppose that I am happy with the fact that I have to give her money, but I am not sure about paying that Mama San for nothing for a month. For what?"

"Now, wait a minute there, Craig. You know that that is Lek's cousin, don't you? Favourite cousin. Oh, be very careful about slagging her off in front of Lek. Lek will side with her cousin, she will have to, believe me and you will lose Lek. Guaranteed. So, please, gently, gently, my friend. You do not know much about Thailand or the East yet. Don't dive in head first and make a tit of yourself. Let's work this out together over the next few days."

"That reminds me, who has been paying my bar finds for Lek then, because I haven't."

"Oh, I paid the first night," said Will, "no problem, but they will have been adding the bar find to your bar bill every night. You do not check, I have seen that, so you never noticed."

They laid back and kept their own counsel until the girls arrived together about thirty minutes later.

The next few days passed idyllically and identically: up at nine or ten in the morning; a shower; breakfast; over to Will's hotel for a swim; lunch; a few beers and a stroll; back to the hotel for a shower; meet up at Daddy's Hobby at eight, drink a lot of beers and go for dinner. Then Will and Goong would go back to their hotel at midnight and Craig and Lek would usually go for a walk and a few more beers.

Lek had 'arranged' the reduction in the bar find, but Craig was still not happy that someone was profiteering from his 'girlfriend' for nothing, like a pimp. He was increasingly seeing Lek as his girlfriend and this bar find bothered him more and more too. One night, after about a week, while waiting for Will and Goong, they had their first row.

"I am not happy about the bar find, Lek, I'm not paying it any more starting tonight and if your cousin doesn't like it then we won't come drinking here any more and I'm going to ask Will to do the same."

Lek was horrified, but she let nothing show on her face. She said nothing rather than say something she would regret and tried to ignore the things that Craig had said until she had had time to analyse them.

"Not now, telak, not now. You don want pay tonight, I pay. No problem. Wait for Will and Goong. We talk later."

Their friends duly arrived and as is custom, the girls sat next to each other and so did the men. Craig started up:

"Will, I told Lek that I'm not paying any more bar fines. I've been paying them for more than a week and I don't like it. Lek got hers reduced by fifty percent, but I still don't like it. It is not the money, it's just that I feel like I'm paying a pimp and I'm stopping tonight."

Looking at Will, who was next to Goong, who was next to Lek, Craig could see that the girls were talking seriously too and he could guess what about.

Will looked concerned as well, but Craig, strengthen by lack of opposition and plenty of beer added:

"And I told Lek that if her cousin doesn't like it, Lek and I will stop drinking in Daddy's Hobby. What do you think, Will?"

"Well, Craig, I told you before, if you go against family, you are on dodgy ground. Lek is sure to stick up for her cousin over you, but now that you have risked your neck on this one, I'll go with you. To Hell with it, there are plenty more girls."

That last bit was not what Craig wanted to hear at all. He had become very, very attached to Lek and he didn't really want to risk losing her for a few pounds a day. It all seemed rather petty now. To lose someone he thought a great deal of because of four pounds a day over a month's holiday? He realized that he was making a big mistake and wanted to back down, but he did not like the principal and he had already made such a fuss.

It was not the first time that speaking hastily had got him into trouble.

Anyway, the night progressed and they got drunker until the time came for Will to go back to the hotel. "Check bin," he shouted to Beou and she came over.

Beou had started a 'new tradition' with Craig and Will of giving them a B52 on the house when they left and today was no exception. Craig and Lek decided to leave at the same time and go to Tom's bar around the corner. Beou handed over the free drinks and took Will's beaker of chits. She added them up and then took out the bill with the bar fine on it and ripped it up:

"No more bar finds for my two lovely lady from my village for you and same for you, Craig. Cheers!"

Craig and Will were flabbergasted. They had been set for an argument that neither of them really saw the sense of having any more and Beou had taken the wind right out of their sales. Defused them. The girls were looking coy, as if butter wouldn't melt in their mouths and the guys felt obliged to buy another round each to acknowledge Beou's generosity.

Everyone went home happy that night.

Especially Craig, who knew that he had come very close to losing a wonderful woman and who also knew that he still had her only because someone was wiser than he was.

14 LEARNING CURVE

Time passed quickly and sweetly for Craig and Lek, but not exactly in the same way. Craig delighted in the company of his new friend and was anxious to learn everything that she had to teach him, whereas Lek was looking for some sign or preferably some words about where all this was going.

They stopped swimming at Will's hotel every day and they even stopped seeing him every night. There were no problems, it was just that both couples wanted to be alone sometimes or go to different places. Sometimes, Will liked to eat early and go to the cinema, whereas Lek and Craig preferred to eat later and stay out later.

Besides that Craig had learned that Lek didn't like being out in the sun much. In common with most Thai women, Lek preferred to keep her skin as white as possible. So she didn't want a sun tan and didn't want to even be outside from about eleven in the morning to about five in the evening. Craig wasn't a sun-worshipper anyway and didn't have the sort of skin that browned easily, so didn't mind that, but he was surprised to see that Lek used skin whitener to bleach her skin a little every day.

However, being unknowledgeable, he assumed that Thai women were emulating Western women and he was embarrassed about it. One day, he asked a couple of expat residents in Pattaya and they said it had nothing to do with the West; that it was because the Thai royal family has pale skin for one reason or another. Many of his assumptions about Thailand and Thais were wrong, because he was looking from a Western point of view.

In order to keep out of the sun, Lek would either go and visit friends or Beou or go home to do some domestic chores during the hours of strong sunlight. This also answered his question why Thai women often hurried down the street during these hours with a newspaper or a hat held up shielding their faces from the sun, whereas Craig had assumed that it was because they had forgotten their sun glasses.

Lek also took on such tasks as dropping their clothes off at the laundry and buying fruit and snacks to be eaten in their, or rather his room. It was increasingly becoming their room and Craig loved sharing it with her. He hadn't lived with anyone for years and it was nice to sit in the room and read or watch TV together.

However, when Lek went off to do her stuff in the shadows at the sun's peak, Craig would maybe have a beer, a bite to eat or sit in an Internet cafe learning about Thailand, Thai culture and picking up emails from back home. He was really into the Internet and computers but, although Lek would come and sit watching for hours without either interfering or complaining, he could not get her interested in it at all.

In order to try to get her involved, one day Craig said:

"Lek, give me your full name and we can set up a free account for you at Hotmail or Yahoo and you can keep in touch with people."

"Keep in touch with who?" she said hopefully.

"Well, your friends and your family, of course."

"Oh, OK," she said forlornly, her little burst of enthusiasm having petered out.

They signed her up, but she never used the account.

It had never crossed Craig's mind that no-one in the village had a computer and that there was no Internet up there anyway and that even if they did have it, no one would know how to use it.

They were very happy though and despite many cultural faux pas, Craig and Lek got on with everyone wherever they went. They were both night birds so staying up late suited them both and neither of them needed much sleep, although Craig suspected that Lek went home to grab a few hours in the afternoon, not that it mattered. It was good to have some time to explore alone in the afternoons, not that Lek ever tried to stop him doing anything and even took him into A-Go-Go bars to show him what went on in there. She never got jealous, which Craig had been told by many ex-pats was very strange for Thai women with a farang boyfriend.

If they did not spend the afternoon together, the rendezvous point was always Daddy's Hobby between four and five, before it got busy. Lek still liked to keep in touch with her friends and Craig loved the attention from all the girls too. He enjoyed watching them put on their make up and get ready for the evening.

It must be what it is like in a chorus girls' dressing room backstage, he thought. It was like being a fly on the wall in a private world where most men are not allowed. Craig was only allowed in because he was with Lek and the girls would coyly ask him to translate text or email messages that they had received from 'old' or even current boyfriends, giggling with a hand before their mouth to hide their smile if the message was a bit saucy or just downright filthy.

Lek's friends would often chat him up and put their arms around him or hold his hand right in front of Lek. He found it a little embarrassing at first, but Lek said they were her friends and she didn't mind and he genuinely believed her.

Craig didn't mind either.

The sorority was making him feel welcome, because they loved their friend Lek and they wanted her to have as much chance as possible of getting out and being happy. Sometimes, people would ask: "When you go home Wales, Craig?," but the question was never pushy or suggestive. "The twelve August," he would say and sometimes one of the girls would tick the days off on her fingers quietly and say: "Oooh..."

Lek thought that she was falling in love with Craig, but she also realized that she may have drawn a dud. Craig knew that he was falling in love with Lek and he knew that he had not drawn a dud, but that seemed to be as far as his thought processes took the matter. It was as if everyday was a new one and he took one day at a time. No forward thinking, no planning, no 'What happens after the 12th?'

It was kind of infuriating, but it was also the way the bar girls were leading their lives, so what could they say? Bar girls lived for the day and hoped that something would 'come along'. Meaning Mr. Right, usually, but not always. Some wanted Mr. Stupid, because Mr. Stupid might shower them with gold and money, before he paupered himself and they had to wait for the next one.

Some girls were stringing six or seven men along, getting money and presents off all of them. One girl had twelve men abroad all sending her money every month and not one of them knew about the others. This could get quite tricky sometimes and took careful planning. Sometimes, she had to go free-lancing in Phuket if two boyfriends arrived at the same time, saying that she was looking after her sick mother back in the village as an excuse.

Craig had wondered whether Lek was like that or had been like that, but had come to the conclusion that whatever had happened before they met was none of his business. In fact, this was the only way to stay sane in such an environment as the bar world of Pattaya. He had managed not to ask a single sensitive question, partly because he was frightened of the answer, but mostly because he realized that it was none of his business.

How can a Westerner with all the advantages of social security and charities ever think they have the right to make a moral judgement about those who do not have those advantages? Take away the safety net in the West and people would die nowadays. People have become so soft .

Whereas they survive very well in places like Thailand, because in places like Thailand, family takes care of family. In the West, a lot of families have become fragmented, because they don't really need each other to survive any more.

Places like Thailand still have what many Westerners have forgotten.

Craig realized after a while that most of the girls in Daddy's Hobby were from the same village as Lek 'up north' and that Lek had known the younger ones since they were toddlers or younger. It was all so different for Craig and to be let into the 'secret world' of how things worked was fascinating.

The learning process was not only one way either. Although Lek had been seeing foreigners, mostly Westerners, for ten years, she had learned surprisingly little about Europe. She didn't know that the United Kingdom consisted of four countries, each of which had its own language. She knew that some Westerners did certain things, like 'touch wood', but she had never asked, and no-one had ever told her, why. She was learning almost as much from Craig as he was from her. They fascinated each other and there was no doubt in either person's mind, that they were falling in love.

But still there were barriers. Craig had had a couple of weeks of afternoons to talk to ex-pat resident foreigners and they often had grim stories to tell. Stories of theft and deception enough to frighten most men off. For her part, Lek had been promised loads of things many times over the years, only never to see the man again or to see him months later with another woman.

They were both resigned to the fact that people lied, especially on holiday and especially to holiday romantic partners. Many men that Lek had been with were probably married back home.

Craig said that he had never been married and Lek wanted to believe him. In fact she did, really.

Craig wanted to believe that Lek was not married, although he had never asked her, but he had heard people in the bars saying that some Thai men pimp their wives because the money is easier and better than working, and why would that not be true here with no social security, reasoned Craig, when it happens in the West too.

So both knew that they could easily love each other, but it was still not easy: neither could ask if the other was married because neither knew the other one well enough to know if he or she was lying. This bothered both equally, but both were enjoying the other's company too much to want to risk spoiling it.

The difference was that Craig didn't think any further than that, whereas it bothered Lek all the time and Craig was blissfully unaware that Lek was being barraged with questions by her girlfriends, to which she had no answers. Questions like: is he married? Does he love you? Will he take you back with him? Does he have a girlfriend in Wales? Has he got any children? What is his job? How much money does he earn?

One night, Lek decided to take the bull by the horns again and try to find out. This relationship was going well and they were both very happy, but Lek could not work out where it was leading, because Craig never talked about his emotions or his plans or even his hopes.

One morning, Lek announced that there was a big family reunion in her village and that she wanted to go.

"Oh, great," said Craig without any trace of irony, "I hope you have a good time. How long will you be away? Don't forget that I have to go home next week and I will miss you."

"Well, I will be away for four days, but I can ask Mum if I can take you with me, if you want. If you trust me."

She had already asked her mother and this was another test.

"Hmm, I'd like to go, Lek," replied Craig, "but I don't want to leave my friends and I am going home a week tomorrow."

As soon as he said it, Craig felt stupid. He could see a flash of hurt on Lek's face and he thought, I may never get an opportunity like this again. In for a penny in for a pound.

"Sorry, Lek. I mean, I would love to come to meet your family at the village. Please ask your Mum if that is all right."

Lek could not stop herself, she threw her arms around Craig and hugged him, sniff-kissing him wherever she could reach with her beautiful head.

They were to leave on Friday, the day after next and return on Monday. They were both looking forward to it already.

Lek left Craig in the room and went off to make the arrangements. Craig knew that Lek's village was about 700 kilometres north of Pattaya, but nothing more than that, so he picked up the phone and rang Will.

"Sorry, Craig, I have no idea where Lek's village is or even what it's called. I have never asked Goong and she's not here at the moment. What is it called again? Baan Suay, north of Phitsanulok? You are going up there are you? I have heard of Phitsanulok, but I have never been there. Look, let's have a chat this evening. I'll see you at six in Daddy's Hobby. Bye."

It was only eleven in the morning, but Craig wanted to find out more right away, so he went down to the bar in the Pig. It was quite busy, as it normally was in the lunch time and the afternoon in general, but he didn't see anyone he had spoken to before. He sat at the bar nearest to the window where a lot of long-time residents of Pattaya sit and waited to get into a conversation. Meanwhile, he ordered a Guinness and a beef sandwich.

It didn't take long, they were a friendly bunch in the Pig and soon he was talking to the three guys around the corner of the bar.

"Have any of you ever been up north?," asked Craig, "I've been invited up by my girl to meet her folks for the celebrations this week-end. What do you reckon?"

"They'll ask you for money to pay for vet's fees or doctor's fees or mechanic's fees for sure. Don't go, it's a con, believe me," said one man. "I went back with a girl a couple of years ago and the whole tribe expected me to pay for everything. Never again. Don't bother, it's an invitation to the ATM, that's all."

Another man chirped in: "I went to Isaan once and it cost me more to stay with the family than it would have if I had stayed in a five star hotel. Waste of time. He's dead right, don't bother."

This was all pretty depressing, but the third one said: "You have to judge the girl who is taking you. If you feel that you are being put upon, get in a taxi and leave. It's that simple. If you like her and you trust her, just go for it."

"Ach, you're too soft, you've been had over too. I know you have," said one of the first two.

Craig pretended to read the paper, leaving them to discuss it amongst themselves. He had another beer while digesting this disappointing feedback and left the Pig to go for a walk.

It seemed that everyone Craig talked to had had problems in Pattaya or in a village somewhere or other. The only thing that he learned for certain was that going north was better-known as going up country. It was all very depressing, but Craig was determined to go anyway. If he was cheated, well, so be it – he would chalk it down to experience.

There was one man who showed him a front door key and said that he had arrived back the day before. He told his story in a dismal, drunken voice. He had hired an apartment for himself and a girl he had known for six months. He had furnished the place out and paid three months rent in advance and left her in there while he went back to Britain to pick up some personal effects and sell all his belongings. He had arrived back the day before but his key hadn't fitted the lock, so he had gone to see the landlord that morning after spending the night in a hotel, thinking that his girlfriend must have been called home urgently.

The landlord had told him two hours ago that she had only paid two weeks rent and promised to pay more; that she had moved all her stuff out three days ago and that he had changed the locks for security reasons. The man he met said, that he had discontinued his whole life in Britain; said 'Goodbye' to his friends and family; given up his apartment, and lost four thousand pounds on the flat and the contents in Pattaya.

He was really angry and pretty drunk and not much fun to be with so Craig moved on.

For want of a happier alternative, Craig decided to go and talk to Noi and so, walked the ten yards or so to Daddy's Hobby. Noi was awake or at least had woken up, because she was not lying down, although she was propped up on a few pillows in the corner with her eyes shut. There were no customers and the music and television were switched off.

Craig purposely scraped the barstool as he sat down opposite her and her eyes opened. "Hello, Craig," she said, "I wasn't asleep. Just thinking, you know. What can I get you? A cold beer Chang? It is vely, ve'y hot today. Maybe forty-th'ee deglee. Later, more hot. Maybe forty-five deglee."

"Yes, go on then, Noi. Can I get you something? No? OK, maybe later."

When she had returned with the beer and chit and sat down again, they both started talking at the same time.

"You go our village…"

"We are going to your…,"

They both smiled and stopped talking.

"Yes, he continued, we are going to your village on Friday. What you think? Good idea? Not good idea?"

"Oh, vely good, I want go too, but cannot. Must work here. You like village, have good time. See everything. Family and friends from me and Lek and from girls here. I think you like, but looooong, looong way. Twelve hours on bus. Long way."

"Jesus," he said, "how far is that? Twelve hours on a bus? How far, Noi? Kilometres?"

"Oh, I not sure, 600, 700 maybe. Maybe more. Long way in the north. I show you."

She rummaged around under the bar, but didn't find what she was looking for, so she went down the far end of the bar by the cashier's desk and bent down behind that. Five minutes later she came back with a dog-eared map, smiling.

"Show you," she said unfolding the map and patting it flat on the bar like an old map to buried treasure, "We are here."

Craig had to take her word for it because the map was in Thai.

"This Pattaya. Go here, north. Not go Bangkok, pass Bangkok. Go here, more north. Road go Ayutthaya, Singburi, Utai Tani, Nakon Sawan, Phichit then Phitsanulok. Pattaya to Phitsanulok is 550 kilo maybe. Then go to village, 95 or 100 kilo more. Stay on bus long time, but good bus. Bus vely good."

"Mmm…," he said, but, 'How good?' he was wondering.

The girls started trickling in and everyone asked where Lek was. It is polite to ask where the partner is in Thailand even if you already know the answer, which Craig suspected they all did. He was probably the only one who didn't, but he enjoyed their company and enjoyed the bits of attention he got and the things they told him, because he knew no Thai whatsoever.

Not long afterwards, Will, Goong and Lek arrived together. Early for Will. Sometimes, Craig got the impression that there was a massive conspiracy going on. Not a malicious one, but a conspiracy nevertheless of Thais and one unwitting European accomplice, Will. Everybody always seemed to know everything before he did. The only things that he could tell anyone about that they did not already know, would have had to have been about Europe. Everybody always seemed to know where he was, where he had been and what he had been doing. It was as if they had RFID'd him and were tracking him like an elephant in an African Safari Park. It was not a problem, but it was certainly a strange experience.

The two girls said 'Hello' and went behind the bar, everybody seemed pretty excited about something and Craig guessed that it was about the impending trip up country.

"Are you going?" Will asked.

"Looks like it. I said I would this morning and I can't see why I shouldn't, although all I've heard today so far is horror stories from people who have been ripped off. Bloody depressing. But yes, I'm still going. I'm looking forward to it actually, although I just found out that it's nearly 700 kilometres away and takes about twelve hours on the bus. Noi said that the buses are very good though."

"Wow. I could not sit on a bus for twelve hours even if I wanted to," said Will. "Two beers, please, darling. Twelve hours there and twelve hours back? That's a day of your holiday gone and you've only got eight left, haven't you?"

"Yes, but I suppose I'll see a bit of Thailand on the way, won't I?"

"Quite a bit of it, I should think, 700 kilometres of it twice. You'll be all right. You're not daft and Lek seems to be on the level. I've been asked a few times, but I have never gone because of the length of time you have to be on the bus. It is just too much for me and I like my comfort anyway… and I'm scared of snakes."

A party was soon under way, it never took much to get them started anyway, but everyone was happy that Craig was going to their village with Lek and they were all looking forward to the weekend themselves. Craig realized that the reason for the family get together was a religious festival called 'Dharma Day' as far as he could work out, no one seemed capable of explaining it properly. Anyway, the whiskey came out and the music got louder and everyone was congratulating Craig and Lek and they were both beaming.

Will took his chance as soon as he could to slip off for a meal with Goong.

Craig received more kisses that night than in any one month in his whole life before and everybody wanted to clink glasses with them both and wish them a lovely weekend. Food appeared as if from nowhere, but most of it was too hot for Craig. Food from the north is not as hot as it is in other parts of Thailand, but when Thai people move to Pattaya they seem to become influenced by the Isaan culture and eat hot. There were also fried insects, which are considered a delicacy. Craig was not up to eating those yet either.

Still there was plenty he could eat and he got stuck in with the revelry.

By the time two o clock came, everybody was ready to go to their bed.

The following day, Lek was up early and gone. She said that she had lots to do and that she wouldn't see Craig much before six in the evening.

Craig had a late breakfast or as late as he could possibly get without having to pay because he was on a bed and breakfast deal. After that, he stayed in the bar and read the English-language Bangkok Post from front page to the back, hardly missing a word. He did not look up for fear of attracting attention and someone speaking to him.

He was hung over.

Some of the waitresses guessed the problem and made fun of him and gradually persuaded him to smile and talk a little. It did make him feel better and he was soon taking a 'hair of the dog'. He filled the time in until six o'clock as usual: walking around, a beer here and a chat; a beer there and a chat, but never wandering very far from the area where Daddy's Hobby was located.

Lek on the other hand was very busy. She first dropped the laundry off making sure that they knew that it had to be ready within twenty-four hours. Then, she went to the bank and withdrew enough money so that she could buy presents to take back and have a few notes in her purse to show that she was 'doing all right'. She had never taken anyone home before and she was really quite nervous, but looking forward to it.

She was worried about Craig: would he like it? Would he get bored? She knew that he would try to fit in, but would he be able to? Lek knew that no-one in the village spoke any European languages and Craig spoke no Asian ones, which could make it rather awkward.

She made numerous phone calls to her friends and family saying that she was bringing her boyfriend back. Not 'boyfriend' in the sense that bar girls usually used the word, but boyfriend as in the dictionary. None of her friends or family had ever met one of her men-friends before, not since her husband in any case. Things had to go right and it made her nervous.

She trusted the villagers to be friendly, but there was still plenty of room for things to go wrong. There was no bed for them, so how would he react to having to sleep on the floor for a few days? The kitchen floor was plain earth and when it rained as it surely would in this monsoon season, it became muddy, so what would he think of that?

The toilet was not a sit-down job, but a French type squat-down; the water for the shower came from a container and there were far more mosquitoes than in Pattaya. There were no bars, no restaurants, no hotels and nowhere to buy Western food or snacks like the chocolate he liked so much.

Oh, yes, there was plenty that could still go wrong. But she did her best to cover as many eventualities as possible.

She also had to get the bus tickets and she was praying that she could get them on the VIP luxury air-conditioned coach, because that would mean that he would get there in a good mood or at least a better mood than if the bus was fan-cooled. Then she had to plan transport from Phitsanulok. The bus would drop them there at two o'clock in the morning and there was no connecting service.

Lek always waited at the terminal until the first bus at five thirty, but she did not want Craig to have to do that. A hotel or a taxi to the village would add expense and that was not her way, although they were reasonable alternative plans.

Yes, there was still plenty that could go wrong all right.

When she met up with Craig at six o'clock, he was having a beer with Will as they would not see each other until Tuesday, although Craig thought it would be Monday. She didn't correct him. Better to let him find out on Monday, she thought.

She was completely exhausted and after a bite to eat and a bottle of beer, she excused herself to go to bed. It was only seven o'clock.

15 THE TRIP UP COUNTRY

The following morning, they got up showered and went down for breakfast at about ten.

"Telak," she began, "you have money for go holiday to my village today? Not have ATM in village, not have bank. You must take from bank today."

"Yes, I have little bit, but I will get more, just in case. I want to take something for present for your family. What can I take?"

"I buy, no problem. You can give me 1,000 for bus now, please? I pay already and for how much you want to buy present? 1,000, 2,000?"

"I have no idea. Here is the one, plus two thousand. Three thousand, OK?"

Yes, very good. With that she jumped up, kissed him on the cheek and said: "See you here in the Pig at four o'clock. Not late, eh? Or we miss bus."

And she was gone again.

First Lek wanted to buy presents for her family, especially for her mother and her daughter, although Craig didn't know about her at the time. Then she had to bring them back to the Pig and wrap them. Next, she had to collect and check the laundry and start packing. After that, she had to go to the her cousin's and Daddy's Hobby to collect all the parcels that the girls wanted taken back to their families and finally, she wanted to spend an hour or so in the beauty salon in order to look her best when they got there.

She hoped that Craig would make an effort as well, but she had her doubts about that.

Craig did his usual rounds but was back waiting in the bar in the Pig by three forty-five; Lek came in as if her trousers were on fire an hour later, but she looked great. They went up to the room together and Craig was dismayed to see his suitcase and four huge shopping bags waiting there for them. It was a good job there was a lift, thought Craig, but what about after that?

The bus would come to the terminal on Sukhumvit Road at six o'clock, but it was the Friday evening before a Bank Holiday weekend, so the traffic was sure to be horrendous. Lek went outside and hailed a taxi immediately and they were off to farewells, waves and smiles from the staff at the Pig.

The traffic was bad. It took them thirty minutes to travel the few kilometres to the terminal, but that still gave them thirty minutes grace. They were both very excited to be going to the village. Lek had not been for more than a year and Craig had no idea what the next few days would bring.

Lek paid the taxi driver when they arrived and installed Craig in one of the empty seats to wait for her. She took the case and a bag, put them down a few metres away and then came back for the rest. While she was hurrying around talking to people, Craig surveyed the bus station. It was not large; it was newish but it was not as busy as he had expected.

The timetable revealed that only a dozen buses a day ran out of the station and that most of them were after six in the evening, so he guessed that they were getting in ahead of the peak period. The buses were going to all the far away places he had heard of: Chang Mai, Chang Rai, Udon, Phuket, et cetera.

When the first bus pulled in, it did Craig a power of good. It certainly looked like a luxury coach and it had 'VIP' and the names of some places on the side, presumably where it was going to, he thought. Lek had already told him that she had been lucky enough to get them on a VIP bus, so things were starting off well. Lek came back and confirmed that the bus would be on time and that their luggage had been checked in, although Craig could still see it in the middle of the floor where Lek had left it. He wondered how safe it all was, but it was in plain sight and there were not many people about.

And not one foreigner besides himself either.

What did that mean, he wondered. Was he the only foreigner in Pattaya stupid enough to go? The only lamb to the slaughter this weekend? He could not help but wonder.

When it was a few minutes to six, Lek jumped up and said she had to go to the shop for something. Craig was amazed at the bad timing. As soon as Lek was out of sight a coach swept in with 'Rayong, Phitsanulok, Chiang Mai' written on the side. Rayong was presumably where it had come from and Chiang Mai was its final destination via Phitsanulok. This was their coach.

Craig didn't know what to do. He could see their luggage and he could see a queue forming at the entrance to the coach. No-one got off and an assistant was opening the sides of the coach up for the storage of luggage. Should he take the bags down to the assistant as others were doing? Was it their coach anyway? What the hell was going on? Where was Lek? Craig was starting to get angry. Her sense of timing had always put him on edge, but this was just too much.

He got up and walked over to the luggage, just as an assistant was checking the labels that Lek had tied on them. He was starting to take them away. No-one could speak English and he didn't know what was going on. He was really starting to get angry, when like a kingfisher, in flew Lek talking rapidly to the porter and pulling Craig's arm towards the bus. She had another two bags of shopping from the station's on site shop.

Lek oversaw the luggage being stowed away and then got on the bus. Craig followed grumpily, although he soon perked up when they were inside. It was cool. The air conditioning was on. A stewardess came up to greet Lek, who showed her her tickets. The stewardess lead them to their seats and Lek motioned Craig to go in first and sit by the window. They were in seats fifteen and sixteen, right at the back, which meant that there were only thirty-two seats on this full-size coach. There was a monitor in the front and six drop-down screens besides.

Craig's mood was improving by the minute and Lek took his hand. Squeezing it, she smiled sweetly and asked: "OK, now?"

Yes, everything was perfect.

Now, it was, anyway.

He hoped that she would never do that to him again. He had had a mild panic attack, although he was not the sort to panic quickly, but he did get embarrassed easily and if he had been made a fool of, it would have taken him ages to live it down, especially after all the warnings. No, it was definitely the last time he wanted to go through anything like that again, but then he still did not fully understand the Thais relation-ship with time yet, so the chances were that he would.

He was blissfully unaware of that at the time.

Minutes later, the coach pulled out of the station. It was six-fif-teen. Not bad, thought Craig and the stewardess came into the cabin, which was separated from the front two feet of the coach where she and the driver sat. She gave a short speech in which Craig caught the words Phitsanulok and Chiang Mai. It was presumably to welcome the latest passengers on board. She then unplugged her mike and set a film in motion, after which she walked up the aisle past them. She disap-peared into the back ten feet of the bus and returned with a bag of crisps, a small packet of biscuits, a litre of cold water and a blanket for each of the new passengers and then she went to sit with the driver in the front.

Lek showed Craig how to work the controls on the seat. It would go back to about 135 degrees. Most of the passengers were already flat

out with their blankets up over their faces. The seats had a lumbar mas-
sager which was really soothing. Lek confided that when she had first
come across this facility, it was still running from the previous occu-
pant of the seat and she had wondered whether there was a ghost living
in her seat. It was a very long time ago she said, but Craig wondered
just how long ago it really was.

She was so beautiful and so attentive; Craig was loving the trip
already.

Lek was trying hard to make Craig happy, because she knew that
he hated being bored. She also knew that there would be nothing to do
for the next eight or nine hours but sleep or look out of the window.
She knew from experience that it would be best to go to sleep, but she
also knew that she would not do so if this were her first time travelling
through Wales.

Once they got out of Pattaya and the surrounding district, the
stewardess served up curry and rice and sweet Chiang Mai sausage. It
was gorgeous, if a little hotter than Craig was used too. It was clear that
most of their fellow passengers had done this trip before, because they
wolfed down their food, put the trays on the floor to be collected,
pulled their blankets up over their heads and went to sleep.

The stewardess collected the polystyrene trays in a bin bag and as
soon as it got dark, she switched the lights and the monitors off
without any more a do.

Craig was still eating.

He and Lek could see the funny side of that and they both had a
laugh about it. He had always eaten slowly, but the curry was too hot
for him to eat quickly anyway. When he had finished, Lek went out the
door behind them and put his tray in the galley. There was also a toilet
out there.

Lek tried to coax Craig to sleep, but he didn't want to. Lek knew
what was ahead and she reasoned that she at least would have to get

some sleep. Craig saw nothing wrong with that, so she kissed him, put the seat back and the foot rest up, pulled the blanket up over her head and joined all the other faceless undulating grey mounds lying at regular intervals around the bus.

But Lek did not go to sleep straight away. First she ran her plans for the following three days through her mind and when she was satisfied that there was not much more she could have done, she reached out for Craig's hand, pulled it under her blanket and went to sleep.

Craig reclined the seat a little for the sake of the arm of his that Lek held and took to staring out of the window. Not that there was much to see. Motorway lights and blackness beyond. A few cars. A few trucks. Deserted roads, deserted streets and deserted towns. Looking for UFO's in the sky was more interesting. He wondered why they had not left hours earlier, so that he could have enjoyed the journey. All in all though, he was quite a reflective soul and he didn't mind having a few hours to just think about things. He had travelled a lot and knew that he couldn't read while in motion without experiencing travel sickness.

The coach rolled a little from side to side in the bends, but it was very quiet and quite soothing. In fact, it was a very pleasant ride and Craig was enjoying it as he wondered about the weekend before him and his life after he got back to the UK the following week. There was still no prospect of a job, and who would want a fifty year old man who had only worked for himself or family for twenty-five years?

He wanted to work on the Internet. Maybe with web sites, but the one he already had was not earning enough to buy a pizza a week. His whole life had been turned upside down by the collapse of their family firm a year before. Now, he was on his own again and it was a bit scary. Thailand was an interlude, but what was to be done after that?

Bright lights. Blackness. Nothing.

He may have dozed off, he didn't know. From time to time a mobile phone would ring and bring him out of his reverie. Why did people take so long to answer a phone? Why was the sound on anyway? Surely, it was for situations like this that the vibrator could be used instead? Some people don't think or just don't care. Why didn't the bus company insist on passengers switching mobiles off in the bus?

Another of life's imponderables sent to make old people grumpy, he thought.

In Britain somebody would have said something about it and everybody else would have thought it, but in Thailand no-one seemed to care. Thais were so easy going. Or was it just that they didn't think that complaining would have any effect?

They arrived in Phitsanulok at two fifteen in the morning and the stewardess handed out a carton of milk and a sweet-smelling towel to everyone who was getting off. She also retrieved their blankets. Once off the bus, they went for their bags and were immediately pounced on by taxi drivers, although none of them could speak English so Craig just ignored them completely. Lek did the same. They took their bags a little way away from the bus and Lek took out her phone.

"Wait a little bit, please, Craig," she said and dialled a number. After a short conversation, she said: "Come, we go eat something."

In fact that was the last thing that Craig wanted to do, but he followed along behind, watched sadly by a group of previously-hopeful taxi-drivers. The first impression of Phitsanulok bus station was that it was four or five times bigger than the one in Pattaya and it was surrounded by small cafes and small guest-houses. Some looked pretty rough, while others looked all right.

Lek led the way into one of the better ones and they sat down in the empty cafe. They took a menu each, but it was only in Thai, so Craig was none the wiser.

"I don't want to eat, thanks, Lek. You go ahead, I'll just have a beer. Do they have beer here?"

"OK," she said, "I order for you. Car come for us after one hour."

Craig assumed that it was a taxi as he had not been made privy to any of the arrangements for the weekend at all. Lek ate her food and Craig drank his beer, all the while fighting off mosquitoes which seemed to have gathered to meet them. "Oh, we have mosquitoes too much in the north," said Lek. She called the waitress and said something. Minutes later a huge fan, salvage from a wrecked hovercraft by the look of it, was placed nearby aimed at their legs under the table.

The mosquitoes were literally blown away by the fan and the problem was temporarily over.

The car came thirty minutes early and the couple were not ready, so the driver came in to join them.

"This is Deo. He is married to my sister." Deo waaied, Craig waaied back and Deo sat down."

"Deo, do you want a beer?" asked Craig.

Lek translated: "No, thank you. Later, he is driving. He want coffee."

So, Deo had a coffee and a plateful of what Lek was eating and Craig had another beer. Craig got a lot of smiles from Deo and Lek, but no conversation. They were obviously very pleased to see each other and were catching up on things. Craig sat back and watched and listened, trying to discern words and attitudes from any foreign words that might have been in Thai, facial expressions and body language. It was one of his favourite pastimes.

Or at least, it had become a favourite pastime since coming to Thailand. He had never been anywhere before where so few people spoke any European languages at all.

When they had finished fifteen minutes later, Lek paid up and they went out to the car, which was a pick-up, the most common vehicle in rural Thailand. Lek got in the back seat and Craig was made comfortable in the front by Deo.

"This is my sister, Chalita, she married to Deo," said Lek and everybody smiled and said 'Hello' again. The three Thais continued talking, leaving Craig to look out of the window again.

Phitsanulok had huge, quite beautiful boulevards with massive pictures of the king and queen. Many of the trees were decorated like Christmas trees. Craig asked why and Lek said that it was a holiday weekend, but it was also the queen's birthday next Thursday, the day Craig was going home. The streets were deserted and the car was soon out of the city and rolling down the highway at a leisurely pace off to who knew where.

Well, everyone but Craig did, presumably.

The motorway was well lit, but not as brightly as it had appeared in the south. Craig could see past these motorway lights into the fields beyond. Miles and miles of grassland interspersed with a few trees and houses. It was all very open. Suddenly, Deo pulled off the motorway and went down a narrow, unlit lane. There was nothing more to see.

Lek on the other hand was having a whale of a time. She had not seen her younger sister nor her brother-in-law for a long time. They lived and worked in Bangkok and were also up for the weekend. They had tried to co-ordinate their arrival from Bangkok with that of the bus in Phitsanulok, but their departure had been delayed, so they were a little late. No-one minded such things in Thailand. Thais have an almost Spanish approach to time.

To say that time does not rule their lives is an understatement.

Lek passed around cold cans to everyone, cola to the three Thais and Heineken to Craig.

"How are you, Telak? You OK? Happy? Sorry, I talk to my sister and brother. No problem for you?" she asked.

"No, Lek. I am fine. No problem. I have a beer and I can look out the window, but I don't know what I am looking at because it is so dark. Grass, I think."

"Thank you. Not grass! You are looking at rice. Everything here is rice. I will show you later in my village. I talk to my sister now, all right?"

"Sure, you carry on."

He wondered if this was how it was going to be all weekend.

Lek was getting all the latest gossip about their mutual friends in Bangkok, because she had often gone there for a weekend to visit since her sister had married and moved there five years before. She was also asking about the arrangements they had made for the weekend and, knowing that Craig could not understand them, they were discussing him.

"Oh, he is big and handsome. He has a lovely smile and his skin is so white. I wish that my skin was as white as that. You know, I can't re-member the last time I was out in the sun and I'm still not as pale as I want to be. He's lovely. Does he have a brother?"

Deo looked at Craig and they smiled at one another. There was nothing else to be done.

Meanwhile, there were peals of laughter from the back seat.

They rounded a corner and there was light. They seemed to be on some sort of 'B' road, running from village to village and it was quite well lit. Craig could see all kinds of structures: houses, wooden and brick, outhouses, barns, sheds and lean-tos. There were cars, pick-ups and farm equipment in every house and dogs lying in every gateway. Between the villages, there was rice as far as the eye could see. Thou-sands of square kilometres of rice illuminated by the moon.

Another can of beer later, and they were back under over-hanging trees and he could only see what got caught in the headlights again — mostly moths and mosquitoes. Then they slowed down and turned left, down a ramp and off the road onto a 'C' road running between fields of rice just metres away on either side, but they were back in the moon-light and Craig could see a large building through the trees a mile ahead.

It looked a little like a Transylvanian Castle, he thought. Eerie. But they passed that and entered a well-lit, but deserted village. There were only dogs to be seen, sleeping in the middle of the road and they were loathe to get up and move out of the way too.

Then there was a right turn and they were in the dark again. It was four-thirty and Craig wondered where on Earth he was not for the first time in the last ten hours. Deo turned the wheel and the car left the road, went up a ramp and stopped in someone's front garden.

The eagle had landed. He guessed that they had arrived in Lek's mother's house in Baan Suay, 700 kilometres from the nearest person he knew.

Except Lek.

Daddy's Hobby

16 BAAN SUAY

No sooner had the pick-up pulled up than lights went on and doors opened. Some people had obviously just got up, but Craig could vaguely make out some others sitting on a table top in the half-light. Deo started to get out, so Craig thought he had better follow suit.

In for a penny, in for a pound.

He got out and held the seat forward for Lek to get out too. Lek moved forward and Craig did too, but he kept a few inches to the left and to the rear of her. They all went forward to meet the half dozen people already there. There was a lot of Thai spoken, some laughing and a small bench was pulled away from the table and Lek told Craig to sit down.

He did as he was told, but he felt awkward about not having greeted everyone, especially Lek's mother, who he assumed was the sixty-odd-year-old woman who was beginning to light a fire. Everyone was looking at him, nodding 'Hello' and smiling. He had expected a lot of waaing, as he had read in a book happens in Thailand, but he did not see a single waai exchanged.

"Lek, please stay by me for a while, I am totally at a loss here," he said. Lek came over and sat on the table opposite him. The table was huge, about ten square metres in size.

"What is problem, Craig?"

"I want to say 'Hello' to everybody but I do not know how. Should I waai? What should I do? I want to say 'Hello' to your mother. Is that her making the fire?"

"Yes, but don' worry. They don' speak English and they know you don' speak Thai. No problem. My mother, she is shy. She never see falang before. Wait little bit. You want another beer?"

"Yes, OK then." In truth, he felt a little awkward drinking beer at that time of the day in front of Lek's family, but seconds after Lek handed him a can she had opened, a man held a small glass up to him with what looked like a double shot of whiskey in it."

"Chee'," he said.

"Cheers," said Craig.

Then he spotted the bottle of Scotch. By five fifteen, there were a dozen men and Lek sitting in a circle on the table drinking whiskey from a small glass that they passed around in rotation, talking and laughing; Craig on the bench drinking beer and about six women cooking. Soon afterwards, plates of food started arriving." Within fifteen minutes there were at least a dozen different dishes on the table with one of two spoons or forks in each for everyone to help themselves, but no individual plates to put the food on. The idea was to eat from the main plate.

He didn't mind that, but Lek was picking out the best bits and feeding him like a baby. He didn't mind that either. People seemed genuinely happy that he was eating and enjoying their food.

"Why no rice, Lek?" he asked.

"This is a holiday, we don' eat rice on special days. You want rice, I get you rice, Mum have over there. Eat in the morning before people go to work. Not work now for two day. This weekend big day for Buddha. Everybody try come home see family. Thank you for come with me. Everybody is very happy to meet you. They say you have good heart – 'jai dee'."

Craig looked up at Lek and smiled at her warmly and then looked around to see that everyone was grinning at him. He held up his can and said: "Chock Dee – Good Luck," a little bit of Thai that he had learned from when he was drinking with the Thai girls in Daddy's

Hobby.

The next time Lek's mother came over, Craig waaied her, she gave a big smile, waaied back and hurried off.

"Thank you," Lek whispered.

From time to time, either one of the men on the table or one of the women cooking would lean over or come over to clink glasses and smile. Nobody could talk to Craig, but it didn't seem to matter. The atmosphere was fantastic; it was only five-thirty and the sun was just beginning to rise.

By six o'clock, Craig had had another tin, the food was nearly all gone and people were starting to drift off, the excitement of meeting Lek's falang boyfriend having waned a little too.

"You want to go shower now and sleep?," she asked.

He had been dreading this part and wanted to put it off a while longer: "No, I am all right. Later, Lek."

"No, I want you go now. Long day and I must do some things for myself. I cannot take care you. Please, shower and sleep."

"OK," he acquiesced, knowing that she was right, "but I want you take me show me everything. OK?"

"Yes, no worry. I show you everything first."

She led him into a large room that he assumed was a kind of family chapel, because first he had to wash his feet in a tray placed outside the door. Once inside, he saw a thin mattress laid out on the floor with several towels on it. The room was beautiful in yellows and deep blue, adding to his belief that they were in a family chapel. The ceiling tiles were large and very ornate.

He got undressed and Lek showed him how to fix a towel around his waist like a sarong. She thought that it was hilarious that he had never done that for himself before. Then she led him back out into the courtyard, past a dozen people looking at him and into the shower.

"You want to go to the toilet first?"

"No, I am all right. I will shower now, please wait outside."

"I help you. You say you want me help you."

"Not with your Mum and all your family outside, I don't," he said.

Laughing, she left him to his own devices. When he was ready, she took him back to the room, covered him with talcum powder, trained a fan on him and left. He was asleep in minutes as happy as a sand boy.

Lek was not at all tired, but she had slept on the bus for seven hours. It was the sleeping on the bus that marked the regular travellers out from the part-timers. The first thing she did was muck in with the ladies. She helped with the washing up and clearing away and then she went to see her daughter. Soom had come down to say 'Hello' to her mother when she arrived, but had gone back to bed again. Lek went up to the communal bedroom / living room in the house and sat on the floor by her daughter, revelling in being with her again.

"If this works out perfectly, Little One," she thought, "we will never be parted again for long until you are married." She stroked her hair and sniff-kissed her forehead, before hurrying out of the room with tears in her eyes. In her heart of hearts, she knew that she had done what had had to be done, when she had left ten years before, but she could not help thinking that her daughter had got a bad deal in life having her as a mother. She desperately wanted to make it up to her as soon as possible.

She helped the women chop vegetables for lunch and happily listened to all the latest gossip for an hour and then went over the road to visit her grandmother who was something over eighty and a little frail these days. Her identity card said that she was 86, but she said that she was at least two years older than that. The fact was that no-one knew and the authorities didn't care. Her age didn't entitle her to any-thing, so it didn't matter.

Lek spent the next couple of hours riding around the village on her mother's motorcycle. Her family was under strict instructions to phone her on her mobile if Craig got up, but she planned to be back by midday anyway. She got back at twelve thirty after making plans with family, friends and neighbours about what to do over the weekend.

Craig was still asleep, so she got undressed, put on a towel and went for a shower. When she got back, she opened the window shutters that faced onto the garden and sat on the mattress to put on her make-up.

She was made up to be home again as well.

Craig woke up at about one o'clock and he felt great. He lie there, with Lek framed by the window, the sounds of birds in the garden and people outside. He felt so at home.

"Good morning! What are we going to do today, telak?" He asked Lek.

"Oh, good morning! Good afternoon. We do what people, what everybody want. You want to go for shower? Then eat? OK. Get up. Party start already."

He could hear it too. It sounded as if there were thirty people outside. He put his towel on and she led him outside back to the toilet and shower. He was wrong, there were only about twenty people there. They stopped and stared as he came out. Some smiled, some looked away quickly, but most just stared.

Craig hurried on to the toilet.

Lek was not waiting for him this time, so he went back to the room alone past all those curious eyes. He was glad to be back within the four walls. He got dressed with the clothes that Lek had laid out on the bed for him, took his book out of his suitcase, lay down on the mattress and read, but really his heart was not in what he was reading. He was listening to the birds in the trees and the people laughing and joking in the garden. He was too shy to go out alone, so he decided to wait for Lek to come and get him when she was ready.

About thirty minutes later, Lek breezed in, saying: "Come on, we go soon. Come eat."

Outside, there were still a couple of dozen people: men on the table drinking and women bustling around cooking. People stopped what they were doing again and stared. "Good afternoon. Sawadee, kap," he announced and went to his bench without waiting for a reply. Seconds later, food and a beer were put in front of him.

"Lek," he said, "this is all very well, but I am not used to eating curry for breakfast washed down with a bottle of beer. What will they think of me?"

"Oh, no problem, Craig. I tell them you like beer. Not breakfast now. Two o'clock. Some people wait you four, five, six hours. You cannot eat Thai food now? Sorry, but no' have European food in the village. Try little bit. It is not hot. Mum make special for you."

So, he had a sip of beer, said 'chock dee - cheers' to those around him and started eating the pork curry. It was really quite nice and as long as he tried to remember that it was a late lunch and not breakfast, it went down well enough. As soon as he had finished, a 'Thailand' pulled up and people started piling on the back of it.

A 'Thailand' is a five or six metre long, four-wheeled vehicle powered by a simple, yet powerful diesel engine. The rear of the Thailand is an open, flat-bedded container of about 5000 by 1500 centimetres with framework walls. It will carry about two tons and is the basic farmers' tractor.

Everybody got on and the women loaded up baskets of food and a few boxes. Lek sat in the back, but Craig had to sit up front. Lek was right behind him.

"Where are we going now, Lek?"

"Go see family and friends," she replied and off they went. Two more Thailands pulled in behind them, both full of people.

It was quite exhilarating travelling at forty miles an hour over rough terrain through rice fields going God knew where. Lek passed him a beer and told him to share it with the driver, who was her uncle. He seemed very happy to be offered a beer by a foreigner.

After about ten miles, the wagon train pulled into a courtyard.

"We go see family my uncle, come on, Craig" and he could see that their contingent of fifty or sixty people were already jumping down and running to greet the hosts.

There were trestle tables laid out, so Craig presumed that they were expected. Lek told him to sit down, gave him a beer and said: "Wait."

She was gone again, but her youngest brother, Ngat, 26, sat opposite him and beamed.

Food came as if from a caterer and everyone was having a good time. Lek returned about thirty minutes later, but by now, Craig was getting used to being without her and relying on her family to look after him. When she returned she said: "Ngat take good care of you? He tell me go away because he want to take care of you. I say: 'OK, but only thirty minutes'. You not mind, eh? My family want to take care you. They like you. Say you have 'jai dee' – good heart."

He could only smile, but he meant it. It was such a totally new experience.

Two hours later, everyone boarded the Thailands and they were off again. Back the way they had come. Suddenly, it started raining and within seconds it had become a storm or a monsoon, but no-one seemed to care. The people in the back were laughing and joking and everybody was soaked through. But it was warm rain. The same temperature as you might expect in a bathroom shower at home on a warm summer's evening.

It was not a shame that it was raining, it was welcome.

By the time they got back, everyone was totally drenched, a little bit tired and ready for a meal again, so the three Thailands went their separate ways and when they had stopped, so did the passengers.

"You OK, Telak?" Lek said when they were back in their room. "You want go shower first? People wait for you go shower first."

Craig felt that he oughtn't to let them do that for him, so he showered first and went back to the room. Lek powdered him down and he lay there to read or dose as the mood took him.

He had not felt so pampered and been so relaxed amongst strangers in his whole life and the funny thing was that nobody that he had met so far had been able to speak to him yet.

He wondered why so many people had said that they had had problems in the villages and he wondered if his were yet to come.

Craig woke up at eight o'clock to see Lek's smiling face not twelve inches from his own.

"Come on, telak, people wait you outside, or you want to sleep some more?"

"No, I am not tired, what time is it now? Why people wait me?"

"It is eight o'clock, people wait you; want to meet you; want you have good holiday in the village. Many people never see falang before too. I want people meet my telak too."

So he got up, had a swig of cold water and allowed Lek to take him outside again.

There were about twenty people out there, about six or eight of whom he recognized: Lek's mother, of course, Lek's sister, her husband, Lek's brother and the uncle who had driven them earlier and a few whose names he could not remember or had never been told. They all grinned at him, pointed to sit down and someone gave him a beer. All the food on the table, eight or ten plates of it, was also moved towards him as well.

"Here we go again!," he thought and smiled at everyone, not even bothering to look around for Lek, because he felt so at home.

Ten minutes later, Deo wheeled in a 27" TV screen and Ngat plugged it into a karaoke set that he had set up nearby. That was to be the evening's entertainment. They threw themselves into it with gusto. People were dancing and everybody took a turn to sing a song.

Everyone except Craig that is, because no-one had a single record in English, which surprised him more than a little. He was glad about it too, because although he was from the Land of Song, he thought of karaoke as a malicious invention of the Japanese to inflict pain on the world in revenge for having lost the Second World War.

Despite his misapprehension over the karaoke, the evening went well and he found that he was still raring to go when the party melted in ten minutes flat at midnight. People just disappeared into the darkness.

"Where is everybody, Lek?" Craig asked.

"People go home. New day tomorrow. Start again tomorrow. Come, have shower. We go to bed too."

And it was done.

And it had been the best day he had ever had and he had spoken about one hundred words all day and to only one person and it did not matter.

He and Lek slept together very happily.

She knew that it had been a success as well.

Craig awoke at eight o'clock on Sunday morning and he was surprised that there was no-one beside him. The shutters were open and he could hear people outside, so he assumed that Lek must have got up early. However, he did not feel inclined to get started that early, so he pulled on his short trousers, lay on the bed and started to read.

When Lek came in an hour later to see what he wanted to do, Craig said:

"Please, telak, just leave me here until midday and then I will gladly join in again, but your family party too much for me. I cannot, I must rest."

It was a half-truth. The real truth was that Craig didn't like being the centre of attention. Not that he had ever been it before except on birthdays. He found it wearing, if the truth be told. He preferred to sit on the periphery and watch. If he went out, he would be on show again. He would do it, for Lek's sake, but he wanted time to recharge his batteries before that. Lek loved it and he liked that about her, it sort of balanced them out. Lek could have the attention and he could have the anonymity.

Although not here in the village. Not yet.

The rest of the day proceeded much the same way as the day before had. It was great fun. There was lots of food, all the drink that an army could ask for and enough smiling faces to make anybody's holiday.

What amused Craig, was that at midnight, everybody just melted into the darkness again without saying good night.

Craig woke up just before eight and again, Lek had already left. It was strange, thought Craig, in Pattaya Lek seemed to be able to survive on just as much sleep as she had time for, but back home in the village, she hardly slept at all. He didn't realize that Lek rarely came home more than once a year and that she was making the most of it. Also she knew that she could sleep on the bus going back to Pattaya that evening.

He put yesterday's clothes on and lay on top of the mattress to read his book and listen to the sounds from outside. He particularly liked the call of one bird, which he later found out to be called 'Nok Ian', or that was what it sounded like anyway.

Meanwhile, Lek had borrowed her mother's motorbike again and had taken Soom to the local town of Fort Phichai. Phichai is not large, but it is famous all over Thailand for the battles that were fought there against the Burmese in the late eighteenth century. The town, once the provincial capital of Uttaradit, was named after Praya Phichai Dap Hak (Broken Sword) who led the last great battle there.

Lek wanted to have some time alone with her daughter and to spoil her a little. She knew that Craig could look after himself and that her family would take care of him too, but she guessed that he would probably just read until she got back.

Lek first took Soom for an ice cream and they talked about Soom's school life, her home life and her social life. Soom seemed to be doing fairly well in school, Lek knew this from her school reports, but Soom genuinely seemed to like school and enjoyed learning. She told her mother that she hoped to be a vet's assistant when she grew up. Life at home with her grandmother, her uncle and her cousin was fine too. The house was not large, but she found it cosy to be with her small family in the village where she knew everyone and felt safe. Lek was more than a little hurt that Soom had not mentioned missing her, but she thought it for the best that way.

In truth, Soom did miss her mother, but she felt that it was kinder not to bring it up, after all, she reasoned, her mother must have chosen not to live with them for some reason. Soom knew dozens of children whose parents were working away. It was quite normal for parents of working age to give their children to their parents to look after so that they could go away to work for better money.

It gave the old people something to do as well. There was no social security and no old age pension, but parents got paid by their children for bringing up their grandchildren. It kept the elderly involved with the family, meant that they didn't have to do back-breaking work and ensured that they didn't go hungry. It was good for everybody.

Soom seemed happy and that was the main thing. Satisfied with that, they went shopping for some clothes. Soom got kitted out from head to toe with new gear and they had great fun choosing it. Both of them thought that this was what it should be like every day, not just once or twice a year, but neither of them mentioned it.

They got back to the village at about midday, and Lek went in to get Craig. "Craig," she said, "quickly have shower, get dressed, I want you meet someone."

He did as he was told and he was introduced to Soom. Soom waaied and Craig waaied back. Then Craig held out his hand and said: "Nice to meet you, Soom."

"Nice to meet you too," she replied without a trace of a foreign accent.

"You did not tell me that your daughter spoke English so well. That was perfect."

As they sat down together, Soom giggled shyly and said: "We learn in school." That was not perfect, but the accent was still very good, thought Craig. "Mae says you come from Wales, they speak English in Wales? Not speak Wales?"

"Yes, we speak English in Wales and about 25% speak Welsh too. Not speak Wales, speak Welsh."

"Oh, OK, thank you," she said. And that was it, Lek took over and began talking to her daughter in Thai. The next hour passed something like this: one of them would say something; the other would look at Craig; they would both start laughing and then the other would reply. Lek's mother put down a bottle of Chang beer for Craig and a container of iced water for the other two. Craig didn't mind being talked about as if he were not even there, in fact he quite liked to see mother and daughter doing well and besides, it meant that he didn't have to think of anything to say.

The inevitable food arrived soon after they sat down. Seven or eight plates of different dishes, but Lek's mother didn't join them. She wanted to go to the Wat as she did every Monday afternoon apparently. The afternoon passed very pleasantly in this manner until Lek got up about two beers later and said: "Soom, you take care Craig for little bit. I mus' do something" and she slipped into the chapel-cum-bedroom.

Soom and Craig chatted a while: "Where is everyone today,

Soom?" asked Craig. "Working. Holiday has finished, so people must go back to work. I do not must go back to school today. I must go back to school tomorrow. Good, neh?"

"'Neh', was the first bit of Thai accent Craig had heard Soom use." He knew now that her English was not as good as he had first thought, but it was still pretty impressive for a ten year old and her accent was almost flawless. The schools must be pretty good up here he reasoned.

Lek came back after twenty minutes with the suitcase and she sent Soom off to get two more beers – one each. "We have to go soon. Drink one more beer and wait for friend finish working, come take us to Phitsanulok bus station." Craig didn't really want to go, but it had been gradually dawning on him all day that he was going home in three days time. He had had a fantastic weekend but now it was over and he regretted it very much.

None of the things that he had been told to look out for had happened. No-one had asked him for money, he had not had to pay for all the drinks and they had not been to the supermarket. In fact, he had not spent one Baht since he paid for the tickets and presents three days ago. Which reminded him: "Lek, did you give your family their presents?" "Oh, yes," she said, "everybody very happy with their presents. Everybody say thank you. I forget tell you. Sorry."

"That's all right," he said, "I was just wondering. Shall I give your mother some money?"

"Why? Why you want to give her money?"

"I just thought, I not buy anything here for three days. I drink beer and eat food for free. Never pay anything."

"That is OK, people happy to see you. You my friend, but if you want to give mum something, you can give no problem. What you think of Soom. She speak English good, eh?"

"Yes, very well, er, good. Did she only learn it at school or did you help?" "Only at school, I can not help. I live in Pattaya and I come home see everybody one time or two time for two or three days every year. I can not help. I want to help, but can not." She looked sad and Craig decided to shut up and let her change the subject.

As a pick-up pulled into the front garden, Lek said: "Come on we go now. Friend come." Lek's mother and a young man got out of the car and Soom and her cousin jumped up on the back. Lek got in the back and the seat was put up for Craig to sit in the front, but he did not feel right just going away without saying anything although he suspected that that was the intention.

Anyway, he decided that he had to do what he thought was right, so he went up to Lek's mother and gave her all the notes in his pocket, about 3,000 Baht, said 'Thank you very much for a wonderful weekend', gave her a kiss on the cheek and turned to walk back to the car. Lek had got out and was smiling. Lek and her mother exchanged a few words and a laugh and then she and Craig got in.

"What you do with my mum?" she asked.

"Oh, I said thank you, gave her some money for the food and the beer and gave her a kiss goodbye. That's all."

Lek got out her phone and made a call. Five minutes later she said: "My mum say thank you for the money, but not necessary and thank for the kiss. It is the first one for more than ten years when my father die." She repeated it in Thai and everyone laughed. "It is the first time I see someone kiss my mother outside the house in my life," said Lek. "Very nice. Very funny. First time. Mum very shy, she say she very happy not have everyone there to see."

Craig had not thought about that aspect and felt a bit foolish. He had not seen anyone kiss or hold hands all weekend, it just struck him. Even Lek, who always held his hand in Pattaya, had not done so in the village.

When they got to the station, they had time to go for a small meal to thank the driver and spend fifteen minutes with Soom and then the

bus arrived and they were on there way. There was no kissing or hug-
ging or even the shaking of hands; just a lot of 'bye-bye's and a few
teary eyes, but Lek was waving at her daughter waving back until they
were out of sight and then Lek covered her head with the blanket and
went to sleep or at least pretended to. Craig was alone again, but that
had never bothered him much and it didn't bother him now either. He
had had a wonderful weekend and he had a lot to think about.

Lek's hand reached for his and drew it under the blanket.

Lek was crying softly because she missed her daughter already, but
she was also pleased with the way that the weekend had gone. She was
pleased that her family liked Craig and that he seemed to like them. The
same with her friends. She had done virtually all she could now to get
this man to fall in love with her, the rest was up to him and Fate. Eventually, she fell asleep as she knew she would. She had always had the
ability to sleep whenever she wanted to

For his part, Craig was thinking about the weekend, Lek, her
mother and her daughter. They had seemed to accept him genuinely.
They had made him more than welcome. Soom had been nice too.
Everyone had been nice. He could not find fault in any part of the
weekend at all, even if he had wanted to.

The problem for him was Thursday. It was coming up fast and he
did not want to go back to his old life having discovered this new and
exciting one. Craig tried to sleep, but sleep never came easy to him and
this day was to be no exception, so he just looked out of the window
and let his mind wander.

Daddy's Hobby

17 THE LAST FEW DAYS

When they arrived back in Pattaya at five o'clock in the morning, both of them were thinking more about how much time they had left together, rather than what time it was. Pattaya never slept completely anyway, so they took a taxi to the Pig, put their bag inside and went for a walk. They held hands as they normally did and walked towards the beach. It was Tuesday, only one full day left together and then they would be 5,500 miles apart.

Lek had been counting the days down for a while, but it was a bit of a shock to Craig. There were still people at Daddy's Hobby, but Lek said that they had been sitting in the bus for eight hours and wanted to stretch their legs.

She also promised to return within twenty minutes.

They walked along the beach feeling sad but neither voiced their emotions for a long time until Craig said: "That was a great weekend, Lek. I loved being on holiday with you and meeting your family and friends. I wish we could do it again soon, but I have to go home the day after tomorrow."

"Yes" was all she could muster up, so they turned around and went back to Daddy's Hobby.

"Oooh, ooh," shouted Beou as they approached the bar. She had obviously had a fair bit to drink, but she seemed stable. "Sit down, join the party, my friends come back from UK tonight. You know David and Ian? No I don' think so. You remember them, Lek?"

Lek did, but she didn't really want to be reminded about it at that precise moment. "Yes, of course," she said, "How are you? You have good flight? I want you meet my friend, Craig." They all shook hands.

Lek shook hands at arm's length, she didn't want to be grabbed and kissed. Or worse.

As quickly as she could, Lek steered them away from the drunken crowd and into the safety of the back of the bar. "I am sorry," she said to Craig, "old friends from Beou from before. I know them long time too, but I don' want to talk to them now. I want talk only to you, be-cause we only have sixty hours left before you go home." She waited for that to sink in and hoped for a response.

"Let's have quick beer and go back to the hotel," was not quite what she was hoping for, but it was good enough.

Back in the hotel, they got undressed, showered together and went to bed. Long after Lek had fallen asleep, Craig lay there thinking about the rest of his life.

The morning followed a fairly typical routine for mornings after staying up late: they got up and showered just in time to get a breakfast without having to pay for it again, but the atmosphere was very sub-dued. When Lek said that she had to go to book a taxi for the day after tomorrow, she left Craig sitting alone.

One of the guys at the bar stopped by the table on his way to the gents: "How did it go up country? Did they sting you?"

"Not at all," Craig replied, "I had a fantastic time and I'd go back any day I was invited."

"Oh, good for you. I'm glad about that. You must've found a good one," but the man moved off crest-fallen.

Craig couldn't understand the ex-pats, but he was more concerned why Lek had not asked him to go with her to book the taxi. Lek was wondering that exact same thing: why hadn't Craig offered to go with her? Neither of them wanted to expose their feelings too much, but the problem was that there was not much time left for subtlety. Lek de-cided that her next move would be to leave him alone for most of the day on some pretext or other hoping that absence may make the heart grow fonder, but then to shower him with reminder gifts before he went home, so she went off looking for inspiration in the shopping malls.

When Lek didn't come back quickly, Craig phoned Will and then went to his hotel for a swim and a chat. "I don't know what to do," he confessed to Will within earshot of Goong. "I love the girl to bits, but I am going home the day after tomorrow and God knows what will happen then. She may forget all about me or someone else may come along and catch her eye. What can you do from 5,500 miles away?"

"I don't know" said Will, "I have loved half-a-dozen of the beauties over the years, but I forget all about them when I get home. This is a holiday, but it's Never-Never Land for me. It doesn't really exist in my world. This is a fantasy place where you can do what you want. Well, let me rephrase that, where any sane fantasies can come true. It is not worth falling in love with your nurse in my opinion. I get a new nurse to administer my fantasies every time, sometimes more than one, although this time I'm back with Goong again."

"First time for me though. Same girl twice in a row. Usually, it's a different girl every week, sometimes more than that. As long as you treat them right and don't make them lose face, they don't mind. They know what most blokes are like and they know that most blokes that come here are already married too. You have to do what you want to do, but I am not the best guy in the world to advise you. I will say this though, I have never seen you looking happier. Sometimes I'd see you after work and you used to look down right miserable. That Lek has certainly perked you up, but she's a lovely girl, so she is too."

None of this was helping much, but then Craig knew enough to know that no-one could help him. He was on his own. Goong was pretending to be asleep, but not very well. She was itching to phone Lek and tell her the good news that she was overhearing, but she didn't want to be too obvious. However, the strain became too much for her, so she made an excuse that she had to go to the Ladies' and hurried off.

"Lek, Lek, great news! Craig loves you to bits!" she whispered down he phone once she was locked in a cubicle. "Craig is here now with us and he is telling Will that he does not know what to do because he has to go home, but he does not want to because he loves you and will miss you too much. Isn't that great? I wish that Will would say the same about me. You like Craig too, don't you?"

"Yes. I do. Very much. I even think that I am falling for him badly, but just talking like that to his friend is not going to help either of us when he gets on that plane the day after tomorrow, is it? He has to get his act together and bloody do something about it. Actually DO something about it. Anyway, thanks for letting me know. Where are you? At your hotel? Listen, do me a favour and don't tell anyone about this conversation. I may come around there later, but I may not. If he leaves though, be sure to let me know. See you this evening, darling Little Sister and thank you."

Goong hurried back to the poolside hoping that she hadn't missed too much.

"… we had a fantastic weekend up in her village, Baan Suay. I have never lived in a village before, they are too quiet, but I could live there, I think. Maybe it's because I'm getting older. Britain doesn't in-terest me and never has done really. I love my family, but we don't live in each other's pockets and it's not really that far to go back if I had to or wanted to. You know..."

"Hang on a sec, this is going to be a long one, I can see. Goong, shout up two beers and something for yourself, please, as soon as pos-sible. OK, I'm with you again."

"Lek said to me when we were in the bus that my journey to south

Wales was 5,500 miles and took twelve and a half hours, but her journey home also took twelve hours or so normally although it is only 700 km. And she's right. She lives as far away from her village as I do from mine, if you measure the distance in time not in feet and inches. A lot more expensive, I'll grant you, but my journey is easier than hers as well."

"You have got it bad, mate. You are even starting to justify or rationalise something. What I am not sure yet. I suppose you are saying that you like Lek enough to come here again are you?"

"I really don't know what I am saying. I am just running off at the mouth, saying what comes into my mind and hoping that when I hear what I have to say that it will make more sense to me. Sorry if I'm boring you."

"It is not a question of boring me, I was getting tired of that book anyway, but I just don't know what to say. Maybe that is better anyway, if you only want to hear yourself speak. No offence meant, Craig."

"None taken. I know that no-one can sort this one out for me."

At that moment, Craig's phone rang. "Hello, Craig, where are you? I am talking with Beou, you want party for go home tomorrow night? Beou want to make party for you, so you, so everybody can say goodbye you. You want? Ah, good! Only 5,000 Baht, is that OK? We take care everything. See you later. Come to Daddy's Hobby when you want to see me. Bye."

He felt as if a bit of wind had left his sails. That was the sting. Not a very big one, granted, but a way of getting something out of him before he left. As if he had not spent enough already. Still, he reasoned, people had been good to him and he did want to say goodbye and 5,000 Baht was not much to him although it was a month's wages to some of the girls. He felt ashamed of himself for thinking like that, but he had thought it.

"Will, Lek just suggested, and I agreed, that we have a going-away party for me tomorrow night in Daddy's Hobby. I hope you and Goong will come along."

"I wouldn't miss it for the world! Beou's parties are legendary, I've been to dozens of them. She will do you proud, don't worry and with Lek as your friend and having been to her village, I'm sure that you will get something really special. How much is she charging you, if you don't mind me asking? 7,500?"

Craig started to feel even more guilty about suspecting Lek's motives: "No, 5,000," he said, "but I don't know what it entails," he added to ameliorate his embarrassment with himself for being suspicious of their motives.

Lek for her part was certainly not looking for a quick buck from him before he left, she was trying to play his heart strings. The money would cover the cost of the party, but it would not give Beou her customary bonanza, she was sacrificing a cut in profits for her cousin as well, but Beou was happy to do almost anything to help her cousin achieve her goals and so were a lot of other people, because Lek was a very popular woman.

"OK, well I'm going to have another swim, have another beer and then go round to pick up Lek at Daddy's Hobby when I'm dry, as I didn't bring a towel with me. What are you doing today?"

"I have no plans, my friend, I'm doing what I really enjoy doing right now. I have a good friend, a beautiful girl, sunshine, a swimming pool and a cold beer. What more could anyone want on holiday? Or off holiday, for that matter? Give us a call later and tell us what you are doing. I'll join you for that dip first though. Goong, shout up two more Heinekens, darling, please."

Craig got to Daddy's Hobby at about four o'clock which was more by accident than by design. It crossed his mind that this might be the last time he would be there at his favourite hour watching the girls get ready for the night. Lek went straight over and gave him a kiss and

Beou greeted him straight away too. In fact, all the girls seemed to be just that little bit more attentive than usual. He was already enjoying it too much.

"OK, Craig," Beou said as she and Lek sat down opposite him. What do you want to eat tomorrow night? For 5,000, you already have one roasting pig on a spit. What else? Sandwiches, soup, er, I mean stew?"

"Well, what a whole pig?"

"Yes, maybe twenty-five, thirty kilos, OK?"

"Yeah, fine," he said not really comprehending how much meat that was. "And some sandwiches, great. I'm not sure about the stew though."

"It is a good idea to have some chicken stew for if Arabs come. Some Arabs not eat pork. Some eat on holiday, but some not eat."

"OK, chicken stew and some spring rolls too, please. Is that all right?"

"Yes, popia. No problem. Lek know what you like, she can tell me; Lek help me make everything tomorrow, OK."

"Yes, fine," he said as his heart sank. That meant that they had already had their last evening out alone together.

He realized it and Lek had hoped that he would.

Will and Goong came down later and they all had a lovely evening. Beou found the time to join in too and all the girls found time to give him a kiss on the cheek or to squeeze his shoulder as they passed. Many wanted to know what he had thought of Baan Suay and whether he had had a good time there.

He went back to the hotel with a heavy heart, although Lek appeared to be in the best of spirits. They showered together and Lek gave him a massage in the nude with some oil that she had bought specially for the occasion.

He was in Seventh Heaven, but the parking metre was running out fast.

They stayed in bed until late on Wednesday morning, but they made it down for breakfast before midday. At breakfast, Lek explained that it was part of her duty to help prepare the bar for the night's party. Craig was rather disappointed, but Lek said that he could come and watch or even help, if he wanted. He said that he might, so she gave him a kiss and left.

Craig was left sitting there wondering what to do, so he picked up the Bangkok Post and went to the bar to read it, freeing up the table for others who were waiting to eat. At the bar he sat on a bar stool, ordered a Guinness for a change and started to read the paper.

When he had finished his beer, the owner of the Pig, who happened to be checking the till receipts for the day before said: "Another one, Craig?" and gave the glass to one of the barmaids. "You're going home tomorrow, aren't you? Have you got a taxi booked yet?"

"Yes, Lek said it would be here for six pm. My flight is at eleven thirty."

"I thought so. Have you enjoyed yourself? Good, good. Look, there's a bloke staying here, Michael, I don't know whether you've met him, nice chap, but he says he's having trouble getting a taxi at the right price. Would you let him share yours for half the fare? You'd be helping him out. Company for you too, if you're going up alone. What do you think?"

"Yes, all right. Tell him that the taxi will leave at six, no later. I don't want to be hanging around waiting for him. Otherwise, no problem."

After finishing the paper, he went down to see Lek, who was laughing and joking with Beou, Noi and half-a-dozen other girls. It was a good atmosphere, but he just felt in the way and restless, so he left Mott and Lek standing on the bar pinning up balloons and walked down to Beech Road. It was nearly three o'clock and he knew that he was going to miss all this and it made him sad.

An A-Go-Go bar was offering pints of beer at half price to fill the place up early, so he allowed himself to be shown in by the tout advertising on the pavement. He sat at a table alone and a waitress asked what he wanted: "A pint of draught Chang, please." He studied the girls who were all completely naked except for a see-through net curtain around their waists. They had numbers on arm bands and they were all looking at him smiling. The bar must have just opened because he was the only one in it. He felt lonelier than ever, even in a male paradise like this.

The music stopped and the girl on the far right of the line of dancers stepped down from the stage and another one got up on the left hand side. They all moved along a spot and the girl who had come down came over to him. "Hello, sir. You like something?" she said, "What your name? Where you come from? Ah, Ankit, er, Engeland? I sit with you talking? Sorry, not speak Engelish so good. Only little bit."

Craig pointed at the stool in front of him. She hopped up smiling and they sat knee-to knee. She was really beautiful, every inch of her and there was nothing left to the imagination. Like most Thai ladies, she was clean shaven - all over. She moved her stool closer so that they could talk over the music and brushed her small breasts against him. "I never see you before. You only come to Thailand not long? You want buy me a drink?"

'Why not?' he thought. 'I'm going home tomorrow and all this will be like a dream. Just a distant memory'. "OK, what you want?," he said. She surprised him by ordering a cheap beer and not an expensive Lady Drink as he was expecting. When it arrived she leaned forward, said cheers, clinked glasses and slipped her free hand up the leg of his short trousers. He was wearing boxers, so her hand found what she was looking for instantly. It was pretty hard to miss anyway, with all these naked women around.

"Ooh," she said, "you horny. Have big cock. You make me horny too. I start wet now. Feel" and she put her glass down, opened her legs and put his hand in there. He had a feel around. "You want to come upstairs? Make love," she asked, still holding his cock. You want make love or I give you very good blow job."

"Nah," he lied "too early. I want drink little bit here, walk little bit, one more drink, walk little bit. Talk to people. Maybe later." He beckoned her off the stool, opened her legs and slipped his thumb into her, she did a little dance and at that point he had to remove her hand, but only because he did not want to have to walk about with wet trousers. Meanwhile, the music had changed again and another dancer was making for them.

He thought it best to leave. That was the first time he had witnessed anything like that and it had all been so easy. He assumed that it would have been different if there had been other customers in the bar, but he was not so sure. It was all very nice, but so unreal, the whole of Pattaya was unreal and his holiday had been like a teenage male fantasy. He paid his bill and went back to Lek. "Where you go, telak?" she asked him.

"I go to A-Go-Go around the corner, have cheap beer. Half price, but only have one. Boring."

"OK, good. I finish in thirty minutes, you want one more beer wait for me then we go back to hotel. Sleep little bit, shower and come back here for seven o'clock?"

"Yes, OK." He felt a little bit guilty, but then there was a very good chance that he would never see Lek again after twenty-six hours or so. He still didn't know what to make of it all.

Lek for her part had played nearly all her cards, but still had one or two up her sleeves. For the moment though, she was just acting as if tomorrow would be just another day and hoping that Craig would make sure that it would not be.

They went back down to Daddy's Hobby at eight o'clock. Lek appeared to be looking forward to the do, but Craig was decidedly down-beat about it. In fact, if Lek had not been so keen on going, he wouldn't have bothered. As soon as they arrived, the party started, but then they were thirty minutes late and it probably would have started without them anyway. Lek showed them to their reserved stools and went off to organise the food.

"All right, Craig? We thought you weren't coming," said Will. "Anything wrong?"

"Not really. I'm just a bit pissed off about going back tomorrow, that's all. I've had such a great time that … well, Barry is never going to be the same again. In fact, I'll probably never be the same again. This time tomorrow, I'll be in Bangkok waiting for the sodding plane to take me home. But home to what?"

"Oh dear! You have got it bad, haven't you? Here get this down you," he said handing him a double gin and tonic to go with the beer that Lek had already put in front of him.

The party went well and dozens of people turned up, but Craig knew none of them. He could see that everyone including Will was having a good time, but he would not have minded leaving after thirty minutes. The food was extremely good, that was the only thing he could find good to say about it, although he knew that that was unfair by the look on everyone elses' faces.

To Craig, there were too many people, it took too long to get served and the music was too loud. That was probably the only legitim-ate complaint because you could not hear anything that anyone said. It was like being deaf but with an extremely bad case of tinnitus. Twice in the evening, Craig made an excuse to go to the Pig to use the toilet, al-though the real reason was to get a bit of peace and quiet and be miser-able on his own.

The truth was that he would rather have stayed in the quiet of the Pig and read his book, but that was not possible, or rather it was, but it

was not the sort of thing that he could do to the people who were trying to give him a good send off.

Luckily for Craig the party could not go on as long as it might otherwise have done, because the next day was August the 12th – the
queen's birthday and Mothers' Day all rolled into one and the drinking
of alcohol was prohibited by law on this day and the king's birthday. It
was also Lek's birthday, but he didn't know that.

However, Beou kept the bar open until she received a warning
from the local bobby on the beat at about one a.m.. That was late
enough for most people anyway. Many of the people partying were
professional balloon-chasers. That is, they watch out for balloons during the day, knowing that that means a party, music and free food in
the evening. Some of them went to strangers' going away parties every
night of the week just for the food.

By one thirty, everyone had gone except the staff, Craig and Lek
and Will and Goong. The staff were cleaning up and the other four
were sitting in the back of the bar out of sight enjoying a few last beers
and finishing off the sandwiches. Lek also had two bags of sandwiches,
spring rolls and pork to take back to the hotel for the next day, Will
had the same.

"Well, me ol' mate, that was a good do. As good as any I've been
to in my fourteen years of coming to Thailand. Beou, Lek and the girls
did you proud."

"Yes, thanks everyone. It was a really good party. Sorry, I had such
a long face for most of the evening, but I am not looking forward to
going home."

"Why?" asked Mott, "Don't you like flying? I want to fly some
day."

"It's not that so much, Mott, although the journey will be boring. I
have made so many new friends here and I just do not want to do
home. That's all."

They were waiting for him to mention Lek by name but he didn't.

They all went their separate ways at four a.m. after lengthy and teary good-byes, kisses and hugs.

Back in the Pig, they showered, got into bed and went straight to sleep, because they were tired and more than a little drunk. The next morning saw them with hangovers and they had to rush to get down before twelve o'clock for breakfast. They ate in virtual silence, but after the plates had been cleared away, Craig reached across the small table and took one of Lek's hands in both of his.

"Well, telak, I go home in six hours. I don't want to go, but I must go. I want to stay here, but I don't see how I can."

"I un'erstand, Craig," Lek replied. "Maybe you come back next year and see me working in Daddy's Hobby. Do you have wife and job go home for?"

"No, telak, nothing like that. I told you before I never marry and not have girlfriend for two years, maybe more and I do not have a job. Job finish two years ago. I try to make new job for me with the Internet, but it is not easy. I am sure many people you see before tell you lies. Say not married, but married. Say not have babies, but have.

No, everything I have told you is the truth. You can believe that, it is just that I have to go back tonight. Maybe if I think before I can delay flight for one or two weeks, but I not think. Stupid, but same, same, one day I must go home. What are you going to do after I have gone, Lek?"

"I have to work. I must pay my mother for take care Soom and Soom must have clothes and things for school, you know. I cannot stop working. Ayr have my job now, but she is good friend, she give me back."

"I don't want you to go back to work in the bar, Lek. Not right away. You have been so good to me, introducing me to your friends and family that I want to give you something."

He handed her 10,000 Baht.

"I know it is not much, but you can have two weeks holiday in your village and take over from Ayr next month. What you think?"

She didn't know what to think. It was something and nothing. It was not a token of affection and, although she could last for two months on that in the village, she still had to relieve Ayr or give up the job. It was not just only money, but an almost completely useless gift.

"Thank you," she said, "if you want to pay for me to go see my daughter for two weeks, I will do that. Thank you from me and from Soom. She will be happy if I stay there for two weeks. Now I go make suitcase for you and you must pay the boss for the room."

That was true, he had only paid a small deposit a month ago and now he would have to pay the balance. Lek went upstairs and packed his suitcase. Hidden under the top layer, she put a silver-framed photo of herself, her favourite one along with a message that one of her friends had helped her write in English. She also put a bag of lam yai in there, Craig's new-found favourite fruit and a few cans of Chang beer, which Craig had said he had never seen in the UK. Then she carried the case and the sandwiches downstairs so that the maids could clean the room.

When she got down to the bar, it was empty except for Craig and the boss. "Hello, Lek," he said, "we are just having a few beers. The bar is closed and the restaurant is closed. I told all the girls to finish at one because it is a Bank Holiday. They can go home and see mama for a surprise. Do you want something to drink?"

After a drink or two, the boss shook their hands, said it was nice to have met them and gave them an open bottle of Thai wine to drink until the taxi came. Will also turned up with Goong and they sat in the back out of the way of prying eyes.

It was not much fun for anyone. They drank the wine and ate the sandwiches and Will bought another bottle of wine from the supermarket nearby, which the receptionist opened for them.

It was a welcome release for Will and Craig when the taxi arrived, but Goong and Lek were left perplexed.

Lek put her hand in a bag and pulled out a garland which she hung around Craig's neck and she threw her arms around him. They both started crying and Will and Goong went outside to tell the taxi driver that he would not be long. Five minutes later, Craig was outside, he kissed Lek again, promised to phone, kissed Goong and shook hands with Will. "I'll see she's all right until I go home next week," he said.

There was already someone sitting in the front seat, whom Craig supposed to be Michael, then the car backed up and they were away. That was the end of that episode, but he felt bad about it. Michael introduced himself, but rather than chat, Craig feigned tiredness and sat back in the rickety taxi to stare out of the window for the next two hours.

Lek couldn't wait to open a bottle of Thai whiskey with her friends. She wanted to get drunk and quickly. The three of them walked down to Daddy's Hobby and sat with Noi. The bar was closed officially, but it still needed Noi there to guard it and some of the girls just did not have anything better to do. There were no customers, but the girls were drinking whiskey out of coffee mugs. The three friends joined in, although Will drank gin and tonic.

After half a bottle of Scotch and thought, Lek phoned Ayr and asked her if she would do the job for another fortnight because she had to go home. Ayr , of course, agreed.

Daddy's Hobby

18 HOME SWEET HOME

Lek woke up fairly early and decided to catch the first bus up country that she could. She didn't care whether it was VIP, First Class, Second Class or a hay wagon, she just wanted to get out of Pattaya and go home. She had no idea whether Craig would ever ring her, she honestly thought that it could go either way. Or that maybe he would phone for a few weeks and then the calls would stop. That was probably the most likely. She had seen it happen many times before and indeed it had happened to her before as well.

She got to the bus station on Sukhumvit Road just before midday and was lucky enough to get a bus to Phitsanulok at twelve thirty. It was not much of a bus, in fact it was the worst kind, but at least she would be moving in the right direction. She looked at her watch for the umpteenth time and calculated what time it would be in the UK and where Craig might be. As it happened, he was just getting off the disembarkation bus at Schiphol airport, but she didn't know that. She assumed that he was still in mid-air.

Lek was sitting on a cramped, sweaty, fan-cooled bus that had the windows wide open for extra cooling, but that let all the dust of the road in too. Worse than that, the soldier sitting next to her kept trying to strike up a conversation, but she really was not interested. This was why, she reminded herself, that she always travelled by VIP AirCon.

Craig had bumped into Michael again in the airport. He had five hours to kill and Michael seven, so they decided to put their bags in lockers and go into Amsterdam by shuttle. There was nothing to do at that time of the morning, so they just walked from the main train station down to Dam Square and then left to Leidse Square, where Craig knew from past experience there would be something open. They found a cake shop that had a few tables where they could stop for a coffee, so that is what they did.

"Did you leave anyone behind, Craig? I left a beautiful lady and I miss her already. She couldn't see me off because she had to go home to take care of her kid. I'm going back as soon as I can get a few shillings together. How about you?"

"Yes, I suppose I did. I'm not sure really." Up until that time, he had tried not to give Lek too much thought, but Michael was beginning to make him consider her. "We'll have to see. I had a great holiday with a woman I met, but…"

"Oh, the one that I saw you with at the Pig. Yeah, she was gorgeous. I'd definitely go back for that one."

"What a strange attitude," thought Craig, "he doesn't even know her, but he's saying that after seeing her just once. No wonder so many foreigners make mistakes and get ripped off."

"Yes, well, she's a looker all right, but we'll have to see."

"Ah, get away with you. You were both mad about each other. Anyone could see that. Go back to her as soon as you can, that's my advice. Send them a few pounds every month, give them a baby to play with and go back as often as you can. That's what I'd do anyway."

He meant well, but he was starting to become annoying and Craig wanted to get away. "Look, Michael, I used to live in Amsterdam, and I want to go to see some friends. You're all right to get back alone are you? It's not far to the station. If you forget the way, a taxi will cost less than a fiver. So, I'll be off now. Nice to meet you. All the best. I'll just pay for the coffee and cake."

"Yes, nice to meet you too, Craig. I'll pay the bill. Leave it to me. Thanks for everything. Bye."

They shook hands and parted amicably. Craig just wanted to be on his own and he had started thinking about Lek again now. He did miss her, there was no question about that.

He flew into Cardiff Airport at three pm and friends were waiting to pick him up in a car. He dropped his bag off at his flat and went straight to the pub. He went home at seven on Friday night and gratefully put his feet up to watch TV. Coincidentally, Lek was arriving in her village at the same moment although there it was one a.m. on Saturday.

When Lek got home, her mother and her daughter were waiting for her with plates of food. They knew when she would be home, because she had phoned ahead and taken a taxi, something she didn't like to do alone normally. Lek decided to come clean with her family and told them that Craig had gone home and that she was not sure whether she would ever see him again.

However, she did go to pains to point out that he had asked her to go home for at least a fortnight and given her the money to be able to do it. They didn't stay up long and slept in the communal room upstairs as a family as they had before Craig arrived.

Craig was just pleased that his obligations to his friends who had picked him up were over so that he could go home. He was a fan of TV and looked forward to being able to understand all the programmes that evening, but he drifted in and out of sleep and that was OK too. He woke up at nearly two a.m. and on a whim, decided to phone Lek to say that he had arrived home safely. Something that Thais did as a matter of course if they had been visiting friends.

Two o'clock a.m. in the UK would be eight a.m. in Thailand – not an unreasonable hour to wake her up.

It rang. "Hello, telak, how are you. I am in Wales now and want to phone you. Are you all right?"

"Yes, I am fine" came the sleepy voice. "I am happy to hear you. I was not sleeping, but I travel all night on a bus. I am in the village now same you tell me to do, telak. I say 'Hello Soom'. Soom say hello, Craig."

She had done as she was bid and seemed genuinely happy to be speaking to him again, although he put it down to her never having made a transcontinental call before, which was probably unfair.

"Craig, I miss you. You take everything out of your case already?"

"No, Lek, my friends take me from the airport and go to bar, but I go home early at seven pm, one o'clock Thai time. Then sleep. Wake up now and I want to phone you, because I miss you already."

"You get in your house one o'clock Thai time? Really? Me same too! I get in Mum's house at one ten in the morning. Wow! Wow! Same, same!"

They both laughed and thought that it wonderful to hear the other laugh again.

He looked around his flat and although it was bigger than his hotel room had been, it felt small and drab without Lek to share it. £23 later they said goodbye. Lek lay back for a few minutes before having to get up, and Craig lay back to go to sleep.

They were 5,500 miles apart, but they were happy again.

This was a difficult time for Craig.

The boot was on the other foot now.

Craig phoned Lek every night at between midnight and two, UK time. That suited Lek, because she always got up early in the village anyway and it gave her the rest of the day to do whatever she wanted, not that she wanted to do anything that Craig would disapprove of, but she was more certain of him now. He on the other hand was beginning to wonder how far he could trust her. After all, her ex was still in the vicinity, or so he thought.

People did not help either. There were the normal stories from people who had been to Thailand before and delighted in running the

Thais down. The wife of one of his old friends called Thai women 'the flat-nosed, flip-flop brigade'. She had never been to Thailand, but her husband had and she had found sexy photos in his luggage. Not hubby's fault, oh no, the Thai sluts had led him astray.

There were many ludicrous examples. The seventy year old wife of a man he barely knew asked whether it was true that a Thai woman would 'make love naked on the beach for a shilling'. Another, normally sensible female friend called 'all Thais pimps and child-molesters'. The venom from people whom he had known for years was quite incredible and they had never mentioned Thailand before he went there.

There were also a few that had good things to say about Thailand, but then they had actually been there. It turned out that one of the sub-contractors he had worked with was married to a Thai and another couple he knew had been going to Thailand together for twenty years. They even wanted to retire to Thailand.

One occasion was particularly embarrassing. A young woman of about thirty-two was telling her boyfriend about all 'those third world prostitutes' and he turned around to her and said: "I met you in a club on a Friday night. I paid for all your drinks and took you for a meal and then slept with you. Your friends are still doing it now. They take a fiver out with them and sleep with whoever fills them up with drink, but you lot can afford to pay for yourselves, those 'third world prosti-tutes' do it to support their families. Move your stuff out of my house tomorrow, you fucking hypocrite."

She didn't know where to look or what to say. She melted a little, then threw her wine over him and they never saw her again.

Craig took the only sensible approach and shunned the people with extreme views who had never even been there. There were also the old men who asked how much it would cost to live there, because they were hoping that their pensions would let them live in the paradise which is Thailand for nothing. The fact was that Craig had met many

who were doing just that, but it was a very big step to take and a cur‑
rency swing could change everything.

Craig phoned Lek every night and sometimes she surprised him
with a call too. After three weeks, she rang him up: "Telak, I need
some money. Can you send me 5,000 Baht or I must go working in
Pattaya again. He didn't like it, but the real truth was that he didn't un‑
derstand village life. The only jobs to be had in a village were farming
jobs. Hard manual labour and Lek was not prepared to do that. Craig
assumed that she could just get a job in the village as a… Well, yes as a
what? He had never lived in a village before and had no idea what went
on in one in the UK or in Thailand, so he sent her the money via
SWIFT into her mother's account.

After a couple of weeks, Craig took his stepmother out for a meal
to one of his favourite Italian restaurants. "Rose," he started when they
were into their second course: "I want to go back to Thailand to live
with a girl that I met when I was out there. In fact, I spent all my time
with her because we met within three hours of my being in Pattaya."

"Oh," she said, "what is her name and what does she do for a liv‑
ing?"

"Her name is Lek, but that is only a nickname, all Thais have
them, it means 'small' or 'little one'. What she does or did for a living is
less clear. I met her working in a bar but I am not sure how far her du‑
ties extended."

She looked him full in the eyes and said: "Craig, there but for the
grace of God go many women. Don't ask her what she did and don't
ask anyone else. When are you going back?"

He was totally stunned by the reply, but so happy. She could not
have stopped him going back and he knew that she would never try,
but what she had said was right. It was more than right, it was perfect
and he couldn't help but cry, although he felt pretty bloody silly in the
middle of the Friday afternoon luncheon set.

That evening, Craig went on line and booked a KLM flight to Bangkok and two months in the 'Siam Sawasdee' Hotel on Soi Buakhao. Later that night he phoned Lek to say that he would be going back 'to see her' in a week's time. After giving her the details of the flight, she promised to pick him up from the airport.

Both of them were ecstatic. Lek threw a small party in her mother's house and told everyone the good news about Craig coming back for a holiday, while Craig went down to the pub and started plotting how he could move to Thailand permanently.

He hadn't mentioned that bit unless in case didn't work out and it was very dodgy on the evidence that he had to hand. His idea was that he should be able to make enough off the Internet to support them both. He had enough cash already to take care of their needs for five years, but after that it was house-selling time, which he would rather put off for twenty years.

The factor that would decide where he would live would be Internet connectivity and his ability to learn how to use it to make a living. He had used computers for twenty years and had been on line for seven or eight, but he didn't know how to make money on line. That would be crucial.

Of course, Lek knew none of this, she just thought that she would get another chance to make Craig fall in love with her, if he hadn't done so already, and take her out of Pattaya. Take her anywhere, but preferably abroad with her daughter.

For the intervening days, Craig took back ups of everything that he thought he might need from his desktop computer. He also took various computer manuals and a 'Teach Yourself Thai' Book. He had used teach yourself books before and found them to be a reliable series. He was also considering teaching English, if he had to.

Suddenly, the day before his departure arrived and his family were giving him a going-away party. His mother even gave him a present to give to Lek, a Welsh brooch and the following day he was flying back to Thailand.

He would never have admitted it, but he felt like Batman going to rescue a robin.

However, Lek was not in need of rescue. She knew how to look after herself better than most, but the truth was that she was fed up with the struggle. She was battle-weary and wanted to get out. Even to let someone else take care of her for a while, to have the comfort and support that most women experienced.

She just wanted to be a normal woman; a normal mother and daughter; and yes, a normal wife for the first real time in her life.

He flew out KLM via Amsterdam again and arrived in Bangkok at three o'clock in the afternoon. After passing through customs, he went outside and was regaled by the normal huddle of touts and taxi drivers, but he walked past them all heading for the taxi ranks. There was no sign of Lek, so he took his place in the queue for a taxi.

After about ten minutes, as he was advancing down the queue, there was a whoop and a touch on the shoulder and there was Lek at his side. He was completely beside himself with joy and so was she. They kissed and hugged and she led him away from the rank to where she had a taxi waiting. Goong was there too and Craig was almost equally glad to see her.

"Oh, thank you for coming, Lek and you, Goong."

"We have a taxi over there" and she pointed. A man jumped out of a taxi, took his bags and they got inside. Goong sat in the front to allow the love birds some privacy.

He was in Seventh Heaven again.

Lek was beaming, but reserved and Craig wondered if everything was as it should be, but it was nothing to worry about, only nerves on Lek's behalf.

"How are you, telak?" he asked, "I missed you so much. I am very happy to see you again. For ten minutes, I not sure if you come or you change your mind."

"No, sorry. Taxi have problem, but OK now."

They sped down to Pattaya with Goong, Lek and the taxi driver doing most of the talking. Craig was on his own again, but he was used to it by now. 'In for a penny, in for a pound', he thought again, 'The worst is yet to come'.

When they arrived at the hotel, Lek and Craig checked in and Goong went off to find Will. They arranged to meet at the Pig at nine o'clock and they both went up to their room.

The room was not as good as the one in the Pig, but the hotel did have a swimming pool, which made it all right.

They showered together and then lay on the bed in each other's arms – it was almost like old times.

19 AN EXCITING FUTURE

Lek picked life up where they had left off a month before. In the morning, she would go out to eat a Thai breakfast somewhere come back for half and hour and then go visiting friends or shopping. Breakfast was not included in this package, but they could partake of the buffet breakfast for fifty Baht each.

Lek thought it expensive for the Thai food on offer. It was pretty good value for the European food, but then Craig didn't want to be tied to having to have a breakfast every day.

When Lek came back the second time, somewhere between twelve and one, Craig would either be swimming or studying Thai from his book. He was determined to learn to read, write and speak Thai as soon as possible, partly because he may need it to earn money, if the Internet idea failed to support them.

Lek liked to watch TV or lie under a parasol in the early afternoon because she did not like being in the direct sun until it had waned a little at around four o'clock. Craig used this time for studying Thai or sitting in the Internet cafe across the road from the hotel studying eBay and HTML, the programming language of web sites.

He had made money on the stock exchange before and was interested in knowing more about Forex, but he also knew how risky it was. Too risky for his new life in Thailand, it could bankrupt him quickly and rob him of the chance of a new life. Others were trying it, he had heard them discussing it in the Internet cafe, but it was not for him any more. Times were too volatile after the Twin Towers disaster.

He already had two web sites, so he thought he might go down that route; he might make some money on eBay and he might have to teach English. They were the three strings he had to his bow. The last thing he wanted to do was teach.

Lek was not sure what was happening. Nothing had been said. They were sort of slipping into a comfy couple's routine, which was nice enough, but she wanted to know what was going on. She wanted to have some degree of control back and besides, there had been no talk of money at all.

One night, over dinner, she said: "Telak, you want me go working in Daddy's Hobby again?"

"No, of course not, Lek. I don't want to be stuck all on my own 5,500 miles from my friends and family for ten hours a day while we sleep different shifts. I didn't come all the way over here to wait for you to come home at two a.m. and then wait for you to wake up eleven. Why do you say that?"

"Well, telak, I must have money and I do not have. You pay for hotel, you pay for food, you pay for drinking, you give me 100 Baht if I ask, OK, but I want MY money. Not must ask you for everything every time. You know?"

He knew. It had been an oversight, and a stupid one. "Yes, of course. Sorry, I was not thinking. But if we stay together long time, I cannot pay you same before. I do not want to 'pay' you. I will 'give' you. Not the same. Do you understand? How is 2,000 Baht every week, but I pay for everything same now?"

It was not much, about the same as she would get in the bar but without the work. She didn't hesitate. "OK. We can try. How long you stay here this time?"

"Well, Lek, that is difficult to say. I want to stay with you for all my life. I love you, but I am not a rich man so I must work, but what can I do in Thailand? Maybe there is no work for me. Then what can I or what can we do?"

"You cannot work in Thailand. You do not have visa for working. Not easy for falang get Thai visa for working. I hear falang say many time."

He had not thought about a work permit either. He made a mental note to check that out the next day on the Internet.

"Telak, that is why I do not know anything. At the moment, I have money. No problem. I can stay for two, three, four, five years, I do not know. We can change your life, change my life. We have an exciting future together, if we want it. If you want to try, Lek. I am here to look for ways to make money in Thailand and see if I can have a good life with you and if you can have a good life with me. What you think?"

"You want to live with me all time? You want to marry me?"

He had thought about the first question and the answer was definitely a 'yes', but he had not thought about the second one, although it seemed a natural enough progression. He had never asked anyone to marry him before and he had thought he probably never would.

"Well, yes, er, yes. Live together first. See if everything is OK and if OK, maybe marry."

She did not seem as ecstatic as he had expected, but she gave him a warm smile. He was beginning to wonder if he was the catch that he thought he was.

"Just think of it, Lek, a new, exciting future together. Start again, you and me start again together. What do you think?"

"Yes, OK. We can try" and she reached out for his hand.

"What you doing tonight, telak?" she asked.

"I though we were doing it already," he said taken aback.

"Doing 'it' already? Doing what? I don' understand what you say? I have a girlfriend coming down from village near me. She come down on the bus at six o'clock. I tell her I see her at eight o' clock in her hotel. She want to come here working in a bar and I take her to Daddy's Hobby show her start and then I take her out show her Pattaya. She never work bar before and she never come to Pattaya before too. Only me and her, two old friends go out together. OK? So what you do?"

"Oh, don't worry about me, I will go sit in the 'Rich Bar' and listen to music. When you are finished, you can come see me there."

"OK, telak. Good idea. Don' drink too much, see you later" and with a peck on the cheek she was gone.

He was a bit shocked. That had not been quite as romantic an acceptance of living together and possibly getting married as he had expected. He had imagined a lingering kiss on the lips, a 'let's have a bottle of Champagne to celebrate' or at the very least 'I want to phone my cousin to tell her the good news'.

He had definitely not expected a 'well, that's great, hon, I have to be going now, see you when I see you'.

Oh, well, it was a good thing he could see the funny side of things.

This just did not seem right though, he was sure she would not have done that to him on his first trip. She was more confident of him and her position now, but that was a good thing too, he reasoned. Still, not very romantic, whichever way you looked at it. Maybe she wasn't a romantic person, not deep down, maybe she had had that knocked out of her or maybe she never had been anyway.

So, he paid up and went out onto the street of Soi Buakhao. Soi Buakhao means 'White Lily Lane' and in the Nineties it was little more than a muddy track. Nowadays it is a thriving commercial street of about two miles in length and has hotels, nightclubs, restaurants, bars, shops and three markets. It is an area populated mostly by Thais and old ex-pats from every country, but there are a lot of Scandinavians there in particular, many of whom cannot speak English despite having been in Thailand, presumably with a Thai girl who does not speak a

Scandinavian language, for decades. The bars are not so touristy as in other areas of Pattaya. Many of the bars are the sorts of places you would go to in your home town for a quite night out.

Except that nowhere in Pattaya is actually quiet and the Rich Bar is no exception. Noise-wise anyway. They have live music from the resident band every evening from about four until one and they can be too loud to talk over, but not as loud as most other places. The girls are un-obtrusive too. They are attentive to an empty glass without pushing themselves on the customers. He liked the Rich Bar, but he thought that now was a good opportunity to do some exploring.

He walked south down Soi Buakhao in the direction of Lek's flat, although he didn't know that and never would. There were quite a few sad, little bars with one falang and a girl inside, presumably the owner and his girlfriend trying to eke out an existence. Some looked at him hopefully as he walked past, others didn't even bother to do that, they had seen the writing on the wall, but much, much too late.

Many of them had sad homey names like 'London's Inn', 'Arthur's Nights' and 'Darts 'n Skittles' and there was no-one in them despite special offers on the beer and food. 'Two for the price of one before midnight' and '30 Baht All Day' signs abounded. How could anyone think that investing several thousand pounds or dollars was going to give them an income here?

There were restaurants offering speciality German dishes or British food, but there was no-one in them. The prices were fantastic, but still no customers.

It was so depressing, he could see for the first time that many other falangs wanted to come to live in paradise too. If he was going to make it here he would have to find something better than that. He came to an A-Go-Go at the top of Soi Diana and was tempted in by the promise of half-price beer, music and nude women. It was crowded inside, but a girl with a tiny torch showed him to a small table and took his order. This was nothing like the place he had been to before. Not more up-market, not more expensive, not even classier, it was busy and doubted that those things went on where people were looking.

He looked around and couldn't see anything more that a bit of petting anyway. Young women bouncing up and down on old men's laps while they held the woman's tits mostly. There were lots of happy faces of both sexes, but it didn't cheer him up so he left. He turned back the way he had come and sat in the Rich Bar.

The Rich Bar was in full swing and there was no shortage of people getting up to sing a karaoke number. For the first time in his life, he had come across a bar full of people who could sing pretty well even with a skinful of ale. So, he sat there and just watched and listened and thought about making money in Thailand.

At the time, he had a web site that offered Welsh products to mainly ex-pats, but that was not doing well, he had a web site on how to promote a web site, which was not doing well either and he had a safelist, which was not doing anything. Not much of a portfolio of virtual real estate, he thought. The first task seemed to be to try to make these profitable and then create more web sites. To do this successfully, he knew he had to take a course on marketing and learn HTML programming or editing as it is rightly called.

In order to be able to spend a lot of time on those tasks, he would need his own computer and that meant a laptop really. So he decided that the first job the next day would have to be to get a laptop. There was nothing more he could do that night but sit and wait.

And it was to be a long wait.

Lek met her friend, Mia, in a small hotel not far from her own flat. In fact, she had asked Ayr to check on availability for her friend. Then she took her to Daddy's Hobby to meet her future colleagues. Mia was a pretty, tall woman of about twenty-five. She was unmarried, had no children and had never been out of the province before. She also spoke next to no English, but she dressed smartly, had a lovely smile and beautiful hair.

When Lek had told her about Craig, she had said 'I want one the same' and Lek had offered to help get her started. That was often how it worked. Mia could not see her life going anywhere, she had no qualifications, didn't want a Thai village husband who would tie her to a life of drudgery but could not see a way out. Then Lek happened along and now she was here about to get her first instructions on being a bit more outgoing and picking up foreigners.

Lek assumed that she would be on safer ground after that.

At Daddy's Hobby, Lek introduced Mia to Beou, Ayr and Goong and then all the other girls. Mia did not drink alcohol, but she was mesmerized by the clothes the girls wore, the lights, the loud music and the men.

"If you are nervous, Mia, it does help to have a beer from time to time. It also boosts your earnings if you can get them to buy you a Lady Drink. If you are buying your own, buy a beer, but if they are getting it for you have a Spritzer or something like that – white wine and soda. They're not strong and you get a commission."

Lek knew that Craig would probably not approve of Lek being this kind of teacher, but it was part of what she had promised Beou that she would do in her capacity as unpaid Agony Aunt.

"How do you feel about letting the men grope you at the bar?"

"OK," she said and looked down.

"Don't worry, I'm only teasing you. You don't have to put up with that. When someone over steps the mark, just tell him, as you normally would. It will happen though. This is a girly bar, this is Pattaya and these are drunken horny men. All I'm saying is that you should be ready for whatever and know what you're going to do when it happens, because it will, as sure as eggs is eggs, every week of your life until you leave here. Sad fact, but true nevertheless. Just remember that it is always, always, always up to you how far you go. Not up to anyone else, only you. Not even Mama San Beou or the paying client, only up to you.

Are you ready for your first beer? On me. Two Changs, please Mott and make them big ones" and they both laughed - chang, meaning elephant in Thai, and elephant, or at least his trunk being a slang word for the part of the male anatomy that Mia was about to become more frequently acquainted with.

They stayed there until ten and then did a mini pub crawl around the area to get Mia a little accustomed to it and to introduce her to a few people. Then they bought a half bottle of scotch and took a motorbike taxi to Xcite, a huge disco. Mia was also introduced to Nong and Bong the Mafia motorbike riders. "You take care of her, boys, she's an old friend of mine from near my village. Don't let anyone mess with her and don't you try either'.

Mia was impressed and grateful to her friend.

They walked into Xcite and it was like walking into an aircraft engine testing bay. It was almost painful, but they found a table ordered a bottle of soda and two glasses and had a scotch and soda each. They had a few dances, finished the bottle and took a motorbike taxi back to Mia's hotel. "OK, Mia, I have to go now. See you at four in Daddy's Hobby. Get a good night's sleep." She jumped back on the bike and went back to her and Craig's hotel. As she passed through the foyer, she saw that it was five a.m..

'Oh shit', she thought, 'this'll be a test'.

And so it was, when she opened the door to the room, Craig woke up and she tripped over her bags. Then she was sick over them. "Telak, what is problem? I go wash first."

He just sat there until she came back. As she was cleaning up the mess on the floor, she said "Why you put my bags here?"

"Guess."

"I don' know. Why, telak?"

"Because I am not living with a woman who comes in at five o' clock in the bloody morning. That's why. I didn't come 5,500 miles to be treated like this. Who the hell do you think you are? Or more to the point, how much of an idiot do you have me pegged at?"

She started to cry, but had to rush back into the toilet as another spasm gripped her. He could hear the splashing and felt foolish already. If she took him at the meaning of her packed bags and left, he would regret it so much, now that he had seen her face to face again. He regretted packing her bags and getting angry.

He put the bags back in the wardrobe and closed the door on them: "Are you all right, Lek?"

"Yes, thank …blughhhhh, I am fine only sick and little drunk. Blughhhh."

Serves you right, he thought rather ungraciously and switched the TV on.

There was always something to watch at any time of the day or night in Pattaya.

Daddy's Hobby

20 REALITY KICKS IN

Craig woke up at seven-thirty still lying on the bed on his own, so in a bit of a panic in case Lek had left, he hurried to the bathroom. She was still there, lying on the floor asleep with mascara dried on her cheeks and sick dried on her front. She looked a real mess, but he still loved her and he was so grateful that she hadn't been well enough to get up and walk out.

He wrung out a flannel and started to dab at the vomit. She woke up slowly and said "I'm sorry, telak, I make a mess everywhere. I clean, not you."

"Well, look, just wait a minute, let's get you cleaned up and out of here first," then he rephrased it "… get you out of the shower and into bed."

He started to help her off with her clothes, but he could feel that she was reluctant to let him help. She was in fact very embarrassed about him seeing her covered in vomit, so he passed her the shower head, turned it on for her and handed her the soap and shampoo and left her to it saying: "Tell me when you want a towel and I give you."

He considered unpacking her clothes, but she would know that they weren't how she had left them even if she didn't remember him packing her bags, so he left them where they were, picked up his book and stared watching TV again.

It was not looking like if he would be getting a laptop first thing that morning.

Twenty minutes and about a hundred gallons of water later, there was a faint tap on the door. He got up to look outside, but there was no-one there. Early for the cleaners, he thought. Then it came again from inside the bathroom.

"Telak, telak, can you give me towel please?"

He did as he was asked, amazed that she was still so shy as not to want to be seen naked under normal circumstances. In bed was all right, in the shower together was all right, but if she was the only one naked then she had to have a towel on instead.

"Sure, here you are" and she opened the door an inch, snatched the towel like Thing in the Addams' Family and closed the door again.

She came out looking very sheepish, quietly sniffling to herself. "Telak, I am sick, I think I eat something bad last night."

"Mmm, I think so too. Alcohol." He didn't really want to be mean to her, but she was rather overplaying her hand. "Come off it, Lek, you were as drunk as a fart when you fell in through the door last night. People don't fall over because they are sick with food poisoning, they fall over because they are pissed, drunk, and inebriated, like you were this morning."

"You put my bags on the floor to make me fall over and when I fall quickly I get sick. I feel sick before, but not sick, keep inside, but when you make me fall, I cannot keep inside no more. It come out."

'Oh, well', he thought, 'it's my fault that she was sick. At least I'm off the hook for packing her bags for a while', but he said:

"OK, darling. Come on get into bed and have a good sleep. Maybe you OK after four or five hours. Come on let me help you."

And she did let him help her and then she kissed him and went to sleep and it was never mentioned again.

Face had been saved.

And she never stayed out until five o'clock without him again either.

He needed Lek to buy the laptop because most Thais do not understand English even in Pattaya and besides, if a falang is shopping on his own the price will rise by ten, twenty, thirty even one hundred per-cent depending on how stupid they are or on how stupid they think the foreigner is, so he had to postpone the shopping expedition. Instead he went over to Shy's Internet cafe at the Welcome Inn across the road to check up on work permits and visas.

That didn't take long, basically he had a cat in hell's chance of get-ting a work permit for any job that a Thai could do, which is everything, even if there are some things that they cannot do very well like speak English. He met one young man who had paid quite a lot of money to go on a course in Pattaya to learn how to teach English to foreigners. There was a guaranteed job with a guaranteed salary and a guaranteed work permit at the end of the course. The young man had completed the course and been working on dreadful wages in local schools ever since, but he was still waiting for the work permit and the guaranteed wage.

Of course, the language school picked up his wages for him as he was sub-contracted to them. Once they had told him that if he had a degree he could demand more money. 'But I haven't got a degree', he had said. 'What are you good at?' they asked and when he said 'yoga', they introduced him to a man in the back room of a pub who asked him ten questions on yoga and then gave him a degree for 5,000 Baht, but he was still waiting for the wage rise to come through.

He was naive enough to think that it and the work permit would come through 'any day now' as they promised him.

The visa to stay in Thailand was different. That was quite straight-forward and he would have no problem qualifying for it. He spent the rest of the morning and afternoon researching laptop computers, HTML editors and marketing strategies.

When he went back to the room at six, Lek was sitting up in bed watching TV.

She didn't want to go out, so for one of the first times ever, they stayed in and watched TV together.

The following day their routine was back to normal: breakfast, swimming, shopping, Internet cafe and room respectively. At three o'clock Craig wanted to go shopping for his laptop and Lek went with him. Having bought a fairly decent, middle of the range model, they went to Daddy's Hobby to see how Mia was getting on. Lek had told him a little of what had happened that night and that she had promised to see her the day before but had been sick.

Craig thought she was really beautiful, really gorgeous and the pair hit it off from the start. Lek said: "Mia, I want to go the beauty salon, will you take care of Craig, please."

"OK" she replied. Mia came around from behind the bar, sat by Craig and took his hand.

This was perplexing. He knew what Lek had said, she had asked dozens of people to look after him for a while, but nobody had interpreted it like this before. Then she laid his hand on her thigh and started rubbing it. He did not know what she wanted, so he made a slight test and lightly squeezed it. She opened her legs a few inches and smiled at him.

Then she moved his hand up and played with each finger one by one, lightly brushing some of them against the front of her skirt. He was sure that Lek had not meant her to look after him like this. He also thought that maybe he was being tested by Mia, by Lek or by both of them. None of the other girls could see what was going on though, so he let it carry on.

When she switched hands and started rubbing his thigh, he thought it was time to stop.

But that was difficult, because it was so nice.

Suddenly she stopped, removed his hand and stood up. She dropped to the floor on her heels and then stood up again, waiving a pair of pink panties at him and tucked them into her bra. She sat down again and resumed what she was doing before.

He didn't know Mia or anything about her but he could feel that her hands were as rough as sandpaper. She must have worked as a labourer in her village and a sex-starved one at that, judging by the way she was carrying on. Her hand moved to the bulge in his trousers and started stroking it. "Mmm," she purred as she turned on her stool to face him and spread her legs so that he could see that she that she was smooth shaven.

He could not resist it. He put his hand up her skirt and stroked her bald pussy. Then he looked at her to see if she was all right about it — she was smiling — and then he looked around to see who was watching — no-one. So he opened her lips and spread the moisture around them. She opened further and then slid off the stool with his hand still up her skirt, so he put a finger up inside her and stroked it up and down its full length slowly. Mia put her hand down the front of his shorts and took his cock.

"Mmm, big chang," she whispered, moving it up and down. "I want see chang falang. I never see before." With that she dropped to her heels again, pulled the front of his trousers down and took his cock out. She didn't even look around to see if anyone was watching. "Big chang," she said and then put it in her mouth and smiled at him. "I never eat chang falang before. Big and white. Very beautiful." She pulled her skirt back so that he could see her fanny.

"Bpai hong naam?," she said, meaning "Do you want to go to the toilet?"

"No, no, thank you." She sucked and chewed on his dick while wanking him off. He knew that he was going to come soon and he didn't want that, so he pulled out of her mouth, but not quite soon enough and he ejaculated all over her face. She seemed to like it and kept wanking him until he was dry. She stood up and smiled at him with cum all over her face.

"Mmm, good. I like water from man," then she took her knickers out of her bra and wiped her face, just as Ayr appeared and asked if there was anything they wanted.

"No, er, it's OK, thanks... Oh, go on then one more beer for me and do you want something to drink Mia?"

"No, thank you, not now," she smiled.

When Lek got back a little while later, she kissed him quickly and then sat the other side of her friend and they chatted, both girls turning to smile at him from time to time. He was alone again, so he took out the manual of his new laptop, ordered a round and began reading it.

On their way home, Lek asked: "Did you like Mia? She is an old friend of mine from school. She said she take care of you. You know at first, I think she too shy for do this job, but I tell her never let man be the boss. It is up to you what you do. I am not sure it is good idea she wear short skirt. I tell her maybe man try touch her if she wear skirt. I tell her same two days ago when I go see her in hotel and tell her about this job. Maybe she not remember, so I tell her again today. She is pretty, no? I think she get someone like her soon."

Craig was quite sure of it. He thought every man would like her.

∞

Five days later, Craig was on line and he was convinced that he would be able to make some money in Thailand. To test the theory, he bought a card reader from the computer shop, photographed it and put it on eBay. He sold seven within a week. Then he bought a pair of jeans, photographed them and sold 17 pairs in a week. He was sending stuff all over the world, but it was not what he really wanted to do.

Some people were making a lot of money sending cigarettes back to the UK. They were sending thousands every day and reckoned that more than 90% were getting through, but he didn't want to do that either. He wanted to publish web sites, so he needed more hosting space, which he bought in America, so that the IP address would be considered more reliable by his future visitors.

He could not wait to tell Lek the good news that he could move to Thailand and still earn a living. However, when he told her she didn't seem that impressed. The problem, as far as she was concerned, was that she wanted to live abroad in order to earn more money. She didn't want to live in Thailand. This living with a foreigner was not working out quite as she had planned. She wanted to move to the UK and even take her daughter over there so that she would get a better education, a better job and a better, or at least a richer, husband.

Craig, on the other hand, had had enough of the UK and wanted to live abroad again, especially in Thailand and with Lek. It just was not working out as either of them had planned, but Craig was determined not to live in the UK any more, but he did have to go back to organize his affairs and rent out his house. "How about a holiday in the UK, in Wales, Lek? We can go there for three months, because I have to clean out my house and rent it out. Do you want to come over with me?"

"Oh, yes, I want to go very much. When do you want to go?"

"My flight home is for the end of October, so that is the best time for me. We can go for Christmas and come back next year. What do you think?"

She rushed over to him and hugged him tightly, kissing him on the lips. "Oh, I cannot wait to go to the UK. I want to go for a very long time. First we must get a visa for the UK for me. Is that easy? People tell me not easy."

"I don't know. What is the problem? Why do people say they have a problem getting a UK visa?"

"I don' know why. Only people say not easy for Thai people to go to UK."

So they sat at the laptop together and looked up the web site of the British embassy in Bangkok. It certainly didn't look difficult so he downloaded the visa application form, VAF1 and went down to reception to have it printed out. That night they filled in the form and sent it off to the embassy in Wireless Road, Bangkok. A week later they were summoned to an interview at the embassy.

They went up two days before the interview in order to get Lek a passport to put the visa in and to get to the embassy early. They were both very nervous about the interview, but Craig was certain that she would get one. In order to settle their nerves, they went to the cafe across the road from the embassy for breakfast before going in.

They also wanted to run through their story one more time. Lek repeated the names of Craig's family. She repeated Craig's address and what he did for a living, well, his new profession of Internet marketer and went through a few facts about Barry and Wales. "What is the name of the month when we met?" she asked, "June or July, I mix them up all the time?"

"July" he said, "just remember the seventh month." Then they crossed over the road to get her visa. They went to the reception, picked up the application forms she had sent them and Craig paid the fee. Then they had to wait their turn to be called in. It was the most nerve-wracking experience of their lives. When they were called, Craig opened the door for Lek to go in.

"You are not part of the interview. We do not require you here," he was told and he had to leave Lek in there alone. She looked terrified. When she came out she still looked pretty bad. "I must go back inside in ten to thirty minutes. They have to think about it."

When she came out, he could see that there was a problem because she was close to tears. "What is the matter, Lek?"

"I cannot have a visa. I am so sorry, Craig. So sorry, I make problems for you. I am not a good lady. British government not want me to go to the UK. I am so very sorry." She was genuinely ashamed and wanted to get back to the hotel as soon as possible to hide her tears.

They went to the bar in the hotel and Lek went straight to the toilet. Twenty minutes later, she had still not come back so he went to look for her. He didn't like to stand outside the ladies' toilet door, but he did and he could hear Lek crying out loud. He didn't know whether to try to get her out or just wait. He settled for going back to the bar and waiting for her to compose herself. Thirty minutes later, she came back to the bar.

"Craig, I'm sorry, but I forget to show you the letter they gave me explaining why I cannot have a visa for the UK. I am so sorry" and she burst into tears again. Sorry, I must go to our room now. I want you to stay here, but come up later. I want to sit alone for sometime. See you later. I am so sorry."

She didn't stop to kiss him, but just hurried away. Craig opened the letter and read the reasons for the refusal:

1] The applicant has not demonstrated reasonable financial or family ties to convince us that she will return to Thailand,

2] The applicant has not been abroad before.

3] The applicant has not demonstrated that she has close personal ties with the sponsor.

4] The applicant attempted to deceive when asked how long she has known her sponsor.

He couldn't understand what had gone wrong. He had done everything that the form had asked for and nowhere had it stated that an applicant who had not been abroad before could not go to the UK. It seemed ridiculous. He had a couple more beers to give Lek some privacy and continued to read his book.

Once in the room, he went over to sit with Lek and put his arm around her. "Don't worry, Lek. I read the letter and it does not speak badly of you. Only that you said you have not known me for a long time. What went wrong?"

"A Thai lady asked me many questions and a British man wrote everything down with a typewriter. She asked me what you do for a living and I said 'promotion or marketing', the stupid woman did not understand, so the man told her advertising. Everything was fine and I thought that I will get a visa. She asked me how long I know you and I remember what you said, so I said 'seven months'.

She said "No, not true. Mr. Williams only came to Thailand in July, so you can not know him for more than three months." "I wanted to say 'Sorry, I mean I meet him in month seven', but I could not say it. It would not come out of my mouth. I did not mean to tell lies, really, I didn't. I am so sorry, Craig."

"Don't worry about it, Lek. What else did they say? Anything?"

"Yes, the man said I can try again after I have known you for six months. After Christmas. In January or February."

So they made plans to reapply in February and to establish proof of a loving relationship in the meantime. She could also go on his next visa run to Cambodia so that they could not use that ridiculous excuse again of not having been abroad before.

After a late breakfast, they took a taxi back to Pattaya and went straight to Daddy's Hobby. They arrived at four thirty and all of her friends were there. When Lek walked up to them behind the bar, she burst into tears again and so did some of the others. They all hugged and huddled together. Noi handed Craig a beer and said: "So sorry for your bad luck. You go back alone now next month?"

"No, of course not. Is that what Lek is thinking? No, I will wait for her. We go back together next year when she gets her visa."

He could see that he was going to be on his own for a while, so he got his laptop out to check his email. Ten minutes later Mia slid onto the stool next to him. "Hello" she said, "Sorry that Lek not get a visa. You try again sometime?" and she turned to face him, crossing her legs as she did so. He could not help looking and she could not help liking that he was looking – no knickers again. "What you thinking?"

"Oh, nothing. You are not cold?"

"Why?" She uncrossed her legs, opened them wide and then lifted the front of her skirt up. "Oh, I forget put my panties on again. You want me to put on now?"

"Don't do it just for my sake."

She smiled and let her skirt fall, but high enough up so that he could still see her crotch. "It is not cold today; I am very hot. Touch me and you see that I am very hot. A little bit thirsty too. You want to give me something to drink?"

"Do you want a beer?" he asked.

"If you have nothing else, OK. Maybe you give me something else salty later. You must take salt when it is hot, neh? Doctor say on TV and I think he is right. I like a little bit salt water sometimes when I am hot."

Craig was growing hot too now.

And growing in stature – about six inches bigger.

When Lek started to come over, Mia moved close to the bar so that Lek could not see that her skirt was up around her waist but so that Craig could still see everything. "Are you all right, telak, Mia can take care of you while I talk to the girls. Some of them have ideas for the visa. You can sit with him, Mia, please?

Mia took his hand, held it up for Lek to see. "As if he was my own man," she said and put his hand in her crotch. Lek could not see, but he retrieved it quickly anyway. When Lek turned around and walked away, Mia put his hand back and put her own hand in his crotch squeezing his cock hard. "Oh, Mr. Chang wake up again." She knocked her beer mat on to the floor, bent over at the waist so that her skirt rode up over her backside, pulled his cock out and started sucking it all in one deft movement.

She was a few inches lower than the bar so no-one could see what she was doing. This was getting out of hand, but he put his hand on her behind and slipped his thumb into her fanny. She bit his cock harder. He was working his thumb inside her and she was pushing back on it and sucking him off. He came in her mouth within a minute or so. It was so sexy, so naughty to be brought to come like that that he could not hold out any longer.

She straightened up, his thumb slipped out of her and she put the beer mat back on the bar. "Thank you for my salt water," she said. Then she turned to face him, lifted up her skirt and started rubbing herself off. She came twice, smiled at him, put her knickers on and walked away. When she was two or three yards away, she bent over and touched her toes, smiling at him through her open legs and showing him her bottom.

That is one naughty woman, he thought.

Lek came over and sat with him. He felt guilty about Mia, but then he was not really happy with Lek's lack of enthusiasm about him coming to live in Thailand either. He tried to console himself with what someone had told him once – 'a standing cock has no conscience'.

The problem was that it was not quite true when it lay down again.

"Hiya, Lek, are you all right? What is the story about Mia?"

"Mia is an old friend of mine from the next village. We are good friends for twenty years, but when we were in school, we both liked the same boy. First he go with her, but then he finish her and go with me. She was very angry with me for two or three weeks, then we start friends again. We said no boy is worth fighting over – there are or were many boys. Why you ask? She say something to you?"

"No, nothing she said. I just wondered about her. What did the girls say about getting a visa?"

"People tell me maybe I never get visa, but I can buy a visa with corruption. There is a lady up the road who bought a visa for 20,000 to go to the UK. She can take my passport to Bangkok and she will bring it back with a visa. What do you think? Maybe I never get a visa. They don' like me now. They think I tell lies."

"No. Never. We will get a visa legitimately. There is nothing in that letter about a problem in the future. We will try again in February and see what happens. Don't worry about things too much. We will stay here for a while and go to Cambodia when I have to renew my visa next month. We can stay a week or a weekend, whatever you want and then the embassy can't say they that you have never been abroad.

"We also need to save all of our hotel and restaurant receipts and take a few more photos together. I also want you to ask your cousin for a letter saying that you can have your job back any time you want it. It might be worth getting a letter from the mayor of the village to say you have a mother and a daughter that you take care of. Then they can't say that you have no financial or family ties with Thailand. We will get you a visa, don't worry."

Lek was not so sure. She would have gladly paid 20,000, or at least let Craig pay it, never to have to go to the embassy again.

Daddy's Hobby

21 BIDING TIME

The next time that Craig had to renew his thirty-day visa, he booked Lek in to go with him. They departed on the minibus at six a.m. from Pattaya Klang and left Thailand five hours later. Lek got her precious exit stamp as did Craig. Over the border they stopped a taxi and asked to go to a hotel in the nearest large town. The Cambodian driver was perplexed. "There is no large town near here. Do you want to go to Pnom Phen?"

They had not done any research, but Craig thought that there must be some town closer than the capital. "No, we just want to go to a town somewhere not far."

"OK," he said "one hundred Baht if you pay in Thai money." They had no Cambodian reals anyway. The taxi driver spoke English, but no Thai. Lek didn't have the confidence to speak English to him, so for the first time in her life, Lek couldn't speak. Later she said that it was a very strange experience and that she couldn't understand the Cambodian accent when applied to English anyway.

They travelled over extremely bad roads, where there were dozens of potholes that were over two feet deep. They didn't travel at more than 20 kph and driving involved swinging from one side of the road to the other to avoid the holes. This was not a problem because there was no other traffic at all. The grass on either side of the road was over eight feet tall, so they couldn't see where they were going and after an hour or so it crossed Craig's mind that they could be being taken to their deaths, when he spotted a bullet hole in the windscreen at about the driver's chest height.

All of a sudden it started getting scary, but Craig didn't say anything to Lek, who was really enjoying herself in the back seat alone.

After three hours, they pulled up onto a paved road and Craig read a sign: 'You have successfully passed through the Battambang minefield'.

That was where they were heading, Batambang, situated one hundred kilometres from the Thai border. As they passed through the town an hour later, they had to drive slowly because of all the pedestrians and when children saw Craig, they tried to open the doors. The driver was getting scared and so wouldn't stop. When he put the central locking on, Craig noticed that he was looking pretty scared of the massing crowd. Cambodia was scary or Battambang was anyway, probably because it was off the tourist track.

The hotel that the driver took them to was very nice; Arabic in style, it was clean and inexpensive. It also had a high wall around it and guards on the gate. They didn't leave the hotel grounds all weekend because Lek was too frightened to go outside. Luckily, there was a bar, a restaurant, an Internet cafe and a karaoke bar within the beautiful hotel grounds, so there was enough to do.

Enough to do for two days anyway. More than that would have been tiresome, especially as they were the only guests at the fairly large hotel. The driver had given them his card so that they could call him to take them back to the Thai border The hotel staff agreed that it was safer to use a taxi that they knew rather than risk trying another, but they took his licence plate and ID number anyway and advised them to phone a friend in Thailand with an estimated time of arrival, in case they got into difficulty. It was not very reassuring.

They were glad to get back to Thailand, but they both knew that they had ticked off one of the boxes that had stopped Lek from going to Britain.

As usual after having been away, they went straight to Daddy's Hobby so that Lek could tell the girls all about her latest adventure.

Craig sat at the back as usual, out of the way of the large speakers that he hated so much and Lek went behind the bar to huddle with her friends. Mia came over and handed him a beer: "Lek tell me to give you. You OK today?"

"Yeah, fine thanks. And you?"

"OK" she said and left.

Ten minutes later she was back but beside him this time. "It is very hot again today, isn't it?"

"Yes" he replied, wondering what she had on. She stood close enough to lean her thighs against him so he tickled her through her skirt. She did not move back, but did not react either so he stopped. When he stopped, she lifted her skirt up and draped it over his leg, pushed her crotch against his knee and moved ever so slightly but rhythmically.

This woman was all sex and danger.

Craig picked up his beer, took a swig and handed it to Mia. She looked at him, licked the top and then slowly finished the bottle making a big show of draining every drop. He slipped his hand over his knee so that she was rubbing herself off on the back of his hand. She became more enthusiastic and lifted her skirt so that he could watch. He was praying for the good luck that no-one would come along because he was not looking out for them; he couldn't, he was mesmerized. She moaned softly and moved off him, but pulled his hand towards her.

He stroked a finger in her moist slit and then pushed his thumb inside her. There was no resistance at all because she was quite wet. She groaned a fair bit louder and put her hand into his shorts grabbing his cock roughly. He thought he might come, even if she had not done that, but she shuddered a little and then went down on him. He shot his load into her mouth in seconds.

Before she walked away, she whispered: "That was the last time. I have my own man now. Nice man from Australia. You meet him one day soon."

'OK', he nodded with a smile, but 'Thank God for that!' was what he was thinking.

∞

Time passed in an idyllic way. They both had certain times of the day that they tended to spend alone. These periods were usually in the morning and early afternoon. Lek liked to get everything done that she needed to and be where she had to be before midday and she did not like to go out again until after four. Craig on the other hand did not mind the blazing heat, although he had never been a sun-worshipper. He liked to swim early and then work on his Thai or on the Internet until about four, when he usually started to feel like an ice-cold beer.

Or even a few of them.

He was getting on well with the Internet, but learning Thai was another kettle of fish. He had learned a few European languages, but they were all vaguely similar – they all had a bit of Latin in them and he had studied Latin for four years in school, to 'A' Level, in fact. However, there were no reference points with Thai whatsoever. Some words had origins in English but they were so heavily disguised and so few in number that they hardly made any difference. 'Sutemp' meaning ' postage stamp' and 'boscar' meaning 'postcard' were good examples.

In addition, he got the impression that no-one really wanted him to learn Thai. Maybe the Thais he knew liked to have a private language or maybe foreigners just made such a hash of speaking Thai that it was easier to struggle on with English. He couldn't make up his mind and he got different answers from different people.

Lek had said that she and he both lost face when he made a pig's ear out of trying to speak the Thai language and she didn't want him to lose face. He couldn't understand why he would lose face for trying to learn a new language. Everyone had to do it, even if they only spoke one language.

"You are falang," she had explained, "You are up from most people. You must be same as boss. No-one must laugh at you. When you speak bad Thai, people don' understand you. Some people think you are stupid, some people laugh at you later when you are not there. I don' want that."

But he persevered with Thai anyway whether people laughed at him behind his back or thought he was stupid or not. Lek was not happy about it though. On the other hand, she often said that she was fed up translating everything back and forth for him.

It seemed that he couldn't win this one whatever he did.

Maybe she just wanted him to shut up, read his book and go to the bank every now and again. It certainly felt like it sometimes.

It was not too much of a problem in Pattaya, but people told him that they had tried living in a village and that they soon became bored rigid because they had no-one to talk to. He could see that this might become a problem. After all, he hadn't spoken much more than a thousand words all weekend when he had gone up country. A six month stretch of that would be like being in solitary, he guessed. The only answer was to learn Thai or live in Pattaya as he presumed many others had worked out before him.

He and Lek had started looking at property prices. It was a treacherous area, because a foreigner could own a condo in a block where 51% of the condos were owned by Thais, but a foreigner could not own land. Therefore, he could rent land and build a house. Or he could lease land for up to thirty years and build a house. There were also a few other dubious, semi-legal ways for a foreigner to acquire land, but they were just too much trouble. Like giving your wife a mortgage, but only accepting a monthly payment of one hundred Baht so that she could never pay it off, with the land being held as security. If the foreigner built a house on this land, he would own the house but not the land.

Craig saw a property in a magazine that he liked: "What do you think of this one, Lek? One thousand rubber trees and a three-bedroomed house on the same plot of land... We would have our own forest and you could run a rubber plantation. One million Baht. It sounds great to me."

"Where is it?" she asked, half-heartedly. "Show me... It is in Isaan! I like Isaan people; I love Isaan food and I love Isaan music, but I am not from Isaan. I will never live in Isaan. Never. You go alone if you want to. I can go back to work."

'Wow', he thought, 'that was a strong reaction'. "Well, where do you want to live?" he asked. "We have to live somewhere."

"I know we have to live somewhere, I am not stupid. I live in Pattaya, but I am from Uttaradit. Two choices. Only two. Pattaya or Uttaradit. Not Isaan, khao jai mai, kha? You un'erstand?"

"Yes, OK, OK, calm down. It was only a suggestion. You do not want to live anywhere else, now I know. You don't have to get angry. Just speak. I only ask you. Jeez! I can't say anything at all now."

"You can speak, but don' speak stupid."

She would definitely not have behaved like this two months ago, he thought.

He also thought that it would be nice to have a house or a condo in Pattaya and a small 'hunting lodge' up in Baan Suay, because he could foresee that they would be going to visit her family quite often. That didn't worry him. If he could produce web sites up there he wouldn't get bored and besides, it was good to have peace and quiet when he was working. No, he was actually looking forward to going up country often.

Will went back home and Craig was getting used to seeing people coming and going. On Loy Kratung in November, a party of fifteen people went over from Barry. Craig met them in Daddy's Hobby by pure accident. He didn't know any of them, but they had been going to Thailand for Loy Kratung for fifteen years. Apparently, they had used to be ten couples, but a few had died, a few had divorced and a few had remarried.

Loy Krathong is the Thai version of St. Valentine's Day except that it is much older. Thai women and some Thai men dress up in traditional costume and, in the evening, two lovers, married or not, push a 'kratong' or 'boat' each out onto the water. Each person has to make a secret wish as they push the boat out. If the boats disappear into the darkness side-by-side the lovers will stay together for another year.

Some people put a small amount of money in their boat to appease the gods, but there are always a few dozen children fifty yards out in the water waiting to rob the kratng of their cargo. It is a very popular time for Thais and tourists alike and that group from Barry were not the only people he met who had been going to Thailand for Loy Krathong with their spouses for years.

November, December and January is the peak season with the fortnights before and after Christmas the peak season of all. Tens of thousands of men flock to Thailand to avoid the European Christmas cold weather. Nick and Barry came back as they had promised, but they got a fairly cool reception from Joy and Deou, because they had not sent any money over.

The girls had lost face quite badly because everyone had been so sure that they were being taken out of the game by two nice men who cared for them. The guys must have realized what would happen to the girls if they were left in Thailand without an income.

The only reasonable answer was that they didn't care enough.

It was an unwelcome, though poignant reminder to Lek what could happen to her if things went wrong with Craig and she resolved to try to be nicer to him.

They took a lot of photographs over this period and saved all the receipts from their restaurant meals and all their used telephone cards. They were building up evidence of a 'strong and lasting relationship' in order to nail another excuse for not having allowed Lek to go to the UK. They decided to ask her cousin and the mayor of the village for help with the other excuse.

They spent Christmas Eve at Daddy's Hobby. Craig didn't really want to go there because he knew that it would be packed and very noisy, but he could not not go really. Lek would want to go and her cousin would feel snubbed if they went anywhere else. They decided to go early, so that they could leave after midnight if they wanted to, although Craig knew that there was not much chance of Lek wanting to leave early, if they stayed there until twelve o'clock.

'Ah well, it is Christmas', he thought.

And it certainly was. All the girls were in Santa costumes with tiny skirts. Some of the bigger bosomed girls were wearing low-cut costumes as well. The only down-side was the din, it was horrific.

Lek gave him a plate of food and a bottle of beer, sat him on a good seat at the back, away from the speakers and went behind the bar to help out on this, the busiest night of the year. He had not expected that, but he didn't mind. It was too loud to talk anyway. The way he looked at it was, the only thing to do was to smile, get drunk and try to remain friendly despite being hustled and jostled by kids trying to sell fairy lights, blokes trying to get you to have a photo taken with their pet snake and women trying to sell you sexy lingerie for your girlfriend.

It was just the sort of night that Craig had come to hate. On top of that, Nick and Barry, with whom he thought he might have tried to have a chat, could not get a seat near him, so took seats way down the bar on the other side. Mia might have been a pleasant distraction a couple of months ago, but that had all stopped and it was too busy now anyway.

Lek was glad to get back behind the bar. She knew dozens of people, especially men, who usually came over for Christmas. It was her favourite time of the year in Pattaya along with the Thai New Year in April, but Craig was being such a wet blanket. She was glad to be shot of him for a few hours, if the truth be known.

She didn't want to go back to work permanently, but she did miss it and she loved to help out from time to time. She had no intention of being unfaithful to Craig, but she loved flirting and most of these people would not know that she was with someone. She was really looking forward to it.

She could keep an eye on him and she would make sure that he had plenty of food and drink. He could take care of himself for company or he could sit there alone and be miserable; it was up to him. She didn't really care this evening. She was going to have some fun again. She only wished that she had remembered that they dressed up for Christmas Eve and Christmas Day, but then again, old misery guts, as she was beginning to think of Craig, wouldn't have liked her doing that anyway. She was looking good, as she always did, and that was the main thing.

She turned around and saw that he was watching her. She smiled, waved and then went off to help her former colleagues.

Craig looked at the clock on the wall and thought 'only nine or ten hours to go', assuming that they could get away by two or three in the morning. As he was drinking his beer, he decided that if he was going to be left at the end of the bar on his own all night, then he was going to be naughty and blame it on the drink. If anyone could remember the next day, which he doubted.

The girls were all drinking whiskey and he was sure they would all be snapped up towards the end of the evening. It was unlikely that they would go early, because the men would want to walk around the bars looking first and having a bit of fun; only taking a girl back to the hotel at around one a.m., when it would be too late for most of them to do anything but wish they hadn't drunk so much, and go to sleep.

He knew he would have to be careful with the old guard, Beou, Goong and Ayr, perhaps Mott, Joy and Deou as well, but from what he had seen so far, the newcomers were only out for themselves, although things were going so badly between them that he didn't really care at that moment anyway. It didn't matter, there were at least twenty other girls working there and he knew that there would be hundreds of freelancers out for a free or paid good night out as well.

He would simply have to sit there and do nothing and dozens of girls would be over to see him during the course of the evening to wish him Merry Christmas. Some would know him, but most would not; they would just see a foreigner with money sitting alone looking bored.

Nid was the first one to arrive and he saw rather than heard her say "Merry Christmas." As she leaned in to kiss him on the cheek, he slipped his arm around her waist, then up her tiny Santa skirt and squeezed her bottom. He could tell that she was surprised, but she didn't pull away. He felt for the elastic at the top of her panties and slipped his hand in. She retreated a little, "Tch, tch. What are you doing?" she asked. He squeezed her bare bottom in reply. She kissed him again and then moved away.

The other two 'N's' came over together and he went for Lek's cousin, Noi, first. He kissed her and patted her bottom. She moved off and he put his arm around Nok. "Hello, Craig," she said, "Merry Christmas." As she kissed him, he slipped his hand up her skirt and into her knickers. When she didn't resist, he quickly started moving it around the front. She shifted round to make it easier for him to gain access to her. She had her back to the bar, facing him. He opened her shaven haven and she put a hand up his trouser leg and squeezed his hard cock. "Merry Christmas," she said and kissed him on the cheek again.

Suddenly Lek was before them: "Are you ready for another?," she asked, not being able to see anything. "Yes, all right, thanks." Lek said something to Nok in Thai and she walked off after kissing him again. "That girl is not nice," said Lek, "she would sleep with a mangy dog for small money" and left.

That is one who was interested, he thought.

Ayr came over next. As she arrived, she jumped up on his lap. As he wriggled to redistribute her weight, he put an arm around her waist and a hand on her bare thigh. He could feel an erection growing under her bottom and he was sure she could as well. As she kissed him Merry Christmas, he tickled the front of her panties. "Oh, no, no, no, no, no. Naughty boy. Can not." She kissed him again and slid off his lap.

That was a dangerous thing to have done, but four beers had given him bravado too.

When the next one came over, it was one of the Isaan girls. As she kissed him, he put his hand down the front of her pants and smiled at her. He opened her lips while looking into her eyes. "Are you OK?," she asked and jumped up onto his lap. Facing forward, she opened his fly and took his cock out. She held it between her thighs and stroked it from the top. Craig put his hand under her bottom and into her pants and stroked her fanny. "Lek, excuse me," she said, "Craig wants one more beer and one for me too." She dug her fingers into his dick.

"Yes, thanks, Lek. Two beers," he said.

He came down her thighs and she scooped some up, hopped off his lap and dabbed it on his nose. Then she kissed it off. "Merry Christmas" she said and winked at him leaving him totally exposed.

He was hoping that no-one would come over until his body had recovered, but as far as he was concerned, so far so good.

The last thing that he remembered the following day was that most of the girls let him touch them to some degree and that about half of them wanted to touch him as well, but no-one else brought him off.

Lek had a good time too, but not in the same way. She drank too much and was kissed a lot and was hugged a lot; one or two tried to touch her intimately, but she stopped them. She was a lot more loyal than Craig, but she left him to his own devices. She could see that her friends were taking care of him and she could see that some 'unknowns' were trying it on, but he did not go anywhere with any of them, so she was satisfied.

When he went to the toilet, she followed him to make sure that everything was as it should be.

She could see that he was very drunk, but she didn't mind about that, it was Christmas.

In the morning they both had very bad hangovers. They said 'Merry Christmas' to each other, but there was no real feeling in it. Craig went down for breakfast, solely because it seemed like a good idea. Lek slept all day, but neither of them went out for a walk or a drink. Craig wondered whether the risks he had taken the night before were worth it. In this moment of good sense, he really thought that it had been a stupid thing to do. He didn't want to lose Lek, but he didn't want to be a doormat to an angry woman either.

Lek, for her part, was wondering whether she wanted to stay with Craig and stay in Thailand or give him up and look for someone that would take her abroad to live. She really didn't know, so she just pretended to be asleep for the whole of Christmas Day.

22 RAPPROCHEMENT

Craig spent most of Boxing Day in the pool and Lek even spent a few hours sleeping there under a parasol. They didn't speak to each other very often, but they were still together. He was quite ashamed of the way he had been behaving on the one hand, but on the other he had come to Thailand to be happy and Lek was not the same person that he had left behind in August. It was all very worrying.

Lek was not happy either. She had been dreaming of living in Europe or America for ten very long years and now that she had someone she liked very much and someone who obviously liked her very much, but he wanted to live in Thailand. It was just her luck. She didn't know whether to stay with Craig or just start again in the bar and look for someone else. She had seen Craig with his arms all over her friends, but she didn't know how far it had gone. She trusted her real friends anyway. She had had a few kisses too, but nothing more, although some men, old acquaintances and strangers, had tried.

At four o' clock, they got dressed and handed the towels back as they had been supplied by the hotel to residents. Craig's swimming trunks were wet, so he posted them into his mailbox in the lobby and went out commando style. They went for a meal nearby, but no sooner had they ordered than Lek had a phone call:

"Hello, Mum. How are you? Is it cold up there? Is everything all right?"

"Yes, darling, everything is all right, but Soom has had a little accident. There is nothing to worry about. She is all right. This morning, still half asleep, I imagine, she slipped off the last few steps of the stairs and broke her right arm. We took her to hospital and she has one of those short forearm plasters, so it can't be all that bad. I waited 'till now to tell you because I didn't want you too worry too much."

"I'll come home tonight, Mum, but if I can't get a bus tonight, then tomorrow for sure. I will probably come up alone, but I am not sure yet. I'll ring you back later, when I know more. Can I speak to Soom? She's sleeping?

Probably the result of the anaesthetic and the shock, I suppose. Tell, her I'm coming up, when she wakes up, please. See you soon. Bye."

"Oh, Craig," she said with tears welling up in her eyes, "Soom has fallen and broken her arm. She is all right, but I want to go to see her tonight or tomorrow. You stay here, I can go more quickly alone. What do you think?"

He thought that he could not understand how she could go more quickly alone by bus and by taxi. Obviously, she did not want him to go and, to be honest, he didn't want to go traipsing all the way up there over the Christmas and New Year's holidays either – they had always meant at least a fortnight of just having fun to him ever since he was a small child and right up until last year.

"OK, telak. You go alone and I will wait here. I can talk to Barry and Nick and make my web sites. You can go quickly alone and come back quickly too. I will miss you, but I understand that you want to see your daughter."

Now she didn't know whether to be happy or sad that he was not going. She also wondered what he would get up to alone. She didn't want him wandering off and meeting someone else. In fact, she realized that she was feeling a little jealous of some unknown woman that he might meet, but it was too late now."

"OK, telak, I go now. Not take more clothes, I have there. I have money. The bus come at six o' clock maybe, maybe seven o'clock. I want to go now.”

He stood up and hugged her. She did not like kissing in public, but she gave him a big lingering kiss on the lips and hugged him tight. Telak, I will miss you. I will come back before New Year. Maybe I will take the bus the night after tomorrow, if I can get a ticket.”

She held him at arms’ length: “Telak, don’ go everywhere, eh? Not drink too much. Only drink here and the Rich Bar and Daddy’s Hobby. Here is not far from the hotel and in my cousin’s bar my friends will take care of you. Please take good care of yourself. Work hard, not drinking all day.”

He promised, gave her three thousand Baht, said to give everyone, especially Soom, his best wishes and she ran for a motorbike taxi.

“Buy Soom a present from us for Christmas,” he shouted after her.

“OK, telak, good idea, Thank you. Bye-bye.”

The two meals arrived and he was alone again.

Half an hour later, Lek phoned to say that she had got a seat on the VIP bus for six fifteen. She also said that she was sorry to leave him alone and that she hoped he would take care of himself because she was worried about him.

He ate the best bits of both meals, but really tried to eat as much of everything as he could and then walked over to the Rich Bar to think about what he was going to do for the next couple of days.

Lek had a long time to think about things too. One thing she was sure of now was that she liked Craig a lot, maybe she even loved him, but the main thing was that she knew that she didn’t want to lose him. It had not escaped her attention that Soom falling down the stairs was similar to her old nightmare. It was not as bad as the nightmare, but it was similar enough to make a superstitious woman worried.

If she were living abroad, she would not be able to be rushing back to help and comfort her daughter at this moment. It was a strong revelation. 'Be careful what you wish for', she thought once more.

She slept on the bus going up so that she would be fresh when she saw Soom early the following morning.

Craig sat in the Rich Bar, which he knew was a 'safe' bar as far as girls were concerned. It was what the Thais call 'old style Thai' meaning that if a man sat alone, a girl would sit with him to talk and pour his beer. She would be unobtrusive and would get up to serve others from time to time, but would return if not asked to leave or made to feel uncomfortable.

She might do more, if she were asked, but she would not suggest it.

He just sat there and listened to the music and wished he had a book to read. Then he remembered that they sold local newspapers in the '7-11' next door, so he indicated to his 'minder' that he would be back soon. Her English was not good enough to fully understand, but she smiled anyway.

He sat in the Rich Bar for a few hours just reading the paper and drinking beer, ably assisted by his female minder. By nine o'clock he was bored and decided to try elsewhere. He didn't want to go far, because he knew from before that most of the bars around there were new, empty and boring. Being Christmas week, there were hundreds of loud male tourists everywhere. He had never seen so many twenty-year-olds in Pattaya before, normally, he was one of the youngest foreigners there at fifty years of age.

Most of them were very loud, singing football songs in the street and some were pretty obnoxious to the girls as well, pulling them about and making sexual remarks that they knew probably were not understood, so Craig just went back to the hotel and sat in the hotel bar, drank alone and watched a football match with the hotel caretaker, who was the only other person in the bar. None of the residents used it at night because there were no resident bar girls. It was always very quiet.

Craig was not keen on football and couldn't understand enough Thai even to know who was playing, but he tried to follow it and hoped that he smiled, nodded and shook his head at all the right moments when the caretaker and the bar keeper passed comments on it to him.

An hour later, he went up to the room to read. He stripped off and lay on the bed naked, but on the eighth floor, there was no chance of anyone seeing him. He put the TV on, read and drifted off to sleep feeling pretty lonely. This is what life would be like for a foreigner in Thailand without a steady girlfriend or wife, he thought, and he didn't think much of it.

At least in Britain he would have friends, family and better TV. He had never minded being alone before he came to Thailand, but it was different being alone outside your own continent, where hardly anybody spoke your language well enough to discuss anything other than football.

He was feeling pretty low and considered going out to find some other lonely sole to talk to but couldn't be bothered to do so, when it came down to it.

Lek phoned at two o' clock: "Hello, telak, how are you? OK? Good. Where are you? In the room? Really? In our room? Wow, good boy! You are not too drunk? Wow, good boy! Sorry, Craig, I have to go now. I am in Phitsanulok bus station and my taxi has come. Thank you for the money, I forgot to say before. I was worried about you on the bus. I think you go out and drink too much. Do something stupid. I am happy, you are in the room. You not go out now? Good. Go sleep. Get up early in the morning; work and swim. Good night. Choop, choop."

"Choop, choop. Kiss, kiss. Take care and thank you for phoning me" he managed to get in before she hung up.

He sat there and thought about the call. It sounded as if it was a mixture of concern for him and concern for herself. She might even have been worried about him finding a new lady. That made him feel happy, because there had not been many signs of affection for the last couple of months. Maybe things were looking up, he thought as he went to sleep with the TV on, as was his habit when he slept alone in hotels, as he normally had done in the past on other holidays.

The next day, he was up bright and early and went down for breakfast with his 'Teach Yourself Thai' book. In fact, Craig spent all of the next couple of days studying. He worked in the room and in the hotel bar on his Thai and on his computer, both learning how to make better web sites and how to market them. He didn't go to any bars except the hotel bar and ate in the restaurant of the hotel as well, although it was not really very good. He was trying to be a 'good boy', so he phoned her every morning and she phoned him every evening.

Lek's time in the village was only fleeting, she spent almost as much time travelling to and fro as she spent there, but it was nice to see her daughter again. There was no real need as far as the injury was concerned, Soom was calm about that, but she did appreciate her mother coming back to check on her. It was while she was with her daughter that she decided that she wanted to live in the village again. However, she did not tell anyone, in case it all went wrong.

Lek got back at five a.m. on New Years Eve and walked into the room with the TV on loud; Craig fast asleep, an open book on his chest. She picked up the book carefully so as not to wake him, but as soon as she turned the TV off he woke up.

"I was listening to that," he said instinctively, then he opened his eyes and saw Lek. "Hello, my beautiful darling, telak suay phom, how are you? Did you have a good trip?"

"Yes. Everything go OK. So, you speak Thai now, eh? Who teach you? You get lady teach you when I go home, eh?" and she tickled him so that he would know that she was kidding.

"Yeah, I talked to the waitresses and the barmaids every day in the hotel, but it is not easy. I do not think that I will ever get the tones right. I just cannot remember which tone goes with which meaning of a word. Come on let's sleep some more."

But Lek wanted a shower first and really was not tired anyway. "You sleep first, telak. I want to take a shower and then I come later," but she had no intention of sleeping really. She showered, put the TV on very quietly and sat there thinking about life in the village after ten years away and about Craig in the village. He had told her that he had never lived in a village before. Would he be able to handle it? Who knew? As long as he had his work, maybe he could last a few months at a time.

They could live in Pattaya, she thought and she could bring Soom to Pattaya to live – she had cousins there, but Craig had said several times that he had not lived with children since he was one himself and that he didn't want to start now at fifty years of age. In fact, he often said that he didn't like children, but she didn't believe that. Surely, he must have been joking on that one. Who could not like children? Especially her little Soom. She looked over at him. He was a nice man. She did like him a lot, but there was so much that she didn't know. So much for him and his 'exciting future', she thought, 'bloody scary future', if you ask me. Very scary.

When Craig woke up at eight, she pretended to be busy, but she went down to breakfast with him and then on to the pool for a swim. Not that she went in, because of the sunshine. At ten o' clock, she told Craig that she wanted to go help the girls do up the bar and prepare the food for the New Years Eve party.

"OK, dear, what time will I see you later?" he asked, but he was thinking: 'leaving me to get on with it alone again. Why should I care? I'm getting very used to it now'.

"At about three-thirty," she replied, "I will come back here to get you, have a shower and then we can go to the party. Bye, bye, telak. Choop, choop. See you later." She knew that she had just upset him again, but she really had to go and help and there was no getting out of it, although after today, there would not be anything big to celebrate until April, so they could spend more time together.

And she was gone again. He really was getting very cheesed off with spending most of his time sitting around alone. This was really not what he had come to Thailand for. He had been alone enough in Britain. OK, it was great to be in Thailand and it was great to be in a warm, new, exciting country with a beautiful new girlfriend, except that he hardly ever saw her during daylight. He knew that if their relationship was to continue, let alone progress, they were going to have to have a serious talk together very soon, either the next day or the day after.

Lek came back on time and after her shower, they went to the party at Daddy's Hobby. It was a very similar affair to the Christmas party, but this time Craig was determined to behave himself. All of the girls came over to wish him happy New Year in their own time. Some wanted a bit of the same as the week before, but only two or three openly suggested anything: "Shall I sit on your lap?" asked the girl from Isaan "and you can buy me another beer, like last time."

"I'll buy you a beer, but it is too hot for you to sit on my lap today."

"Oh, that's a shame. Do you want me to blow it cool for you?"

"No, it's all right on its own, thank you. Don't be naughty. I'm trying to be a good boy today." "Lek", he called out, "a beer for me and one for our friend here, if she wants one later, please."

Lek said something to the girl and she went back to the front of the bar.

He hoped that he hadn't got her into trouble, but she was trouble for him – far too tempting to have near him. The rest of the evening passed fairly easily though, although he was bored rigid.

Not that he could have told the Isaan girl that, he thought.

The main problem was that it was just too loud. He couldn't speak to anyone without shouting into their ear and he didn't find that a lot of fun any more. Lek took breaks this time though which helped, but they were only ten or fifteen minutes every hour and they couldn't talk together either. Still, she was trying.

That was precisely what she was doing too. She was consciously trying to make the party more enjoyable or at least less boring for him, by going over for a chat every now and again. As she got up to go back to 'work', he said: "Lek, I'm going to the Pig to use the toilet. I'll have to have a drink there too so I won't be back for thirty minutes. All right."

"Sure," she said and walked off.

It took a while to get to the Pig because of the crowds and because girls were on the look out for single foreign men, but he got there eventually, sat at the bar and checked the time, so that he could get the thirty minutes more or less right. The difference in the noise and the heat levels was fantastic. It was a real pleasure to just sit there and look out of the window at the passing crowds. One or two of the waitresses came over to wish him Happy New Year, but he didn't have to strain to hear them. It was lovely, but unfortunately soon over.

Once more into the fray, he thought.

He managed to make another two trips to the Pig before midnight.

At midnight everyone wanted to kiss everyone else and there was a fair bit of groping going on as well, although not by Craig and Lek as she had come around to make sure he was not left out. There were fire-works going off everywhere and even a few very loud bangs, which Lek said were handguns. They sang 'Olde Lang's Ayne' holding hands in a circle and then went back to the bar. "Lovely, eh" said Lek. "Craig nodded, but he was just hoping that that was the worst of it over with. He never had liked New Year's parties,

New Year's Day was not as bad as Christmas Day had been as far as hangovers went, although when Craig went for breakfast and a swim, Lek stayed in bed. She didn't get up until the maid wanted to clean the room at one o' clock so that she could have the afternoon off to be with her family. She laid down on a sun bed and went straight to sleep.

While swimming about lazily, Craig reckoned that it would probably be best to broach the subject of always being left alone the next day rather than then because Lek didn't really seem up to it.

The following day, Lek joined him for breakfast. That was usually a bad sign, because it meant she was going somewhere. "Where are you going today, telak?"

"Wherever you are going, telak. I not see too much of you for one or two weeks. I want to sit with you. What do you want to do today? Swim a little; learn Thai a little and then go Internet? Same as usual?"

"Yes, I have to do that every day. Maybe, for the rest of my life. It is my job now. Not very interesting for you though, is it? You see, I am fifty years old and if I lived in the UK, I would have to work until I am sixty-five, so I have to do it here too or I do not have enough money to stay here for a long time."

"Yes, I un'erstand, telak, I am not speaking bad for you. I know and I want to help. I do not un'erstand computers or the Internet – nothing at all, zero percent, maybe you can teach me… and I can help you learn Thai and sit watch you when you go swimming. I don' want black skin, so I don' want to swim, but I will come watch you. OK?"

He was flabbergasted. He could not have hoped for anything more really.

"One more thing that we have to start doing soon is to reapply for your visa, so maybe while I am working on line, you could start putting all the information together for that. What do you say to that? A good idea or not?"

"Yes, all right," she said, "starting this afternoon. Let us go swimming or you can go swimming and I will watch you and read the newspaper."

The rest of the day went really well and Craig was happier than he had been for weeks. Lek looked happy too, but she was better at hiding her true feelings than Craig. In truth, she was very worried about applying for a visa and even going to the UK. She just could not bear the thought of being refused again; she was sure she would die of shame if it happened too, but she was also frightened of going to the UK.

She had not mentioned it to Craig and probably never would, but friends of hers had warned her to be careful, because some foreigners came to Thailand, befriended a beautiful woman and then took her back home to sell her into slavery or the sex industry. This had really frightened her very much. Craig would not do that, she had said to her friends. You cannot tell, they had said, you will never know if he is a good con-man until it is too late and you are locked up in a room and forced to sleep with ugly, fat, old foreigners who like beating beautiful, young, foreign women.

They had really scared her and she was secretly watching Craig like a hawk for signs that he was a sex trafficker. They had said that much of the organising was done over the Internet and Craig did like using the Internet a great deal. That was very suspicious, they had told her. If you love your daughter and want to see her children, maybe it would be better not to go to the UK.

It was seeming like a good option to her at the moment and it would also mean not having to risk another refusal at the embassy as well. She was trying to work out a way of finding out exactly what he was doing on the Internet all those hours every day, which was why she

had suggested that he teach her something about how to access the Internet on her own.

23 AND IF AT FIRST YOU DON'T SUCCEED…

After the New Year, the couple started to get on well again, almost as well as when they had first met. Craig concentrated more on learning how to make money on line, putting learning Thai on the back burner, while Lek worked on her new visa application and learning how to use the Internet. They were aiming to make their next application in the first week of February and both were quite aware that it had to go well or Lek would never try again.

She had a large bag of every restaurant bill that they had ever been given since the first attempt; she also had hotel bills, phone cards and dozens of happy photographs of them together at many locations all dated and annotated on the back. She also learned as much about Craig's family, home town and life as he could tell her.

Or would tell her, she sometimes still thought.

She had not uncovered any real evidence yet that he was involved with human trafficking, although there was a lot of pornography in his email. She had asked him about that and he had said that it was just spam – something that everyone who used the Internet had to put up with. However, he never tried to hide it from her, so she tended to believe his explanation. Some of the younger girls in Daddy's Hobby used the Internet and they said that what Craig said was quite true, but she could not help bearing in mind what some of the older women in the village had warned her about.

She had discussed it with some of the girls in the bar and with

Beou, naturally, but they had told her that the women in the village were just jealous. They had never been anywhere and they didn't want her to go anywhere either. Beou was very supportive. She had come across this kind of jealousy before and she despised the women who tried to drag everyone and everything down to their level of ignorance and banality.

One day, Craig discovered Skype. It was purely by accident and he sent access details to all his family. He had been emailing his mother and three brothers for years and often read their emails out to Lek, who always listened politely, but somehow not really in an interested way. What he did not know was that she thought that they may be fakes that he had sent himself as part of his confidence trick.

A few days later, he received confirmation that his mother had set up Skype, so he arranged to call her at a set time. When that time arrived, he and Lek were going through his email and he phoned his mother without telling Lek what he was doing. The computer made the sound of a phone ringing and Lek looked at him surprised. Then there was a click and the image of a woman appeared on the screen:

"Hello, Craig," the image said, "how lovely to see and talk to you again. Isn't technology wonderful? Is that Lek by the side of you? She is beautiful. Hello, Lek. How are you, my dear?"

Lek looked at Craig as if she had just seen a ghost walk through the wall.

"Who is that?" she stammered.

"That is Rose, my mother. She is in Barry, but we can talk over the Internet. I did it as a surprise for you. Say 'Hello'."

"Er, hello, Mum, how are you today?"

"I'm fine, thank you. It is cold here. What is the weather like over there in Thailand, Lek?"

She could not speak.

"Er, OK, Mum. Er, thank you. Bye, bye" she said and went out of view of the camcorder.

Craig and his mother chatted for about twenty minutes and Lek listened, but she did not join in.

After they were finished, he asked her: "Well, what did you think? Good surprise or not? We will go to see her next month when you have got your visa."

"That was your Mum? Really? In the UK? Wow … Someone tell me before you can talk on the Internet the same as on the telephone but with pictures, but I never see before. It was a big shock. Why you not warn me? Now your Mum thinks I am very stupid and very rude. Please tell her next time that I was sick. She is very beautiful, your Mum. I like her."

That surprise chat with Craig's mother had unforeseen consequences. It went a very long way to dispelling Lek's fears that Craig might be a recruiting officer for the slave sex industry in the UK. She was more determined than ever to get a visa and go to Wales to meet Craig's mother and family. In fact, they talked to all the family over the next few days and Lek became more confident talking to them using VOIP.

She was even looking forward to going now whole-heartedly. She wanted to meet Craig's Mum more than anything, because family was everything to her. Over the months, she had tried to impress on Craig that he should never nod at or say hello to any Thai that he didn't know – and she would prefer it if he never said hello to anyone that she had not introduced him to, but he was incapable of doing what she advised. He went on about being fifty years of age and being able to look after himself 'thank you very much' but in reality, he had just been lucky in Thailand so far.

She shuddered at the things that happened to some people. She was only trying to look after him, but he saw it as trying to boss him about. He could be so childish sometimes. Surely, he realized that he could not even understand what people were saying? And that they knew that too? Men had such big egos – they always thought they were the boss. Why didn't they realize that if two people are on the same side, it doesn't matter who is in charge? The right person for the job at all times was what counted, not egos.

They waited until the last week of January and then sent off their application for a visa. Everyone in Daddy's Hobby wished them well as did the few other friends that they had made. They knew that it would take a few days to get there and a few days to process, so they went up to Bangkok on the following Sunday, hoping to be called in for an interview a few days later. They tried to be more laid-back about the situation than the first time, after all, they were old hands now.

Hitherto unsuccessful old hands maybe, but old hands nevertheless.

Craig wanted to do it that way because she had people to talk to and drink with in Pattaya, whereas in Bangkok he would have had to bear the brunt of her stress alone and he knew that would mean fight after fight until they got an answer. On the Monday, Craig telephoned the embassy and explained that if they needed to speak to the applicant for the visa, they would now have to contact their Bangkok hotel as they had moved on from Pattaya. The fact was noted and on Tuesday Lek was told to present herself at the embassy on Wednesday morning.

They were there at seven-thirty, not having slept all night and having had three coffees each in the cafe across the road as well. When Lek was called up for the interview she was a bag of nerves, but so was Craig.

Maybe so much coffee had not been a good idea.

She came out of the small interview room about fifteen minutes later, and it was obvious to everyone in the room that she was happy. She had probably never been happier since the birth of her daughter. She tried to act with some decorum, but after letting the interview room door go behind her, she looked for Craig, took three lady-like steps and then gave up. She ran over to him and burst into tears:

"I have a visa! I have a visa! Your government says I can go there for six months holiday!" and she showered his face in kisses. "Oh, come on, we must go to Pattaya now. Right now!"

"OK, darling, we can give up the room and go back today, no problem. Wow, good for you. Well done, you get a visa!"

They went back to the restaurant over the road for an early lunch, a few beers to celebrate and to order a taxi. Craig also wanted to check the documentation as soon as possible, so that he knew exactly what was going on and that if there was a mistake, it could be corrected.

They clinked glasses and then Lek handed over the paperwork she had been given and her passport. Her face was like a child's on Christmas day. She kept saying: 'Your government believes me now. I am so happy'.

Craig checked the passport first and it was true. She had a six month, multiple entry visa valid from that day. There was also a piece of paper stapled to it saying that she had to go back to the embassy on her return to have any unused portion of the visa cancelled. It also said that she had no right of access to any government funds. That was all right, he thought, although he had never seen a visa to the UK before. Two more beers later, he had gone through the rest of the paperwork and it was clear that she had a valid visa to visit the UK.

"You did it, girl," he said, "I am taking you back to the UK. Whoopee!"

They hurried back to the hotel, packed in minutes, paid, got into a taxi and were on their way to Daddy's Hobby again. Both slept off and on on the way back, but they got to the bar at three o'clock and Noi welcomed Lek with a teary hug: "I knew you could do it, Lek. Good for you. Craig, I am very happy for you both. You take good care of her in the UK. Understand? My darling here take good care of you in our country, now you must take good care of her in your country."

As the girls came in, there was a marked difference in the way that some of them treated him. Everyone was all over Lek, but only the old sorority seemed truly happy to Craig when they spoke to him. It was as if the new girls had had slender hopes of stealing him away from the older Lek, but now they knew that they could not. Her old friends were genuinely happy for both of them.

Beou came down straightaway to congratulate them and even put on an impromptu party. Lek cried from time to time, but he didn't have a lot of opportunity to speak to her about anything. Not that he really needed to because she didn't let go of his hand except to go to the toilet. He had not felt so loved since he had came back five months before. She looked like she had done the previous July, really happy and without a care in the world.

As always though, there was more going on in Lek's head than showed on her face. She had resigned herself to the 'trafficking' – if he was a trafficker, then so be it, she would risk it, but what about her daughter and food and speaking English and travel sickness? She had always suffered from travel sickness, but she could cope with it on a bus. She was worried about how she would cope on a plane? She tried to tell herself that she was worrying about too much that she could not change, but it was not easy. She also wanted to go to the village for a few days before departing, but she had not discussed that with Craig yet. Would he mind? She wanted to see her family before she left, just in case.

They had the best night together out of their room, or in it, for months. They woke up fairly early and went for a shower together before going down for breakfast.

"OK, Lek, what do you have to do before we can leave? We have plenty of time, but I want to set a schedule. Is two weeks enough for you?"

She made a few calculations in her head and on her fingers and thought that she only needed a week really. "Yes, all right, two weeks is plenty. I only want to go home for three days and then we can go."

After breakfast, they went to a travel agent and booked the first flight out that they could get on. Craig had lost his return ticket months ago, so it was just a question of buying two new return tickets at about the end of February because they were booked in until the end of the month on a special monthly rate and they didn't have to be back until early August when the visa expired. Craig intended going for three months so they had loads of time.

They bought two return tickets with Etihad Airways to leave on the 27th of February. Lek had to take them down to show Noi immediately, but Craig went for a swim instead, although he was just as happy as Lek and promised to meet her at Daddy's Hobby for lunch at one o' clock.

Because they had so much time, Lek decided that she wanted to go home for a week, if they were going to the UK for twelve. She offered Craig the chance to go with her, but phrased it in such a way that she hoped that he wouldn't go. She also said that she was only going for three days, but she intended to tell him later that her daughter wanted her to stay longer. She doubted that he wanted to spend a week in Baan Suay anyway.

She was quite right, in this case, not because he didn't like the village, but because he didn't want to spend one of the last two weeks of his 'holiday' somewhere that closed at eight o' clock every night. He justified his decision by telling himself that Lek needed some time alone with her family and although he arrived at it via an excuse, it was the exact truth of the matter.

She wanted to say a serious goodbye to all her family as a soldier might before going into battle. She also wanted to spend some considerable time in the village Wat for the first time in ten years. It worked out right for both of them but only because Lek had lied and because Craig was trying to kid himself that he wasn't being selfish. Craig was not going to get up to his old tricks again and, in fact, he supposed that he would be very bored without her, but maybe not as bored as if he had to sit on the bus for a day going up and a day coming back and not speaking to anyone for two or three days more.

Lek left two days later and Craig actually went up to the bus station to see her off. He was genuinely sad to see her go, but she was quite happy to see him stay there. On the way back to the hotel, Craig had a brainwave and instructed the taxi to stop at a block of private condos not far from the hotel where they had spent the last six months. The Diana Estate was somewhere that they had both admired for six months, so he went in and booked a private apartment from the day that the flight touched down for three full months – June until August.

He couldn't wait to tell her so he phoned her while having a beer in the Rich Bar. "Hi Lek, I have a surprise. I have booked a room for when we come back in June. The Diana Estate. I have booked an apartment for three months for when we get back! What do you think? I have paid a deposit already. Great, eh?"

"Yes" she said half-heartedly, "I am sleeping. I take tablet already for travelling, I cannot think good. Please let me sleep. Take care yourself, Craig. Sorry. I am stupid now. I will speak to you tomorrow morning. Choop, choop, telak. Faan dee; sweet dreams, don' drink too much." Click. And she was gone.

He knew the tablets that she took when she travelled. They really knocked her out, but if she didn't take them she would be sick after ten or fifteen minutes of travelling. Her attitude had been disappointing, but it didn't upset him. He could have, even should have predicted it. After all, he knew that she was a rotten traveller… and then it hit him. How was she going to get 5,500 miles to the UK if she had trouble after fifteen minutes on a bus? It was quite a thought and he had no idea how she was going to accomplish it.

He would have to leave that one to her.

He would also have to leave something else to her – her spiritual salvation as she saw it. She wanted to pray that she would return to Thailand and to her daughter at the allotted hour or at least the allotted day. She wanted to be back on the day that they had arranged, the first of June. She didn't want trouble with the police, the customs, the Mafia, racists or anyone else and she prayed that Craig's mother and family would like her and that she would like them. She prayed every day in the Wat, usually twice a day and she was normally accompanied by a couple of friends or her mother. She promised Buddha that if she returned unharmed on the right day, she would put on a Likay in the Wat's grounds; a Likay being a bawdy, folksy, popular, slapstick play based on a traditional court story, but brought up-to-date by references to current affairs. A bit like a pantomime. Likay was very popular in Baan Suay and the whole village would attend a performance by a famous troupe.

She took the question of leaving Thailand to go so far very seriously and didn't have an alcoholic drink for the whole week – the first time since her baby had been born, ten years before.

Craig decided to behave himself for the week, not that the girls in Daddy's Hobby seemed that much interested in him any more. They were polite and even shook his hand, but there were no more kisses or hugs. A shame, he thought, but just as well. He went to Daddy's Hobby every day after having had lunch at the Pig. He got into the routine of going back to the hotel at about six or seven and reading in the room until Lek phoned at about midnight.

One afternoon, someone was talking about a Thai massage and never having had a massage in his life before, he decided to try one on his way home from Daddy's Hobby that evening. There were plenty of massage parlours, but he had no idea which would be a good one or how to tell. He decided to pick one situated about half-way home in case he was aching as much as the man had told him he would be if he had never had a Thai massage before. He was quite looking forward to it.

When he got to the road that he had always judged to be half-way, he thought that he would choose the third one he came across just to make it a random choice. When he got to the third one, he slowed down outside and looked at the prices – 300 Baht, about the same as all the others he had passed. The girls noticed his interest and one of them came over to help him make up his mind. He allowed himself to be led over to the table where there were three young ladies and a lady boy,

"Do you wan' me massage you or you wan' someone else" she asked looking at the lady boy.

They all looked up at him with their most winsome smiles.

"Maybe this lady."

She got up took his hand and led him inside. She took him upstairs past a few small rooms and annexes to a room with three cubicles, but as far as he could see they were empty. He was pleased about that. He didn't like the idea of being half-naked with a lot of other half-naked men.

"My name is Lee. What massage do you want?" she asked.

"Nice to meet you Lee. My name is Craig. An oil massage, please."

"Oil massage? OK. Please take off all your clothes." She slightly turned away from him, but took his things from him as he handed them to her, folded them up and placed them on a chair. Then she passed him a towel, which he wrapped around his waist.

"OK, ready. Now we go for a shower" and she led him back down the corridor. He was immediately worried about him wallet. It made him uncomfortable and he thought about how a fool and his money are soon parted. She helped wash his arms and back in the shower, but she did not get undressed. She helped dry his back and his legs and then with his towel on, she led him back to their cubicle. "Lie down on your fron', please." He did as he was bid and he could feel her pulling at the towel. He lifted his middle up and it came away, then she laid it over his bottom.

She started with his legs, then arms before jumping up onto the table to straddle him as she worked on his neck and back. He could feel the oil being worked into his skin and muscles. It was wonderful. She didn't say much as she worked, but she half hummed and half sang a Thai song that he didn't know – a traditional one, he supposed. She hopped off and removed the towel. She poured a lot of oil into the small of his back and used it as a reservoir to oil his buttocks.

He had been doing well up until that point, but once she started doing that, it didn't take long to get a large erection, which embarrassed him as she had done everything correctly with no innuendo. He hoped she would realize that it was only because he was new to massage.

"OK, turn over." She said. "Oh, big cock" and she looked at him, then it.

"You have a big cock for me? Why, I do nothing sexy." She took it in her hand, stood it upright and pulled the skin down tight. "I like big cocks, I like to kiss and suck them." She licked the top of it slowly, then kissed it quickly, pulled it back towards his feet and let it go so that it slapped down on his stomach. She giggled, patted it like a puppy and started work on his arms and legs, getting very close to his balls, just touching the hairs on them sometimes with her finger tips. He decided to try to ride it out, hoping that his erection would get bored and just go away, but it didn't.

Especially when she sat on it to massage his chest.

Her skirt was not particularly short, maybe six inches above the knee, but when she straddled him to work on his chest, he could see her underwear and the movements of her working on his groin, demolished his resistance. When she had finished, she said: "Do you want me to take care of him? 200 for hand, 500 for mouth or 1,000 for sex."

"Hand, please."

She did her job pretty clinically and then led him away for a shower. This time she did undress and get in with him and they washed each other down quite intimately. As they got dried and dressed together he started to feel quite an affection for this twenty-something from Isaan. He checked his pockets and at least his wallet was still there.

She sat him down into an ornate corner that had been behind a screen and made them a cup of tea. "Where do you come from in the UK, Craig? Wales? Oh, I want to go to the UK one day"

"Have you been here long, Lee?" he asked, checking the contents of his wallet and passing her a five hundred Baht note. It was all there. She took it and waaid her thanks.

"No, not long. Three months. The mama san is a good lady and I like the job more than working in a bar. I do that for six months but it was horrible."

"You have children at home, Lee and husband?" He knew from experience that Thai girls did not mind these questions, although he would never have asked in Europe.

"Yes, I have a beautiful little girl. She is five, but she is not here. She is with my Mum in Isaan. I was married before and had a good job with my husband in a bank, but he sleep with everyone like some king, so I finished him. He made me lose my job, but I can earn more here. It is good for my daughter."

They chatted, but time was money and so she stood up to lead him out. She led him by the hand to the bottom rung of stairs where she said that he should go on alone. She followed close behind.

Once in the foyer, mama san said, everything to your satisfaction, sir? She is a good girl, yes? Please come back again."

"Yes, I will" he lied, as he turned to look at Lee who was handing over three one-hundred Baht notes to the mama san. She smiled at him, and guided him to the door, which was opened by one of the girls outside. They all smiled and waaid at him as he walked away, leaving Lee in the doorway waving after him.

They had given him a really warm feeling all over, all of them, but particularly Lee.

That was the first and last time that he went for a massage that week. He had not expected to have any form of sex while Lek was away, but he supposed that he had been naive or fooling himself if he thought that nothing sexual was going to happen in a massage parlour. They are famous covers for the sex industry all over the world, although to be fair, he had never been in one before. Maybe it had been naivety.

The rest of the week passed without event and Lek came back seeming happy to have been home and spend some time alone with her friends and family. One night he tried to explain about Wales in the winter. "Lek it will be very cold and very windy in March, probably very wet in April and you never can tell about May these days. You have to take appropriate clothing. It will cost twice as much or three times as much over there."

"It is OK, Craig, it is cold here too sometimes. I bring clothes for cold from my home. Look." And she laid them out on the bed. They were the sort of things a woman might wear in April or September on a chilly evening in Spain. No use whatsoever against a March wind in the UK. The nearest thing she had to a coat was a thin denim jacket, made to look pretty rather than keep someone warm.

The next day, he took her out to buy a few pairs of warm trousers, jumpers and a coat, but they came back with a new bag and shoes as well. The night before they left, her cousin gave a free going away party for them and started calling Craig 'my cousin'.

And then the big day was upon them. They checked out of the hotel after a stay of six months and the staff lined the foyer to shake their hands, or waai or both and wish them a pleasant flight. All the girls there wanted to be Lek. They walked over to the Rich Bar where some friends were waiting for lunch and a few farewell drinks, because the flight was not until eight and the taxi was coming at four.

Lek took two tablets an hour before the taxi was due and they started to take effect before it arrived making her drowsy, a little as if she were tipsy and a little childlike. They loaded three-quarters of their luggage into Lek's cousin's car to store at her house, because they only wanted to take the bare necessities back with them.

Lek slept all the way to Bangkok airport, while Craig worried about whether everything would go well. He worried particularly about getting into the UK, although the visa was legitimate and no lies had been told to get it. They had their passports and he had his money and credit cards and essentially that was all they needed all the rest was luxury and could be replaced if necessary.

Lek may have been the experienced traveller within Thailand, but Craig did not know many people personally who had spent more time abroad than he had. He had been all over Europe and northern Africa, but had also been to south America and the old Soviet Union and been on several cruises.

Craig was a confident traveller.

24 GETTING THERE

The fast driver in the old taxi was nothing out of the ordinary for Thailand, but the journey was uneventful. When they arrived at the airport, the driver helped them with their bag, Lek gave him a tip and they went inside. Craig remembered the layout of the airport, so they went more or less straight up to the Etihad counter, handed over their bags at baggage control and checked in. Lek looked awestruck and more than a little intimidated.

She was visibly frightened when they had to pass through separate aisles at passport control, although everything went quite smoothly. Craig got through first and he waited for Lek behind the customs officer checking her queue of Thai passport holders. She brightened up when she saw him nearby. She passed through control and they went to find somewhere to sit down.

"I want something to drink. Some beer," she said. I am nervous, sorry, Craig. How long must we wait now?"

"Well, we have about two hours. We can stay here in Duty Free for an hour and then go on to Boarding. In that section we are close to the plane for when they call us in. Do you want anything in Duty Free?" He explained what it was, but it wasn't much cheaper than outside the airport, so they didn't bother. They found a bar not far from the route to their boarding gateway, so they could stay there for an hour. They took two beers to sit by the window and watched the planes coming and going.

He showed her how to read the flight monitor and showed her their flight reference number so that she could track what was going on. They had three beers and then moved on to a bar closer to Boarding. They had two there and they decided to spend all their Thai money on cigarettes to sell in the UK. They bought five cartons although they were only allowed one each. Lek was not worried about British customs, but that was only because of the tablets and the beer.

Then they progressed to boarding control, took their boarding cards and were called up ten minutes later. Lek was worried again, but it was too late now. Twenty minutes later, they were rolling down the runway and Craig took Lek's hand to comfort her, but there was no need. She thought that he was doing it because he was nervous, so she squeezed it back. In fact, she had taken another three tablets and now that they were starting to work she would not have been frightened of fighting a raging bull in a Spanish bullring.

She enjoyed being waited on and she enjoyed the wine, but when the menus were handed around and Craig translated for her, there was nothing on it that she wanted to eat. There were four choices, two of which contained beef, which she wouldn't eat ever (her family didn't eat beef); there was an Indian chicken curry, but she hated the 'smelly' spices that Indians used and there was a vegetarian pie.

The vegetarian part was all right, but she didn't eat wheat flour: no bread, no cakes and no pastry. He wished now that he had ticked the box on the booking form for 'special dietary requirements'. Eventually, she settled for the pie, but left the pastry. Craig swapped his chips for her pastry and his ice cream for her cake. He also ate her bread roll and then asked for two more ice creams. That and more wine did the trick.

A man died in Club Class. He had a heart attack and died very suddenly. They didn't know that until afterwards, but they were told that the plane would have to put down in Mumbai for a medical emergency. Lek thought it was very exciting. It was the first time in 36 years of flying that anything like this had happened to Craig and Lek got it on her first flight. After thirty minutes, the pilot switched the air conditioning off and opened the doors for some fresh air. Mosquitoes the size of matchsticks came in and attacked in squadrons.

Everyone wanted cabin service at the same time. It was really hot and uncomfortable and people were worried about malaria and dengue. Craig and Lek were dehydrating and wanted more beer, but the staff wouldn't serve alcohol, so they said, although they could see them handing out bottles of whisky to Arabs in Arabic dress a few yards away. Instead, they were given an ice cream and a plastic cup of warm water each.

They were there for three hours and missed their connecting flight from Bahrain to London, so Etihad put them up in a hotel in Bahrain. Craig's nationality allowed him to just walk through passport control, but Lek's meant something special had to be done and they had to have someone special to do it. However, there was no-one there who could – they had all gone home, so all ninety onward bound passengers had to wait for this special official, maybe special because he could read Thai, to be found, dragged out of bed and brought to see Lek's passport.

It was a lovely hotel when they eventually got there. Five Star, but the staff had already gone home too: there was no bar and no food. They didn't even have any local currency to buy anything outside, if there was anything open, which was dubious at three o' clock in the morning. In addition, the only TV station that was broadcasting was in Arabic - Craig was totally cheesed off.

However, Lek didn't care because she was so out of it that she just went to sleep without even showering, which was extremely rare for her. Twin beds too that could not be pushed together and no beer in the mini-bar. He just read for five hours until it was time to go for breakfast.

The five hour flight to London left late in the morning and all went well. They were treated in an exceptionally special manner on board the airplane, but every other Etihad flight goes to Gatwick and every other flight goes to Heathrow. This one was going to Heathrow, whereas Craig had studied how to get home from Gatwick. He had also missed the bus from there the night before that he had booked and paid for online from Thailand.

Lek was worried about customs and again she had to use a different aisle from Craig, but he waited for her as before and even had to help Lek and customs with some words because of their accents.

"Welcome to the UK, Lek! We made it; you made it! How do you feel?"

"I am so happy I could cry. I was scared that the UK did not want me to come, but my Buddha take care of me" and she took the amulet from inside her blouse and touched it to her forehead.

It was pretty cold. Lek said she was warm enough, but Craig was not. He had planned to have been making this journey with Lek the previous October, which is often still fairly warm these days, whereas February / March is wet and cold. He had a suit on but it was only a thin one and he wanted to get on a bus or a train soon.

They got lost several times in Heathrow, but eventually found the platform to Paddington from where they could get a train to South Wales. Lek loved every minute of it. When they got to Cardiff, it was eleven fifteen pm, freezing cold and the bars were shut again. It was the worst trip Craig had ever made, but Lek had loved every second of it. In addition to all that, he felt ashamed of the shabbiness of the station and its environs. They were supposed have just come from a Third World country not arriving in one.

Nick had offered to pick them up from Cardiff 'at whatever time' and Craig had phoned him when they had left Newport. He was sitting in his car outside Cardiff Central Station. When he saw Lek he jumped out and hugged her. "Welcome to Wales! The Land of Song welcomes the Land of Smiles." He shook hands with Craig and they got into the car out of the rain.

Nick dropped them off at Craig's place just before midnight, but he wouldn't go in: "I'll see you tomorrow in the usual place," he said and left.

Lek wanted to see everything. She wanted to see the garden, she wanted to walk on the street and she wanted to look inside all at the same time. Because it was cold and raining, Craig persuaded her to look inside first.

It could have been a nice flat. It had its own front door at street level although it was on the first of a two-floor block and so was technically a maisonette. It was on the brow of a hill overlooking Barry, Barry Docks, the Bristol Channel, Flat Holm and Steep Holm islands and towns such as Weston-Super-Mare on the English side of the Severn, which was about twelve miles across at that point. It needed redecorating and a lot of TLC, none of which he had bothered to give it for years.

However, that did not matter one jot to Lek, she loved everything that she had seen so far: shabby old, run-down Heathrow airport, where they had desperately needed an ATM only to find that most of them were out-of-order; the run-down train that took them to shabby Cardiff Central and then the miserable weather that greeted them and on top of all that, Craig's run-down flat. He found it all terribly embarrassing and terribly depressing, but Lek said that everything she had seen so far was 'too beautiful'.

Once again, she thanked her Buddha, Craig and the British government in her heart for getting her to Britain.

There was six months' dust over everything and nothing in the fridge, because it had been turned off. He had left the heating on a thermostat though so the place was tolerable and after turning it up to 20c, it was soon warm. Craig went around plugging everything in and showed Lek around. She said that it was the most beautiful house that she had ever been in.

They were both hungry and thirsty, not having eaten since the meal on the flight, so Craig threw the ingredients for a loaf into the bread-maker for himself and they went through the tins for something for her. They settled on sharing a tin of soup; a tin of green beans for her; bread for him; and a tin of tapioca to finish. They decided to open a bottle of wine rather than make tea or coffee and took it through to watch TV while waiting for the bread.

It was too late to phone anyone, but he plugged his computer in and sent emails to everyone that they had arrived safely. They didn't know anyone in Thailand with a computer. The bed was damp, so they made one up on the floor and were both fast asleep long before the wine or the bread were finished - both very happy people indeed.

In the morning, Craig went to the corner shop early to get some provisions and left Lek sleeping. He wanted to surprise her that he could cook, so he prepared a vegetable Biriani with real saffron rice. When she finally woke up, came out of the shower and got dressed, he presented her with his meal and a cup of tea. She drank the tea, but eyed the Biriani with suspicion. "I am sorry, Craig, but I cannot eat that."

"Why, what is the matter with it?"

"You make a problem with the rice, it has gone bad. It is yellow, not white and smells not right. Sorry. I will cook later."

"It is not bad! It is white Thai rice that I made go yellow with saffron flowers to make special!"

"So sorry, Craig, but Thai rice is special to Thai people. We like rice white, not yellow or green. You see any colour rice in Thailand not white?" And it was true, he hadn't, but hadn't noticed at the time.

"All right," he said, "today is the day of the Saint of my country, Wales. His name is Saint David, meaning Buddha David. We can go out to the pub and see friends and eat in the restaurant, but first I want to phone Mum and say we are home safe."

Rose couldn't leave the house to join them that day, so they arranged to meet her the next and then they headed off into the bright sunlight of a bitterly cold March midday.

'The Old School', the pub was not far away. It was very popular at lunch times and usually you had to be there early or be lucky to get a seat between twelve and two. Nick and Barry were already there reserving a table for six. "Will's coming later, as soon as he can get away," said Barry as they sat down.

Lek and Craig ordered a full English breakfast while Nick ordered a round. Lek wanted to try best bitter, so they brought her a half. Craig had a Guinness. She wolfed the breakfast down and loved it; she swigged the bitter and loved it and she tried Craig's Guinness and liked that too. Within the first thirty minutes, dozens of regulars had stopped by to wish them well so that they could meet this beautiful Thai lady that they had heard so much about. Everybody wanted to buy her a drink and talk to her and she was lapping the attention up. A bit too much at times, Craig thought.

He was the only man in the bar to think so, although a few of the women agreed with him.

He wondered whether she was aware of the effect she was having on these people, but he reasoned that being a beautiful woman she must be. She just liked attracting men and she was in her element. Craig sat back and went practically unnoticed, not that he minded. Not too much anyway. Over the course of the next six hours, it seemed as if everyone he had ever met in Barry, except his mother, who was otherwise engaged, came to say 'Hello'.

Word was getting around quickly. His brothers came in after work and they took to her immediately, as most people did. Will came and went after they had made a big fuss over each other. There were a few catty comments about that from some of the women, but Lek held a special place in her heart for Will because she gave him the credit for introducing her to Craig and ultimately fulfilling a dream, even if only temporarily, by getting her to the UK for a holiday.

At about six o' clock, she tried to whisper subtly in his ear: "Take me home. Take me home, please," but it came out loud enough for everyone to hear. She was either still jet-lagged or those six or seven pints of mixed ales were having an adverse effect on her. He did as he was told. She was as sick as a dog on arrival at the flat, got undressed and went to bed.

Craig sat there alone again watching TV, but very happy with the way things had gone. She had made a great first impression and everyone loved her as he knew they would. She liked them too and he knew that they were going to have a lovely holiday in Wales.

He ate the Biriani and had an early night. The Biriani was gorgeous, he thought, she doesn't know what she's missing – even if it is cold.

25 GOING TO SEE MUM

At about eight o'clock the next morning, Craig woke up to hear Lek groaning close by his right ear: "What's the matter, telak, Hangover? I thought you were drinking too much of too many types of beer. You must not mix the beers in Europe. Only drink one type of beer on one day. It is better."

"No, darling, you don' understand, I am sick. Not sick from beer, not hangover. I am sick from flying and sick from not eat rice too. More. I am more sick from not eat Thai rice."

"Oh, come on, Lek. You have a hangover. You cannot be sick from not eating Thai rice. Can you?" He was not sure himself now, but it didn't sound right.

"I have eaten Thai rice for breakfast for thirty-two years, but I have not eaten it now for three days. I must eat Thai rice soon or maybe I die same junkie. Help me to go to the kitchen and make some rice. Thank you, darling."

He helped her to the kitchen and sat her on a bar stool at the counter then he put a bag of Thai rice in front of her and a small sauce-pan. She studied the bag carefully which had a bit of writing in Thai on the bottom. Then she tipped some onto her hand sniffed it and inspec-ted it carefully. She put a grain in her mouth and tasted it."

"Mmm, not best rice. Thai rice? Yes, I think so, but bad, old Thai rice. Maybe rubbish from the floor. Not grade one, two or three. Maybe grade ten for cows." She laughed at her joke. She put some tap water with it and Craig transferred it to a gas ring. She moved her stool over so she could keep a close eye on it.

"It is true what you say, eh? The water from the tap is very good. Can drink and not make sick? Very good, not must buy water. Thai people can drink water in my village, but they drink for long time. Maybe make you sick, I don' know. You can try one day."

He didn't relish the prospects, but put it down to one of her jokes.

She stirred the rice as it simmered. The rice melted into a slush a bit like porridge and she put the lid on the pan. "OK, darling, nearly ready. Do you have a bowl and a spoon for me? And some salt, some sugar and some chillis from our bag?" He went to get one of the two one-kilo bags of chillis that her mother had given her from her garden to take with her. One was her present to her counterpart in Wales.

Lek stirred some of the ingredients in, poured some into a bowl and took it through to watch TV. "Mmm, alloy, good. It makes me strong again. Not the best, all right, but not bad. Try." He tried and it was quite nice. He preferred porridge, but it was a good substitute.

She took two aspirins and disappeared into the bathroom for half an hour. When she came out she was as right as rain.

"What are we going to do today, darling?"

"Well, we can go and see Mum at about three, until then, we can clean this place up a bit and unpack." He could see that the cleaning bit did not go down very well, but they both knew that it had to be done, so they set about it. Lek loved using the vacuum cleaner; she had never seen one before.

Most of the general cleaning had been done by one thirty, so they had another shower and started to walk up to Mum's house. Lek loved everything about Barry. She thought that the gardens were beautiful (even in March); she thought the paved streets were beautiful because there was no dust on them and she liked the trees lining the streets although she did not know that they normally had leaves on them.

Halfway to their destination, it started snowing. Craig had told her not to expect snow, because she had set her heart on seeing it. She had been disappointed at the time, because she had never seen snow and thought that it looked so pretty in the photographs. Neither of them could believe that she had been lucky enough to see snow on her second day on her first trip. Sometimes it didn't snow for four or five years on the trot.

By the time they had walked the more than two miles to Mum's house, Lek was worn out, but ever so happy to see and be in the snow. Craig knocked the door and walked in with Lek just behind him. Mum hugged him and kissed him, which greatly impressed Lek. Then he introduced Mum to Lek and she did the same to her. Lek didn't know how to behave or what to do, but she hugged Craig's mother and kept repeating: "Hello, Mum. Nice to meet you, Mum." Craig took their coats to the cloakroom, while his mother and Lek walked off towards the kitchen arm in arm. It was so typical of them both to just get on with other people. They were both naturally likeable.

"Can I help with the cooking, Mum?" she asked.

"Of course not, Lek. You are a guest. Sit down and rest. Do you want a drink? Craig, get her a drink while I finish off."

"OK, Mum, but it's just that a Thai guest especially a son's girlfriend would expect and be expected to help in Thailand. She really does want to help."

Rose hated anyone helping her in her kitchen. She liked to do everything herself because she was a perfectionist as far as her cooking was concerned.

"Can't she peel some potatoes or chop something for you. She will soon learn how you like it done."

"Yes, Mum, I want to learn how you cook. Craig tells me you are a very good cook and I wan' to cook the same for him like you later in our house."

It made sense and she wanted to make Lek feel at home, so Rose set her up with a few jobs and showed her how she wanted them completed. They were soon talking and chopping and ignoring him, so he took a beer out of the fridge and went into the living room to watch television.

Craig could hear all sorts of happy noises coming from the kitchen before he turned the sound up on the TV. He started reading the paper, but he didn't know whether to gaze out of the large picture window, which had a similar view to his own; read the paper or to watch TV.

He was just so happy to be there again and especially with Lek; and Lek, for her part, had everything she had been dreaming of for ten years – except her daughter again.

The End

(for now)

Look out for the sequel:

"An Exciting Future"

Glossary

These are a few commonly used terms in this book:

Auw: to want; I want; you want etc..

Baan Suay: properly called Baan Suay, 'Beautiful Village', Lek's home village in northern Thailand

Baht: Thai currency: 1 Baht = 2p or 3c, but also 15.2 grammes of gold

Baht Bus: most common form of transport – a covered pick-up with bench seats, now 5 Baht for Thais and 10 Baht for foreigners

Beer Chang: Thailand's most popular beer – 6.4 % ABV

Daddy's Hobby: bar in Pattaya where Lek works

Dam: the colour black

Deng: the colour red

Falang: properly 'farang', white foreigners, Caucasians. Confusingly 'man falang' means crisps (potato chips). It comes from the name given to the first white foreigners in Thailand, the French or 'Falangset' ('Farangset').

Kapun Ka: or just 'Ka', 'thank you', spoken by a woman.

Kapun Kap: or just 'Kap', 'thank you', spoken by a man.

Khao: can mean rice, or food in general or the colour white or just 'clear'.

Lao: can mean Laos, but usually means alcohol 30-40% ABV – clear (white) or red

Lek: means small or 'Little One"; but is short for Leynou Suksawat,

Lek's full name

Ma: a dog, a horse or the verb 'to come'

Maak: or 'maak, maak', much, many or too (much)

Mai: makes a negative like 'not' – 'mai auw' – 'I don't want' (or he, she, he , we, they).

Mee: to have

Naam: water

Neh?: Thai equivalent of 'Eh?'

Nid Noi: little bit, some

Phitsanulok: city 'not far' from Lek's village

Phom: I, me, mine or my

Pig and Whistle: Pub-restaurant in Pattaya Soi 7 where Craig stayed first time.

Satang: money – 'mai mee satang' = 'I don't have any money'.

Soi: a lane or narrow street. Soi 7 is the busiest soi in Pattaya, if you don't count Walking Street.

Soi Buakhao: White Lily Lane, a street where may ex-pats hang out

Soom: Lek's daughter

Uttaradit: city 'not far' from Lek's village

Suay: beautiful or pretty.

Telak: Darling

Wat: Buddhist Temple

Review Request

Please leave a short review where you bought this book. This kind of feedback is extremely important to authors and other readers, so please make your voice heard, and join me as my fiend on

BlueSky: owen-author.bsky.social
Facebook: **AngunJones**
Instagram: owen_author
LinkedIn: owencerijones
Pinterest: owen_author
TikTok: @owen_author
X: @owen_author
Blog: Megan Publishing Services

Thanks,
Owen.

Daddy's Hobby

Bonus: The first chapter of the sequel:

Behind The Smile:
An Exciting Future

The story of Lek, a bar girl in Pattaya

1 Starting Again

As the wheels of the aircraft touched down on the runway at the new Bangkok International Airport called Suvarnabhumi, Craig knew that he was going to have his hands full with Lek. She suffered badly from travel sickness – it was her one big weakness, but she even got sick on the bus going to the market, so a flight of 11,500 kilometres and fifteen hours was always going to be a problem.

Lek had taken five of the green tablets which were her favourite anti-travel sickness pills. She always seemed to have about twenty of them in her bag. One tablet would make her appear a little drunk, but five made her seem like an escapee from a lunatic asylum. He had seen it on the outward flight. He looked at her sitting next to him; her eyes were glassy and she was humming something quietly to herself.

"Are we there yet?" she asked, "That was quick. Have we stopped off somewhere?"

"We're in Thailand," he replied a little too testily.

Craig was fifty years old and had never asked a woman to marry him so far, but he thought he might like to ask this one. She was a handful, as they say, that was to be sure, but there was also something about her that he found very special.

He didn't like her taking those pills though, but he knew how badly affected by travel-sickness she could get. She'd had to throw up in her new crocodile skin handbag once – her pride and expensive joy – because they had gone on a short bus ride and she had forgotten to transfer all her paraphernalia into the new bag. It was either be sick in her new bag or on the floor of the bus and she would rather die than do that and lose face.

Later, she would have to be assisted like a drunk through the air-port, baggage control and immigration and suffer the stern stares from the Thai officials who would assume that she had drunk too much cheap alcohol on the plane.

He was glad that she had chosen to wear long, baggy trousers.

The plan of the day was Lek's usual one whenever anything un-usual or exciting happened to her, namely to get down to 'Daddy's Hobby' in Pattaya and tell her friends all about it. In fact, it didn't have to be anything unusual at all, it was just the place where Lek felt most at home in the world. 'Daddy's Hobby' was the name of the bar that Lek's cousin owned and where he had met her. Craig didn't mind going there one little bit. The two dozen bar girls always made a big fuss of him and Lek even encouraged them to do it.

Within a couple of hours, he'd have girls hanging off his shoulders, sitting on his lap and plying him with drinks while Lek recounted the details of her recent adventure in the UK. She should have come round a bit by then too.

Just in time to share a couple of bottles of whiskey with her ex-col-leagues.

Still, it would be very pleasant and the apartment that he had booked before they had left was not far from the bar.

He was wondering whether that would be a good time to propose – in front of her friends, when she least expected it and when she would get the maximum amount of attention and admiration. It would certainly give her face a boost, not that it was flagging in Pattaya. All her friends thought she was a star - one in a million.

Craig thought so too.

However, first things first, he thought; people were starting to dis-embark. Craig thought it best to wait for most people to get off before he tried to coax and manhandle Lek down the aisle, so they just sat there and he tried to get her to get a grip on herself.

Without much success.

The cabin staff were helpful – they understood about the tablets – and Lek and Craig eventually made it to immigration, which was pretty straightforward, although Lek did attract a few of the expected stern looks from the Thai officials and Craig got more than a couple of knowing nods from them too. He just smiled back weakly in reply.

They made it to the carousel, where Lek fell into a chair and Craig picked up the luggage, which he loaded onto a trolley. He considered putting Lek on it too, but that would have been just too embarrassing, so he settled for letting her push it, so that she had something to lean against. No problems at baggage control and then out into the heat.

He had more or less forgotten the overpowering heat and the everyday bustle outside a Thai airport. Taxi drivers and their touts all shouting at once for your custom. This was one of the occasions where having a Thai girlfriend helped a lot. She shooed them all away and they stood in the queue for a proper meter taxi to take them to Pattaya, which was only about an hour away.

They were supposed to go to the British Embassy to have Lek's six-month visa cancelled as it was still valid for three months and allowed multiple entries into the UK, but the Embassy would be closed now and Lek was in no fit state anyway. They would have to do something about it another day.

They arrived in Daddy's Hobby after an uneventful journey. Lek had tried to talk to the driver a few times, but he thought that she was drunk so he ignored her and tried to speak to Craig, but in Thai, which Craig could not speak, so that quickly fizzled out too and Lek, being ignored, soon fell asleep, which was probably the best thing she could have done anyway.

Lek had wanted to speak Thai though. She was excited to be back in her own country, where she could hold a proper conversation in her own language and where she could feel that she belonged again. They had had a few months in Craig's home town of Barry in South Wales and everyone had made her feel very welcome. She liked European food and she could speak English reasonably well, but …

It wasn't her town, it wasn't her favourite food, it wasn't her language and they were not her people. She had had a fantastic holiday – her first trip to Europe – but she was glad to be home and she just wanted everyone to know it. She couldn't wait to see her old mates.

They got to Daddy's Hobby at a good time: nearly six o'clock. All the girls had arrived and were ready for action, but there were no customers yet and so the music was low. It would seem like a totally different place in two hours time. Once it got dark, the punters would be out and the volume would rise to deafening.

But between four and eight o'clock, the girls had time to talk and the volume was low enough to be able to hear them. It had been Craig's favourite time to visit the bar before they had gone on holiday. He had come down to the bar for an early drink and a chat almost every day then and he and the girls had got to know each other pretty well.

He often translated messages, texts and letters from and to their 'boyfriends' for them. Not that he could speak Thai, but he translated good English into pigeon and vice versa. It was fun although sometimes the messages were rather intimate and the girls would blush and giggle and run around telling each other in fits of laughter.

It was a good 'job' to have: It earned him a lot of brownie points from the girls, even if it went unpaid in monetary terms. They genuinely liked to see him, although he was quite well aware that he had only gotten his foot in the door because he was Lek's boyfriend. Many of the girls were from Lek's village in the north and she had worked with others for years. She was like a big sister to them and many of them called her just that.

At thirty-two years of age, Lek was also the oldest woman in the bar or at least joint oldest with her two best friends: Goong and Ayr. Her cousin, Beou, was a few years older again, but no-one ever mentioned that – she was the boss anyway. Despite her 'advancing' years (most of the girls were in their early twenties or younger), Lek was acknowledged to be the most beautiful woman in the bar by everyone, although no-one ever mentioned the obvious fact that that would not be true for many more years to come.

However, for now, she was still the beauty queen amongst beauty queens, for they were all very good-lookers in their own right.

When the taxi pulled up outside the bar, it was as if a film star had arrived, all the girls crowded around Lek, took her handbag, led her up to the bar by the arm, fired a dozen questions at her and whooped and whooped and whooped.

Craig paid the taxi driver and carried the luggage to the bar. He had expected a bit more attention for himself than that.

Once he was at the bar, a few of the girls noticed him and flung their arms around him, kissing him repeatedly on the cheek and arms. A few of the girls took the luggage to store behind the bar and Lek and

Craig sat down for the start of what they both knew would be a long and lively session.

All the women were talking at once and, although Craig wasn't being totally ignored, he wasn't getting served either. He was dying for an ice-cold beer. He couldn't follow the conversation, maybe nobody could, but he could see how happy they all were, so he went behind the bar and got three beers. The first one didn't touch the sides. He downed it in two mouthfuls, but the other two he took back to the bar and handed one to Lek.

"Oh, so sorry, telak! Nobody take care of you. So sorry."

She said something and a few girls were detailed to 'take care' of Craig. Then she said loudly:

"You only buy two beers, this is not enough!" and she leaned over and rang the bell, signalling a drink for everyone at her expense.

Craig finished his beer quickly and accepted another.

Two of the girls detailed to 'take care' of Craig were unknown to him. They had obviously joined the crew while he and Lek had been away. They were very friendly, but when Ayr thought they were getting a bit too familiar, she sent them behind the bar to serve.

"So, sorry, Craig," she said, "these girls new. They don' know Lek and you together. I tell them later. Nice to see you again. You have good time in Wale'?" and she was gone without waiting for the answer.

Ayr and Goong were Lek's oldest friends, came from the same village and had shared a room in Pattaya before Craig came on the scene. Neither of them held any ill will against Craig for taking their friend away though. They were happy that she was happy, because they were true friends.

"Oh, well," he joked with himself, "Shame about that. Still, never mind. At least, I didn't get into trouble on my first day back. Saved from myself by Lek's friend. Saved from whatever-their- names were too."

It did the trick though. He was not ignored by Lek, her friends or the strangers again. Everyone was keeping an eye on him now. He was served, kissed and complimented without long intervals in between and it suited him fine.

The girls quietened after about twenty minutes and they all sat around Lek, or as near as they could get, to listen to her favourite stories. It wasn't long after that that the first bottle of whiskey was broken out and a few small glasses appeared. The girls preferred whiskey because it was less fattening than a bottle of beer and it was easier to finish quickly if a punter wanted to talk with one of them.

Craig sat nearby too and listened out for landmark words like: Barry, Wales and family names. Sure enough, they were all mentioned often and he was sometimes called upon to corroborate the details, although no-one actually waited for him to finish speaking. He just about had the time to nod and smile, even though he didn't know what was being said. He trusted Lek though.

She was speaking softly so that the girls would have to listen hard:

"We set off on a typically beautiful, balmy Pattaya evening... a bit like this evening, in fact, and at about the same time of day, to catch the overnight flight to Britain. We were going to Wales, where Craig's family lives, but we had to go to London first, of course.

"Naturally we had to be at the check-in desk two to three hours before the flight, but there was nearly a disaster! Really! We nearly couldn't go! All because, unfortunately, Craig had forgotten that he was carrying an old souvenir pen-knife in his pocket that his father had given to him twenty years before.

"I thought they were going to arrest him. I was horrified! I thought I might have to go alone and wait for him over there and I didn't want to have to do that now, did I? Anyway, we were lucky, they only confiscated it. He was very sad about it, especially as the airline gave us metal cutlery to eat with anyway and the knives that they gave us were bigger than the one they had taken off Craig. Weren't they, Craig? Bigger knives?

"Craig said it was stupid to take his one-inch blade from him under such circumstances and I think that I have to agree with him, don't you?

"Anyway, the ten-and-a-half hour flight to Bahrain was very comfortable. The food was not to my liking because I am a Buddhist that does not eat beef or dairy products and the only two other choices were Indian curry or vegetable pie. I didn't mind though. It all looked very nice and I swapped my main course for Craig's ice cream.

"Bahrain was a shock from Suvarnabhumi airport. Oh, my God! It was OK, really, but we didn't have any of their money, Dinar, I think, so we just had to sit there and watch people for the two hours until the connecting flight to Gatwick. That is in the UK. The time passed slowly and I was a little cold because it was 20°c there, much colder then Bangkok. Virtually freezing!

Did I tell you that a man died on the flight? I nearly forgot. Shock or travel-sickness, I think. When they opened the doors to take him off mosquitoes as big as birds flew in! Oh my Buddha! I was sure we'd get malaria…

"Anyway, the second leg flight was also OK; not as good as the first, but at least I could eat the scrambled egg and pork sausage. I had Craig's too, because he took my feta salad. Feta is cheese by the way. Greek cheese, isn't it, Craig? Craig? He's not listening again... Anyway, they eat a lot of cheese in Europe. The coffee was much stronger than I am used to too, but it was lovely. All in all, I liked Etihad Airways and would fly with them again, wouldn't we, telak?

"It took five hours to get to Gatwick and if Bahrain was a shock, Gatwick's 5°c was as good as icy to me. As soon as I got off the plane, I was looking for the Ladies! It was that cold, honest. If you haven't been abroad, darlings, you have no idea what cold is. We are so lucky here in good old Thailand. Anyway, fortunately we only had twenty-five minutes to wait for the bus to Cardiff via Victoria Coach Station – that's in London again, of course.

"The tour coach was good and the driver was friendly, but the weather turned so bad as we crossed the Severn Bridge, into Wales, that is, over the Bristol Channel, isn't it dear? that we were late arriving in Cardiff. We got there just in time for the eleven o'clock traffic jam. Just as bad as Bangkok, but you're in the dark, which makes it a lot worse!

"It was hor-ren-dous!

"So, then our friend Nick, you know Nick, he comes in here sometimes took us in his car through Dinas Powys and Penarth before coming into Barry through Cadoxton.

"Craig suggested getting out at the King William IV – called The Billy – that's a pub, so that we could have a drink. It was typical of him; well, you know my Craig, but it was bitterly cold, and it was close. We had been travelling for thirty-three hours and now we were ten minutes from my Welsh Mum's house.

"Ooh, I'm parched, well, when we got to Mum's, which was a day and a half after we started out from here… No, more about that later.

"I met so many handsome men, Oh my gosh! Our friends Colin, Ray, Billy, Digger, Danny, Sam, Paul and Selby, the father of two famous Welsh boxers, Andrew and Lee (he gave me one of Andrew's jackets – I'll show it to you one day) - they were in O'Brien's and Mike, or Henry as his friends call him, in the Buccaneer and so many others. Those places are in the centre of the town of Barry, of course, Holton Road, near the King's Square. When they come over to visit us, we could introduce you, if you like…."

Lek had them spellbound. It was exactly what it must have been like to watch Hans Christian Andersen telling fairy stories to kids in Denmark, although Lek's stories were true even if a little dramatised.

They just stared at her, sometimes looking at Craig as if to say 'What with him?', but actually saying "Ooh, really?" and "Ahhh, really? None of them had been to Europe before, although it was the dream that every single one of them had.

In fact, they would happily go to live anywhere abroad so long as the job was better and there was more money, which everybody believed that it was 'abroad' – meaning Europe, Australia and the USA. Not many of them had heard of Canada or New Zealand. Second choice was northern Africa, but most of the girls had heard rumours of sex slaves there and none of them fancied that.

Beou arrived on her motorbike and the commotion started all over again. Some girls jumped up to pretend they were working and others got out of the way to allow the boss easier access to her favourite cousin. She put one arm around Lek and, as she leaned in to exchange kisses, took Craig's hand with the other.

"Hello, both! How the devil are you? Did you have a good time? Sorry that I couldn't be here to greet you when you arrived, but someone was late coming to see me. (They'll never do it again though). So, he didn't sell you into slavery then? Or did you do a bit of part-time sex-slaving? Did she tell you, Craig? She was rather worried that you would sell her as a sex-slave to a bunch of old men in a nursing home! She might not have minded if it was to a football team. Or what do you play over there in Wales? Ah, rugby, is it? Yes, rugby."

Lek was blushing deeply and she thought she would die if any of the girls knew what was actually being said about her, but it was a bit too fast for most them.

"No, she didn't say anything. What's this all about, Beou? And how are you anyway?"

"Oh, I'm fine. A few of the old women back home warned Lek to be careful that you didn't sell her into the sex industry. A lot of people are worried about it, but I told her that the old biddies in the village were just jealous."

Lek could still barely speak so she covered her face below her eyes with a hand to hide her blushes.

"Oh, Beou! How could you? I didn't really believe them, but you hear such terrible things, don't you? And I never said anything about an old men's home or a football team! And I didn't even know what rugby was until a few months ago." Then in English: "Don't believe her, Craig..... Well, not all of it anyway."

"I don't know what you are all talking about. Don't believe all of what? What did Beou say?" asked Craig

"Oh, don't worry, I tell you later. It is not important now. Ladies in the village tell me to take care nobody sell me into sex slavery, that's all. Don't worry."

"Oh, is that all," he replied, still not completely understanding. One thing he had learned though was that if Lek said 'later', it usually meant either 'no' or 'never', so he just let it drop. He trusted her and her judgement and, besides that, they were back on her turf now where she knew far more than he ever would.

Beou sat down and a gin and tonic was put in front of her, she lit a cigarette and rang the bell, which was an uncommon thing for her to do. Half-a-dozen of the girls jumped up to see to their boss' order, but they all came back to find out how the story would develop. Beou didn't mind that, she was a pretty good employer and the majority of these girls were not there to clean glasses anyway.

Lek recovered quickly from her embarrassment and she seemed to have thrown off the effects of the tablets too. The adrenaline and ex-citement of being with her friends again had 'sobered' her up faster than a cold shower, a coffee or even a car crash ever could have. She was flying high and everybody else was up there with her, so Craig just settled back to drink his beer and watch the proceedings.

Customers came and went and girls got up to keep them company and either came back when the man had left or went with him. Some girls had their regulars, whom they were grooming so that they too might have an adventure like Lek's. Everybody wanted what Lek had and they were hoping that she would pass on some secret, insider tips on how to accomplish it.

No-one was surprised that Lek had been the first to manage going abroad in years and no-one begrudged her her good fortune either. She was their big sister, the legendary heroine Lek, and they all wanted to be like her. Even the new girls had heard of her, they had just never met her in the flesh. This put Craig on a pedestal, because they all assumed that a woman like Lek would have had many chances to get out, but just didn't take them for one reason or another. That meant that Craig must be something special.

No Adonis, so must be kind and wealthy, most of them assumed. Or at least well-off.

Sometimes, Lek wasn't sure why either. Some things were coming to a head in her life, it was true: she was no spring chicken any more; but more than that, her daughter, Soomsomai, was twelve, and she didn't want her to know that her mother was associated with the seamier side of life. She also liked Craig a lot, even loved him and he was kind. Not wealthy, but well-off by her standards and still of an age that he could work.

For his part, Craig really loved Lek. He had never met anyone like her before. True, he had worked, studied and travelled nearly all his life and had never been married, but he wasn't totally inexperienced with women either. He had just never met one quite like Lek before. Or maybe he just happened to meet her when the time was right. He didn't know and was not much interested in why anyway. He knew that he wanted to stay with her and that he wanted to stay in Thailand, a place he had come to prefer over his own country.

The only problems from his point of view were that he had always been wary of marrying someone from abroad because of his limited financial resources and the huge travelling costs involved with visiting two sets of parents on two different continents regularly. He would not be able to work in Thailand except perhaps as a teacher and he was sure that he lacked the patience and confidence for that. There was savings money and a few investments for the time being but how long would it last?

That was the big question.

He would have to get out of central Pattaya as soon as possible; that much was clear, but go where? He only knew Pattaya. Bangkok was sure to be even more expensive and he didn't like big cities anyway. They both liked Pattaya, so maybe they could move to the suburbs. He and Lek had not broached the subject yet, but they had pre-booked an apartment for two months, so they had some time to work something out.

Craig spent the next six or seven hours day dreaming and drinking, while Lek spent them drinking and talking. It wasn't boring.

Not at all. It was peaceful. Relaxing.

He had even managed to filter out the awful, loud music that he so detested. He was just so pleased to be back in Pattaya and Thailand. He was tempted to go and look at the sun setting on the sea, but couldn't be bothered.

At sometime near one o'clock, the official closing time in Pattaya, jet lag and the alcohol were winning out over the excitement and adrenaline and Lek reluctantly wanted to call it a day and go to their room. Beou called them a taxi which arrived too soon. They had hoped it would take ten or twenty minutes to get there, but it arrived in two. Lek knocked her whiskey back in one and Craig took his bottle with him. The driver put their bags in the boot and they were off. Glad to be going to their new home for the next few months.

Their apartment was in the Diana Estate which was not far away in Soi Buakhao so they were there in less than ten minutes despite the busy streets. The security guard on the gate was waiting for them with the key to the apartment, because the concierge had already gone to bed. Not that that was a problem. They refused the security guards offer to show them the way as Craig had inspected the apartment three months previously before paying the deposit.

They went up to the room, stripped off and showered together. When they fell onto the bed, Craig was starkers and Lek was in her customary towel; pleased to be wrapped in a towel like she had been for some time every day of her life in Thailand and which she had missed in the UK. She had never thought that such a simple thing like a towel could bring so much pleasure. She hadn't realised that she had missed it in Britain, but now that she had its protection around her again, she knew that she had.

Or maybe it was just Thailand and her friends that she had missed when she was in Europe, despite the fact that it had been her ambition for ten years to make that journey.

It didn't matter for now really; neither of them had much chance to analyse anything because they were both fast asleep in minutes.

That would have to wait until the next day, the real start of their new life, their exciting future, together.

Behind The Smile Series

The Story of Lek, A Bar Girl in Pattaya

The seven-part **Behind The Smile** Series is the story of Lek, a bar girl in Pattaya, Thailand. Lek was born the eldest child of four in a typical rice farming family in the northern rice belt of Thailand. A catastrophe occurred out of the blue one day – her father died young with huge debts that the family knew nothing about. Lek was just twenty years of age, and the only one who could prevent the foreclosure of the family farm, and allow her younger sister and two brothers to continue their education. However, the only way she knew how was to go to work in her cousin's bar in Pattaya.

Can a Pattaya bar girl ever go back to being a regular girlfriend or wife?

Behind The Smile is a look into one part of Thailand, a country known around the world as 'The Land of Smiles'.

1] Daddy's Hobby

Daddy's Hobby: Lek went to the bar 'Daddy's Hobby', in Pattaya, as a waitress-cum-cashier, until she realised that she was pregnant by her estranged husband, and everything changed. After having the baby, a girl, whom she left with her mother on the farm, she needed real money to provide a better life for her child and drifted into the tourist sex industry.

The adventures, dreams and sometimes nightmares, this is Lek's point of view of what it's really like to be a Thai bar girl... the exhilarating hopes that cover up the frustrations, let-downs, lies and deceit of daily life, give way to the dream of a normal life when she meets a new man, yet again.

When this new man returns for a real life relationship, Lek finds it's not so easy going through the good and bad of couplehood.

Will they stay together, and for how long? Will she ever be able to trust a man enough again either? Or will she go back to the bar girl life?

2] An Exciting Future

An Exciting Future starts where volume one ends. Lek and Craig, her new 'permanent' boyfriend are flying back to Bangkok from Craig's home in Wales. The holiday atmosphere continues in Pattaya for months, but then reality dawns, and they have important decisions to make such as: where are they going to live, and how are they going to make a living. They start squabbling, and both wonder whether they have done the right thing in joining forces.

They persevere, and, after many trials, tribulations and happy times, begin to settle down into, what, for them at least, could be called a normal life. One of the trio dies tragically, but gives the other two new hope. However, will the old villagers forgive Lek for going to Pattaya? And will Lek and Craig be able to adapt to rural village life after all that Lek has seen and done, and Craig being used to living in large towns? What chance do they have of really fitting in?

3] Maya – Illusion

Maya – Illusion refers to the Buddhist concept that life on Earth is not real. More than 95% of Thais are Buddhist, and so have a totally different outlook to most Christian Westerners. Lek and her best friend Ayr go into business together, when she retires from Pattaya, and brings a surprise Australian fiancé with her. A natural disaster occurs in the village but the two friends come up with an innovative form of help. Ayr proves to be quite a business woman, and teaches Lek, a willing student, how to make money and fit into the community, while Craig plods along with his books and websites.

4] The Lady in the Tree

The Lady in the Tree continues straight on from book three, Maya - Illusion. Lek is still in business with her old friend Ayr and they mean business as well, especially when rivals from nearby try to intimidate them. The two friends come up with a daring solution, which they can't even discuss with their friends, family or husbands. Soom is still at university in Bangkok and doing well in spite of having problems of her own, let alone looming final exams, which political upheaval in the capital threatens to disrupt. Craig continues to write, but he realises all of a sudden that he has bigger problems than finishing and selling his books. An old friend and an old lady give the three women some remarkably similar and accurate advice, but where will it get them?

5] Stepping Stones

Stepping Stones picks up the story of Lek, her family and friends in the village of Baan Suay four years on from where The Lady in The Tree finished. Lek and Ayr are still looking to expand, but especially Lek's career in the political arena, where she finds evidence of disturbing activity. Craig is still trying to write a best seller and Soom has graduated from university. In Stepping Stones, we are introduced to the Champunot family from Bangkok, the members of which have a profound effect on Lek, Craig and Soom - one which none of them will ever be able to forget. Stepping Stones reveals more in-depth details of life in a Thai family that has been affected by the inclusion of a falang like how they deal with the strange mixture of traditional and modern Thai life that that situation often creates.

6] The Dream

The Dream takes up the story of Lek, her family and friends from two years further down the line. In the past, it has always been Lek who issued the ultimata, but this story opens with her having received one and it throws her. She is offered the fulfilment of her oldest dream, but can she take it? The fulfilment of any dream requires sacrifices, but is Lek prepared to make them now that her goal is within her grasp? It is a tough one, which means a hard time for her, although her family and friends are behind her as always. Which way will she go? The instinct to follow her dream and the inertia of a comfortable life in the village, as she gets older vie for supremacy in her mind. As is usual in this series, nothing is hidden from the reader, we are privy to all of Lek's agonizing thoughts.

7] The Beginning

The Beginning... At twenty-one years of age, Lek, an ordinary, contemporary, farm girl from the northern Thai rice belt, had to go to Pattaya to work in the leisure industry to help her widowed mother pay off the mortgage to save the farm from foreclosure, and keep her siblings in school. This book, The Beginning, shows what her life was like before she had to leave her small, hard-working, but happy village and the only people she had ever known. It depicts the events that made her happy and those that saddened her in her early life from living with her grandmother to surviving with her husband, Tom. At the very last moment, some friends step up to make Lek's transition to life in Thailand's number one sex city just that little bit easier.

Books by Owen Jones

Alien House
A Story of Love, Hope and Alien Intervention

-

Andropov's Cuckoo
A Story of Love Intrigue and The KGB

-

Annwn – Heaven - *series*
A Night in Annwn
The Strange Story of Old Willy Jones's NDE
Life in Annwn
Thhe Story of Willy Jones's Life in Heaven
Leaving Annwn
Returning to Earth on a Mission!

-

Asian Shorts
An Anthology of Short Stories Involving Asians or Asia

-

Behind The Smile - *series*
The Story of Lek, a Bar Girl in Pattaya
Volume I: **Daddy's Hobby**
Volume II: **An Exciting Future**
Volume III: **Maya – Illusion**

Daddy's Hobby

Volume IV: **The Lady in the Tree**
Volume V: **Stepping Stones**
Volume VI: **The Dream**
Volume VII: **The Beginning**

-

Daisy's Chain
A Story of Love, Intrigue and the Underworld on the Costa del Sol

-

Dead Centre - *series*
Dead Centre
Not All Suicide Bombers Are Religious!
Dead Centre II
Even The Wrong Can Be Right Sometimes!

-

The Disallowed
The Story of a Contemporary Vampire Family

-

Fate Twister
The Strange Story of Wayne Gamm

-

The Bull at the Gate
The Day the Sky Fell!

-

The Ghouls of Calle Goya
When Malice Results From Good Intentions!

-

The Psychic Megan Series
A Spirit Guide, A Ghost Tiger, and One Scary Mother!
The Misconception
Megan's Thirteenth
Megan's School Trip

Megan's School Exams
Megan's Followers
Megan and the Lost Cat
Megan and the Mayoress
Megan Faces Derision
Megan's Grandparents' Visit
Megan's Father Falls Ill
Megan Goes on Holiday
Megan and the Burglar
Megan and the Cyclist
Megan and the Old Lady
Megan's Garden
Megan Goes to the Zoo
Megan Goes Hiking
Megan and the W. I. Cooking Competition
Megan Goes Riding
Megan and the Radio One Beach Party
Megan Goes Yachting
Megan at Carnival
Megan's Christmas
Megan Catches Covid-19

-

The Bull at the Gate
The Day the Sky Fell !

-

Tiger Lily of Bangkok *– Series*
Volume I: **Tiger Lily of Bangkok**
When the Seeds of Revenge Blossom!
Volume II: **Tiger Lily of Bangkok in London**
The Tiger Re-awakens!

-

Non-Fiction

How to Give Your Dog a Real Dog's Life
(and make him love you for it)

-

The Eternal Plan
— Revealed
(written by Colin Jones, compiled by Owen Jones)

-

Authorship
Publishing Your Book On You Own

Plus 150 self-help manuals.

www.ingramcontent.com/pod-product-compliance
Lightning Source LLC
Chambersburg PA
CBHW070801120726
47910CB00001B/252